*Praise for*

Bernard Cornwell's

# THE NATHANIEL STARBUCK
# CHRONICLES

"The battle scenes are gripping and realistic and Cornwell has
studded the narrative with colorful and . . . accurate portraits of
real civilian and military figures. . . . [He]'s particularly skillful
at portraying the complexity of men in . . . inner conflict. . . .
A superb series." —*San Jose Mercury News*

"Fast-paced . . . [and] gripping entertainment."
—*Daily Telegraph*

"The most entertaining military historical novels. . . . Always
based on fact, always interesting . . . always entertaining."
—*Kirkus Reviews*

"[A] wonderful series. . . . A rollicking treat for Cornwell's
many fans." —*Publishers Weekly*

"Highly successful." —*The Times* (London)

Photograph by Cristine Clarke

## About the Author

**BERNARD CORNWELL** is a native of England, where he worked as a journalist in newspapers and television. In addition to *Rebel, Copperhead, Battle Flag,* and *The Bloody Ground,* the four novels in the Nathaniel Starbuck Chronicles, he also wrote the bestselling Sharpe series, featuring the adventures of Captain Richard Sharpe of the British Army in the wars against Napoleon, which has been dramatized for television by *Masterpiece Theatre;* the Warlord Chronicles, about Arthurian England; *Stonehenge: 2000 B.C., a Novel;* and *The Archer's Tale.* A resident of the United States for fifteen years, Bernard Cornwell now lives with his American wife on Cape Cod.

# BOOKS BY BERNARD CORNWELL

## ~ The Sharpe Novels ~
*(in chronological order)*

### Sharpe's Tiger
*Richard Sharpe and the Siege
of Seringapatam, 1799*

### Sharpe's Triumph
*Richard Sharpe and the Battle
of Assaye, September 1803*

### Sharpe's Fortress
*Richard Sharpe and the Siege
of Gawilghur, December 1803*

### Sharpe's Trafalgar
*Richard Sharpe and the Battle
of Trafalgar, 21 October 1805*

### Sharpe's Rifles
*Richard Sharpe and the French
Invasion of Galicia, January 1809*

### Sharpe's Eagle
*Richard Sharpe and the
Talavera Campaign, July 1809*

### Sharpe's Gold
*Richard Sharpe and the Destruction
of Almeida, August 1810*

### Sharpe's Battle
*Richard Sharpe and the Battle
of Fuentes de Onoro, May 1811*

### Sharpe's Company
*Richard Sharpe and the Siege
of Badajoz, January to April 1812*

### Sharpe's Sword
*Richard Sharpe and the Salamanca
Campaign, June and July 1812*

### Sharpe's Enemy
*Richard Sharpe and the Defense
of Portugal, Christmas 1812*

### Sharpe's Honor
*Richard Sharpe and the Vitoria Campaign, February to June 1813*

### Sharpe's Regiment
*Richard Sharpe and the Invasion of France, June to November 1813*

### Sharpe's Siege
*Richard Sharpe and the Winter Campaign, 1814*

### Sharpe's Revenge
*Richard Sharpe and the Peace of 1814*

### Sharpe's Waterloo
*Richard Sharpe and the Waterloo Campaign, 15 June to 18 June 1815*

### Sharpe's Devil
*Richard Sharpe and the Emperor, 1820–21*

## ~ The Nathaniel Starbuck Chronicles ~

### Rebel
*(Book One)*

### Copperhead
*(Book Two)*

### Battle Flag
*(Book Three)*

### The Bloody Ground
*(Book Four)*

## ~ Other Novels ~

### Stonehenge: 2000 B.C., a Novel

### The Archer's Tale

### Redcoat

# Bernard Cornwell

# COPPERHEAD

### THE
### NATHANIEL STARBUCK
### CHRONICLES
~ BOOK TWO ~

HARPER ⬤ PERENNIAL

NEW YORK ● LONDON ● TORONTO ● SYDNEY

A hardcover edition of this book was published in 1993 by HarperCollins Publishers.

COPPERHEAD. Copyright © 1993 by Bernard Cornwell. All rights reserved. Printed in the United States of America. No part of this book may be used or reproduced in any manner whatsoever without written permission except in the case of brief quotations embodied in critical articles and reviews. For information address HarperCollins Publishers Inc., 10 East 53rd Street, New York, NY 10022.

HarperCollins books may be purchased for educational, business, or sales promotional use. For information please write: Special Markets Department, HarperCollins Publishers Inc., 10 East 53rd Street, New York, NY 10022.

First Perennial edition published 2001.

*Designed by David Lane*

Library of Congress Cataloging-in-Publication Data

Cornwell, Bernard.
    Copperhead / by Bernard Cornwell.— 1st Perennial ed.
      p. cm.— (The Nathaniel Starbuck chronicles ; bk. 2)
    ISBN 0-06-093462-X
      1. Starbuck, Nathaniel (Fictitious Character)—Fiction.
    2. United States—History—Civil War, 1861–1865—Fiction.
    3. Richmond (Va.)—History—Civil War, 1861–1865—Fiction.
    I. Title.

PR6053.O75 C66 2001
823'.914—dc21

                                                      2001021409

13  14  15  RRD  20  19

*Copperhead* is for Bill and Anne Moir.

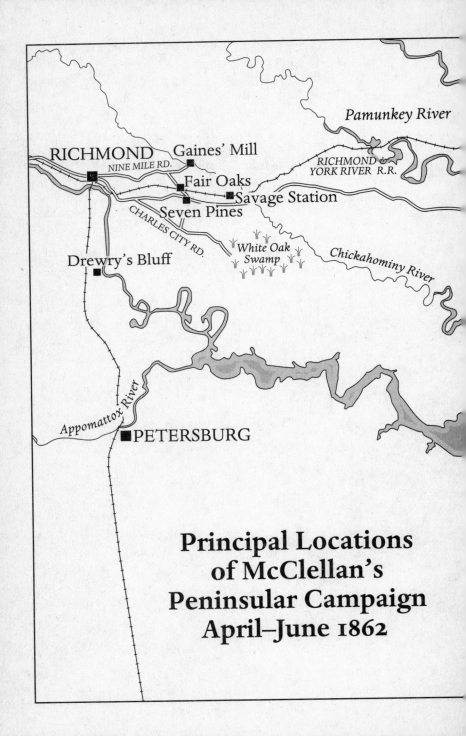

**Principal Locations
of McClellan's
Peninsular Campaign
April–June 1862**

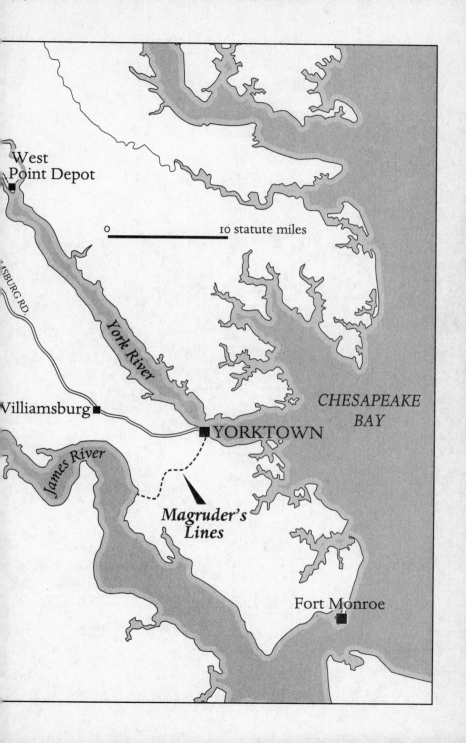

West
Point Depot

0          10 statute miles

SBURG RD.

York River

CHESAPEAKE
BAY

Williamsburg

James River

YORKTOWN

Magruder's
Lines

Fort Monroe

~ PART ONE ~

THE INVASION BEGAN AT MIDNIGHT.

It was not truly an invasion, just a heavy raid on a rebel encampment that a patrol had spotted among the thick woods that crowned the high bluffs on the Virginia side of the river, but to the two thousand men who waited to cross the bleak slate-gray swirl of the Potomac River this night's exertions seemed more momentous than a mere raid. This fight across the river was their opportunity to prove their critics wrong. Nursery soldiers, one newspaper had called them; wonderfully trained and beautifully drilled, but much too precious to be dirtied in battle. Yet tonight the despised nursery soldiers would fight. Tonight the Army of the Potomac would carry fire and steel to a rebel encampment and if all went well they would march on to occupy the town of Leesburg, which lay two miles beyond the enemy camp. The expectant soldiers imagined the shamefaced citizens of the Virginia town waking to see the Stars and Stripes flying over their community again, and then they imagined themselves marching south, ever farther south, until the rebellion was crushed and America was reunited in peace and brotherhood.

"You bastard!" a voice shouted loudly from the river's edge where a work party had been launching a boat carried from the nearby Chesapeake and Ohio Canal. One of the work party had slipped in the clay, dropping the boat's stern onto a sergeant's foot. "You no-good son of a bitch goddamn bastard!" The Sergeant hopped away from the boat.

"Sorry," the man said nervously.

"I'll give you sorry, you bastard!"

"Silence! Keep it quiet now!" An officer, resplendent in a new gray overcoat that was handsomely lined in red, clambered down the steep bank and helped lift the skiff toward the river's gray water from which a small mist crept to hide the lower slopes of the far bank. They labored beneath a high moon, no clouds, and a spread of stars so bright and clean they seemed like an augury of success. It was October, the fragrant month when the air smelt of apples and woodsmoke, and when the sweltering dog days of summer gave way to clear sharp weather that held just enough promise of winter to persuade the troops to wear their fine new overcoats that were the same color as the river's drifting mist.

The first boats pushed clumsily off the bank. The oars clattered in the oarlocks, then dipped and splashed as the boats receded into the mist. The men, who a moment before had been cursing and cumbersome creatures clambering down the clay bank into the clumsy boats, were mysteriously transformed into warrior silhouettes, spiky with weapons, who glided silent and noble through the vaporous night toward the misted shadows of the enemy shore. The officer who had remonstrated with the Sergeant stared wistfully across the water. "I suppose," he said softly to the men around him, "that this was how Washington felt on the night he crossed the Delaware?"

"A much colder night, that one, I think," a second officer, a young student from Boston, replied.

"It'll be cold enough here soon," the first officer, a major, said. "There's only two months till Christmas." When the Major had marched to war, newspapers had promised that the rebellion would be over by fall, but now the Major was wondering whether he would be home with his wife and three children for the family rituals of Christmas. On Christmas Eve they sang carols on Boston Common, the children's faces lit by lanterns hung on poles, and afterward there were warm punch and slivers of cooked goose in the church vestry. Then on Christmas Day they went to his wife's parents' farm in Stoughton, where they harnessed the horses and the children laughed in delight as they trotted down country roads in a cloud of snow and a tinkling of sleigh bells.

"And I rather suspect General Washington's organization was superior to ours," the student-turned-lieutenant said in an amused voice. His name was Holmes and he was clever enough to awe his superiors, but usually intelligent enough not to let that cleverness alienate their affections.

"I am sure our organization will suffice," the Major said just a little too defensively.

"I am sure you're right," Lieutenant Holmes said, though he was not sure of that fact at all. Three regiments of northern troops waited to cross, and there were just three small boats to carry them from the Maryland shore to the island that lay close to the river's far bank, upon which island the troops must land before reembarking on two more boats for the final short crossing to the Virginia mainland. Doubtless they were crossing the river at the spot closest to the enemy encampment, but Lieutenant Holmes could not really understand why they did not cross a mile upstream where no island obstructed the river. Maybe, Holmes surmised, this was such an unlikely crossing place that the rebels would never think to guard it, and that seemed the best explanation he could find.

But if the choice of crossing place was obscure, at least the night's purpose was clear. The expedition would climb the Virginia bluffs to attack the rebel camp and capture as many Confederates as possible. Some rebels would get away, but those fugitives would find their flight blocked by a second Yankee force that was crossing the river five miles downstream. That force would cut the turnpike that led

from Leesburg to the rebel headquarters at Centreville, and by trap-
ping the defeated rebel forces it would provide the North with a small
but significant victory to prove that the Army of the Potomac could
do more than just drill and train and mount impressive parades. The
capture of Leesburg would be a welcome bonus, but the night's real
purpose was to prove that the newly trained Army of the Potomac
was ready and able to whip the rebels ragged.

To which end the small boats struggled back and forth in the
mist. Each crossing seemed to take forever, and to the impatient men
on the Maryland shore the waiting files seemed to get no shorter. The
15th Massachusetts was crossing first, and some men in the 20th Massachusetts feared that their sister regiment would capture the enemy
camp long before the few boats succeeded in ferrying the 20th across
the river. Everything seemed so slow and clumsy. Rifle butts clattered on gunwales and bayonet scabbards snagged themselves on the
bushes at the water's edge as the men clambered into the row boats.
At two in the morning a larger boat was discovered upstream and
brought down to the crossing place, where it was greeted with an
ironic cheer. It seemed to Lieutenant Holmes that the waiting men
were making a lot of noise, enough surely to alert any rebels who
might be guarding the Virginia bank, but no challenge sounded
through the mist and no rifle shots echoed from the high wooded
slope that loomed so ominously beyond the island. "Does the island
have a name?" Lieutenant Holmes asked the Major who had spoken
so wistfully of Christmas.

"Harrison's Island, I think. Yes, Harrison's."

It sounded an undramatic name to Lieutenant Holmes. He
would have preferred something nobler to have marked the 20th
Massachusetts's baptism of fire. Maybe a name with the iron ring of
Valley Forge, or the simple nobility of Yorktown. Something that
would ring through history and look fine when it was embroidered
on the regiment's battle flag. Harrison's Island sounded much too
prosaic. "And the hill beyond it?" he asked hopefully. "On the far
bank?"

"That's called Ball's Bluff," the Major said, and that was even less heroic. The battle of Ball's Bluff sounded like a poker game rather than the signal event that would mark the resurgence of northern arms.

Holmes waited with his company. They would be the first of the 20th Massachusetts to cross and so the likeliest of their regiment to be in a fight if the 15th had not already captured the encampment. That possibility of battle made the men nervous. None of them had fought before, though all had heard tales of the battle fought at Bull Run three months before and how the ragged gray-clad rebel ranks had somehow clung together long enough to drive the larger Federal army into panicked retreat, but none of the 20th Massachusetts believed they would suffer a similar fate. They were superbly equipped, well-trained, led by a professional soldier, and confident they could out-fight any rebel born. There would be danger, of course—they expected and even wanted some danger—but the night's work would be crowned with victory.

One of the boats coming back from Harrison's Island brought a captain of the 15th Massachusetts who had crossed with the very first troops and who now returned to report to the commanding officers of the waiting regiments. The Captain slipped as he jumped from the boat's bows and would have fallen if Lieutenant Holmes had not reached out a steadying hand. "All quiet on the Potomac?" Holmes asked jocularly.

"All's quiet, Wendell." The Captain sounded disappointed. "Too quiet. There's not even an enemy encampment up there."

"No tents?" Lieutenant Holmes asked in surprise. "Truly?" And he hoped his voice sounded properly disappointed as befitted a warrior denied a chance of battle, and in part he was disappointed because he had been looking forward to the excitement, but he was also aware of a shameful relief that perhaps no enemy waited on the far bluff.

The Captain straightened his coat. "God knows what that patrol thought they saw last night, but we can't find anything." He walked away with his news while Lieutenant Holmes passed the word on to his company. There was no enemy waiting across the river, which meant the expedition would most probably march on to occupy Leesburg. A sergeant wanted to know if there were any rebel troops in Leesburg and Holmes had to confess he did not know, but the Major, overhearing the conversation, volunteered that at best there would be only a handful of the Virginia Militia probably armed with the same guns with which their grandfathers had fought the British. The Major went on to say that their new task would be to capture the harvest that would have been newly gathered into the barns and storerooms of Leesburg, and that while such supplies were a legitimate military target, other private property should be respected. "We're not here to make war on the homes of women and children," the Major said sternly. "We must show the seceshers that northern troops are their friends."

"Amen," the Sergeant said. He was a lay preacher who was trying to rid the regiment of the sins of card-playing, liquor, and womanizing.

The last of the 15th Massachusetts crossed to the island and Holmes's gray-coated men shuffled down the bank to wait their turn in the boats. There was a feeling of disappointment among the men. They had anticipated a whooping hunt through the woods, but instead it seemed they would merely be disarming a town's old men of muskets.

In the shadows of the Virginia bank a fox pounced and a rabbit died. The beast's cry was sudden and shrill, gone almost as soon as it had begun, to leave nothing behind but the scent of blood and the echo of death in the dark, sleeping, and unsuspecting woods.

Captain Nathaniel Starbuck reached his regiment's campsite at three in the morning. It was a clear night, star-bright and moonlit, with just a hint of mist showing in the hollows. He had walked from Leesburg and was dog-tired by the time he reached the field where the Legion's tents and shelters were lined in four neat rows. A sentry from C Company nodded companionably at the young black-haired officer. "Hear the rabbit, Captain?"

"Willis? You're Willis, right?" Starbuck asked.

"Bob Willis."

"Aren't you supposed to challenge me, Bob Willis? Aren't you supposed to level your rifle, demand the password, and shoot me dead if I get it wrong?"

"I know who you are, Captain." Willis grinned in the moonlight.

"The way I feel, Willis, you would have done me a favor by shooting me. What did the rabbit say to you?"

"Shrieked like he was dying, Captain. Reckon a fox got him."

Starbuck shuddered at the relish in the sentry's voice. "Good night, Willis, and may sweet angels sing thee to thy rest." Starbuck walked on between the remnants of the night's fires and the handful of Sibley tents where a few men of the Faulconer Legion slept. Most of the regiment's tents had been lost in the chaos of the Manassas battlefield, so now the majority of the regiment slept either in the open air or in neat shelters made of branches and sod. A fire flickered among the shelters of Starbuck's K Company and a man looked up as Starbuck approached.

"Sober?" the man asked.

"Sergeant Truslow is awake," Starbuck declaimed. "Do you never sleep, Truslow? I am perfectly sober. Sober as a preacher, in fact."

"I've known a few drunk preachers in my time," Sergeant Truslow said sourly. "There's a snake-oil Baptist down in Rosskill who can't say the Lord's Prayer without taking a gut-ful of pine-top whiskey first. He nearly drowned once, trying to baptize a passel of weeping women in the river behind the church. Them all praying and him so full of liquor he couldn't stand up straight. So what were you doing, caterwauling?"

"Caterwauling" was the Sergeant's disapproving word for womanizing. Starbuck pretended to consider the question as he settled beside the fire, then he nodded. "I was caterwauling, Sergeant."

"Who with?"

"A gentleman does not tell."

Truslow grunted. He was a short, squat, hard-faced man who ruled K Company with a discipline born of pure fear, though the fear was not of Truslow's physical violence, but rather of his scorn. He was a man whose approval other men sought, maybe because he seemed such a master of his own brutal world. In his time he had been a farmer, a horse thief, a soldier, a murderer, a father, and a husband. Now he was a widower and, for the second time in his life, a soldier, who brought to his trade a pure, uncomplicated hatred of Yankees. Which made his friendship with Captain Nathaniel Starbuck all the more mysterious, for Starbuck was a Yankee.

Starbuck came from Boston, second son of the Reverend Elial Starbuck, who was a famous excoriator of the South, a fearsome opponent of slavery, and an impassioned preacher whose printed sermons had shivered guilty consciences throughout the Christian world. Nathaniel Starbuck had been well on the path to his own ordination when a woman had tempted him from his studies at Yale College's seminary. The woman had abandoned him in Richmond, where, too scared to go home and face his father's terrible wrath, Starbuck had joined the army of the Confederate States of America instead.

"Was it the yellow-haired bitch?" Truslow now asked. "The one you met in the prayer meeting after worship service?"

"She is not a bitch, Sergeant," Starbuck said with pained dignity. Truslow responded by spitting into the fire, and Starbuck shook his head sadly. "Did you never seek the solace of female company, Sergeant?"

"Do you mean did I ever behave like a tomcat? Of course I did, but I got it out of my system before I grew a beard." Truslow paused, maybe thinking of his wife in her lonely grave in the high hills. "So where does the yellow bitch keep her husband?"

Starbuck yawned. "With Magruder's forces at Yorktown. He's an artillery major."

Truslow shook his head. "You'll be caught one of these days and have your giblets beaten out of you."

"Is that coffee?"

"So they say." Truslow poured his captain a mug of the thick, sweet, treacly liquid. "Did you get any sleep?"

"Sleep was not the purpose of the evening."

"You're just like all preachers' sons, aren't you? Get one smell of sin and you wallow like a hog in mud." There was more than a hint of disapproval in Truslow's voice, not because he disliked womanizers, but because he knew his own daughter had contributed to Starbuck's education. Sally Truslow, estranged from her father, was a whore in Richmond. That was a matter of bitter shame to Truslow, and while he was uncomfortable with the knowledge that Starbuck and Sally had been lovers, he also saw in their friendship his daughter's only chance of salvation. Life could sometimes seem very complicated even for an uncomplicated man like Thomas Truslow. "So what happened to all your Bible reading?" he now asked his officer, referring to the half-hearted attempts at piety that Starbuck still made from time to time.

"I am a backslider, Sergeant," Starbuck said carelessly, though in truth his conscience was not as easy as his flippant tone suggested. At times, assailed by the fears of hell, he felt so trapped in sin that he suspected he could never find God's forgiveness, and at such moments he would suffer agonies of remorse, but come the evening, he would find himself being impelled back to whatever tempted him.

Now he rested against the trunk of an apple tree and sipped the coffee. He was tall, thin, hardened by a season's soldiering, and had long black hair that framed an angular, clean-shaven face. When the Legion marched into a new town or village, Truslow always noticed how the girls looked at Starbuck, always at Starbuck. Just as his own daughter had been drawn to the tall northerner with his gray eyes and quick grin. Keeping Starbuck from sin, the Sergeant reflected, was like keeping a dog out of a butcher's shop. "What time is reveille?" Starbuck now asked.

"Any minute."

"Oh, sweet Jesus." Starbuck groaned.

"You should have come back earlier," Truslow said. He threw a billet of wood onto the small fire. "Did you tell the yellow-haired bitch that we're leaving?"

"I decided not to tell her. Parting is such sweet hell."

"Coward," Truslow said.

Starbuck thought about the accusation, then grinned. "You're right. I'm a coward. I hate it when they cry."

"Then don't give them cause to cry," Truslow said, knowing it was like asking the wind not to blow. Besides, soldiers always made their sweethearts cry; that was the way of soldiers. They came, they conquered, and then they marched away, and this morning the Faulconer Legion would march away from Leesburg. In the last three months the regiment had been a part of the brigade that was camped close to Leesburg and guarded a twenty-mile stretch of the Potomac River, but the enemy had shown no signs of wanting to cross, and now, as the fall slipped toward winter, rumors were multiplying of a last Yankee attack on Richmond before the ice and snow locked the armies into immobility, and so the brigade was being weakened. The Legion would go to Centreville, where the main body of the Confederate army defended the primary road that led from Washington to the rebel capital. It had been on that road, three months before at Manassas, that the Faulconer Legion had helped bloody the nose of the North's first invasion. Now, if rumors spoke true, the Legion might be required to do the work all over again.

"But it won't be the same." Truslow picked up the unspoken thought. "I hear there's nothing but earthworks at Centreville now. So if the Yankees come, we'll cut the bastards down from behind good thick walls." He stopped, seeing that Starbuck had fallen asleep, mouth open, coffee spilt. "Son of a bitch," Truslow growled, but with affection, for Starbuck, for all his preacher's-son caterwauling, had proved himself a remarkable officer. He had made K Company into the best in the Legion, doing it by a mixture of unrelenting drill and imaginative training. It had been Starbuck who, denied the gunpowder and bullets needed to hone his men's marksmanship, had led a patrol across the river to capture a Union supply wagon on the road outside Poolesville. He had brought back three thousand cartridges that night, and a week later he had gone again and fetched back ten sacks of good northern coffee. Truslow, who knew soldiering, recognized that Starbuck had instinctive, natural gifts. He was a clever fighter, able to read an enemy's mind, and the men of K Company, boys mostly, seemed to recognize the quality. Starbuck, Truslow knew, was good.

A beat of wings made Truslow look up to see the black squat shape of an owl flit across the moon. Truslow supposed the bird had been hunting the open fields close to the town and was now returning to its roost in the thick stands of trees that grew above the river on Ball's Bluff.

A bugler mishit his note, took a breath, and startled the night with his call. Starbuck jerked awake, swore because his spilt coffee had soaked his trouser leg, then groaned with tiredness. It was still deep night, but the Legion had to be up and doing, ready to march away from their quiet watch on the river and go to war.

"Was that a bugle?" Lieutenant Wendell Holmes asked his pious Sergeant.

"Can't say, sir." The Sergeant was panting hard as he climbed Ball's Bluff and his new gray coat was hanging open to reveal its smart scarlet lining. The coats were a gift from the Governor of Massachusetts, who was determined that the Bay State's regiments would be among the best equipped in all the Federal army. "It was probably one of our buglers," the Sergeant guessed. "Maybe sending out skirmishers?"

Holmes assumed the Sergeant was right. The two men were laboring up the steep and twisting path that led to the bluff's summit where the 15th Massachusetts waited. The slope was about as steep as a man could climb without needing to use his hands, though in the dark many a man missed his footing and slid down to jar painfully against a tree trunk. The river below was still shrouded by mist in which the long shape of Harrison's Island showed dark. Men were crowded onto the island as they waited for the two small boats that were ferrying the troops across the last stretch of river. Lieutenant Holmes had been surprised at the speed of the river's current that had snatched at the boat and tried to sweep it away downstream toward distant Washington. The oarsmen had grunted with the effort of fighting the river, then rammed the small boat hard into the muddy bank.

Colonel Lee, the 20th Massachusetts's commanding officer, caught up with Holmes at the bluff's summit. "Almost sunrise," he said cheerfully. "All well, Wendell?"

"All well, sir. Except I'm hungry enough to eat a horse."

"We'll have breakfast in Leesburg," the Colonel said enthusiastically. "Ham, eggs, cornbread, and coffee. Some fresh southern butter! That'll be a treat. And no doubt all the townsfolk will be assuring us that they aren't rebels at all, but good loyal citizens of Uncle Sam." The Colonel abruptly turned away, startled by a sudden barking cry that echoed rhythmically and harshly among the trees on the bluff's summit. The heart-stopping noise had made the nearest soldiers whip round in quick alarm with rifles raised. "No need to worry!" the Colonel called. "It's just an owl." He had recognized the call of a barred owl and guessed the bird was coming home from a night's hunting with a belly filled with mice and frogs. "You keep going, Wendell"—Lee turned back to Holmes—"down that path till you come to the left-flank company of the 15th. Stop there and wait for me."

Lieutenant Holmes led his company behind the crouching men of the 15th Massachusetts. He stopped at the moon-bright tree line. Before them now was a brief meadow that was dotted with the stark shadows of small bushes and locust trees, beyond which rose another dark stand of trees. It was about there on the previous night that the patrol had reported seeing an enemy encampment, and Holmes guessed that frightened men could easily have mistaken the pattern of moonlight and black shadow in the far woods for the shapes of tents.

"Forward!" Colonel Devens of the 15th Massachusetts shouted the order and his men moved out into the moon-whitened meadow. No one fired at them; no one challenged them. The South slept while the North, unhindered, marched.

The sun rose, glossing the river gold and lancing scarlet rays through the misted trees. Cocks crowed in Leesburg yards where pails were pumped full of water and cows came in for the day's first milking. Workshops that had been closed for the Lord's Day were unlocked and tools picked up from benches. Outside the town, in the encampments of the Confederate brigade that guarded the river, the smoke of cooking fires sifted into the fresh fall morning.

The Faulconer Legion's fires had already died, though the Legion was in no great hurry to abandon its encampment. The day promised to be fine and the march to Centreville comparatively short, and so the regiment's eight hundred men took their time in making ready, and Major Thaddeus Bird, the regiment's commanding officer, did not try to hurry them. Instead he wandered companionably among his men like an affable neighbor enjoying a morning stroll. "My God, Starbuck." Bird stopped in amazement at the sight of K Company's captain. "What happened to you?"

"I just slept badly, sir."

"You look like the walking dead!" Bird crowed with delight at the thought of Starbuck's discomfort. "Have I ever told you about Mordechai Moore? He was a plasterer in Faulconer Court House. Died one Thursday, widow bawling her eyes out, children squalling like scalded cats, funeral on Saturday, half the town dressed in black, grave dug, the Reverend Moss ready to bore us all with his customary inanities, then they hear scratching or the coffin lid. Open it up, and there he is! One very puzzled plasterer! As alive as you or I. Or me, anyway. But he looked like you. Very like you, Nate. He looked half decayed."

"Thank you very much," Starbuck said.

"Everyone went home," Bird went on with his tale. "Doc Billy gave Mordechai an examination. Declared him fit for another ten years and, blow me, didn't he go and die again the very next day. Only this time he was properly dead and they had to dig the grave all over again. Good morning, Sergeant."

"Major," Truslow grunted. Truslow had not been known to address any officer as "sir," not even Bird, the regiment's commanding officer, whom Truslow liked.

"You remember Mordechai Moore, surely, Truslow?"

"Hell yes. Son of a bitch couldn't plaster a wall to save his life. My father and I redid half the Cotton house for him. Never did get paid for it either."

"So no doubt the building trade's better off for having him dead," Bird said blithely. Pecker Bird was a tall, ragged, skeletal man who had been schoolmaster in the town of Faulconer Court House when Colonel Washington Faulconer, Faulconer County's grandest landowner and Bird's brother-in-law, had established the Legion. Faulconer, wounded at Manassas, was now in Richmond, leaving Bird to command the regiment. The schoolmaster had probably been the least soldierly man in all Faulconer County, if not in all Virginia, and had only been appointed a major to appease his sister and take care of the Colonel's paperwork; yet, perversely, the ragged schoolmaster had proved an effective and popular officer. The men liked him, maybe because they sensed his great sympathy for all that was most fallible in humankind. Now Bird touched Starbuck's elbow. "A word?" he suggested, drawing the younger man away from K Company.

Starbuck walked with Bird into the open meadow that was scarred with the pale round shapes showing where the regiment's few tents had been pitched. Between the bleached circles were smaller scorched patches where the campfires had burned, and out beyond those scars were the large cropped circles marking where the officers' horses had grazed the grass out to the limit of their tethering ropes. The Legion could march away from this field, Starbuck reflected, yet for days afterward it would hold this evidence of their existence.

"Have you made a decision, Nate?" Bird asked. He was fond of Starbuck, and his voice reflected that affection. He offered the younger man a cheap, dark cigar, took one himself, then struck a match to light the tobacco.

"I'll stay with the regiment, sir," Starbuck said when his cigar was drawing.

"I hoped you'd say that," Bird said. "But even so." His voice trailed away. He drew on his cigar, staring toward Leesburg, over which a filmy haze of morning smoke shimmered. "Going to be a fine day," the Major said. A splutter of distant rifle fire sounded, but neither Bird nor Starbuck took any notice. It was a rare morning that men were not out hunting.

"And we don't know that the Colonel really is taking over the Legion, do we, sir?" Starbuck asked.

"We know nothing," Bird said. "Soldiers, like children, live in a natural state of willful ignorance. But it's a risk."

"You're taking the same risk," Starbuck said pointedly.

"Your sister is not married to the Colonel," Bird answered just as pointedly, "which makes you, Nate, a great deal more vulnerable than I. Allow me to remind you, Nate, you did this world the signal service of murdering the Colonel's prospective son-in-law, and, while heaven and all its angels rejoiced at your act, I doubt that Faulconer has forgiven you yet."

"No, sir," Starbuck said tonelessly. He did not like being reminded of Ethan Ridley's death. Starbuck had killed Ridley under the cover of battle's confusion and he had told himself ever since that it had been an act of self-defense, yet he knew he had cradled murder in his heart when he had pulled the trigger, and he knew, too, that no amount of rationalizing could wipe that sin from the great ledger in heaven that recorded all his failings. Certainly Colonel Washington Faulconer would never forgive Starbuck. "Yet I'd still rather stay with the regiment," Starbuck now told Bird. He was a stranger in a strange land, a northerner fighting against the North, and the Faulconer Legion had become his new home. The Legion fed him, clothed him, and gave him intimate friends. It was also the place where he had discovered the job he did best and, with the yearning of youth to discern high purpose in life, Starbuck had made up his mind that he was destined to be one of the Legion's officers. He belonged.

"Good luck to us both, then," Bird said, and they would both need luck, Bird reflected, if his suspicions were right and the order to march to Centreville was part of Colonel Washington Faulconer's attempt to take the Legion back under his control.

Washington Faulconer, after all, was the man who had raised the

Faulconer Legion, named it for himself, kitted it with the finest equipment his fortune could buy, then led it to the fight on the banks of the Bull Run. Faulconer and his son, both wounded in that battle, had ridden back to Richmond to be hailed as heroes, though in truth Washington Faulconer had been nowhere near the Legion when it faced the overpowering Yankee attack. It was too late now to set the record straight: Virginia, indeed all the upper South, reckoned Faulconer a hero and was demanding that he be given command of a brigade, and if that happened, Bird knew, the hero would expect his own Legion to be at the heart of that brigade.

"But it isn't certain the son of a bitch will get his brigade, is it?" Starbuck asked, trying in vain to suppress a huge yawn.

"There's a rumor he'll be offered a diplomatic post instead," Bird said, "which would be much more suitable, because my brother-in-law has a natural taste for licking the backsides of princes and potentates, but our newspapers say he should be a general, and what the newspapers want, the politicians usually grant. It's easier than having ideas of their own, you see."

"I'll take the risk," Starbuck said. His alternative was to join General Nathan Evans's staff and stay in the camp near Leesburg where Evans had command of the patchwork Confederate brigade that guarded the riverbank. Starbuck liked Evans, but he much preferred to stay with the Legion. The Legion was home, and he could not really imagine that the Confederate high command would make Washington Faulconer a general.

Another flurry of rifle fire sounded from the woods that lay three miles to the northwest. The sound made Bird turn, frowning. "Someone's being mighty energetic." He sounded disapproving.

"Squabbling pickets?" Starbuck suggested. For the last three months the sentries had faced each other across the river, and while relations had been friendly for most of that time, every now and then a new and energetic officer tried to provoke a war.

"Probably just pickets," Pecker Bird agreed, then turned back as Sergeant Major Proctor came to report that a broken wagon axle that had been delaying the Legion's march was now mended. "Does that mean we're ready to go, Sergeant Major?" Bird asked.

"Ready as we'll ever be, I reckon." Proctor was a lugubrious and suspicious man, forever fearing disaster.

"Then let us be off! Let us be off!" Bird said happily, and he strode toward the Legion just as another volley of shots sounded, only this time the fire had not come from the distant woods, but from the road to the east. Bird clawed thin fingers through his long, straggly beard. "Do you think?" he asked of no one in particular, not bothering to articulate the question clearly. "Maybe?" Bird went on with a note of growing excitement, and then another splinter of musketry echoed from the bluffs to the northwest and Bird jerked his head back and forth, which was his habitual gesture when he was amused. "I think we shall wait awhile, Mr. Proctor. We shall wait!" Bird snapped his fingers. "It seems," he said, "that God and Mr. Lincoln might have sent us other employment today. We shall wait."

The advancing Massachusetts troops discovered the rebels by blundering into a four-man picket that was huddled in a draw of the lower woods. The startled rebels fired first, sending the Massachusetts men tumbling back through the trees. The rebel picket fled in the opposite direction to find their company commander, Captain Duff, who first sent a message to General Evans and then led the forty men of his company toward the woods on the bluff's summit where a scatter of Yankee skirmishers now showed at the tree line. More northerners began to appear, so many that Duff lost count. "There are enough of the sumbitches," one of his men commented as Captain Duff lined his men behind a snake fence and told them to fire away. Puffs of smoke studded the fence line as the bullets whistled away up the gentle slope. Two miles behind Duff the town of Leesburg heard the firing, and someone thought to run to the church and ring the bell to summon the militia.

Not that the militia could assemble in time to help Captain Duff, who was beginning to understand just how badly his Mississippians were outnumbered. He was forced to retreat down the slope when a company of northern troops threatened his left flank, which withdrawal was greeted by northern jeers and a volley of musket fire. Duff's forty men went on doggedly firing as they backed away. They were a ragged company dressed in a shabby mix of butternut-brown and dirty gray uniforms, but their marksmanship was far superior to that of their northern rivals, who were mostly armed with smoothbore muskets. Massachusetts had taken immense pains to equip its volunteers, but there had not been enough rifles for everybody, and so Colonel Devens's 15th Massachusetts regiment fought with eighteenth-century muskets. None of Duff's men was hit, but their own bullets were taking a slow, steady toll of the northern skirmishers.

The 20th Massachusetts came to the rescue of their fellow Bay Staters. The 20th all had rifles, and their more accurate fire forced Duff to retreat still farther down the long slope. His forty men backed over a rail fence into a field of stubble where stooked oats stood in shocks. There was no more cover for a half mile, and Duff did not want to yield too much ground to the Yankees, so he halted his men in the middle of the field and told them to hold the bastards off. Duff's men were horribly outnumbered, but they came from Pike and Chickasaw counties, and Duff reckoned that made them as good as any soldiers in America. "Guess we're going to have to give this pack of black-assed trash a lesson, boys," Duff said.

"No, Captain! They're rebs! Look!" one of his men shouted in warning, then pointed to the tree line where a company of gray-clad troops had just appeared. Duff stared in horror. Had he been firing at his own side? The advancing men wore long gray coats. The officer leading them had his coat open and was carrying a drawn sword that he used to slash at weeds as he advanced, just as though he were out for a casual stroll in the country.

Duff felt his belligerent certainties drain away. He was dry-mouthed, his belly was sour, and a muscle in his thigh kept twitching. The firing all across the slope had died away as the gray-coated company marched down toward the oat field. Duff held up his hand and shouted at the strangers, "Halt!"

"Friends!" one of the gray-coated men called back. There were sixty or seventy men in the company, and their rifles were tipped with long shining bayonets.

"Halt!" Duff tried again.

"We're friends!" a man shouted back. Duff could see the nervousness on their faces. One man had a twitching muscle in his cheek, while another kept looking sideways at a mustachioed sergeant who marched stolidly at the flank of the advancing company.

"Halt!" Duff shouted again. One of his men spat onto the stubble.

"We're friends!" the northerners shouted again. Their officer's open coat was lined with scarlet, but Duff could not see the color of the man's uniform because the sun was behind the strangers.

"They ain't no friends of ours, Cap'n!" one of Duff's men said. Duff wished he could feel the same certainty. God in His heaven, but suppose these men were friends? Was he about to commit murder? "I order you to halt!" he shouted, but the advancing men would not obey, and so Duff shouted at his men to take aim.

Forty rifles came up into forty shoulders.

"Friends!" a northern voice called. The two units were fifty yards apart now, and Duff could hear the northern boots breaking and scuffing the oat stubble.

"They ain't friends, Cap'n!" one of the Mississippians insisted, and just at that moment the advancing officer stumbled and Duff got a clear view of the uniform beneath the scarlet-lined gray coat. The uniform was blue.

"Fire!" Duff shouted, and the southern volley cracked like a canebreak burning and a northerner screamed as the rebel bullets slapped home.

"Fire!" a northerner shouted and the Massachusetts's bullets whipped back through the smoke bank.

"Keep firing!" Duff shouted and emptied his revolver into the haze of powder smoke that already obscured the field. His men had taken cover behind the shocks of oats and were steadily reloading. The northerners were doing the same, except for one man who was twitching and bleeding on the ground. There were more Yankees off to Duff's right, higher up the slope, but he could not worry about them. He had chosen to make his stand here, plumb in the middle of the field, and now he would have to fight these bastards till one side could stand no more.

Six miles away, at Edwards Ferry, more northerners had crossed the Potomac and cut the turnpike that led to Centreville. Nathan Evans, thus caught between the two invading forces, refused to show any undue alarm. "One might be trying to fool me while the other one gets ready to rape me, ain't that how it's done, Boston?" "Boston" was his nickname for Starbuck. They had met at Manassas where Evans had saved the Confederacy by holding up the northern attack while the rebel lines reformed. "Lying, thieving, black-assed, hymn-singing bastards," Evans said now, evidently of the whole northern army. He had ridden with an order for the Faulconer Legion to stay where it was, only to discover that Thaddeus Bird had anticipated him by canceling the Legion's departure. Now Evans cocked his ear to the wind and tried to gauge from the intensity of the rifle fire which enemy incursion offered the most danger. The church bell in Leesburg was still ringing, summoning the militia. "So you're not going to stay with me, Boston?" Evans remarked.

"I like being a company officer, sir."

Evans growled in response, though Starbuck was not at all sure the small, foulmouthed South Carolinian had heard his answer. Instead Evans was switching his attention back and forth between the competing sounds of the two northern incursions. Otto, his German orderly, whose main duty consisted of carrying a barrel of whiskey for the General's refreshment, also listened to the gunfire so that the two men's heads twitched back and forth in unison. Evans was the first to stop, clicking his fingers for a drop of whiskey instead. He drained the tin mug, then looked back at Bird. "You'll stay here, Pecker. You're my reserve. I don't reckon there's so many of the bastards, they're not making enough noise for that, so we might as well stay put and see if we can't give the bastards a bloody nose. Killing Yankees is as good a way to start the week as any, eh?" He laughed.

"Of course, if I'm wrong we'll all be stone dead by nightfall. Come on. Otto!" Evans put spurs to his horse and galloped back toward the earth-walled fort that was his headquarters.

Starbuck climbed onto a wagon loaded with folded tents and slept as the sun burned the mist off the river and dried the dew off the fields. More northern troops crossed the river and climbed the bluff to mass under the trees. General Stone, the commander of the Federal forces guarding the Potomac, had decided to commit more troops to the crossing and sent orders that the invaders should not just occupy Leesburg but reconnoiter the whole of Loudoun County. If the rebels had gone, Stone commanded, then the Yankees should occupy the area, but if a strong Confederate force opposed the reconnaissance, then the Federal forces were free to withdraw across the river with whatever foodstuffs they might confiscate. Stone dispatched artillery to add firepower to the invading force, but also made plain that he was leaving the decision whether to stay in Virginia to the man he now placed in command of the whole northern operation.

That man was Colonel Ned Baker, a tall, clean-shaven, silver-haired, golden-tongued politician. Baker was a California lawyer, a United States senator from Oregon and one of President Lincoln's closest friends, so close that Lincoln had named his second son after the Senator. Baker was an impetuous, emotional, warmhearted man, and his arrival at the river crossing sent ripples of excitement through those men of the 15th Massachusetts who still waited with the New York Tammany Regiment on the Maryland bank. Baker's own regiment, the 1st Californian, now joined the invasion. The regiment was from New York, but had been recruited from men who had ties to California, and with them came a fourteen-pounder rifled cannon from Rhode Island and a pair of howitzers manned by U.S. Army regulars. "Take everything across!" Baker shouted ebulliently. "Every last man and gun!"

"We'll need more boats," the Colonel of the Tammanys cautioned the Senator.

"Then find them! Build them! Steal them! Fetch gopher wood and build an ark, Colonel. Find a beautiful woman and let her face launch a thousand ships, but let us press on to glory, boys!" Baker strode down the bank, cocking his ear to the staccato crackle of musketry that sounded from the river's far shore. "Rebels are dying, lads! Let's go and kill some more!"

The Tammany Colonel attempted to ask the Senator just what his regiment was supposed to do when it reached the Virginia shore, but Baker brushed the question aside. He did not care if this was a mere raid or a historic invasion marking the beginning of Virginia's occupation, he only knew that he had three pieces of artillery and four regiments of prime, unbloodied troops, which gave him the necessary power to offer President Lincoln and the country the victory they so badly needed. "On to Richmond, boys!" Baker shouted as he pushed through the troops on the riverbank. "On to Richmond, and may the devil have no mercy their souls! On for the union, boys, on for the union! Let's hear you cheer!"

They cheered loud enough to obliterate the splintering sound of musketry that came from the river's far bank where, beyond the wooded bluff, powder smoke lingered among the stooked oats where the day's long dying had begun.

MAJOR ADAM FAULCONER ARRIVED AT THE FAULCONER Legion a few moments after midday. "There are Yankees on the turnpike. They gave me a chase!" He looked happy, as though the hard riding of the last few minutes had been a cross-country romp rather than a desperate flight from a determined enemy. His horse, a fine roan stallion from the Faulconer Stud, was flecked with white foam, its ears were pricked nervously back, and it kept taking small nervous sidesteps that Adam instinctively corrected. "Uncle!" he greeted Major Bird cheerfully, then turned immediately back to Starbuck. They had been friends for three years, but it had been weeks since they had met, and Adam's pleasure at their reunion was heartfelt. "You look as if you were fast asleep, Nate."

"He was at a prayer meeting late last night," Sergeant Truslow interjected in a voice that was deliberately sour so that no one but he and Starbuck would know he made a joke, "praying till three in the morning."

"Good for you, Nate," Adam said warmly, then turned his horse back toward Thaddeus Bird. "Did you hear what I said, Uncle? There are Yankees on the turnpike!"

"We heard they were there," Bird said casually, as though errant Yankees were as predictable a feature of the fall landscape as migrating wild fowl.

"The wretches fired at me." Adam sounded astonished that such a discourtesy might occur in wartime. "But we outran them, didn't we, boy?" He patted the neck of his sweating horse, then swung down from the saddle and tossed the reins to Robert Decker, who was one of Starbuck's company. "Walk him for a while, will you, Robert?"

"Pleased to, Mr. Adam."

"And don't let him drink yet. Not till he's cooled," Adam instructed Decker, then he explained to his uncle that he had ridden from Centreville at dawn, expecting to encounter the Legion on the road. "I couldn't find you, so I just kept going," Adam said cheerfully. He walked with a very slight limp, the result of a bullet he had taken at the battle at Manassas, but the wound was well-healed and the limp hardly noticeable. Adam, unlike his father, Washington Faulconer, had been in the very thick of the Manassas fight even though, for weeks before, he had been assailed by equivocation about the war's morality and had even doubted whether he could take part in the hostilities at all. After the battle, while he was convalescing in Richmond, Adam had been promoted to major and given a post on General Joseph Johnston's staff. The General was one of the many Confederates who was under the misapprehension that Washington Faulconer had helped stem the surprise northern attack at Manassas, and the son's promotion and staff appointment had been intended as a mark of gratitude to the father.

"You've brought us orders?" Bird now asked Adam.

"Just my good self, Uncle. It seemed too perfect a day to be stuck with Johnston's paperwork, so I came for a ride. Though I hardly expected this." Adam turned and listened to the sound of rifle fire that came from the far woods. The gunfire was fairly constant now, but it was nothing like the splintering crackle of battle. Instead it was a methodical, workmanlike sound that suggested the two sides were merely trading ammunition because it was expected of them rather than trying to inflict slaughter upon each other. "What's happening?" Adam demanded.

Major Thaddeus Bird explained that two groups of Yankees had crossed the river. Adam had already encountered one of the invading parties, while the other was up on the high ground by Harrison's Island. No one was quite sure what the Yankees intended by the double incursion. Early on it had seemed they were trying to capture Leesburg, but a single company of Mississippi men had turned back the Federal advance. "A man called Duff," Bird told Adam, "stopped the rascals cold. Lined his fellows up in the stark middle of a field and traded them shot for shot, and damn me if they didn't go scuttling back uphill like a flock of frightened sheep!" The story of Duff's defiance had spread through Evans's brigade to fill the men with pride in southern invincibility. The remainder of Duff's battalion was in place now, keeping the Yankees pinned among the trees at the bluff's summit. "You should tell Johnston about Duff," Bird told Adam.

But Adam did not seem interested in the Mississippian's heroism. "And you, Uncle, what are you doing?" he asked instead.

"Waiting for orders, of course. I guess Evans doesn't know where to send us, so he's waiting to see which pack of Yankees is the more dangerous. Once that's determined, we'll go and knock some heads bloody."

Adam flinched at his uncle's tone. Before he had joined the Legion and unexpectedly became its senior officer, Thaddeus Bird had been a schoolmaster who had professed a sardonic mockery of both soldiering and warfare, but one battle and a few months of command had turned Adam's uncle into an altogether grimmer man. He retained his wit, but now it had a harsher edge, a symptom, Adam thought, of how war changed everything for the worse, though Adam sometimes wondered if he alone was aware of just how the war was coarsening and degrading all it touched. His fellow aides at the army headquarters reveled in the conflict, seeing it as a sporting rivalry that would award victory to the most enthusiastic players.

Adam listened to such bombast and held his peace, knowing that any expression of his real views would be met with scorn at best and charges of chickenhearted cowardice at worst. Yet Adam was no coward. He simply believed the war was a tragedy born from pride and stupidity, and so he did his duty, hid his true feelings, and yearned for peace, though how long he could sustain either the pretense or the duplicity, he did not know. "Let's hope no one's head needs to be bloodied today," he told his uncle. "It's much too fine a day for killing." He turned as K Company's cooks lifted a pot off the flames. "Is that dinner?"

The midday dinner was cush: a stew of beef, bacon fat, and cornbread that was accompanied by a mash of boiled apples and potatoes. Food was plentiful here in Loudoun County where the farmland was rich and Confederate troops few. In Centreville and Manassas, Adam said, supplies were much more difficult. "They even ran out of coffee last month! I thought there'd be a mutiny." He then listened with pretended amusement as Robert Decker and Amos Tunney told of Captain Starbuck's great coffee raid. They had crossed the river by night and marched five miles through woods and farmland to raid a sutler's stores on the outskirts of a northern camp. Eight men had gone with Starbuck and eight had come back, and the only northerner to detect them had been the sutler himself, a merchant whose living came from selling luxuries to troops. The sutler, sleeping among his stores, had shouted the alarm and pulled a revolver.

"Poor man," Adam said.

"Poor man?" Starbuck protested his friend's display of pity. "He was trying to shoot us!"

"So what did you do?"

"Cut his throat," Starbuck said. "Didn't want to alert the camp, you see, by firing a shot."

Adam shuddered. "You killed a man for some coffee beans?"

"And some whiskey and dried peaches," Robert Decker put in enthusiastically. "The newspapers over there reckoned it was secesh sympathizers. Bushwhackers, they called us. Bushwhackers! Us!"

"And next day we sold ten pounds of the coffee back to some Yankee pickets across the river!" Amos Tunney added proudly.

Adam smiled thinly, then refused the offer of a mug of coffee, pleading that he preferred plain water. He was sitting on the ground and winced slightly as he shifted his weight onto his wounded leg. He had his father's broad face, squarecut fair beard, and blue eyes. It was a face, Starbuck had always thought, of uncomplicated honesty, though these days it seemed Adam had lost his old humor and replaced it with a perpetual care for the world's problems.

After the meal the two friends walked eastward along the edge of the meadow. The Legion's wood and sod shelters were still in place, looking like grass-covered pigpens. Starbuck, pretending to listen to his friend's tales of headquarters life, was actually thinking how much he had enjoyed living in his turf-covered shelter. Once abed he felt like a beast in a burrow: safe, hidden, and secret. His old bedroom in Boston with its oak paneling and wide pine boards and gas mantels and solemn bookshelves seemed like a dream now, something from a different life. "It's odd how I like being uncomfortable," he said lightly.

"Didn't you hear what I said?" Adam demanded.

"Sorry, dreaming."

"I was talking about McClellan," Adam said. "Everyone agrees he's a genius. Even Johnston says McClellan was quite the cleverest man in all the old U.S. Army." Adam spoke enthusiastically, as though McClellan were the new southern commander and not the leader of the north's Army of the Potomac. Adam glanced to his right, disturbed by a sudden crescendo in the sound of musketry coming from the woods above the distant river. The firing had been desultory in the last hour, but now it rose to a sustained crackle that sounded like dry tinder burning fierce. It raged for a half minute or so, then fell back to a steady and almost monotonous mutter. "They must cross back to Maryland soon!" Adam said angrily, as though he were offended by the stubbornness of the Yankees in staying on this side of the river.

"So tell me more about McClellan," Starbuck said.

"He's the coming man," Adam said in a spirited voice. "It happens in war, you know. The old fellows begin the fight, then they get winnowed out by the young ones with new ideas. They say McClellan's the new Napoleon, Nate, a stickler for order and discipline!" Adam paused, evidently worried that he maybe sounded too enamored of the enemy's new general. "Did you really cut a man's throat for coffee?" he asked awkwardly.

"It wasn't quite as cold-blooded as Decker makes it sound," Starbuck said. "I tried to keep the man quiet without hurting him. I didn't want to kill him." In truth he had been scared to death of the moment, shaking and panicked, but he had known that the safety of his men had depended on keeping the sutler silent.

Adam grimaced. "I can't imagine killing a man with a knife."

"It's not something I ever imagined myself doing," Starbuck confessed, "but Truslow made me practice on some ration hogs, and it isn't as hard as you'd think."

"Good God," Adam said faintly. "Hogs?"

"Only young ones," Starbuck said. "Incredibly hard to kill, even so. Truslow makes it look easy, but then he makes everything look easy."

Adam pondered the idea of practicing the skills of killing as though they were the rudiments of a trade. It seemed tragic. "Couldn't you have just stunned the poor man?" He asked.

Starbuck laughed at the question. "I had to make sure of the fellow, didn't I? Of course I had to! My men's lives depended on his silence, and you look after your men. That's the first rule of soldiering."

"Did Truslow teach you that too?" Adam asked.

"No." Starbuck sounded surprised at the question. "That's an obvious rule, isn't it?"

Adam said nothing. Instead he was thinking, not for the first time, just how unlike each other he and Starbuck were. They had met at Harvard, where they had seemed to recognize in each other the qualities each knew he lacked in himself. Starbuck was impetuous and mercurial, while Adam was thoughtful and painstaking; Starbuck was a slave to his feelings, while Adam tried desperately hard to obey the harsh dictates of a rigorous conscience. Yet out of those dissimilarities had grown a friendship that had endured even the strains that had followed the battle at Manassas. Adam's father had turned against Starbuck at Manassas, and Starbuck now raised that delicate subject by asking whether Adam thought his father would be given command of a brigade.

"Joe would like him to get a brigade," Adam said dubiously. "Joe" was Joseph Johnston, the commander of the Confederate armies in Virginia. "But the President doesn't listen to Joe much." Adam went on, "He likes Granny Lee's opinion better." General Robert Lee had started the war with an inflated reputation, but had earned the nickname "Granny" after an unsuccessful minor campaign in western Virginia.

"And Lee doesn't want your father promoted?" Starbuck asked.

"So I'm told," Adam said. "Lee evidently believes Father should go as a commissioner to England"—Adam smiled at the notion— "which Mother thinks is a dandy idea. I think even her illnesses would disappear if she could take tea with the Queen."

"But your father wants his brigade?"

Adam nodded. "And he wants the Legion back," he said, knowing exactly why his friend had raised the subject. "And if he gets it, Nate, then he'll demand your resignation. I guess he's still convinced you shot Ethan." Adam was referring to the death of the man who would have married Adam's sister.

"Ethan was killed by a shell," Starbuck insisted.

"Father won't believe that," Adam said sadly, "and he won't be persuaded of it either."

"Then I'd better hope your father goes to England and takes tea with the Queen," Starbuck said carelessly.

"Because you're really going to stay with the Legion?" Adam asked, sounding surprised.

"I like it here. They like me." Starbuck spoke lightly, disguising the fervid nature of his attachment to the Legion.

Adam walked a few paces in silence while the gunfire splintered remote and distant like a skirmish in someone else's war. "Your brother," Adam said suddenly, then paused as though he suspected he was trespassing on a difficult area. "Your brother," he started again, "is still hoping you'll go back north."

"My brother?" Starbuck could not hide his surprise. His elder brother, James, had been captured at Manassas and was now a prisoner in Richmond. Starbuck had sent James gifts of books, but he had not asked for any furlough to visit his brother. He would have found any confrontation with his family too difficult. "You've seen him?"

"Only as part of my duties," Adam said, and explained that one of his responsibilities was to match lists of captured officers who were to be exchanged between the North and the South. "I sometimes visit the prison in Richmond," Adam went on, "and saw James there last week."

"How is he?"

"Thin, very pale, but hoping to be released on exchange."

"Poor James." Starbuck could not imagine his worried and pedantic brother as a soldier. James was a very good lawyer, but had always hated uncertainty and adventure, which were the very things that compensated for the dangerous discomforts of soldiering.

"He worries about you," Adam said.

"I worry about him," Starbuck said lightly, hoping to deflect what he suspected was an imminent sermon from his friend.

"He'll certainly be pleased to hear you're attending prayer meetings," Adam said fervently. "He worries for your faith. Do you go to church every week?"

"Whenever I can," Starbuck said, then decided this was a subject best changed. "And you?" he asked Adam. "How are you?"

Adam smiled, but did not answer at once. Instead he blushed, then laughed. He was clearly full of some piece of news that he was too embarrassed to tell outright, but nevertheless wanted prised out of him. "I'm really fine," he said, leaving the opening dangling.

Starbuck caught the inflection exactly. "You're in love."

Adam nodded. "I really think I might be, yes." He sounded surprised at himself. "Yes. Really."

Adam's coyness filled Starbuck with affectionate amusement. "You're getting married?"

"I think so, yes. We think so, indeed, but not yet. We thought we should wait for the war's end." Adam still blushed, but suddenly he laughed, hugely pleased with himself, and unbuttoned a tunic pocket as though to take out a picture of his beloved. "You haven't even asked what her name is."

"Tell me her name," Starbuck demanded dutifully, then turned away because the sound of rifle fire had swollen again to a frantic intensity. A slight haze of powder smoke was showing above the trees now, a gauzy flag of battle that would thicken into a dense fog if the guns kept up their present rate of fire.

"She's called . . ." Adam began, then checked because hooves thumped loud on the turf behind him.

"Sir! Mr. Starbuck, sir!" a voice hailed, and Starbuck turned to see young Robert Decker galloping across the field on the back of Adam's stallion. "Sir!" He was waving excitedly to Starbuck. "We've got orders, sir! We've got orders! We're to go and fight them, sir!"

"Thank God," Starbuck said, and started running back to his company.

"Her name's Julia," Adam said to no one, frowning at his friend's back. "Her name's Julia."

"Sir?" Robert Decker asked, puzzled. He had slid out of the saddle and now offered the stallion's reins to Adam.

"Nothing, Robert." Adam took the reins. "Nothing at all. Go and join the company." He watched Nate shouting at K Company, seeing the excitement of men stirred from repose by the prospect of killing. Then he buttoned his pocket to secure the leather-cased photograph of his girl before climbing into the saddle and riding to join his father's Legion. Which was about to fight its second battle.

On the quiet banks of the Potomac.

---

The two Yankee river crossings were five miles apart and General Nathan Evans had been trying to decide which offered his brigade the greater danger. The crossing to the east had cut the turnpike and so appeared to be the bigger tactical threat because it severed his communications with Johnston's headquarters at Centreville, but the Yankees were not reinforcing the handful of men and guns they had thrown over the river there, while more and more reports spoke of infantry reinforcements crossing the river at Harrison's Island and then climbing the precipitous slope to the wooded summit of Ball's Bluff. It was there, Evans decided, that the enemy was concentrating its threat, and it was there that he now sent the rest of his Mississippians and his two Virginia regiments. He sent the 8th Virginians to the near side of Ball's Bluff, but ordered Bird to make for the farther western flank. "Go through the town," Evans told Bird, "and come up on the left of the Mississippi boys. Then get rid of the Yankee bastards."

"With pleasure, sir." Bird turned away and shouted his orders. The men's packs and blanket rolls were to be left with a small baggage guard, while every one else in the Legion was to march west with a rifle, sixty rounds of ammunition, and whatever other weapons they chose to carry. In the summer, when they had first marched to war, the men had been weighed down with knapsacks and haversacks, canteens and cartridge boxes, blankets and groundsheets, bowie knives and revolvers, bayonets and rifles, plus whatever other accoutrements a man's family might have sent to keep him safe, warm, or dry. Some men had carried buffalo robes, while one or two had even worn metal breastplates designed to protect them from Yankee bullets, but now few men carried anything more than a rifle and bayonet, a canteen, a haversack, and a groundsheet and blanket rolled into a tube that was worn slantwise around their chests. Everything else was just impediment. Most had discarded their pasteboard-stiffened caps, preferring slouch hats that protected the backs of their necks from the sun. Their tall stiff boots had been cut down into shoes, the fine twin rows of brass buttons on their long jackets had been chopped away and used as payment for apple juice or sweet milk from the farms of Loudoun County, while many of the skirts of the long coats had been cut away to provide material to patch breeches or elbows. Back in June, when the Legion had trained at Faulconer Court House, the regiment had looked as smart and well-equipped as any soldiers in the world, but now, after just one battle and three months picket duty along the frontier, they looked like ragamuffins, but they were all far better soldiers. They were lean, tanned, fit, and very dangerous. "They still have their illusions, you see," Thaddeus Bird explained to his nephew. Adam was riding his fine roan horse while Major Bird, as ever, walked.

"Illusions?"

"We think we're invincible because we're young. Not me, you understand, but the boys. I used to make it my business to educate the more stupid fallacies out of youth; now I try to preserve their nonsense." Bird raised his voice so that the nearest company could hear him. "You'll live forever, you rogues, as long as you remember one thing! Which is?"

There was a pause, then a handful of men returned a ragged answer. "Aim low."

"Louder!"

"Aim low!" This time the whole company roared back the answer, then began laughing, and Bird beamed on them like a schoolmaster proud of his pupils' achievements.

The Legion marched through the dusty main street of Leesburg where one small crowd of men was gathered outside the Loudoun County Court House and another, slightly larger, outside Make-peace's Tavern across the street. "Give us guns!" one man shouted. It appeared they were the county militia and had neither weapons nor ammunition, though a handful of men, privately equipped, had gone to the battlefield anyway. Some of the men fell in with the Legion, hoping to find a discarded weapon on the field. "What's happening, Colonel?" they asked Adam, mistaking the scarlet trim and gold stars on his fine uniform as evidence that he commanded the regiment.

"It's nothing to be excited about," Adam insisted. "Nothing but a few stray northerners."

"Making enough noise, ain't they?" a woman called, and the Yan-

kees were indeed much noisier now that Senator Baker had succeeded in getting his three guns across the river and up the steep, slippery path to the bluff's peak, where the gunners had cleared their
weapons' throats with three blasts of canister that had rattled into the
trees to shred the leaves.

Baker, taking command of the battle, had found his troops sadly
scattered. The 20th Massachusetts was posted in the woods at the
summit while the 15th had pushed across the ragged meadow,
through the far woods and into the open slopes overlooking Leesburg. Baker called the 15th back, insisting that they form a battle line
on the left of the 20th. "We'll form up here," he announced, "while
New York and California join us!" He drew his sword and whipped
the engraved blade to slash off a nettle's head. The rebel bullets
slashed overhead, occasionally clipping off shreds of leaf that fluttered down in the warm, balmy air. The bullets seemed to whistle in
the woods, and somehow that odd noise took away their danger. The
Senator, who had fought as a volunteer in the Mexican War, felt no
apprehension; indeed he felt the exhilaration of a man touched by the
opportunity for greatness. This would be his day! He turned as
Colonel Milton Cogswell, commander of the Tammany Regiment,
panted up to the bluff's summit. " 'One blast upon your bugle horn is
worth a thousand men!' " Baker greeted the sweating Colonel with a
jocular quotation.

"I'll take the goddamn men, sir, begging your pardon," Cogswell
said sourly, then flinched as a pair of bullets slapped through the
leaves above his head. "What are our intentions, sir?"

"Our intentions, Milton? Our intentions are victory, fame, glory,
peace, forgiveness of our enemies, reconciliation, magnanimity, prosperity, happiness, and the assured promise of heaven's reward."

"Then might I suggest, sir," Cogswell said, trying to sober the
ebullient Senator, "that we advance and occupy that stand of trees?"
He gestured at the woods beyond the patch of ragged meadowland.
By pulling the 20th Massachusetts out of those woods Baker had
effectively yielded the trees to the rebels, and already the first gray-
coated infantry were well-established among the undergrowth.

"Those rogues won't bother us," Baker said dismissively. "Our artillerymen will soon scour them loose. We'll only be here a moment or two, just long enough to assemble, and then we'll advance. On to glory!"

A bullet whipsawed close above both men, causing Cogswell to curse in angry astonishment. His anger arose not from the near miss, but because the shot had come from a high knoll on the eastern end of the bluffs. The knoll was the highest part of the bluff and domi- nated the trees where the northern troops were gathering. "Aren't we occupying that height?" Cogswell asked Baker in horror.

"No need! No need! We'll be advancing soon! On to victory!" Baker strolled away, blithe in his self-assurance. Tucked inside the sweatband of his hat, where he had once stuffed his legal notes before going into court, he had pushed the orders he had received from Gen- eral Stone. "Colonel," the order read in a hurried scribble, "in case of heavy firing in front of Harrison's Island, you will advance the Cali- fornia regiment of your brigade or retire the regiments under Colonels Lee and Devens upon the Virginia side of the river, at your discretion, assuming command on arrival." All of which, in Baker's view, meant very little, except that he was in command, the day was sunny, the enemy lay before him, and martial fame was in his grasp. " 'One blast upon your bugle horn,' " the Senator chanted the lines from Sir Walter Scott as he marched through the northern troops gathering under the trees, " 'were worth a thousand men!' Fire back, lads! Let the rascals know we're here! Fire away, boys! Give them fire! Let them know the North is here to fight!"

Lieutenant Wendell Holmes took off his gray greatcoat, folded it carefully, then placed it beneath a tree. He drew his revolver, checked that its percussion caps were properly in place over the cones, then fired at the far, shadowy shapes of the rebels. The Senator's fine voice still echoed through the woods, punctuated by the crack and cough of Holmes's revolver. " 'Hail to the chief,' " Holmes quietly spoke the line from the same poem Baker was declaiming, " 'who in tri- umph advances.' "

Senator Baker pulled out an expensive watch that had been a gift from his associates and friends of the California bar on the occasion of his appointment to the U.S. Senate. The day was hurrying by, and if he wanted to capture and consolidate Leesburg before nightfall he would need to hurry. "Forward now!" Baker pushed the watch back into his fob pocket. "All of you! All of you! On, my fine boys, on! On to Richmond! On to glory! All for the union, boys, all for the union!"

The colors were lifted, the glorious Stars and Stripes, and beside them the white silk colors of Massachusetts with the arms of the Commonwealth embroidered on one flank and the motto *Fide et Constantia* stitched bright on the other. The silk streamed in the sunlight as the men cheered, broke cover, and charged.

To die.

"Fire!" Two whole regiments of Mississippi men were in the trees now, and their rifles whipped flames across the clearing to where the northerners had suddenly appeared. Bullets splintered the locust trees and shredded the bright yellow leaves of the maples. A dozen northerners went down in the volley. One, a man who had never sworn in his life, began cursing. A Boston furniture maker stared astonished at the blood spreading on his uniform, then called for his mother as he tried to crawl back to cover.

"Fire!" Colonel Eps of the 8th Virginia had the high ground that dominated the Yankees' eastern flank and his riflemen poured a slaughtering fusillade down onto the northerners. So many bullets whined and sang off the bronze barrels of the Yankee howitzers that the gunners fled down the precipice of the bluff to where they were safe from the hornets' whine and hissing slash of the rebel bullets.

"Fire!" More Mississippians opened fire. They lay flat among the trees, or knelt behind trunks and peered through the powder smoke to see that their volleys had sent the northern attack reeling back. Scattered among the Mississippians were men from Leesburg and from the surrounding farms who fired fowling pieces and shotguns at the faltering Yankees. A New York sergeant cursed at his men in Gaelic, but the curses did no good and a bullet shattered his elbow. The northerners were retreating back into the trees, seeking shelter behind trunks and fallen logs where they reloaded their muskets and rifles. Two of the Massachusetts companies had been recruited from German immigrants, and their officers shouted in that language, exhorting them to show the world how Germans could fight. Other northern officers feigned indifference to the storm of bullets that whipped and hissed across the bluff's crest. They strolled among the trees, knowing that a display of insouciant bravery was the quality necessary for rank. They paid for the display with blood. Many of the men from the 20th Massachusetts had hung their fine new scarlet-lined coats from branches and the garments twitched as the bullets plucked and tore at the rich gray cloth. The sound of the battle was constant now, like calico tearing or a canebrake burning, but under that splintering crackle came the sobbing of wounded men and the screams of hurt men and the rattle of dying men.

Senator Baker shouted at his staff officers to man one of the abandoned howitzers, but none of them knew how to prime a vent and the hail of Virginia bullets drove the officers back into the shadows. They left a major dead and a lieutenant coughing up blood as he staggered back from the gun. A bullet slashed a shard of wood from a howitzer's wheel spoke, another smacked on the muzzle's face, and a third punctured the water bucket.

A group of Mississippi men, enraged because their Colonel had been shot, tried to charge across the patch of rough meadowland, but as soon as they showed themselves at the tree line the frustrated northerners poured fire at them. It was the rebels' turn to pull back, leaving three men dead and two wounded. At the right flank of the Massachusetts line the fourteen-pound cannon was still firing, but the Rhode Island gunners had used up their small stock of canister and now had nothing to fire but solid iron bolts. The canister, tearing itself apart at the cannon's muzzle to scatter a lethal spray of musket balls into the enemy ranks, was ideal for close-range killing work, but the solid bolts were intended for long-range accurate fire and were no good for scouring infantry out of woodland. The bolts, which were elongated iron cannonballs, screamed across the clearing and either vanished into the distance or else struck slivers of freshly splintered timber from tree trunks. The smoke from the cannon pumped its foul-smelling cloud twenty yards in front of the muzzle, forging a smokescreen that hid the right flank companies of the 20th Massachusetts. "Come on, Harvard!" an officer shouted. At least two-thirds of the regiment's officers had come from Harvard, as had six of its sergeants and dozens of its men. "Come on, Harvard!" the officer shouted again and he stepped forward to lead his men by example, but a bullet took him under the chin and jerked his head sharply back. Blood misted around his face as he slowly crumpled to the ground.

Wendell Holmes, dry-mouthed, watched the stricken officer kneel and then slump forward. Holmes ran forward to help the man, but two other soldiers were closer and dragged the body back into the trees. The officer was unconscious, his bloodied head twitching, then he made a harsh rattling sound and blood bubbled at his throat. "He's dead," one of the men who had pulled the body back to cover said. Holmes stared at the dead man and felt a sour surge of vomit rise in his throat. Somehow he kept the vomit down as he turned away and forced himself to stroll with apparent carelessness among his company. He really wanted to lie down, but he knew he needed to show his men that he was unafraid and so he paced among them, his sword drawn, offering what help he could. "Aim low, now. Aim carefully! Don't waste your shots. Look for them now!" His men bit cartridges, souring their mouths with the salty taste of the gunpowder. Their faces were blackened with the powder, their eyes redrimmed. Holmes, pausing in a patch of sunlight, suddenly caught the sound of rebel voices calling the exact same advice. "Aim low!" a Confederate officer called. "Aim for the officers!" Holmes hurried on, resisting the temptation to linger behind the bullet-scarred trunks of the trees.

"Wendell!" Colonel Lee called.

Lieutenant Holmes turned to his commanding officer. "Sir?"

"Look to our right, Wendell! Maybe we can outflank these rogues." Lee pointed to the woods beyond the field gun. "Find out how far the rebel line extends. Hurry now!"

Holmes, thus given permission to abandon his studied and casual air, ran through the trees toward the open right flank of the northern line. To his right, below him and through the trees, he glimpsed the bright, cool surprise of the river, and the sight of the water was oddly comforting. He passed his gray greatcoat folded so neatly at the foot of a maple tree, ran behind the Rhode Islanders manning their cannon and on toward the flank, and there, just as he emerged from the smoke and could see that the far woods were indeed empty of rebel enemy and thus offered a way for Colonel Lee to hook around the Confederate left flank, a bullet struck his chest.

He shuddered, his whole frame shaken by the bullet's whipsaw strike. The breath was knocked hard out of him, leaving him momentarily unable to breathe, yet even so he felt oddly cool and detached, so that he was able to register just what he was experiencing. The bullet, he was sure it was a bullet, had struck him with the impact he imagined equal to the kick of a horse. It had left him seemingly paralyzed, but when he tried to take a breath he was pleasantly surprised to discover his lungs were working after all, and he realized it was not true paralysis, but rather an interruption of his mind's control over physical motion. He also realized that his father, Professor of Medicine at Harvard, would want to know of these perceptions, and so he moved his hand toward the pocket where he kept his memorandum book and pencil, but then, helpless to stop himself, he began to topple forward. He tried to call for assistance, but no sound would come, and then he tried to raise his hands to break his fall, but his arms seemed suddenly enfeebled. His sword, which he had been carrying unsheathed, fell to the ground, and he saw a drop of blood splash on the mirror-bright blade and then he fell full-length across the steel and there was a terrible pain inside his chest so that he cried aloud in pity and agony. He had a vision of his family in Boston and he wanted to weep.

"Lieutenant Holmes is down!" a man shouted.

"Fetch him now! Take him back!" Colonel Lee ordered, then went to see how badly wounded Holmes was. He was delayed a few seconds by the Rhode Island artillerymen who shouted for the infantry to stand clear as they fired. Their cannon crashed back on its trail, jetting smoke and flame far out into the sunlit clearing. Each time the gun fired it recoiled a few feet farther back so that its trail left a crudely plowed furrow in the leaf-covered dirt. The gun's crew was too busy to haul the weapon forward again and each shot was fired a few feet farther back than the one before.

Colonel Lee reached Holmes just as the Lieutenant was being lifted onto a stretcher. "I'm sorry, sir," Holmes managed to say.

"Be quiet, Wendell."

"I'm sorry," Holmes said again. Lee stopped to retrieve the Lieutenant's sword and wondered why so many men assumed that being wounded was their own fault.

"You've done well, Wendell," Lee said fervently, then a burst of rebel cheering turned him around to see a rush of new rebel troops arriving in the woods opposite, and he knew he had no chance now of hooking around the enemy's open flank. Indeed, it looked as if the enemy might hook around his. He swore softly, then laid Holmes's sword beside the wounded Lieutenant. "Take him down gently," Lee said, then flinched as a corporal began screaming because a bullet had plowed into his bowels. Another man reeled back with an eye filled with blood, and Lee wondered why in God's name Baker had not ordered a retreat. It was time to get back across the river before they all died.

On the far side of the clearing the rebels had begun making the demonic sound that northern veterans of Bull Run claimed had presaged the onset of disaster. It was a weird, ulullating, inhuman noise that sent shivers of pure terror up Colonel Lee's spine. It was a prolonged yelp like a beast's cry of triumph, and it was the sound, Lee feared, of northern defeat. He shuddered, gripped his sword a little tighter, and went to find the Senator.

The Faulconer Legion climbed the long slope toward battle. It had taken longer than anyone expected to march through the town and find the right track toward the river, and now it was late afternoon and some of the more confident men were complaining that the Yankees would all be dead and looted before the Faulconer Legion could get its share of the spoils, while the timid noted that the battle still crackled on unabated. The Legion was close enough to smell the bitter stench of gunpowder carried on the small north wind that sifted the gunsmoke through the green leaves like a winter fog shifting through branches. At home, Starbuck thought, the leaves would all have changed color, turning the hills around Boston into a glorious surprise of gold, scarlet, flaming yellow, and rich brown, but here, on the northern edge of the southern Confederacy, only the maples had turned gold and the other trees were still heavy with green leaves, though their greenness was being plucked and twitched by the storm of bullets being fired from somewhere deep inside the woods.

The Legion marched across the leprous scatter of scorched stubble that showed where Duff's company of Pike and Chickasaw County men had fought the advancing Yankees to a standstill. The burning wads of their rifles, coughed out with the bullets, had started the small fires that had burned and died away to leave ashy scars in the field. There were a couple of patches of blood too, but the Legion was too distracted by the fight at the hilltop to worry about those signs of earlier battle.

More detritus of battle showed at the woodland's edge. A dozen officers' horses were picketed there, and a score of wounded men were being tended by doctors. A mule loaded with fresh ammunition was led into the trees while another, its panniers empty, was brought out. A slave, come to the battle as his master's servant, ran uphill with canteens he had refilled at the wellhead in the nearest farm. At least a score of children had come from Leesburg to watch the battle and a Mississippi sergeant was attempting to chase them out of range of the northern bullets. One small boy had fetched his father's huge shotgun to the field and was pleading to be allowed to kill one Yankee before bedtime. The boy did not even flinch as a fourteen-pound solid bolt streaked out from the trees and slapped close overhead. The shot appeared to fly halfway to the Catoctin Mountain before it fell with a mighty splash into a stream just beyond the Licksville Road. The Legion had now come to within sixty yards of the trees, and those officers who still rode horses dismounted and hammered iron picket pins into the turf while Captain Hinton, the Legion's second-in-command, ran ahead to establish exactly where the left flank of the Mississippi boys lay.

Most of Starbuck's men were excited. Their relief at surviving Manassas had turned to boredom in the long weeks guarding the Potomac. Those weeks had hardly seemed like war, but instead had been a summer idyll beside cool water. Every now and then a man on one or other riverbank would take a potshot across the water and for a day or two thereafter the pickets would skulk in the shadows, but mostly the two sides had lived and let live. Men had gone swimming under the gunsights of their enemies, they had washed their clothes and watered their horses, and inevitably they had struck up acquaintances with the other side's sentries and discovered shallow places where they could meet in midstream to exchange newspapers or swap southern tobacco for northern coffee. Now, though, in their eagerness to prove themselves the best soldiers in all the world, the Legion forgot the summer's friendliness and swore instead to teach the lying, thieving, bastard Yankees to come across the river without first asking for rebel permission.

Captain Hinton reappeared at the edge of the trees and cupped his hands. "A Company, to me!"

"Form on A Company's left!" Bird shouted to the rest of the Legion. "Color party to me!"

One of the cannon bolts slashed through the trees, showering the advancing men with leaves and splinters. Starbuck could see where an earlier shot had ripped a branch from a trunk, leaving a shocking scar of fresh clean timber. The sight gave him a sudden catch in the throat, a pulse of fear that was the same as excitement.

"Color party to me!" Bird shouted again and the standard-bearers raised their flags into the sunlight and ran to join the Major. The Legion's own color was based on the Faulconer family's coat-of-arms and showed three red crescents on a white silken field above the family motto "Forever Ardent." The second color was the national flag of the Confederacy, two red horizontal stripes either side of a white stripe, while the upper quadrant next to the staff showed a blue field on which was sewn a circle of seven white stars. After Manassas there had been complaints that the flag was too similar to the northern flag and that troops had fired on friendly units believing them to be Yankees, and rumor had it that a new design was being made in Richmond, but for today the Legion would fight beneath the bullet-torn silk of its old Confederate color.

"Dear sweet Jesus save me, dear sweet Jesus save me," Joseph May, one of Starbuck's men, prayed breathlessly as he hurried behind Sergeant Truslow. "Save me, O Lord, save me."

"Save your breath, May!" Truslow growled.

The Legion had been advancing in columns of companies and now it peeled leftward as it turned itself from a column of march into a line of battle. A Company was first into the trees and Starbuck's K Company would be the last. Adam Faulconer rode with Starbuck. "Get off that horse, Adam!" Starbuck shouted up to his friend. "You'll be killed!" He needed to shout for the crackle of musketry was loud, but the sound was filling Starbuck with a curious elation. He knew as well as Adam that war was wrong. It was like sin, it was terrible, but just like sin it had a terrible allure. Survive this, Starbuck felt, and a man could take anything that the world might hurl at him. This was a game of unimaginably high stakes, but also a game where privilege conferred no advantages except the chance to avoid the game altogether, and whoever used privilege to avoid this game was no man at all, but a lickspittle coward. Here, where the air was foul with smoke and death whipped among green leaves, existence was simplified to absurdity. Starbuck whooped suddenly, filled with the sheer joy of the moment. Behind him, their rifles loaded, K Company spread among the green leaves. They heard their Captain's whoop of joy and they heard the rebel yell sounding from the troops on the right, and so they began to make the same demonic wailing screech that spoke of southern rights and southern pride and southern boys come to make a killing.

"Give them hell, boys!" Bird shouted. "Give them hell!"

And the Legion obeyed.

Baker died.

The Senator had been trying to steady his men whose nerves were being abraded by the whooping, vengeful, southern fiends. Baker had made three attempts to break out of the woods, but each northern advance had been beaten bloodily back to leave another tide mark of dead men on the small meadow that lay like a smoke-palled slaughter field between the two forces. Some of Baker's men were abandoning the fight; hiding themselves on the steep escarpment that dropped down to the riverbank or sheltering blindly behind tree trunks and outcrops of rock on the bluff's summit. Baker and his aides rousted such timid men out from their refuges and sent them back to where the brave still attempted to keep the rebels at bay, but the timid crept back to their shelters just as soon as the officers were gone.

The Senator was bereft of ideas. All his cleverness, his oratory, and his passion had been condensed into a small tight ball of panic-stricken helplessness. Not that he showed any fear. Instead he strolled with drawn sword in front of his men and called on them to aim low and keep their spirits high. "There are reinforcements coming!" he said to the powder-stained men of the 15th Massachusetts. "Not much longer, boys!" he encouraged his own men of the 1st Californian. "Hot work now, lads, but they'll tire of it first!" he promised the men of New York Tammanys. "If I had one more regiment like you," he told the Harvards, "we'd all be feasting in Richmond tonight!"

Colonel Lee tried to persuade the Senator to retreat across the river, but Baker seemed not to hear the request and when Lee shouted it, insisting on being heard, Baker merely offered the Colonel a sad smile. "I'm not sure we have enough boats for a retreat, William. I think we must stand and win here, don't you?" A bullet spat inches above the Senator's head, but he did not flinch. "They're only a pack of rebels. We won't be beaten by such wretches. The world is watching and we have to show our superiority!"

Which was probably what an ancestor of Baker's had said at Yorktown, Lee reflected, but wisely did not say aloud. The Senator might have been born in England, but there was no more patriotic

American. "You're sending the wounded off?" Lee asked the Senator instead.

"I'm sure we are!" Baker said firmly, though he was sure of no such thing, but he could not worry about the wounded now. Instead he needed to fill his men with a righteous fervor for the beloved union. An aide brought him news that the 19th Massachusetts had arrived on the river's far bank and he was thinking that if he could just bring that fresh regiment across the Potomac he would have enough men to throw an attack against the knoll from which the rebels were decimating his left flank and preventing his howitzers from doing their slaughtering work. The idea gave the Senator instant hope and fresh enthusiasm. "That's what we'll do!" he shouted to one of his aides.

"We'll do what, sir?"

"Come on! We have work!" The Senator needed to get back to his left flank and the quickest route lay in the open where the gun-smoke offered a fogbank in which to hide. "Come on," he shouted again, then hurried down the front of his line, calling to the riflemen to hold their fire until he had passed. "We're being reinforced, boys," he shouted. "Not long now! Victory's coming. Hold on there, hold on!"

A group of rebels saw the Senator and his aides hurrying in the shifting smoke, and though they did not know Baker was the northern commander, they knew that only a senior officer would carry a tasseled sword and wear a uniform so tricked out with braid and glitter. A gold watch chain hung with seals was looped on the Senator's coat and caught the slanting sun. "There's their gang boss! Gang boss!" a tall, stringy, redheaded Mississippian called aloud, pointing to the striding figure who marched so confidently across the battle's front. "He's mine!" the big man shouted as he ran forward. A dozen of his companions scrambled after him in their eagerness to plunder the bodies of the rich northern officers.

"Sir!" one of Baker's aides called in warning.

The Senator turned, raising his sword. He should have retreated into the trees, but he had not crossed a river to flee a rabble of seceshers. "Come on then, you damn rebel!" he shouted, and he held the sword out as though ready to fight a duel.

But the red-haired man used a revolver and his four bullets thudded into the Senator's chest like axe blows hitting softwood. The Senator was thrown back, coughing and grasping at his chest. His sword and hat fell as he tried to stay on his feet. Another bullet ripped his throat open and blood spilt in a scarlet wash down the brass-buttoned tunic of his double-breasted coat and clogged in the links of the gold watch chain. Baker was trying to breathe and was shaking his head as though he could not believe what was happening to him. He looked up at the lanky killer with a puzzled expression, then collapsed onto the grass. The red-haired rebel ran to claim his body.

A rifle shot spun the red-haired man around, then another bullet put him down. A volley drove the other Mississippians back as two of the Senator's aides dragged their dead master back into the trees. One of the men retrieved the Senator's hat and took out the sweaty, folded message that had launched this madness across a river.

The sun was low in the west. The leaves might not have turned, but the nights were drawing on and the sun would be quite gone by half past five, but darkness could not save the Yankees now. They needed boats, but there were only five small craft, and some of the wounded had already drowned as they tried to swim back to Harrison's Island. More wounded were climbing clumsily down the bluff to where the northern casualties already filled the small area of flatland that lay between the base of the steep hill and the riverbank. Two aides carried the Senator's body through the press of moaning men to one of the boats and ordered a space cleared for the corpse. The Senator's expensive watch fell from his pocket as his carcass was manhandled down the bank. The watch swung on its bloody chain, first dragging in the mud, then striking hard against the boat's timbers. The blow broke the watch's crystal and scattered small sharp scraps of glass into the bilges. The Senator's bloody corpse was rolled on top of the glass. "Take him back!" an aide ordered.

"We're all going to die!" a man screamed on the hilltop, and a Massachusetts sergeant told him to shut his damn noise and die like a man. A group of rebels tried to cross the clearing and were hurled back by a crescendo of musket fire that twisted them around and plucked scraps of wood from the trees behind them. A Massachusetts color bearer was hit and his great, beautiful, bullet-beaten silk flag fluttered down toward the dirt, but another man seized its tasseled fringe and lifted the stars back toward the sun before the stripes had touched the ground.

"What we'll do," said Colonel Cogswell, who had finally established that he was the senior officer alive and thus had command of the four Yankee regiments stranded on the Virginia shore, "is fight our way downstream to the ferry." He wanted to take his men out of the murderous shadows and into the open fields where their enemies would no longer be able to hide behind trees. "We'll march fast. It means we'll have to abandon the guns and the wounded."

No one liked that decision, but no one had a better idea, and so the order was relayed back to the 20th Massachusetts, who lay at the right-hand flank of the Yankee line. The fourteen-pounder James rifle would have to be abandoned anyway for it had recoiled so far that at last it had toppled back over the bluff. As it had fired its final shot a gunner had shouted in alarm, then the whole heavy cannon had tilted over the escarpment's crest and crashed sickeningly down the steep slope until it smashed against a tree. Now the gunners gave up their attempts to haul the gun back to the crest and listened instead as Colonel Lee explained to his officers what the regiment was about to do. They were to leave their wounded to the mercy of the rebels and gather at the left-hand flank of the northern line. There they would make a mass charge through the rebel forces and so down to the water meadows which led to where the second Yankee force had crossed the river to cut the turnpike. That second force was covered by artillery on the Maryland bank of the river. "We can't cross back into Maryland here," Lee told his officers, "because we don't have enough boats, so we'll have to march the five miles downstream and fight the rebels off all the way." He looked at his watch. "We'll move in five minutes."

Lee knew it would take that long for the orders to reach all his companies and for the casualties to be gathered under a flag of truce. He hated leaving his wounded, but he knew none of his regiment would reach Maryland this night if he did not abandon the casualties. "Hurry now," he told his officers and tried to sound confident, but the strain was telling now and his sanguine appearance was fraying under the constant whip and whistle of the rebel bullets. "Hurry now!" he called again, then he heard a terrible screaming noise from his open right flank and he turned, alarmed, and suddenly knew that no amount of hurrying could help him now.

It seemed the Harvards would have to fight where they were. Lee drew his sword, licked dry lips, then committed his soul to God and his beloved regiment to its desperate end.

W E'RE TOO FAR LEFT." TRUSLOW HAD GROWLED AT
Starbuck as soon as K Company reached the battle line.
"Bastards are that way." Truslow pointed across the clearing to
where a veil of smoke hung in front of the trees. That smoke lay well
to the right of K Company, while directly across from Starbuck's men
there was no gunsmoke, just empty trees and long, darkening shadows among which the maple trees looked unnaturally bright. Some
of K Company had begun firing into those empty trees, but Truslow
snarled at them to stop wasting powder.

The company waited expectantly for Starbuck's orders, then
turned as another officer came running through the brush. It was
Lieutenant Moxey, who had reckoned himself a hero ever since taking a slight wound in his left hand at Manassas. "The Major says
you're to close on the center." Moxey was filled with the moment's
excitement. He waved a revolver toward the sound of musketry. "He
says you're to reinforce Murphy's company."

"Company!" Truslow shouted at his men, anticipating Star-buck's orders to move.

"No! Wait!" Starbuck was still gazing directly across the clearing to the undisturbed trees. He looked back to his right again, noting how the Yankee fire had momentarily died down. For a few seconds he wondered if that lull in the firing signified that the northern forces were retreating, but then a sudden charge by a yelping group of rebels triggered a furious outburst of northern rifle fire. For a few seconds the gunfire splintered in a mad tattoo, but the moment the rebels retreated the fusillade died away. Starbuck realized that the northerners were holding their fire until they could see targets while the southerners were keeping up a steady fusillade. Which meant, Starbuck decided, that the Yankees were worried about having enough ammunition.

"The Major says you're to move at once," Moxey insisted. He was a thin, pale-faced youth who resented that Starbuck had received a captaincy while he remained a lieutenant. He was also one of the few men in the Legion who begrudged Starbuck's presence, believing that a Virginia regiment had no need of a renegade Bostonian, but it was an opinion he kept to himself, for Moxey had seen Starbuck's temper and knew the northerner was more than willing to use his fists. "Did you hear me, Starbuck?" he demanded now.

"I heard you," Starbuck said, yet still he did not move. He was thinking that the Yankees had been fighting in these woods nearly all day, and presumably they had just about used up all the cartridges in their pouches, which meant they were now relying on whatever small amounts of ammunition could be brought across the river. He was also thinking that troops worried about having sufficient cartridges were troops that could be panicked very quickly. He had seen panic at Manassas and reckoned it could bring a victory just as swift and complete here.

"Starbuck!" Moxey insisted on being heard. "The Major says you're to reinforce Captain Murphy."

"I heard you, Mox," Starbuck said again, and still did nothing.

Moxey made a great play of pretending that Starbuck had to be particularly stupid. He tapped Starbuck's arm and pointed through the trees to the right. "That way, Starbuck."

"Go away, Mox," Starbuck said, and he looked back across the clearing. "And on your way tell the Major we're crossing over here and we'll be rolling the bastards up from the left. Our left, got that?"

"You're doing what?" Moxey gaped at Starbuck, then looked up at Adam who was on horseback a few paces behind Starbuck. "You tell him, Adam," Moxey appealed to higher authority. "Tell him to obey orders!"

"We're crossing the field, Moxey," Starbuck said in a kind, slow voice, as though he addressed a particularly dull child, "and we're going to attack the nasty Yankees from inside the trees over there. Now go away and tell that to Pecker!"

The maneuver seemed the obvious thing to do. The two sides were presently blazing away from either side of the clearing, and though the rebels had a clear advantage, neither side seemed capable of advancing straight into the concentrated rifle fire of the other. By crossing the clearing at this open flank Starbuck could take his men safe into the northerners' trees and then advance on their undefended wing. "Make sure you're loaded!" Starbuck shouted at his men.

"You can't do this, Starbuck," Moxey said. Starbuck took no notice of him. "Do you want me to tell the Major you're disobeying his orders?" Moxey asked Starbuck cattily.

"Yes," Starbuck said, "that's exactly what I want you to tell him. And that we're attacking their flank. Now go away and do it!"

Adam, still on horseback, frowned down at his friend. "Do you know what you're doing, Nate?"

"I know, Adam, I really do know," Starbuck said. In truth the opportunity to turn the Yankee flank was so straightforward that the dullest fool might have seized it, though a wise man might have sought permission for the maneuver first. But Starbuck was so certain he was right and so confident that his flank attack would finish the Yankee defense that he reckoned seeking permission would simply be a waste of time. "Sergeant!" he called for Truslow.

Truslow once again anticipated Starbuck's order. "Bayonets on!"

he called to the company. "Make sure they're fixed firm! Remember to twist the blade when you drive home!" Truslow's voice was as calm as though this were just another day's training. "Take your time, lad! Don't fumble!" He spoke to a man who had dropped a bayonet in his excitement, then he checked that another man's bayonet was firmly slotted onto the rifle's muzzle. Hutton and Mallory, the company's two other sergeants, were similarly checking their squads.

"Captain!" one of Hutton's men called. It was Corporal Peter Waggoner, whose twin brother was also a corporal in the company. "You staying or going, Captain?" Peter Waggoner was a big, slow man of deep piety and fierce beliefs.

"I'm going over there," Starbuck said, pointing across the clearing and deliberately misunderstanding the question.

"You know what I mean," Waggoner said, and most of the other men in the company knew too for they stared apprehensively at their Captain. They knew Nathan Evans had offered him a job, and many of them feared that such a staff appointment might be attractive to a bright young Yankee like Starbuck.

"Do you still believe that people who drink whiskey will go to hell, Peter?" Starbuck asked the Corporal.

"That's the truth, isn't it?" Waggoner demanded sternly. "God's truth, Mr. Starbuck. Be sure your sins will find you out."

"I've decided to stay here until you and your brother get drunk with me, Peter," Starbuck retorted. There was a second's silence as the men understood just what he had meant and then there was a cheer.

"Quiet!" Truslow snapped.

Starbuck looked back at the enemy side of the clearing. He did not know why his men liked him, but he was hugely moved by their affection, so moved that he had turned away rather than betray his emotion. When he had first been made their Captain he knew the men had accepted him because he had come with Truslow's approval, but they had since discovered that their Yankee officer was a clever, fierce, and combative man. He was not always friendly, not like some of the officers who behaved just like the men they commanded, but K Company accepted Starbuck's secretive and cool manner as the trait of a northerner. Everyone knew that Yankees were queer cold fish and none were stranger or colder than Bostonians, but they had also learned that Starbuck was fiercely protective of his men and was prepared to defy all the Confederacy's authorities to save one of his company from trouble. They also sensed he was a rogue, and that made them think he was lucky, and like all soldiers, they would rather have a lucky leader than any other kind. "You're really staying, sir?" Robert Decker asked.

"I'm really staying, Robert. Now get yourself ready."

"I'm ready," Decker said, grinning with pleasure. He was the youngest of the fifty-seven men in the company, almost all of whom came from Faulconer County, where they had been schooled by Thaddeus Bird and doctored by Major Danson and preached at by the Reverend Moss and employed, like as not, by Washington Faulconer. A handful were in their forties, a few were in their twenties and thirties, but most were just seventeen, eighteen, or nineteen years old. They were brothers, cousins, in-laws, friends, and enemies, not a stranger to each other among the lot of them, and all were familiar with each other's houses and sisters and mothers and dogs and hopes and weaknesses. To a stranger's eye they looked as fierce and unkempt as a pack of winter hounds after a wet day's run, but Starbuck knew them better. Some, like the Waggoner twins, were deeply pious boys who witnessed nightly with the other soldiers and who prayed for their captain's soul, while others, like Edward Hunt and Abram Statham, were rogues who could not be trusted a short inch. Robert Decker, who had come from the same high Blue Ridge valley as Sergeant Truslow, was a kind, hardworking, and trusting soul, while others, like the Cobb twins, were lazier than cats.

"You're supposed to reinforce Murphy's company!" Lieutenant Moxey still lingered close to Starbuck.

Starbuck turned on him. "Go and give Pecker my message! For God's sake, Mox, if you're going to be a message boy, then be a good one. Now run!" Moxey backed away and Starbuck looked up at

Adam. "Will you please go and tell Pecker what we're doing? I don't trust Moxey."

Adam spurred away and Starbuck turned back to his men. He raised his voice over the noise of the musketry and told the company what he expected of them. They were to cross the clearing at the double, and once on the far side they would wheel to their right and make a line that would sweep up through the far woods like a broom coming at the open edge of the Yankee's line. "Don't fire unless you have to," Starbuck said, "just scream as loud as you can and let them see your bayonets. They'll run, I promise you!" He knew instinctively that the sudden appearance of a pack of screaming rebels would be sufficient to send the Yankees packing. The men grinned nervously. One man, Joseph May, who had been praying as he climbed the hill, peered at his bayonet's fixture to make sure it was properly secure. Starbuck saw the boy squint. "Where are your spectacles, Joe?"

"Lost 'em, Captain." May sniffed unhappily. "Got broke," he finally admitted.

"If any of you see a dead Yankee with specs, bring them to Joseph!" Starbuck instructed his men, then put his own bayonet onto his rifle's muzzle. At Manassas, at Washington Faulconer's insistence, the Legion's officers had gone into battle with swords, but those officers who survived had learned that enemy sharpshooters liked nothing better than a sword-bearing target and so they had exchanged their elegant blades for workmanlike rifles and their braid-encrusted sleeves and collars for undecorated cloth. Starbuck also carried an ivory-handled, five-shot revolver that he had taken as plunder from the battlefield at Manassas, but for now he would leave that expensive English-made revolver in its holster and depend on his sturdy Mississippi rifle with its long, spikelike bayonet. "Are you ready?" Starbuck called again.

"Ready!" the company answered, wanting to get the battle over with.

"No cheering as we go across!" Starbuck warned them. "We don't want the Yankees knowing we're coming. Go fast and be real quiet!" He looked around at their faces and saw the mixture of excitement and nervous anticipation. He glanced at Truslow, who nodded curtly as though adding his approval to Starbuck's decision. "So come on!" Starbuck called and led the way into the dappled golden-green sunlight that slanted across the clearing and shimmered through the pearly gunsmoke that rested like layered skeins of misty veils between the trees. It was turning into a lovely fall evening and Starbuck felt a sudden and terrible fear that he would die in this sweet light and he ran harder, fearing a blast of canister from a cannon or the sickening mulekick of a bullet's strike, but not one northerner fired at the company as they pounded over to the inner stand of trees.

They trampled their way into the undergrowth on the Yankees' side of the clearing. Once he was safe under the trees Starbuck could see a glint of water where the river turned away from the bluff, and beyond that bright curve he could see the long, green, evening-shadowed fields of Maryland. The sight gave him a moment's pang, then he called to his men to swing right and form a line and he swung his left arm around to show how he wanted them to form the new line of battle, but the men were not waiting for orders; instead they were already pounding through the trees toward the enemy. Starbuck had wanted them to advance on the Yankee flank in a steady line, but they had chosen to race forward in small excited groups, and their enthusiasm more than made up for the raggedness of their deployment. Starbuck ran with them, unaware that he had begun to scream the high-pitched banshee scream. Thomas Truslow was to his left, carrying his bowie knife with its nineteen-inch blade. Most of the Legion's men had once owned such wicked-looking blades, but the weight of the ponderous knives had persuaded almost all of the soldiers to abandon them. Truslow, out of perversity, had kept his and now carried it as his weapon of choice. Alone in the company he made no noise, as if the job at hand was too serious for shouting.

Starbuck saw the first Yankees. Two men were using a fallen tree as a firing position. One was reloading, working the long ramrod down his rifle while his companion aimed across the trunk. The man fired and Starbuck saw the kick of the rifle on the man's shoulder and the puff of spark-lit smoke where the percussion cap exploded.

Beyond the two men the woods suddenly seemed thick with blue uniforms and, more oddly, gray coats that hung from trees and twitched as rebel bullets struck home. "Kill them!" Starbuck screamed, and the two men by the fallen tree turned to stare in horror at the rebel charge. The man who had reloaded his rifle swung it to face Starbuck, aimed, then pulled the trigger, but in his panic he had forgotten to prime his rifle. The hammer fell with a click onto bare steel. The man scrambled to his feet and ran past an officer who stood with drawn sword and a look of appalled bewilderment on his whiskered face. Starbuck, seeing the officer's expression, knew he had done the right thing. "Kill them," he screamed, completely unaware that he was uttering anything so bloodthirsty. He just felt the elation of a man who has outwitted an enemy and so imposed his will on a battlefield. That feeling was intoxicating, filling him with a manic elation. "Kill them!" he screamed again, and this time the words seemed to spur the whole Yankee flank into disintegration.

The northerners fled. Some threw themselves off the bluff's edge and slithered down the slope, but most ran back along the line of the summit and, as they ran, more men joined the flight, and the retreat became ever more crowded and chaotic. Starbuck tripped on a wounded man who screamed foully, then ran into the clearing where the Rhode Island cannon had plowed its ragged furrow back and over the bluff's crest. He jumped a box of ammunition, still screaming his challenge at the men running ahead.

Not all the northerners ran. Many of the officers reckoned that duty was more important than safety and, with a bravery that was close to suicide, stayed to fight the rebels' flanking attack. One lieutenant calmly aimed his revolver, fired once, then went down under two bayonets. He tried to fire the revolver even as he was dying, then a third rebel put a bullet into his head and there was a spray of blood as the shot struck home. The Lieutenant died, though the men with the bayonets still savaged his corpse with the ferocity of hunting dogs rending a fallen buck. Starbuck shouted at his men to let the dead man alone and hurry on. He did not want to give the Yankees time to recover.

Adam Faulconer was riding his horse in the sunlit clearing, shouting for the rest of the Legion to cross over and support Starbuck's company. Major Bird led the color party across into evening woods full of the shrill sound of rebels attacking, of gunshots and of northern officers shouting orders that stood no chance of being obeyed in the panic.

Truslow told a northerner to drop his rifle, the man either did not hear or decided to defy the demand, and the bowie knife chopped down once with a horrid economy of effort. A group of Yankees, their retreat blocked, turned and ran blindly back toward their attackers. Most stopped when they saw their mistake and raised their hands in surrender, but one, an officer, sliced his sword in a wild blow at Starbuck's face. Starbuck checked, let the blade hiss by, then rammed his bayonet forward and down. He felt the steel hit the Yankee's ribs and cursed that he had stabbed down instead of up.

"Nate!" The Yankee officer gasped. "No! Please!"

"Jesus!" The blasphemy was torn from Starbuck. The man he was attacking was a member of his father's church, an old acquaintance with whom Starbuck had endured an eternity of Sunday school lessons. The last news Starbuck had heard of William Lewis was that he had become a student at Harvard, but now he was gasping as Starbuck's bayonet scored down his ribs.

"Nate?" Lewis asked. "Is it you?"

"Drop your sword, Will!"

William Lewis shook his head, not out of obstinate refusal, but out of puzzlement that his old friend should appear in the unlikely guise of a rebel. Then, seeing the look of fury on Starbuck's face, he let the sword drop. "I surrender, Nate!"

Starbuck left him standing over the fallen sword and ran on to catch his men. The encounter with an old friend had unnerved him. Was he fighting a Boston battalion? If so, how many more of this beaten enemy would recognize him? What familiar households would he plunge into mourning by his actions on this Virginia hilltop? Then he forgot his qualms as he saw a giant bearded man howling at the rebels. The man, dressed in shirtsleeves and suspenders, was using one hand to swing an artillery rammer like a club, while in his other he held a short Roman-pattern stabbing sword that was standard issue to gunners. His retreat had been cut off, but he was refusing to surrender, preferring to die like a hero than yield like a coward. He had already felled one of Starbuck's men; now he challenged the others to fight him. Sergeant Mallory, who was Truslow's brother-in-law, fired at the huge man, but the bullet missed and the bearded gunner turned like a fury on the wiry Mallory.

"He's mine!" Starbuck shouted and pushed Mallory aside, lunged forward, then swayed back as the huge man whirled the rammer. This, Starbuck reckoned, was his duty as an officer. The company must see that he was the least afraid, the most ready to fight. Besides, today he felt unbeatable. The scream of battle was in his veins like a splash of fire. He laughed as he lunged with the bayonet, only to have the blade knocked hard aside by the short sword.

"Bastard!" the gunner spat at Starbuck, then slashed the short sword in quick vicious sweeps, trying to keep Starbuck's attention on the blade while he swung the rammer. He thought he had tricked the rebel officer and bellowed with a kind of joy as he anticipated the clublike wooden head smashing his enemy's skull, but Starbuck ducked hard down so that it hissed over his slouch hat and the momentum of the great swing was sufficient to sway the big man off-balance. Then it was Starbuck's turn to shout in triumph as he rammed the bayonet up, hard up, pushing against the astonishing resistance of skin and flesh, and he was still screaming as the big man jerked and fell, twitching on the blade's long shank like a gaffed fish dying.

Starbuck was breathless as he tried to pull his bayonet free, but the gunner's flesh had closed tight on the steel and the blade would not move. The man had dropped his own weapons and was clawing feebly at the rifle in his gut. Starbuck also tried to twist the steel free, but the flesh's suction gripped like stone. He pulled the rifle's trigger, hoping to blast the bayonet loose, but still it would not move. The gunner gasped horribly as the bullet struck, then Starbuck abandoned the weapon and left the gunner dying on the forest floor. He unholstered his fine ivory-handled revolver instead and ran after his company only to discover that K Company was no longer alone in the woods, but was merely a small part of a gray and butternut tide that was overwhelming the northern defenders and driving the survivors in a terrible stampede off the bluff's summit and down to the narrow, muddy ledge beside the river. A New York sergeant screamed as he lost his precarious footing and tumbled down the slope to break his leg on a rock.

"Nate!" Adam had spurred his stallion into the trees. "Call them off!"

Starbuck stared uncomprehendingly at his friend.

"It's over! You've won!" Adam said and gestured at the mass of rebels who had begun firing down the bluff's steep slope at the Yankees trapped beneath. "Stop them!" Adam said, as if he blamed Starbuck for this display of gleeful, vengeful victory, then he turned his horse savagely away to find someone with the authority to finish the killing.

Except no one wanted to end the killing. The northerners were trapped beneath the bluff and the southerners poured a merciless fire into the writhing, crawling, bleeding mass below. A rush of Yankees tried to escape the slaughter by trampling over the wounded to the safety of a newly arrived boat, but the weight of the fugitives overturned the small craft. A man called for help as the current dragged him away. Others tried to swim the channel, but the water was churning and spattering with the strike of bullets. Blood soured the stream and was carried seaward. Men drowned, men died, men bled, and still the remorseless, unending slaughter went on as the rebels loaded and fired, loaded and fired, loaded and fired, jeering all the while at their beaten, cowed, broken enemy.

Starbuck edged his way to the bluff's edge and stared down at a scene from the inferno. The base of the bluff's escarpment was like a wriggling, sensate mass; an enormous beast dying in the gathering dusk, though it was not yet a fangless beast for shots still came up the slope. Starbuck pushed his revolver into his belt and cupped his hands and shouted downhill for the Yankees to cease fire. "You're prisoners!" he shouted, but the only answer was a splintering of rifle flames in the shadows and the whistle of a fusillade past his head. Starbuck pulled his revolver free and emptied its chambers down the hill. Truslow was beside him, taking loaded rifles from men behind and firing at the heads of men trying to swim to safety. The river was being beaten into a froth, looking just as though a school of fish were churning frantically to escape a tidal shallow. Bodies drifted downstream, others snagged on branches or lodged on mudbanks. The Potomac had become a river of death, blood-streaked, bullet-lashed, and body-filled. Major Bird grimaced at the view, but did nothing to stop his men firing.

"Uncle!" Adam protested. "Stop them!"

But instead of stopping the slaughter, Bird gazed down on it like some explorer who had just stumbled upon some phenomenon of nature. It was Bird's view that war involved butchery, and to engage in war but protest against butchery was inconsistent. Besides, the Yankees would not surrender but were still returning the rebel fire, and Bird now answered Adam's demand by raising his own revolver and firing a shot into the turmoil.

"Uncle!" Adam cried in protest.

"Our job is to kill Yankees," Bird said and watched as his nephew galloped away. "And their job is to kill us," Bird went on, even though Adam had long since gone from earshot, "and if we leave them alive today then tomorrow their turn might come." He turned back to the horror and emptied his revolver harmlessly into the river. All around him men grimaced as they fired and Bird watched them, seeing a blood lust raging, but as the shadows lengthened and the return fire stuttered to nothing and as the fear and passion of the long day's climax ebbed away, so the men ceased firing and turned away from the twitching, bloodied river.

Bird found Starbuck pulling a pair of spectacles from a dead man's face. The lenses were thick with clotted blood that Starbuck wiped on his coat hem. "Losing your vision, Nate?" Bird asked.

"Joe May lost his glasses. We're trying to find a pair that suits."

"I wish you could find him a new brain. He's one of the dullest creatures it was ever my misfortune to teach," Bird said, holstering his revolver. "I have to thank you for disobeying me. Well done." Starbuck grinned at the compliment, and Bird saw the feral glee on the northerner's face and wondered that battle could give such joy to a man. Bird supposed that some men were born to be soldiers as others were born to be healers or teachers or farmers, and Starbuck, Bird reckoned, was a soldier born to the dark trade. "Moxey complained about you," Bird told Starbuck, "so what shall we do about Moxey?"

"Give the son of a bitch to the Yankees," Starbuck said, then walked with Bird away from the bluff's crest, back into the trees where a company of Mississippi men was gathering prisoners. Starbuck avoided the sullen-looking northerners, not wanting to be recognized by a fellow Bostonian. One Mississippi soldier had picked up a fallen white banner which he paraded through the twilight, and Starbuck saw the handsome escutcheon of the Commonwealth of Massachusetts embroidered on the blood-flecked silk. He wondered whether Will Lewis was still on the bluff's summit or whether, in the chaos of the defeat, the Lieutenant had sneaked off down to the river and made a bid for the far bank. And what would they say in Boston, Starbuck wondered, when they heard that the Reverend Elial's son had been screaming the rebel yell and wearing the ragged gray and shooting at men who worshipped in the Reverend's church? Damn what they said. He was a rebel, his lot thrown in with the defiant South and not with these smart, well-equipped northern soldiers who seemed like a different breed to the grinning, long-haired southerners.

He left Bird with the Legion's own colors and went on hunting through the woods, looking for spectacles or any other useful plunder that the corpses might yield. Some of the dead looked very peaceful, most looked astonished. They lay with their heads tipped back, their mouths open, and their outreaching hands contracted into claws. Flies were busy at nostrils and glazed eyes. Above the dead the discarded, bullet-torn gray coats of the northerners were still suspended from branches to look like hanged men in the fading light. Starbuck found one of the scarlet-lined coats neatly folded and placed at the bole of a tree and, thinking it would be useful in the coming winter, picked it up and shook out the folds to see that it was unscarred by either bullet or bayonet. A nametape had been neatly sewn into the coat's neck, and Starbuck peered to read the letters that had been so meticulously inked onto the small white strip. "Oliver Wendell Holmes Jr.," the label read, "20th Mass." The name brought Starbuck a sudden and intense memory of a clever Boston family, and of Professor Oliver Wendell Holmes's study with its specimen jars on high shelves. One such jar had held a wrinkled, pallid human brain, Starbuck remembered, while others had strange, big-headed homunculi suspended in cloudy liquid. The family did not worship at Starbuck's church, but the Reverend Elial approved of Professor Holmes, and so Starbuck had been allowed to spend time in the doctor's house where he had become friendly with Oliver Wendell Junior, who was an intense, thin, and friendly young man, quick in debate and generous in nature. Starbuck hoped his old friend had survived the fight. Then, draping Holmes's heavy coat about his shoulders, he went to find his rifle and to discover just how his men had fared in the battle.

In the dark, Adam Faulconer vomited.

He knelt in the soft leaf mold beneath a maple tree and retched till his belly was dry and his throat sore, and then he closed his eyes and prayed as though the very future of mankind depended on the intensity of his petition.

Adam knew that he had been told lies, and, what was worse, knew that he had willingly believed those lies. He had believed that one hard battle would be a sufficient bloodletting to lance the disease that beset America, but instead the single battle had merely worsened the fever, and today he had watched men kill like beasts. He had seen his best friend, his neighbors, and his mother's brother kill like animals. He had seen men descend into hell, and he had seen their victims die like vermin.

It was dark now, but still a great moaning came from the foot of the bluff where scores of northerners lay bleeding and dying. Adam had tried to go down and offer help, but a voice had screamed at him to get the hell away and a rifle had fired blindly up the slope toward him, and that one defiant shot had been sufficient to provoke another rebel fusillade from the bluff's crest. More men had screamed in the dark and wept in the night.

Around Adam a few fires burned, and around those fires the victorious rebels sat with grinning devil faces. They had looted the dead and rifled the pockets of the prisoners. Colonel Lee of the 20th Massachusetts had been forced to surrender his fine braided jacket to a Mississippi muleskinner who now sat wearing it before a fire and wiping the grease from his hands on the coat's skirts. There was the raw smell of whiskey in the night air and the sour stench of blood and the sweet-sick odor of the rotting dead. A handful of southern casualties had been buried in the sloping meadow that looked south toward Catoctin Mountain, but the northern bodies were still unburied. Most had been collected and stacked like cordwood, but a few undiscovered corpses were still hidden in the undergrowth. In the morning a work party of slaves would be fetched from the nearby farms and made to dig a trench big enough to hold the Yankee dead. Near the stack of bloody corpses a man played a fiddle beside a fire and a few men sang softly to his mournful tune.

God, Adam decided, had abandoned these men, just as they had abandoned Him. Today, on the edge of a river, they had arrogated God's choice of life and death. They were, Adam decided in his wrought state, given to evil. It did not matter that some of the victorious rebels had prayed in the dusk and had tried to help their beaten enemy; they were all, in Adam's view, scorched by the devil's breath.

Because the devil had taken America in his grip and was dragging the fairest country on earth down to his foul nest, and Adam, who had let himself be persuaded that the South needed its one moment of martial glory, knew he had come to his own sticking point. He knew he had to make a decision, and that the decision involved the risk of severing himself from his family and his neighbors and his friends and even from the girl he loved, but it was better, he told himself as he knelt in the death- and vomit-scented air of the bluff's crest, to lose his Julia than to lose his soul.

The war must be ended. That was Adam's decision. He had tried to avert the conflict before the fighting ever began. He had worked with the Christian Peace Commission and he had seen that band of pious worthies swamped by the fervent supporters of war, so now he would use the war to end the war. He would betray the South because only by that betrayal could he save his country. The North must be given all the help he could give it, and as an aide to the South's commanding general Adam knew he could give the North more help than most other men.

He prayed in the dark and his prayer seemed to be answered when a great peace descended on him. The peace told Adam that his decision was a good one. He would become a traitor and would yield his country to its enemy in the name of God and for America.

Bodies floated downstream in the dark, carried toward the Chesapeake Bay and the distant ocean. Some of the corpses were trapped on the weirs by Great Falls where the river turned south toward Washington, but most were carried through the rapids and floated through the night to snag on the piles of the Long Bridge that carried the road south from Washington into Virginia. The river washed the corpses clean so that by the dawn, when the citizens of Washington walked beside the waters and looked down at the mud-shoals by its banks, they saw their sons all clean and white, their dead skins gleaming, though the bodies were now so swollen with gas that they strained the buttons and stretched the seams of their lavish new uniforms.

And in the White House a president wept for the death of Senator Baker, his dear friend, while the rebel South, seeing the hand of God in this victory by the waters, gave thanks.

The leaves turned and dropped, blowing gold and scarlet across the new graves at Ball's Bluff. In November the rebel troops moved away from the river, going to winter quarters nearer Richmond where the newspapers warned of the swelling northern ranks. Major-General McClellan, the Young Napoleon, was said to be training his burgeoning army to a peak of military perfection. The small fight at Ball's

Bluff might have filled northern churches with mourners, but the North consoled itself with the thought that their revenge lay in the hands of McClellan's superbly equipped army, which, come the springtime, would descend on the South like a righteous thunderbolt.

The North's navy did not wait for spring. In South Carolina, off Hilton Head, the warships blasted their way into Port Royal Sound and landing parties stormed the forts that guarded Beaufort Harbor. The North's navy was blockading and dominating the southern coast and though the southern newspapers tried to diminish the defeat at Port Royal, the news provoked cheers and singing in the Confederacy's slave quarters. There was more celebration when Charleston was almost destroyed by fire—a visitation from the angel of revenge, the northern preachers said—and the same preachers cheered when they learned that a Yankee warship, defying the laws of the sea, had stopped a British mail ship and removed the two Confederate commissioners sent from Richmond to negotiate treaties with the European powers. Some southerners also cheered that news, declaring that the snub to Britain would surely bring the Royal Navy to the American coast, and by December Richmond's jubilant newspapers were reporting that redcoat battalions were landing in Canada to reinforce the permanent garrison in case the United States chose to fight Britain rather than return the two kidnapped commissioners.

Snow fell in the Blue Ridge Mountains, covering the grave of Truslow's wife and cutting off the roads to the western part of Virginia that had defied Richmond by seceding from the state and joining the Union. Washington celebrated the defection, declaring it to be the beginning of the Confederacy's dissolution. More troops marched down Pennsylvania Avenue and so out to the training camps in occupied northern Virginia where the Young Napoleon honed their skills. Each day new guns arrived on trains from the northern foundries to be parked in giant rows in fields close to the Capitol Building that gleamed white in the winter sun beneath the spidery scaffolding of its unfinished dome. One good hard push, the northern newspapers claimed, and the Confederacy would collapse like a dead, rotted tree.

The rebel capital felt no such confidence. The winter had brought nothing but bad news and worse weather. Snow had come early, the cold was bitter, and the Yankee noose seemed to be tightening. That prospect of imminent northern victory at least cheered Adam Faulconer who, two weeks before Christmas, rode his horse down from the city to the stone quay at Rockett's Landing. The wind was chopping the river into short, hard, gray waves and whistling in the tarred rigging of the truce ship which sailed once a week from the Confederate capital. The ship would journey down the James River and under the high guns of the rebel fort on Drewry's Bluff and so through the low, salt-marsh fringed meanders to the river's confluence with the Appomattox and from there eastward along a broad, shallow fairway until, seventy miles from Richmond, it reached the Hampton Roads and turned north to the quays of Fort Monroe. The fort, though on Virginia soil, had been held by Union forces since before the war's beginning and there, under its flag of truce, the boat discharged captured northerners who were being exchanged for rebel prisoners released by the North.

The cold winter wind was stinging Rockett's Landing with snatches of thin rain and souring the quay with the smell of the foundries that belched their sulfurous coalsmoke along the riverbank. The rain and smoke turned everything greasy; the stones of the quay, the metal bollards, the lines berthing the ship, and even the thin, ill-fitting uniforms of the thirty men who waited beside the gangplank. The waiting men were northern officers who had been captured at Manassas and who, after nearly five months in captivity, were being exchanged for rebel officers captured in General McClellan's campaign in what now styled itself the state of West Virginia. The prisoners' faces were pale after their confinement in Castle Lightning, a factory building which stood on Cary Street next to the two big storage tanks that held the gas supply for the city's street lighting. The clothes of the released prisoners hung loose, evidence of the weight they had lost during their confinement in the commandeered factory.

The men shivered as they waited for permission to board the

truce boat. Most carried small sacks holding what few possessions they had managed to preserve during their imprisonment: a comb, a few coins, a Bible, some letters from home. They were cold, but the thought of their imminent release cheered them and they teased each other about their reception at Fort Monroe, inventing ever more lavish meals that would be served in the officers' quarters. They dreamed of lobster and beefsteak, of turtle and oyster soup, of ice cream and apple butter, of venison steak with cranberries, of duck and orange sauce, of glasses of Madeira and flagons of wine, but above all they dreamed of coffee, of real, good, strong coffee.

One prisoner dreamed of no such things, but instead paced with Adam Faulconer up and down the quay. Major James Starbuck was a tall man with a face that had once been fleshy, but now looked pouchy. He was still a young man, but his demeanor, his perpetual frown, and his thinning hair made him look old far beyond his years. He had once boasted a very fine beard, though even that had lost its luster in Castle Lightning's damp interior. James had been a rising Boston lawyer before the war and then a trusted aide to Irvin McDowell, the General who had lost the battle at Manassas, and now, on his way back north, James did not know what was to become of him.

Adam's duty this day was to make certain that only those prisoners whose names had been agreed between the two armies were released, but that duty had been simply discharged by a roll call and head count, and once those duties were done he had sought James's company and asked to talk with him privately. James, naturally enough, assumed Adam wanted to talk about his brother. "There is no chance, you think, that Nate could change sides?" James asked Adam wistfully.

Adam did not like to answer directly. In truth he was bitterly disappointed with his friend Nathaniel Starbuck, who, he believed, was embracing war like a lover. Nate, Adam believed, had abandoned God, and the best he could hope for was that God had not abandoned Nate Starbuck, but Adam did not want to state that harsh judgment, and so he tried to find some shard of redeeming goodness that would buoy James's hopes for his younger brother. "He told me he attends prayer meeting regularly," he answered lamely.

"That's good! That's very good!" James sounded unusually animated, then he frowned as he scratched his belly. Like every other prisoner held in Castle Lightning he had become lousy. At first he had found the infestation terribly shaming, but time had accustomed him to lice.

"But what will Nate do in the future?" Adam asked, then answered his own question by shaking his head. "I don't know. If my father resumes command of the Legion, then I think Nate will be forced to look for other employment. My father, you understand, is not fond of Nate."

James jumped in alarm as a sudden eruption of steam hissed loudly from a locomotive on the nearby York River Railroad. The machine jetted another huge gout of steam, then its enormous driving wheels screamed shrilly as they tried to find some traction on the wet and gleaming steel rails. An overseer bellowed orders at a pair of slaves who ran forward to scatter handfuls of sand under the spinning wheels. The locomotive at last found some purchase and jerked forward, clashing and banging a long train of boxcars. A great gust of choking, acrid smoke wafted over Adam and James. The locomotive's fuel was resinous pinewood that left a thick tar on the rim of the potlike chimney.

"I had a particular reason for seeing you today," Adam said clumsily when the locomotive's noise had abated.

"To say farewell?" James suggested with an awkward misunderstanding. One of his shoe soles had come loose and flapped as he walked, making him stumble occasionally.

"I have to be frank," Adam said nervously, then fell silent as the two men skirted a rusting pile of wet anchor chain. "The war," Adam finally explained himself, "must be brought to a conclusion."

"Oh, indeed," James said fervently. "Indeed, yes. It is my prayerful hope."

"I cannot describe to you," Adam said with an equal fervor, "what tribulation the war is already bringing to the South. I dread to think of such iniquities being visited on the North."

"Amen," James said, though he had no real idea what Adam was talking about. In prison it had sometimes seemed as if the Confederacy were winning the war, an impression that had been heightened when the disconsolate prisoners from Ball's Bluff had arrived.

"If the war continues," Adam said, "then it will degrade us all. We shall be a mockery to Europe; we shall lose whatever moral authority we possess in the world." He shook his head as if he had not managed to express himself properly. Beyond the quay the train was picking up speed, its boxcar wheels clattering over the rail joints and the locomotive's smoke showing white against the gray clouds. A guard jumped onto the platform of the moving caboose and went inside out of the cold wind. "The war is wrong!" Adam finally blurted out. "It is against God's purpose. I've been praying on this matter and I beg you to understand me."

"I do understand you," James said, but he could say no more because he did not want to offend his new friend by saying that the only way God's purpose could be fulfilled was by the Confederacy's defeat, and though Adam might be voicing sentiments very close to James's heart, he was still wearing a uniform of rebel gray. It was all very confusing, James thought. Some of the northern prisoners in Castle Lightning had openly boasted of their adultery, they had been blasphemers and mockers, lovers of liquor and of gambling, Sabbath-breakers and libertines; men whom James had deemed to be of the crudest stamp and vilest character, yet they were soldiers who fought for the North while this pained and prayerful man Adam was a rebel.

Then, to James's astonishment, Adam proved that supposition wrong. "What is necessary," Adam said, "and I beg for your confidence in this matter, is for the North to gain a swift and crushing victory. Only thereby can this war be halted. Do you believe me?"

"I do, I do. Of course." James felt overwhelmed by Adam's sentiments. He stopped and looked down into the younger man's face, oblivious to a bell that had begun ringing to summon the prisoners aboard the truce ship. "And I join my prayers to yours," James said sanctimoniously.

"It will take more than prayers now," Adam said, and he took from his pocket an India-paper Bible that he handed to James. "I am asking you to take this back to the North. Hidden behind the endpapers is a full list of our army's units, their strength as of this week, and their present positions in Virginia." Adam was being modest. Into the makeshift slipcase made by the Bible's leather cover he had crammed every detail concerning the Confederate defenses in northern Virginia. He had listed the ration strengths of every brigade in the rebel army, and discussed the possibility of conscription being adopted by the Richmond government in the spring. His staff job had enabled Adam to reveal the weekly total of newly manufactured artillery reaching the army from the Richmond foundries, and to betray how many of the cannons facing the northern pickets from the rebel redoubts around Centreville and Manassas were fakes. He had sketched the Richmond defenses, warning that the ring of earth forts and ditches was still under construction and that every passing month would render the obstacles more formidable. He told the North of the new ironclad ship being secretly built in the Norfolk dockyard, and of the forts which protected the river approaches to Richmond. Adam had included all that he possibly could, describing the South's strengths and weaknesses, but always urging the North that one strong attack would surely crumble secession like a house of cards.

Adam desperately hoped this one inclusive betrayal would be sufficient to end the war, yet he was sensible enough to know that whoever received this letter might well demand more information. Now, pacing the greasy quay in the cold rain, Adam told James precisely how a message could reach him from the North. Adam had worked hard on his scheme, attempting to foresee every liability that might reveal his identity to the southern authorities, and he knew that the greatest danger would be posed by northern messages coming south. "Which is why I'd rather you never contacted me," he warned James, "but if you must, then I beg you never to use my name on the letters."

"Of course." James closed his cold hands over the Bible's leather cover, guiltily aware of an unseemly happiness. It was right and proper that he should be glad of Adam's espousal of the North's cause, yet he felt it shameful that he should see in that espousal an advantage for himself, for he was guiltily aware that the letter concealed in the Bible could well assist his military career. Instead of returning North as the humbled aide of a failed general, he was suddenly the carrier of northern victory. His prayers had been answered a hundredfold.

"If necessary I can send you more information," Adam went on, "but only to you. Not to anyone else. I cannot trust anyone else." Both sides were riddled with informers who would betray anyone for the price of a bottle of whiskey, but Adam was certain he could trust this Boston lawyer who was as pious and godly a man as any in either army. "Will you give me your Christian word that you will keep my identity secret?"

"Of course," James said, still dazed by this stroke of good fortune.

"I mean a secret from everyone," Adam insisted. "If you reveal my identity to General McClellan I have no faith he will not tell someone else, and that someone else could be my ruin. Promise me this. No one but you and I must ever know."

James nodded again. "I promise." He turned as the ship's bell rang again. His fellow prisoners were climbing the gangway, but still James made no move to join them. Instead he delved into an inside pocket of his faded, dirty jacket and brought out an oilcloth-covered packet. The oilcloth was loosely wrapped and James let it fall away to reveal a small, much-thumbed pocket Bible with a worn cover. "Will you give this to Nate? Ask him to read it?"

"With pleasure." Adam took the thick Bible and watched as James wrapped his new Scriptures in the patch of oilcloth.

"And tell him," James added in a heartfelt voice, "that if he returns north I will do my best to reconcile him to Father and Mother."

"Of course," Adam said, though he could not imagine Starbuck responding to his brother's generosity.

"You want to stay here, mister?" a sailor called to James from the ship.

"Remember your promise," Adam said. "Tell no one who gave you that letter."

"You can trust me," James assured Adam. "I'll tell no one."

"God bless you." Adam felt a sudden great warmth for this good, clumsy man who was so obviously a brother in Christ. "And God bless the United States."

"Amen to that," James responded, then held out his hand. "I shall pray for you."

"Thank you," Adam said, and he shook James's hand before walking the northerner to the waiting ship.

The gangplank was heaved inboard and the warps cast off. James stood at the rail, the new Bible clutched tight in his hands. As the last warp dropped away and the boat perceptibly moved into the river's current, the freed prisoners cheered. The sidewheels began to turn, their great paddles churning the greasy water white. The motion of the paddles made the released prisoners cheer again, all but James, who stood silent and apart. A plume of dirty smoke sagged from the ship's tall funnel to blow across the river.

Adam watched as the ship dropped past the navy yard, its progress helped by a cold, wind-fretted current. He gave James a last wave, then looked down at the pocket Bible to see that its margins were smothered in tightly written notes. It was the Bible of a man who wrestled with God's will, the Bible of a good man. Adam closed and held the book tightly, as though he could take strength from the word of God, and then he turned and limped back toward his tethered horse. The wind gusted fresh and cold, but Adam felt an immense calm because he had done the right thing. He had chosen the course of peace, and by so doing he would bring nothing but blessings on his country; it would be one country again, North and South, united in God's purpose.

Adam rode toward the city. Behind him the truce boat splashed and smoked its way around the bend and so headed south carrying its cargo of treachery and peace.

~ PART TWO ~

GEORGE WASHINGTON'S BIRTHDAY WAS FIXED AS THE day of Jefferson Davis's formal inauguration as President of the Confederate States of America. He had been inaugurated once before, in Montgomery, Alabama, but that ceremony had only made Davis into the President of a provisional government. Now, hallowed by election and properly installed in the Confederacy's new capital, he would be inaugurated a second time. The choice of Washington's birthday as the date of this second ceremony was intended to invest the occasion with a symbolic dignity, but the auspicious day brought nothing but miserable and incessant rains which drove the huge crowd gathered in Richmond's Capitol Square to shelter beneath a host of umbrellas so densely packed that it seemed as if the speech-makers orated to a spread of glistening black lumps. The drumming of the rain on carriage roofs and tightly stretched umbrella skins was so loud that no one except the platform party could hear any of the orations, prayers, or even the solemn presidential oath of office. After taking the oath President Davis invoked God's help to the South's just cause, his prayer punctuated by the sneezing and coughing of the dignitaries around him. Gray February clouds scudded low over the city, darkening everything except the new battle flags of the Confederate's eastern army. The flag, which was hanging on staffs behind the platform and from every rooftop within sight of Capitol Square, was a fine red banner, slashed with a blue St. Andrew's cross on which were sewn thirteen stars to represent the eleven rebellious states as well as Kentucky and Missouri, whose loyalty both sides claimed. Southerners who looked for auguries were pleased that thirteen states founded this new country, just as thirteen had founded a different country eighty-six years before, though some in the crowd perceived the number as unlucky, just as they perceived the drenching rain as an omen of ill fortune for the newly inaugurated president.

After the ceremony a procession of bedraggled notables hurried along Twelfth Street to attend a reception in the Brockenborough House on Clay Street which had been leased by the government to serve as the presidential mansion. The house was soon crowded with dripping people who draped wet coats on the twin statues of Comedy and Tragedy that graced the entrance hall, then edged their way from one room to another to appraise and criticize the new President's taste in furniture and pictures. The President's slaves had placed protective covers over the expensive carpets in the reception rooms, but the visitors wanted to inspect the patterns and pulled the cotton sheets aside, and soon the beautifully patterned carpets were trodden filthy with muddy boots, while the twin arrays of peacock feathers on the mantel of the ladies' drawing room were ravaged by people wanting souvenirs of the day. The President himself stood frowning beside the white marble fireplace in the state dining room and assured everyone who offered him congratulations that he conceived of the day's ceremony as a most solemn occasion and his presidency as a mighty heavy duty. Some army musicians were supposed to be entertaining the guests, but the crowd was so tightly pressed that the violinist did not even have room to draw his bow, and so the soldiers retired to the kitchen where the cooks regaled them with good Madeira wine and cold jellied chicken.

Colonel Washington Faulconer, resplendent in an elegant Confederate uniform that was made even more dashing by the black sling supporting his right arm, congratulated the President, then went through the small fuss of not being able to shake hands with his wounded right arm and offering his left instead.

President Davis finally managed a limp, awkward handshake, then muttered that he was honored by Faulconer's presence on this solemn occasion which was ushering in these days of heavy duty.

"Heavy duties call for great men, Mr. President," Washington Faulconer responded, "which means we are fortunate indeed in you."

Davis's thin mouth twitched to acknowledge the compliment. He had a piercing headache that made him seem even more remote and cold than usual. "I do regret," he said stiffly, "that you did not feel able to accept the duty of commissioner."

"Though I certainly saved myself some inconvenience thereby, Mr. President," Faulconer responded lightly, before realizing that in war all men were supposed to welcome inconvenience, even if that inconvenience did mean being kidnapped by the U.S. Navy from the comfortable staterooms of a British mail ship. The two commissioners had now been released, thus saving the North from battling the British as well as the Confederacy, but their arrival in Europe had not fetched good news. France would not support the South unless the British made the first move, and the British would not intervene unless the South gave clear signs of being able to win the war without outside help, which all added up to meaningless nonsense. The President, reflecting on the diplomatic failure, had concluded that the wrong men had been chosen as commissioners. Slidell and Mason were raw-mannered and blunt men, accustomed to the homespun texture of American politics, but hardly slippery enough for the sly chanceries of a suspicious Europe. A more elegant commissioner, the President now believed, might have achieved a greater success.

And Washington Faulconer was certainly an impressive man. He had flaxen hair and a frank, honest face that almost glowed with handsomeness. He had broad shoulders, a trim waist, and one of the greatest fortunes in all Virginia; a fortune so large that he had raised a regiment with his own money and then equipped it to a standard equal to the best in either army, and rumor claimed that he could have repeated that generosity a dozen times over and still not have felt the pinch. He was, by any man's standard, a fortunate and striking man, and President Davis once again felt irritation that Faulconer had turned down diplomatic office to pursue his dream of leading a brigade into battle. "I'm sorry to see you're not recovered, Faulconer." The President gestured at the black sling.

"Some small loss of dexterity, Mr. President, but not sufficient to prevent me from wielding a sword in my country's defense," Faulconer said modestly, though in truth his arm was entirely mended and he wore the sling only to give an impression of heroism. The black sling was especially inspiring to women, an effect that was made more convenient by the absence from Richmond of Faulconer's wife, who lived an invalid's nervous existence on the family's country estate. "And I trust the sword will be so employed soon," Faulconer added in a heavy hint that he wanted the President's support for his appointment as a brigadier.

"I suspect we shall all soon be fully employed in our various duties," the cadaverous President answered vaguely. He wished his wife would come and help him deal with these eager people who wanted more enthusiasm than he felt able to give. Varina was so good with small talk, while on these social occasions the President felt the words shrivel on his tongue. Was Lincoln similarly afflicted by office seekers? Davis wondered. Or did his fellow President have a greater ease of manner with importunate strangers? A familiar face suddenly appeared beside Faulconer, a man who smiled and nodded at the President, demanding recognition. Davis scrabbled for the man's name which, thankfully, came in the very nick of time. "Mr. Delaney," the President greeted the newcomer unenthusiastically. Belvedere Delaney was a lawyer and gossip whom Davis did not remember inviting to this reception, but who had typically come anyway.

"Mr. President." Delaney inclined his head in recognition of Jefferson's high office. The Richmond lawyer was a small, plump, smiling man whose bland exterior concealed a mind as sharp as a serpent's tooth. "Allow me to extend my sincere felicitations on your inauguration."

"A solemn occasion, Delaney, leading to heavy duties."

"As the weather seems to intimate, Mr. President," Delaney said, appearing to take an unholy glee in the day's damp character. "And now, sir, if I might, I have come to request Colonel Faulconer's attention. You cannot monopolize the company of our Confederate heroes all day, sir."

Davis nodded his grateful assent for Delaney to take Faulconer away, though the release only permitted a plump congressman to heartily congratulate his fellow Mississippian on being inaugurated as the Confederacy's first President.

"It is a heavy duty and solemn responsibility," the President murmured.

The Mississippi Congressman gave Jefferson Davis's shoulder a mighty slap. "Heavy duty be damned, Jeff," the Congressman bellowed in his President's ear. "Just send our boys north to cut the nuts clean off old Abe Lincoln."

"I must leave strategy to the generals." The President tried to move the Congressman on and accept the more limpid good wishes of an Episcopalian clergyman instead.

"Hell, Jeff, you know as much 'bout war as any of our fine soldier boys." The Congressman hawked a tobacco-rich gob toward a spittoon. The stream of brown spittle missed, spattering instead on the rain-soaked hoop skirt of the clergyman's wife. "Time we settled those chicken-shit Yankees once and forever," the Congressman opined happily, then offered the new President a pull on his flask. "Finest rot-skull whiskey this side of the Tennessee River, Jeff. One slug will cure whatever ails you!"

"You're demanding my company, Delaney?" Faulconer was irritated that the short, sly lawyer had taken him away from the President.

"It ain't me who wants you, Faulconer, but Daniels, and when Daniels calls, a man does best to respond," Delaney said.

"Daniels!" Faulconer said in astonishment, for John Daniels was one of the most powerful and reclusive men in Richmond. He was also famously ugly and foulmouthed, but important because it was Daniels who decided what causes and men the powerful Richmond *Examiner* would support. He lived alone with two savage dogs that it was his pleasure to make fight while he cackled from the vantage point of a high barber's chair. He was no mean fighter himself; he had twice faced his enemies on the Richmond dueling ground in Bloody Run and had survived both fights with his malevolent reputation enhanced. He was also regarded by many southerners as a first-rate political theorist, and his pamphlet, "The Nigger Question," was widely admired by all those who saw no need to modify the institution of slavery. Now, it seemed, the formidable John Daniels waited for Faulconer on the elevated back porch of the new Executive Mansion where, horsewhip in hand, he stared moodily at the rain.

He gave Faulconer a sideways glance, then flicked his whip toward the water dripping off the bare trees. "Is this weather an augury for our new President, Faulconer?" Daniels asked in his grating, hard voice, eschewing any more formal greeting.

"I hope not, Daniels. You're well, I trust?"

"And what do you think of our new President, Faulconer?" Daniels ignored Faulconer's courtesy.

"I think we are fortunate in such a man."

"You sound like an editorial writer on the *Sentinel*. Fortunate! My God, Faulconer, the old U.S. Congress was full of mudsills like Davis. I've seen better men drop out the backside of a hog. He impresses you with his gravity, does he? Oh, he's grave, I'll grant you that, because there's nothing alive inside him, nothing but notions of dignity and honor and statesmanship. It ain't notions we need, Faulconer, but action. We need men to go and kill Yankees. We need to soak the North in Yankee blood, not make fine speeches from high platforms. If speeches won battles we'd be marching through Maine by now on our way to taking Canada. Did you know Joe Johnston was in Richmond two days ago?"

"No, I didn't."

"Know what Johnston calls you, Faulconer?" Daniels asked in his unpleasant voice. It did not matter to Daniels that Faulconer was one of the South's richest men, so rich that he could have bought the *Examiner* a dozen times over; Daniels knew his own power, and that power was the ability to mold public opinion in the South. That same power gave him the right to lounge in the President's wicker rocking chair with his shabby boots up on the President's back rail while Faulconer, in his gaudy colonel's uniform, stood beside him like a supplicant. "He calls you the hero of Manassas," Daniels said sourly. "What do you say to that?"

"I'm most grateful," Faulconer said. In truth the soubriquet was a mistake, for General Johnston had never discovered that it was not Faulconer who led the Legion against the North's surprise flank attack at Manassas, but the unsung Thaddeus Bird, nor had Johnston ever learned that Bird had made that decision in deliberate disobedience of Faulconer's orders. Instead, like so many other folk in the Confederacy, Johnston was convinced that in Washington Faulconer the South had a brilliant and fitting hero.

That belief had been carefully nurtured by Washington Faulconer himself. The Colonel had spent the months since Manassas lecturing on the battle in halls and theaters from Fredericksburg to Charleston. He told his audiences a tale of disaster averted and victory snatched from certain defeat, and his tale was given drama and color by a small group of wounded musicians who played patriotic songs and, at the more dramatic moments of the narration, played imitation bugle calls that gave the audience the impression that ghostly armies maneuvered just outside the lecture hall's dark windows. Then, as the story reached its climax and the whole fate of the Confederacy hung in history's balance, Faulconer would pause and a snare drum would rattle a suggestion of musketry and a bass drum crash the echoes of distant cannon fire before Faulconer told of the heroism that had saved the day. Then the applause would ring out to drown the drummers' simulated gunfire. Southern heroism had defeated dull-witted Yankee might, and Faulconer would smile modestly as the cheers surrounded him.

Not that Faulconer had ever actually claimed to be the hero of Manassas, but his account of the fight did not specifically deny the accolade. If asked what he had done personally, Faulconer would refuse to answer, claiming that modesty was becoming to a warrior, but then he would touch his right arm in its black sling and he would see the men straighten their backs with respect and the women look at him with a melting regard. He had become accustomed to the adulation; indeed, he had been making the speech for so long now that he had come to believe in his own heroism, and that belief made his memory of the Legion's rejection of him on the night of Manassas hard to bear.

"Were you a hero?" Daniels now asked Faulconer directly.

"Every man at Manassas was a hero," Faulconer replied sententiously.

Daniels cackled at Faulconer's answer. "He should have been a lawyer like you, eh, Delaney? He knows how to make words mean nothing!"

Belvedere Delaney had been cleaning his fingernails, but now offered the editor a swift, humorless smile. Delaney was a fastidious, witty, clever man whom Faulconer did not wholly trust. The lawyer was presently in Confederate uniform, though quite what his martial duties entailed, Faulconer could not guess. It was also rumored that Delaney was the owner of Mrs. Richardson's famous brothel on Marshall Street and of the even more exclusive house of assignation on Franklin Street. If true, then the collected gossip of the two brothels doubtless provided Delaney with damaging knowledge about a good number of the Confederacy's leaders, and doubtless the sly lawyer passed all that pillow talk on to the scowling, diseased, twisted-looking Daniels.

"We need heroes, Faulconer," Daniels now said. He stared sourly down at the flooded paths and muddy vegetable beds of the soaking garden. A wisp of smoke twisted up from the presidential smokehouse where a dozen Virginia hams were being cured. "You heard about Henry and Donelson?"

"Indeed," Faulconer said. In Tennessee Forts Donelson and

Henry had been captured and now it looked as if Nashville must fall, while in the east the Yankee navy had again struck from the sea; this time to capture Roanoke Island in North Carolina.

"And what would you say, Faulconer"—Daniels shot an unfriendly look at the handsome Virginian—"if I were to tell you that Johnston is about to abandon Centreville and Manassas?"

"He can't be!" Faulconer was genuinely aghast at the news. Too many acres of northern Virginia were already under enemy occupation, and yielding more of the state's sacred turf without a fight appalled Faulconer.

"But he is." Daniels paused to light a long black cheroot. He spat the cheroot's tip over the railing, then blew smoke into the rain. "He's decided to pull back behind the Rappahannock. He claims we can defend ourselves better there than in Centreville. No one's announced the decision yet, it's supposed to be a secret, which means Johnston knows, Davis knows, you and I know, and half the goddamn Yankees probably know too. And can you guess what Davis proposes doing about it, Faulconer?"

"I trust he'll fight the decision," Faulconer said.

"Fight?" Daniels mocked the word. "Jeff Davis doesn't know the meaning of the word. He just listens to Granny Lee. Caution! Caution! Caution! Instead of fighting, Faulconer, Davis proposes that a week tomorrow we should all have a day of prayer and fasting. Can you believe that? We are to starve ourselves so that Almighty God will take note of our plight. Well, Jeff Davis can tighten his belt, but I'll be damned if I shall. I shall give a feast that day. You'll join me, Delaney?"

"With enormous pleasure, John," Delaney said, then glanced around as the door at the end of the verandah opened. A small boy, maybe four or five years old and carrying a hoop, appeared on the porch. The boy smiled at the strangers.

"Nurse says I can play here," the boy, whom Washington Faulconer guessed was the President's oldest son, explained himself.

Daniels shot a venomous look at the child. "You want a whipping, boy? If not, then get the hell out of here, now!"

The boy fled in tears as the editor turned back to Faulconer. "Not only are we withdrawing from Centreville, Faulconer, but as there isn't sufficient time to remove the army's supplies from the railhead at Manassas, we are torching them! Can you credit it? We spend months stocking the army with food and ammunition and at the very first breath of spring we decide to burn every damn shred of material and then scuttle like frightened women behind the nearest river. What we need, Faulconer, are generals with balls. Generals with flair. Generals not afraid to fight. Read this." He took from his vest pocket a folded sheet of paper that he tossed toward Faulconer. The Colonel needed to grovel on the porch's rush matting to retrieve the folded sheet, which proved to be the galley proof of a proposed editorial for the Richmond *Examiner*.

The editorial was pure balm to Faulconer's soul. It declared that the time had come for bold action. The spring would surely bring an enemy onslaught of unparalleled severity and the Confederacy would only survive if it met that onslaught with bravery and imagination. The South would never prevail by timidity, and certainly not by digging trenches such as those with which General Robert Lee seemed intent upon surrounding Richmond. The Confederacy, the editorial proclaimed, would be established by men of daring and vision, not by the efforts of drainage engineers. The writer grudgingly allowed that the Confederacy's present leaders were well-meaning men, but they were hidebound in their ideas and the time had surely come to appoint new officers to high position. One such man was Colonel Washington Faulconer, who had been unemployed since Manassas. Let such a man loose on the North, the article concluded, and the war would be over by summer. Faulconer read the editorial a second time and pondered whether he should go to Shaffers this very afternoon and order the extra braid for his sleeves and the gilded wreaths that would surround the stars on his collar wings. Brigadier General Faulconer! The rank, he decided, sat well on him.

Daniels took the editorial back. "The question is, Faulconer, do we publish this?"

"Your decision, Daniels, not mine," Faulconer said modestly, hiding his elation as he shielded a cigar from the wind and struck a light. He wondered if publication would offend too many senior officers, then realized he dared not express such a timid reservation to Daniels or else the editorial would be changed to recommend that some other man be given a brigade.

"But are you our man?" Daniels growled.

"If you mean, would I attack and attack and go on attacking, yes. If you mean, would I abandon Manassas? No. If you mean, would I employ good men to dig drainage ditches around Richmond? Never!"

Daniels was silent after Faulconer's ringing declaration. Indeed he was silent for so long that Washington Faulconer began to feel rather foolish, but then the small, black-bearded editor spoke again. "Do you know the size of McClellan's army?" He asked the question without turning to look at Faulconer.

"Not precisely, no."

"We know, but we don't print the figure in the newspaper because if we did we might just cause people to despair." Daniels twitched the long whip as his voice rumbled just a little louder than the seething and incessant rain. "The Young Napoleon, Faulconer, has over a hundred and fifty thousand men. He has fifteen thousand horses, and more than two hundred and fifty guns. Big guns, Faulconer, slaughtering guns, the finest guns that the northern foundries can pour, and they're lined up wheel to heavy wheel to grind our poor southern boys into bloody ruin. And how many poor southern boys do we have? Seventy thousand? Eighty? And when do their enlistments run out? June? July?" Most of the southern army had volunteered for just one year's service, and when that year was over the survivors expected to go home. "We'll have to conscript men, Faulconer," Daniels went on, "unless we beat this so-called genius McClellan in the spring."

"The nation will never stand for conscription," Faulconer said sternly.

"The nation, Colonel, will damn well stand for whatever brings us victory," Daniels said harshly, "but will you lead those conscripted men, Faulconer? That's the proper question now. Are you my man?

Should the *Examiner* support you? After all, you're not the most experienced officer, are you now?"

"I can bring new ideas," Faulconer suggested modestly. "New blood."

"But a new and inexperienced brigadier will need a good and experienced second-in-command. Ain't that right, Colonel?" Daniels looked malevolently up at Faulconer as he spoke.

Faulconer smiled happily. "I should expect my son Adam to serve with me. He's on Johnston's staff now, so he has the experience, and there isn't a more capable or honest man in Virginia." Faulconer's sudden sincerity and warmth were palpable. He was desperately fond of his son, not just with a father's love, but also out of a gratified pride in Adam's undoubted virtues. Indeed, it sometimes seemed to Faulconer that Adam was his one undoubted success, the achievement that justified the rest of his life. Now he turned smilingly to the lawyer. "You can vouch for Adam's character, can't you, Delaney?"

But Belvedere Delaney did not respond. He just stared down into the sopping garden.

Daniels hissed in a dubious breath, then shook his ugly head warningly. "Don't like it, Faulconer. Don't like it one goddamn little bit. Stinks of favoritism to me. Of nepotism! Is that the word, Delaney?"

"Nepotism is the very word, Daniels," Delaney confirmed, not looking at Faulconer, whose face was like that of a small boy struck brutally hard.

"The *Examiner* could never stand for nepotism, Faulconer," Daniels said in his grating voice, then he threw a curt gesture toward Delaney, who obediently opened the verandah's central door to admit onto the porch a gaunt and ragged creature dressed in a wet, threadbare uniform that made the newcomer shiver in the day's raw cold. The man was in his early middle age and looked as though life had served him ill. He had a coarse black beard streaked with gray, sunken eyes, and a tic in his scarred cheek. He was evidently suffering from a cold for he cuffed his dripping nose, then wiped his sleeve on his ragged beard that was crusted with flakes of dried tobacco juice. "Johnny!" this unprepossessing creature greeted Daniels familiarly.

"Faulconer?" Daniels looked up at the Colonel. "This is Major Griffin Swynyard."

Swynyard gave Faulconer a brisk nod, then held out his left hand, which, Faulconer saw, was missing its three middle fingers. The two men made an awkward handshake. The spasm in Swynyard's right cheek gave his face a curiously indignant look.

"Swynyard," Daniels said to Faulconer, "served in the old U.S. Army. He graduated from West Point, when?"

"Class of twenty-nine, Johnny." Swynyard clicked his heels together.

"Then served in the Mexican and Seminole wars. Is that right?"

"Took more scalps than any white man alive, Colonel," Swynyard said, grinning at Faulconer and revealing a mouthful of rotted yellow teeth. "I took thirty-eight headpieces in one day alone!" Swynyard boasted. "All with my own hands, Colonel. Squaws, papooses, braves! I had blood to my elbows! Spattered to the armpits! Have you ever had the pleasure of taking a scalp, Colonel?" Swynyard asked with a fierce intensity.

"No," Faulconer managed to say. "No, I haven't." He was recovering from Daniels's refusal to countenance Adam's appointment, and realizing that promotion would carry a price.

"There's a knack to it," Swynyard went on. "Like any other skill, there's a knack! Young soldiers always try to cut them off and, of course, it don't work. They end with something which looks like a dead mouse." Swynyard believed this was funny, for he opened his gap-toothed mouth to breathe a sibilant laugh at Faulconer. "Cutting don't work for a scalp, Colonel. No, you have to peel a scalp off, peel it like the skin of an orange!" He spoke lovingly, demonstrating the action with his wounded, clawlike hand. "If you're ever in the Tidewater I'll show you my collection. I've three cabin trunks full of prime scalps, all cured and tanned proper." Swynyard evidently felt he had made a good impression on Faulconer for he smiled ingratiatingly while the tic in his cheek trembled fast. "Maybe you'd like to see a scalp now, Colonel?" Swynyard suddenly asked, pawing at the button of his top pocket as he spoke. "I always keep one about my person. As a good-luck charm, you understand? This one's from a Seminole squaw. Noisy little bitch she was, too. Savages can squeal, I tell you, how they can squeal!"

"No, thank you." Faulconer managed to prevent the trophy from being produced. "So you're a Virginia man, Major?" he asked, changing the subject and disguising his distaste for the wretched-looking Swynyard. "From the Tidewater, you say?"

"From the Swynyards of Charles City Court House," Swynyard said with evident pride. "The name was famous once! Ain't that so, Johnny?"

"Swynyard and Sons," the editor said, staring into the rain, "slave traders to the Virginia gentry."

"But my daddy gambled the business away, Colonel," Swynyard confided. "There was a time when the name Swynyard meant the selfsame thing as nigger trading, but Daddy lost the business with the sin of gambling. We've been poor men ever since!" He said it proudly, but the boast suggested to Washington Faulconer exactly what proposition was being made to him.

The editor drew on his cigar. "Swynyard's a cousin of mine, Faulconer. He's my kin."

"And he has applied to you for employment?" Faulconer guessed shrewdly.

"Not as a newspaperman!" Major Swynyard intervened. "I don't have skill with words, Colonel. I leave that to the clever fellows like cousin Johnny here. No, I'm a soldier through and through. I was weaned on the gun's muzzle, you might say. I'm a fighter, Colonel, and I've got three cabin trunks crammed full of heathen topknots to prove it."

"But you are presently unemployed?" Daniels prompted his cousin.

"I am indeed seeking the best place for my fighting talent," Swynyard confirmed to Faulconer.

There was a pause. Daniels took the editorial from his pocket and pretended to cast a critical eye over its paragraphs. Faulconer took the hint. "If I should find employment for myself, Major," he told Swynyard hastily, "I should count it as a great honor and a privilege if you would consider being my right-hand man?"

"Your second-in-command, don't you mean?" John Daniels interjected from the President's rocking chair.

"My second-in-command indeed," Faulconer confirmed hurriedly.

Swynyard clicked his heels. "I'll not disappoint you, Colonel. I might lack the genteel graces, by God, but I don't lack fierceness! I ain't a soft man, my God, no. I believe in driving soldiers like you drive niggers! Hard and fast! Bloody and brutal, no other way, ain't that the truth, Johnny?"

"The entire truth, Griffin." Daniels folded the editorial, but did not yet return it to his vest pocket. "Unfortunately, Faulconer," Daniels went on, "my cousin impoverished himself in the service of his country. His old country, I mean, our new enemies. Which also means he has come to our new country with a passel of debts. Ain't that so, Griffin?"

"I'm down on my luck, Colonel," Swynyard confessed gruffly. A tear appeared at one eye and the tic in his cheek quivered. "Gave my all to the old army. Gave my fingers too! But I was left with nothing, Colonel, nothing. But I don't ask much, just a chance to serve and fight, and a grave of good Confederate soil when my honest labors are done."

"But you are also asking for your debts to be settled," John Daniels said pointedly, "especially that portion of the debt which is owed to me."

"I shall take great pleasure in establishing your credit," Faulconer said, wondering just how much pain that pleasure would cost him.

"You're a gentleman, Colonel," Swynyard said, "a Christian and a gentleman. It's plain to see, Colonel, so it is. Moved, I am. Touched deep, sir, very deep." And Swynyard cuffed the tear from his eye, then straightened his back as a sign of respect to his rescuer. "I'll not disappoint you. I ain't a disappointer, Colonel. Disappointing ain't in the Swynyard nature."

Faulconer doubted the truth of that assertion, yet he guessed his best chance of being named a general was with Daniels's help, and if Daniels's price was Swynyard, then so be it. "So we're agreed, Major," Faulconer said, and held out his left hand.

"Agreed, sir, agreed." Swynyard shook Faulconer's offered hand. "You move up a rank, sir, and so do I." He smiled his decayed smile.

"Splendid!" Daniels said loudly, then delicately and pointedly inserted the folded editorial back into his vest pocket. "Now if you two gentlemen would like to improve upon each other's acquaintance, Mr. Delaney and I have business to discuss."

Thus dismissed, Faulconer and Swynyard went to join the throng which still crowded the President's house, leaving Daniels to flick his whip out into the rain. "Are you sure Faulconer's our man?"

"You heard Johnston," Delaney said happily. "Faulconer was the hero of Manassas!"

Daniels scowled. "I heard a rumor that Faulconer was caught with his pants around his ankles? That he wasn't even with the Legion when it fought?"

"Mere jealous tales, my dear Daniels, mere jealous tales." Delaney, quite at his ease with the powerful editor, drew on a cigar. His stock of precious French cigarettes was exhausted now, and that lack was perhaps the most pressing reason why he wanted this war to end quickly. To which end Delaney, like Adam Faulconer, secretly supported the North and worked for its victory by causing mischief in the South's capital, and today's achievement, he thought, was a very fine piece of mischief indeed. He had just persuaded the South's most important newspaperman to throw his paper's massive influence behind one of the most foppish and inefficient of the Confederacy's soldiers. Faulconer, in Delaney's caustic view, had never grown up properly, and without his riches he would be nothing but an empty-headed fool. "He's our man, John, I'm sure of it."

"So why has he been unemployed since Manassas?" Daniels asked.

"The wound in his arm took a long time healing," Delaney said vaguely. The truth, he suspected, was that Faulconer's inordinate pride would not allow him to serve under the foulmouthed, lowborn Nathan Evans, but Daniels did not need to know that.

"And didn't he free his niggers?" Daniels asked threateningly.

"He did, John, but there were extenuating reasons."

"The only extenuating reason for freeing a nigger is because the bastard's dead," Daniels declared.

"I believe Faulconer freed his slaves to fulfill his father's dying wish," Delaney lied. The truth was that Faulconer had manumitted his people because of a northern woman, an ardent abolitionist, whose good looks had momentarily enthralled the Virginia landowner.

"Well, at least he's taken Swynyard off my hands," Daniels said grudgingly, then paused as the sound of cheering came from inside the house. Someone was evidently making a speech and the crowd punctuated the oration with laughter and applause. Daniels glowered into the rain that still fell heavily. "We don't need words, Delaney, we need a goddamn miracle."

The Confederacy needed a miracle because the Young Napoleon was at last ready, and his army outnumbered the southern troops in Virginia by two to one, and spring was coming, which meant the roads would be fit once more for the passage of guns, and the North was promising its people that Richmond would be captured and the rebellion ended. Virginia's fields would be dunged by Virginia's dead and the only way the South could be saved from an ignominious and crushing defeat was by a miracle. Instead of which, Delaney reflected, he had given it Faulconer. It was enough, he decided, to make a sick cat laugh.

Because the South was doomed.

Just after dawn the cavalry came galloping back across the fields, their hooves splashing bright silver gouts of water from the flooded grass. "Yankees are at Centreville! Hurry it up!" The horsemen spurred past the earthen wall that was notched with gun embrasures, only instead of cannon in the embrasures there was nothing but Quaker guns. Quaker guns were tree trunks painted black and then propped against the firing steps to give the appearance of cannon muzzles.

The Faulconer Legion would be the last infantry regiment to leave the Manassas positions, and the last, presumably, to march into the new fortifications that were being dug behind the Rappahannock River. The retreat meant ceding even more Virginia territory to the northerners, and for days now the roads south through Manassas had been crowded with refugees heading for Richmond.

The only defenses left behind at Manassas and Centreville would be the Quaker guns, the same fake weapons that had brooded across the landscape all winter to keep the Yankee patrols far from Johnston's army. That army had been wondrously supplied with food that had been painstakingly hauled to the Manassas depot by trains all winter long, but now there was no time to evacuate the depot and so the precious supplies were being burned. The March sky was already black with smoke and rich with the smell of roasting salt beef as Starbuck's company torched the last rows of boxcars left in the rail junction. The cars had already been primed with heaps of tinder, pitch, and gunpowder, and as the burning torches were thrust into the incendiary piles, the fire crackled and bellowed fiercely upward. Uniforms, bridles, cartridges, horse collars, and tents went up in smoke, then the boxcars themselves caught fire and the flames whipped in the wind and spewed their black smoke skyward. A barn full of hay was torched, then a brick warehouse of flour, salt pork, and dry crackers. Rats fled from the burning storehouses and were hunted down by the Legion's excited dogs. Each company had adopted at least a half-dozen mongrel mutts that were lovingly cared for by the soldiers. Now the dogs seized the rats by their necks and shook them dead, scattering blood. Their owners cheered them on.

The boxcars would burn till there was nothing left but a pair of blackened wheels surrounded by embers and ash. Sergeant Truslow had a work party pulling up rails and stacking them on burning piles of wooden ties soaked in pitch. The burning stacks generated such a fierce heat that the steel rails were being bent into uselessness. All about the regiment were the pyres of other fires as the rearguard destroyed two months' worth of food and a winter's worth of stored equipment.

"Let's be moving, Nate!" Major Bird strode across the scorched depot, jumping in alarm as a box of ammunition caught fire in one of the boxcars. The cartridges snapped like firecrackers, forcing an incandescent blaze in one corner of the burning wagon. "Southward!" Bird cried dramatically, pointing in that direction. "You hear the news, Nate?"

"News, sir?"

"Our behemoth was met by their leviathan. Science matched wits with science, and I gather that they fought each other to a standstill. Pity." Bird suddenly checked and frowned. "A real pity."

"The Yankees have a metal ship too, sir?" Starbuck asked.

"It arrived the day after the *Virginia's* victory, Nate. Our sudden naval superiority is all for naught. Sergeant! Leave those rails, time to be on our way unless you wish to be a guest of the Yankees tonight!"

"We lost our ship?" Starbuck asked in disbelief.

"The newspaper reports that it floats still, but so does their monstrous metal ship. Our queen is now matched by their queen, and so we have stalemate. Hurry up, Lieutenant!" This injunction was to Moxey, who was using a blunt knife to cut through the hemp rope of a well bucket.

Starbuck's spirits sank. It was bad enough that the army was yielding Manassas Junction to the Yankees, but everyone had been cheered by the sudden news that a southern secret weapon, an ironsided ship impervious to cannon fire, had sailed into the Hampton Roads and decimated the northern blockading squadron of wooden warships. The U.S. Navy's ships had turned and fled, some going aground, others sinking, and the rest simply making what desperate speed they could to escape the clanking, smoke-dark, plodding, but vengeful *Virginia*, the ironclad fashioned from the hulk of an abandoned U.S. Navy ship, the *Merrimack*. The victory had seemed compensation for Manassas's abandonment and promised to destroy the strangulation of the U.S. Navy's blockade, but now it seemed that the

North had a similar beast which had succeeded in fighting the CSS *Virginia* to a standstill.

"Never mind, Nate. We'll just have to settle the war on land," Bird said, then clapped his hands to encourage the last of the men to leave the burning railyard and form up on the road leading south.

"But how in God's name did they know we had an iron ship?" Starbuck asked.

"Because they have spies, of course. Probably hundreds of them. You think everyone south of Washington suddenly changed their patriotism overnight?" Bird asked. "Of course they didn't. And some folks undoubtedly believe that any accommodation with the Yankees is better than this misery." He gestured toward another group of piti- ful refugees and was suddenly assailed by an image of his own dear wife being forced from her home by the invading Yankees. That was hardly a likely fate, for Faulconer County lay deep in the heart of Vir- ginia, yet Bird still touched the pocket in which Priscilla's portrait was carefully wrapped against the rain and damp. He tried to imagine their small house with its untidy piles of music and its scatter of vio- lins and flutes being burned by jeering Yankee troops.

"Are you all right?" Starbuck had seen the sudden grimace on Bird's face.

"Enemy horse! Look lively!" Sergeant Truslow shouted at his company, but he also intended the sudden bellow to startle Major Bird out of his reverie. "Yankees, sir." Truslow pointed north to where a group of horsemen was silhouetted against the pale trunks of a far wood.

"March on!" Bird shouted toward the head of the Legion's col- umn, then he turned back to Starbuck. "I was thinking of Priscilla."

"How is she?" Starbuck asked.

"She says she's very well, but she wouldn't say anything else, would she? The dear girl isn't one to worry me with complaints." Bird had married a girl half his age and, in the manner of a confirmed bachelor falling at last to the enemy, regarded his new bride with an adoration that verged on worship. "She says she's planted onions. Is it too early to plant onions? Or maybe she means she planted them last year? I don't know, but I am so impressed that the dear thing knows about onions. I don't. Lord knows when I'll see her again." He sniffed, then turned to look at the distant horsemen who seemed very wary of the lavish display of wooden guns that threatened their approach. "Onward, Nate, or backward rather. Let us yield this field of ashes to the enemy."

The Legion marched past the burning storehouses, then through the small town. A few of the houses were empty, but most of the inhabitants were staying behind. "Hide your flag, man!" Bird called to a carpenter who was defiantly flying the new Confederate battle flag above his shop. "Fold it away! Hide it! We'll be back!"

"Is anyone behind you, Colonel?" The carpenter inadvertently gave Bird a promotion.

"Just some cavalry. After that it's all Yankees!"

"Give them bastards a good whipping, Colonel!" the carpenter said as he reached for his flag.

"We'll do our best. Good luck to you!"

The Legion left the small town behind and marched stolidly along a wet and muddy road that had been torn apart by the passage of refugee wagons. The road led to Fredericksburg, where the Legion would cross the river, then destroy the bridge before joining the bulk of the southern army. Most of that army was retreating on a road farther west which went direct to Culpeper Court House where General Johnston had his new headquarters. Johnston was assuming that the Yankees would swing wide in an attempt to turn the river line and that a great battle would therefore need to be fought in Culpeper County; it would be a battle, Bird observed to Starbuck, which would make the fight at Manassas look like a skirmish.

The Legion's retreat took them through that old battlefield. To their right was the long hill down which they had fled in disorder after stalling the Yankees' surprise attack, and to their left was the steeper hill where Stonewall Jackson had finally held, turned, and repelled the northern army. That battle was eight months in the past, yet still the steep hill showed the scars of artillery strikes. Close by the road was a stone house where Starbuck had watched the surgeons slash and saw at wounded flesh, and in the yard of the house was a shallow grave trench that had been washed thin by the winter's rain so that the knobbly-headed stumps of bones showed white above the red soil. There was a well in the yard where Starbuck remembered slaking his thirst during the day's terrible, powder-exacerbated heat. A group of stragglers, sullen and defiant, now squatted beside the well.

The stragglers, all of them from regiments that were marching ahead of the Legion, annoyed Truslow. "They're supposed to be men, ain't they? Not women." The Legion passed more and more such laggards. A few were sick and could not help themselves, but most were simply tired or suffering from blistered feet. Truslow snarled at them, but even Truslow's savage scorn could not persuade the stragglers to ignore the blood filling their boots and to keep on marching. Soon some of the men from the Legion's leading companies began dropping back. "It ain't right," Truslow complained to Starbuck. "Go on like this and we'll lose half the army." He saw three men from the Legion's A Company and he stormed over to them, bellowing at the chickenhearted bastards to keep walking. The three men ignored him, so Truslow punched the tallest of the three, dropping him to the ground. "Get up, you son of a bitch!" Truslow shouted. The man shook his head, then squirmed in the mud as Truslow kicked him in the guts. "Get up, you slime-bellied bastard! Up!"

"I can't!"

"Stop it!" Starbuck called the order to Truslow, who turned in astonishment at receiving a direct reprimand from his officer.

"I ain't letting these sons of bitches lose the war because they're gutless weaklings," Truslow protested.

"I don't intend to allow that to happen either," Starbuck said. He walked over to the man from A Company, watched by a score of other stragglers who wanted to see just how the tall, dark-haired officer could succeed where the squat, fierce sergeant had failed.

Truslow spat into the mud as Starbuck approached. "You plan on talking reason to the sumbitch?"

"Yes," Starbuck said, "I do." He stood above the fallen man, watched by the whole of K Company, who had paused to enjoy the confrontation. "What's your name?" Starbuck asked the straggler.

"Ives," the man said warily.

"And you can't keep up, Ives?"

"Reckon I can't."

"He always was a useless sumbitch," Truslow said. "Just like his pa. I tell you, if the Ives family were mules you'd have shot the whole damn lot at birth."

"All right, Sergeant!" Starbuck said reprovingly, then smiled down at the wet, miserable Ives. "You know who's following us?" he asked.

"Some of our cavalry," Ives said.

"And behind the cavalry?" Starbuck asked gently.

"Yankees."

"Just hit the no-good bastard," Truslow growled.

"You leave me alone!" Ives shouted at the Sergeant. Ives had been emboldened by Starbuck's gentle and considerate manner and by the support of the other stragglers, who murmured their resentment of Truslow's brutality and their appreciation of Starbuck's reasonable tone.

"And do you know what the Yankees will do to you?" Starbuck asked Ives.

"Reckon it can't be worse than this, Captain," Ives said.

Starbuck nodded. "So you can't go on?"

"Reckon I can't."

The other stragglers murmured their agreement. They were all too tired, too pained, too wet, too desperate, and too unhappy even to think of continuing the march. All they wanted was to collapse beside the road, and beyond that thought of immediate rest they had no cares or fears.

"You can stay here then," Starbuck told Ives.

Truslow growled in protest. The other stragglers grinned with pleasure as Ives, his battle apparently won, struggled to his feet.

"There is just one other thing," Starbuck said pleasantly.

"Captain?" Ives was eager to please now.

"You can stay here, Ives, but I can't let you keep any equipment that belongs to the government. That wouldn't be fair, would it? We don't want to give the Yankees our precious guns and uniforms, do we now?" He smiled.

Ives was suddenly wary. He shook his head very cautiously, but clearly he did not really understand what Starbuck was saying.

Starbuck turned to his company. "Amos, Ward, Decker, come here!" The three men ran over to Starbuck, who nodded toward Ives. "Strip the gutless bastard naked."

"You can't . . ." Ives began, but Starbuck took one pace and thumped him in the belly, then brought his other hand up to slap his head hard back. Ives collapsed in the mud again.

"Strip him!" Starbuck said. "Cut the bastard's clothes clean off."

"Jesus Christ," one of the other stragglers blasphemed in disbelief as Starbuck's men ripped and tore Ives's clothes away. Truslow, grinning now, had taken the man's rifle and ammunition. Ives was screaming that he wanted to stay with the Legion, but Starbuck knew he needed to make an example of one man, and it was Ives's misfortune to be that man. Ives thrashed and fought, but he was no match for Starbuck's men who pulled off his boots, his pack, and his blanket roll, dragged his pants down, and cut away his jacket and shirt. Ives was left in nothing but a grimy pair of frayed drawers. He staggered to his feet, blood oozing from the blow Starbuck had given his nose.

"I'll keep going, Captain!" Ives pleaded. "Really I will!"

"Take your drawers off," Starbuck said harshly.

"You can't!" Ives backed away, but Robert Decker tripped him, then leaned over and ripped the frayed undergarment away to leave Ives stark-naked in the rain and mud.

Starbuck looked at the other stragglers. "If any one of you wants to stay here and get acquainted with the Yankees, then get undressed now! If you don't, then get walking."

They all began walking. Some exaggerated their limps to show that they had genuine cause to be laggards, but Starbuck shouted that he could strip a cripple far faster than he could rip the clothes off a whole man, and that encouragement made the stragglers walk faster.

Some even half ran as they hurried to get clear of Starbuck and Truslow, spreading the word as they went that there was no mercy to be had at the rear of the Legion's column.

Ives pleaded for his clothes. Starbuck drew his pistol. "Get the hell away from here!"

"You can't do this!"

Starbuck fired. The bullet splashed mud onto Ives's fish-belly-white calves. "Run!" Starbuck shouted. "Go to the Yankees, you son of a bitch!"

"I'll kill you!" Ives shouted. He was running now, splashing jaybird-naked down the road toward Manassas. "I'll kill you, you Yankee bastard!"

Starbuck holstered the revolver and grinned at Truslow.

"You see, Sergeant? Sweet reason always works, every time."

"You're a smart son of a gun, ain't you?"

"Yes, Sergeant, I am. Forward now!" Starbuck called to the company and they marched on, grinning, while Truslow handed out Ives's ammunition. The number of stragglers dropped to a handful, and that handful seemed composed of men who were genuinely crippled. Starbuck had his men take their weapons and cartridges, but otherwise left them alone. There were no more malingerers.

In the early afternoon the Legion trudged past what had once been the largest meat-curing factory in the Confederacy, but was now an inferno of yellow and blue flames. Fat hissed and crackled and sent molten streams pouring down through the hovels where the factory's slaves lived. The Negroes watched the soldiers pass and betrayed not a flicker of emotion. Soon, they knew, the northerners would come, but they dared show no pleasure at that prospect. Children clung to their mothers' aprons, the men watched from shadows, while behind them the burning meat roasted and fried to send a tantalizing aroma of beef and bacon across a wide swath of damp country.

The smell of bacon stayed with the Legion right into the middle of the afternoon when the cavalry rearguard at last caught up with the retreating infantry. The troopers dismounted and led their tired, sweat-whitened horses by the reins. Some of the troopers had no saddles and were using folded squares of heavy cloth instead, while others had bridles made of knotted ropes. The men scanned the road verges as they walked south, looking for anything useful among the equipment that had been thrown aside by the infantry battalions ahead. There were coats, tents, blankets, and weapons, all of them taken from the stores abandoned at Manassas, but then found to be too heavy to carry and so simply thrown away. The Legion's dogs gorged themselves on food that had been snatched from the burning depots but that now was being jettisoned as the men's weariness increased. "It feels more like a defeat than a retreat," Starbuck grumbled to Thaddeus Bird.

"I believe the textbooks describe it as a tactical withdrawal," Bird said with relish. He was enjoying the day. The sight of so much material being burned was proof of the essential idiocy of mankind and especially that portion of mankind which was in authority, and Bird always enjoyed such proofs of general stupidity. Indeed his enjoyment was so great that he sometimes felt guilty for it. "Though I don't suppose you ever feel guilty, do you, Starbuck?"

"Me?" Starbuck was startled by the question. "All the time."

"For enjoying the war?"

"For being a sinner."

"Ha!" Bird liked that confession. "You mean that blacksmith's wife in Manassas? What a fool you are! To feel guilty for doing what is natural? Does the tree feel guilty for growing? Or the bird for flying? Your fault is not the commission of sins, Starbuck, but your fear of loneliness."

That cut too close to the bone, so close that Starbuck ignored the comment altogether. "Your conscience is never tender?" he asked Bird instead.

"I never allowed my conscience to be confused by the bleating of God's ministers," Bird said. "I never listened long enough, you understand. Good Lord, Starbuck, if it had not been for this war you might well be an ordained man of God by now! You'd be marrying people instead of killing them!" Bird laughed, jerking his head back and forth, then suddenly turned as a rifle fired far behind the Legion. A bullet whipped through the trees and the dismounted rebel cavalry immediately turned to meet the threat. A troop of Yankee horsemen had appeared in the distance. The rain made the enemy difficult to see, though every now and then a puff of white smoke betrayed the spot where a carbine had been fired. The sound of the gun would come flat and dull a few seconds later, just after the bullet had slapped into the wet road or flicked harmlessly through the pine needles. The northern cavalry was firing at very long range, relying on luck rather than marksmanship for any effect.

"This calls for your fellows, Nate," Major Bird said with an unholy relish. Bird had firm beliefs about musketry. He liked to hold his regimental volleys until the very last moment and he believed his skirmishing companies should be sharpshooters, and Starbuck's insistence on constant practice had made K Company into the Legion's most lethal skirmishers. A handful of the men, like Esau Washbrook and William Tolby, were natural marksmen, but even the most inept members of the company had improved in the months of training. Joseph May was one of the inept men, though in his case the improvement in his marksmanship was owed to the pair of gold-rimmed spectacles that had been taken from a dead Yankee captain at Ball's Bluff.

Major Bird now stared down the long road that led straight between dark evergreen trees. "One well-aimed volley, Nate. The rascals won't risk coming close, and once they know we can shoot they'll drop even farther back, so the omnipotent, all-seeing God is only giving us one chance to send their miserable souls to hell." He rubbed his thin hands. "Would you be offended if I gave the orders, Nate?"

Starbuck, amused by Bird's bloodthirsty enthusiasm, assured his commanding officer that no offense would be taken, then told his company to find themselves firing positions and to load their rifles. There were about a dozen Yankee cavalrymen in sight, but more were probably hidden by the ruins of a clapboard tavern which stood at the bend in the road where the enemy had appeared. The northerners were firing their carbines from their saddles in the evident belief that they were too far from the rebel rearguard to be in real danger. Their fire was not so much a threat as a mockery, a parting, derisive gesture to the retreating rebels. The Confederate cavalry were firing back, but their makeshift collection of revolvers, sporting guns, and captured carbines was proving even more inaccurate than the northern gunfire.

"A quarter mile!" Truslow shouted. That was very long range for the Legion's rifles. As a rule Starbuck reckoned that shots fired at distances greater than two hundred yards were probably wasted unless one of the company's best marksmen was firing, but a quarter mile was not an impossible distance. He loaded his own rifle, first biting the bullet off the top of the paper-wrapped cartridge, then pouring the powder down the barrel. He stuffed the empty paper into the barrel as wadding, then spat the bullet into the muzzle. The bitter, salty taste of gunpowder lingered in his mouth as he pulled out the rifle's steel ramrod. He thrust the cone-shaped bullet hard down onto the wadding and powder, then slotted the ramrod back into its place. Finally he fished out a small copper percussion cap that he fumbled over the rifle's breech cone. The cap was filled with a pinch of fulminate of mercury, a chemical unstable enough to explode when struck sharply. The rifle's hammer, cracking on the cap, would cause the fulminate to explode and so lance a needle of fire down through the pierced cone into the gunpowder he had rammed into the rifle's breech.

An enemy bullet spat into a puddle thirty yards short of the company and spewed up a splash of dirty water. Ned Hunt, ever the company's clown, jeered at the distant cavalry until Truslow told him to curb his damn tongue. Starbuck knelt beside a tree on which he could steady his aim. He lifted the rear leaf sight to four hundred yards, then, because cold rifles fired short, added an extra hundred for good measure.

"Give us room, boys!" Major Bird called out to the rebel cavalry, and the gray-coated, long-haired horsemen pulled their horses back past Starbuck's company.

"You won't hit a thing, boys!" one of the horsemen shouted good-naturedly. "You might as well chuck rocks at the bastards."

There were more Yankees visible at the bend in the road now, maybe a score altogether. Some had dismounted to kneel beside the tavern while others still aimed and fired from the saddle. "We'll shoot at the group on the right!" Bird called. "Remember to aim off for the wind, and wait for my order!"

Starbuck edged his barrel leftward, so allowing for the wind that gusted out of the east. Rain beaded the rifle's barrel as he laid the foresight on a horseman in the center of the Yankee group. "I'll count to three, then give the order," Major Bird announced. He was standing in the very center of the roadway and staring at the enemy through one half of a pair of field glasses he had taken from a corpse at Manassas. "One," he sang out, and Starbuck tried to control the wavering of his rifle's muzzle. "Two!" Major Bird called, and the rain stung Starbuck's eyes, making him blink as he raised the stock so that the leaf sight framed the foresight. "Three," Bird cried, and the company held their collective breath and tried to freeze their muscles into rigidity. Starbuck held the foresight exactly over the blurred figure of a mounted man a quarter mile away and kept it there until at last Bird shouted the order. "Fire!"

Fifty rifles cracked almost in unison, spitting a ragged cloud of white powder smoke across the wet road. The butt of Starbuck's rifle slammed into his shoulder while a bitter spew of exploding fulminate seared his nostril. Major Bird ran clear of the powder smoke and trained his broken glass at the far bend in the road. A horse was galloping loose there, a man was down on the road, a second was limping toward the wood, while a third crawled in the mud. Another horse was down, kicking and thrashing, while beyond the dying beast a score of Yankees scattered like chaff. "Well done!" Bird shouted. "Now form up and march on!"

"How did we do?" Starbuck asked.

"Three men and a horse," Bird said. "Maybe one of the three men dead?"

"Out of fifty shots?" Starbuck asked.

"I read somewhere," Bird said happily, "that it took two hundred musket shots to cause one casualty in Napoleon's wars, so three men and a horse from fifty bullets doesn't seem a bad tally to me." He gave an abrupt bark of laughter, jerking his head back and forth in the mannerism that had earned him his nickname. He explained his merriment as he put the broken field glass away. "Just six months ago, Nate, I was full of scruples about killing. Now, dear me, I seem to regard it as a measure of success. Adam is right, war does change us."

"He had that conversation with you, too?"

"He allowed his conscience to leak all over me, if that's what you mean. It was hardly a conversation as he regarded any contribution of mine as irrelevant. Instead he moaned at me, then asked me to pray with him." Bird shook his head. "Poor Adam, he really should not be in uniform."

"Nor should his father," Starbuck said grimly.

"True." Bird walked in silence for a few paces. A small farm had been cut from the trees by the side of the road and the farmer, a white-bearded man with a tall ragged hat and hair that fell past his shoulders, stood in his door and watched the soldiers pass. "I keep fearing that Faulconer will reappear among us," Bird said, "full of bluster and dignity. Yet every day that passes and he is not reappointed or, God help us, given a brigade, serves to astonish me that perhaps there is some common sense in our high command after all."

"But none in our newspapers?" Starbuck observed.

"Don't remind me, please." Bird shuddered to recall the editorial in the Richmond *Examiner* that had called for Washington Faulconer's promotion. Bird wondered how newspapers could get things so utterly wrong, then pondered how many of his own prejudices and ideas had been shaped by similarly mistaken journalism. But at least no one in Richmond seemed to have heeded the editorial. "I've been thinking," Bird said after a while, then promptly fell silent.

"And?" Starbuck prompted the Major.

"I've been wondering why we call ourselves the Faulconer Legion," Bird said. "After all, we're no longer in his lordship's pay.

We are charges on the Commonwealth of Virginia, and I think we should find ourselves a new name."

"The 45th? The 60th? The 121st?" Starbuck suggested sourly. State regiments were given numbers according to their seniority, and somehow being the 50th Virginia or the 101st Virginia was not quite the same as being the Legion.

"The Virginia Sharpshooters," Bird suggested proudly.

Starbuck thought about the name, and the more he thought the more he liked it. "And what about the colors?" he asked. "You want the Virginia Sharpshooters to go into battle under the Faulconer coat of arms?"

"A new color, I think," Bird said. "Something bold, bloody, and resolute. Maybe with the state motto? *Sic semper tyrannis!*" Bird declaimed the words dramatically, then laughed. Starbuck laughed too. The motto meant that anyone who tried to oppress the Commonwealth of Virginia would meet the same humiliating defeat as King George III, but the threat could equally well refer to the Colonel who had abandoned his own Legion when it marched against the enemy at Manassas. "I like the idea," Starbuck said, "very much."

The company breasted a small rise in the road to see the smoke of a bivouac rising from a ridge half a mile away. The rain and clouds were masking the setting sun to bring on an early dusk in which the campfires on the ridge showed bright. The ridge was where the division's rearguard would spend the night, protected by a stream and two batteries of artillery that stood silhouetted on the far skyline. Most of the Legion had already reached the encampment, far ahead of Starbuck's company, which had been delayed by its encounter with the stragglers and its brush with the Yankee cavalry. "Home comforts in sight," Bird said happily.

"Thank God," Starbuck said. The sling of his rifle was chafing through his soaking uniform, his boots squelched with rain, and the prospect of resting by a fire was like a foretaste of heaven.

"Is that Murphy?" Bird squinted through the rain at a horseman who was galloping down the road from the ridge. "Looking for me, I daresay," Bird said, and he waved to attract the Irishman's atten-

tion. Murphy, a fine horseman, spurred through a shallow ford, galloped up to K Company, then turned his horse in a flurry of hooves
and mud to rein in beside Bird. "There's a man waiting for you in
the encampment, Pecker. He's kind of demanding you hurry up and
see him."

"Does his rank make his demand important to me?"

"I reckon it does, Pecker." Murphy curbed his excited horse.
Mud splashed up from the beast's hooves to spatter Bird's trousers.
"His name's Swynyard. Colonel Griffin Swynyard."

"Never heard of him," Bird said cheerfully. "Unless he's a Swynyard of the old slaver family? They were a nasty set. My father always
reckoned you needed to stay well upwind of a Swynyard. Does this
fellow smell, Murphy?"

"No worse than you or me, Pecker," Murphy said. "But he wants
you on the chop, he says."

"You can tell him to boil his head, perhaps?" Bird suggested
happily.

"Reckon not, Pecker," Murphy said sadly. "Reckon not. He's got
new orders for us, you see. We're changing brigades."

"Oh God, no." Bird said, guessing the awful truth. "Faulconer?"

Murphy nodded. " 'Fraid so, Pecker. Faulconer himself isn't here,
but Swynyard's his new second-in-command." Murphy paused, then
looked at Starbuck. "He wants you too, Nate."

Starbuck swore. But swearing would do no good. Washington
Faulconer had secured his brigade, and with it he had taken back his
Legion.

And suddenly the day really did feel like defeat.

A group of men, some in civilian clothes and some in uniforms,
walked slowly along the line of abandoned fortifications north of the
rail depot at Manassas. The day was ebbing fast, draining a wet land
of what small gray light had illuminated its misery. The rain was helping to reduce the fires set by the retreating Confederates into damp
smoking piles of evil-smelling ash through which the newly arrived
northern troops raked in hopes of salvaging souvenirs. The towns-

people looked sourly on these invading Yankees who were the first free northerners seen in Manassas since the war had begun. A few free blacks offered a better welcome to the Federal troops, bringing out plates of hoecakes and dodgers, though even that generosity was offered cautiously for the town's northern sympathizers could not be certain that the wind of battle would not turn south once more and bring the Confederate army back.

Yet for now the northern army controlled the rail junction and the commander of that army was inspecting the earthworks abandoned by the retreating Confederates. Major General George Brinton McClellan was a small man, stoutly built, with a full, fresh-colored, and boyish face. He was just thirty-five years old, but made up for his youthfulness with a stiff dignity and a permanent scowl that helped compensate for his diminutive stature. He also cultivated a small mustache that he mistakenly supposed added authority to his looks, but which only made his youth more apparent. Now, in the smoky air of the rail junction, he stopped to examine one of the black-painted logs that jutted like a cannon's muzzle across the wet embrasure.

A dozen staff officers paused behind the Major General and stared with him at the dripping, black-painted log. No one spoke until a weighty civilian broke the portentous silence. "It's a log, General," the civilian said in heavy sarcasm. "What we folk back in Illinois call a tree trunk."

Major General George Brinton McClellan did not dignify the remark with a reply. Instead, and taking fastidious care to avoid placing his polished boots in the deeper puddles, he walked to the next embrasure, where he gave an almost identical log another earnest examination. A rebel had chalked two small words on the fake gun's muzzle: "Ho Ho."

"Ho ho," the man from Illinois said. He was middle-aged, red-faced, and a Congressman known to be close to President Lincoln. Such a relationship would have inhibited most officers from offending the politician, but McClellan despised the Congressman for being one of the Republican mudsills who had spent the winter mocking the Army of the Potomac for its inactivity. "All quiet on the Potomac," the mockers sang, demanding to know why the most expensive army in America's history had waited somnolent throughout the winter before advancing on the enemy. It was men like this Congressman who were nagging the President to find a more combative soldier to lead the northern armies, and McClellan was tired of their criticism. He showed his contempt by pointedly turning his back on the Congressman and glaring at one of his staff officers instead. "The Quakers were placed here this morning, you think?"

The staff officer, an engineer colonel, had examined the Quaker guns and deduced from the rotted state of their butt ends that the logs had been in place since the previous summer at least, which meant that the Federal Army of the United States, the largest force ever assembled in America, had spent the last few months being scared away by a bunch of felled trees smeared with pitch. The Colonel, however, knew better than to confirm such a view to General McClellan. "Maybe they were emplaced yesterday, sir," he said tactfully.

"But there were real guns here last week?" McClellan demanded fiercely.

"Oh, undoubtedly," the Colonel lied.

"For sure," another officer added, nodding sagely.

"We saw them!" a third northern officer claimed, though in truth he was wondering whether his patrolling cavalry had been fooled by these painted logs which, from a distance, did look astonishingly like real cannon.

"These tree trunks"—the Illinois Congressman put a derisive spin on the words—"look pretty well-established to me." He clambered over the muddy embrasure, streaking his clothes with dirt, then slid heavily down beside the Quaker gun. There must have been real guns in the embrasures once, for the fake guns rested on gently ramped earth slopes that had been faced with wooden planks up which a firing gun would have recoiled before rolling gently back into position. The Congressman almost lost his footing on the old wooden planks that were slick with a greasy, damp mold. He kept his balance by holding on to the Quaker's barrel, then hacked down with his right foot. The heel of his shoe broke clean through the rotted planks of the platform to disturb a colony of sowbugs that crawled desperately away from the daylight. The Congressman took a wet chewed stump of a cigar from his mouth. "Don't see as how a real gun could have stood here in months, General. I reckon you've been wetting your pants because of a bunch of sawn-off tree trunks."

"What you are witnessing, Congressman"—McClellan wheeled fiercely on the politician—"is a victory! Maybe an unparalleled victory in the annals of our country! A magnificent victory. A triumph of scientifically employed arms!" The general threw a dramatic hand toward the pyres of smoke and the scattered pairs of blackened box-car wheels and the tall brick chimney stacks that had been left gaunt among the smoldering embers. "Behold, sir," McClellan said, waving his arm at the dispiriting landscape, "a defeated army. An army that has retreated before our victorious advance like hay falling before the scythe."

The Congressman obediently surveyed the scene. "Precious few bodies, General."

"A war won by maneuver, sir, is a merciful war. You should fall to your knees and thank Almighty God for it." McClellan made that his parting shot and strode briskly away toward the town.

The Congressman shook his head, but said nothing. Instead he just watched as a lean man wearing a threadbare and tarnished French cavalry uniform climbed over the embrasure to look at the Quaker gun. The Frenchman wore a monstrous straight sword at his side, had a missing eye disguised with a patch, and displayed a cheerful demeanor. His name was Colonel Lassan and he was a French military observer who had been attached to the northern army since before the previous summer's battle at Bull Run. Now he jabbed his toe against the planks of the gun platform. His spurs jingled as the rotted wood broke apart under his half-hearted kick. "Well, Lassan?" the Congressman demanded. "What do you make of it?"

"I am but a mere guest in your country," Lassan said tactfully, "a foreigner and an observer, and so my opinion, Congressman, is of no importance."

"You've got eyes, ain't you? Well, one anyway," the Congressman added hastily. "You don't have to be an American to decide whether this piece of lumber was put in place just yesterday."

Lassan smiled. His face was foully scarred, but there was something indomitable and mischievous in his expression. He was a sociable man who spoke perfect English with a British accent. "I've learned one thing about your wonderful country," he said to the Congressman, "which is that we mere Europeans should keep our criticisms to ourselves."

"Patronizing frog son of a goddamn bitch," the Congressman said. He liked the Frenchman, even though the one-eyed bastard had taken two months' salary off him at a poker game the night before. "So you tell me, Lassan. Were these logs put here yesterday?"

"I think the logs have been here somewhat longer than General McClellan assumes," Lassan said tactfully.

The Congressman glowered at the General's party which was now a hundred paces off. "I reckon he doesn't want to get his nice clean army dirty by getting into a brawl with some nasty, ill-mannered southern boys. Is that what you reckon, Lassan?"

Lassan reckoned the war could be over in a month if the northern army just marched straight ahead, took some casualties, and kept on marching, but he was far too diplomatic to pick sides in the disagreements that were argued so fiercely in Washington's offices and across the capital's well-stocked dining tables. So Lassan simply shrugged off the question, then was saved from further interrogation by the arrival of a newspaper sketch artist who began making a drawing of the rotted planks and the decaying log.

"You're seeing a victory, son," the Congressman said sarcastically, peeling off the damper parts of his cigar before thrusting it back into his mouth.

"It sure ain't a defeat, Congressman," the artist said loyally.

"You think this is victory? Son, we didn't throw the rebels out, they just strolled away in their own sweet time! They're getting their wooden guns ready someplace else by now. We won't have real victory till we string Jeff Davis up by his scrawny heels. I tell you, son, these here guns have been rotting here since last year. I reckon our Young Napoleon's just been humbugged again. Wooden guns for a timberhead." The Congressman spat into the mud. "You make a sketch of these wooden cannon, son, and be sure to show the wheel-marks where the real guns were towed away."

The artist frowned at the mud beyond the decaying firing ramps. "There ain't any wheel-marks."

"You got it, son. And that means you're one long jump ahead of our Young Napoleon." The Congressman stumped away, accompanied by the French observer.

A hundred paces away another man in civilian dress stood frowning at another of the Quaker guns. This man had a tough, squat, thick-bearded face out of which a blackened pipe jutted belligerently. He wore a shabby riding coat, tall boots, and a round, narrow-brimmed hat. He carried a small horsewhip that he suddenly cut viciously across the fake muzzle of one of the wooden guns, then turned and shouted for an assistant to bring his horse.

Later that night the bearded man received a visitor in the parlor of the house that was his quarters. Houses were scarce in Manassas, so scarce that most men beneath the rank of lieutenant general were forced to live in tents, so the fact that this civilian had a whole house for his own use was proof of his importance. The chalk inscription on the house door read "Major E. J. Allen," though the man was neither a soldier nor bore the surname Allen, but instead was a civilian who liked to use pseudonyms and disguises. His true name was Allen Pinkerton and he had been a detective in Chicago's police force before General McClellan had appointed him as head of the Army of the Potomac's Secret Service Bureau. Now, in the guttering light of candles, Pinkerton looked up at the tall, nervous officer who had been fetched from the tail of the army into his presence. "You're Major James Starbuck?"

"Yes, sir," James Starbuck responded in the cautious manner of a man who expects any summons to presage trouble. These days James looked a disconsolate soul. From being a lofty staff officer, privy to the secrets of the army's commander, he had been relegated to a job with the commissary department of the 1st Corps. His new duties were concerned with the supply of dried vegetables, flour, jerked beef, salt pork, hardtack, and coffee beans, duties he discharged conscientiously, but however much food he managed to supply it was never enough, so that officers from every regiment and battery and troop felt free to swear at him as a useless, black-assed son of a pious bitch. James knew he should ignore such insults, but instead they overwhelmed and humiliated him. He had rarely felt so miserable.

Now, to James's astonishment, he saw that the man called Allen was studying Adam's long letter which James had sent to Major General McClellan's headquarters back in the old year. As far as James was aware, the letter had been utterly ignored by the army's high command, and since James had neither the authority nor the character to persuade anyone of the letter's importance, he had assumed the letter was long forgotten, yet now this unprepossessing Major Allen had finally realized its value. "So who gave you this letter, Major?" Pinkerton demanded.

"I promised not to say, sir." James wondered why he was calling this shabby little man "sir." It was not as though Allen outranked James, yet something in the man's pugnacious demeanor brought out James's natural subservience, though at the same time it also triggered a tiny streak of stubbornness as he decided he would not use the honorific again.

Pinkerton stabbed at the tobacco in his pipe with a callused finger, then placed the bowl by a candle flame and sucked it alight. "You've got a brother with the rebels?"

James blushed, and no wonder, for Nate's treason was a matter of immense shame to the Starbuck family. "Yes, si— . . . Major. I do, alas."

"Did he write this letter?"

"No, si— . . . Major. No, he didn't. I wish he had."

Pinkerton's pipe bubbled as he sucked on the short stem. Wind gusted at the window and howled in the short chimney, driving a billow of thick smoke back into the room. "If I assure you that I can be trusted, Major," Pinkerton said, his voice retaining the soft burr of his native Scotland, "and if I cross my heart and hope to die, and if I swear to you upon my dear departed mother's soul and upon the soul of her own dear mother and upon all the Bibles in all of North America as well, and if by so swearing I promise you that I will never, not ever, reveal your informant's name to any man, will you tell me?"

James felt the temptation. Maybe, if he gave Adam's name, he might be relieved of his foul commissary duty, but he had given his word and he would not break it, and so he just shook his head. "No, Major, I would not tell you. I would trust you, but I could not break my word."

"Good for you, Starbuck. Good for you." Pinkerton hid his disappointment and frowned at Adam's letter again. "Your man was right," he went on, "and all the rest were wrong. Your man told us the truth, or something close to it. He got Johnston's numbers wrong, we know for a fact the rebel army's at least twice the size he told you, but everything else here is spot on the mark, straight on the target, good as gold!" What had impressed Pinkerton was Adam's description of the wooden Quaker guns. He had given their exact number and location, and Pinkerton, coming on the guns in the rainy twilight, had remembered the discarded report and had ordered it dug out of his files. There were hundreds of such discarded reports, many the work of imaginative patriots, some mere suppositions based on newspaper stories, while others undoubtedly were sent by southerners attempting to mislead the North. So much information flowed north that Pinkerton was forced to throw much away, yet now he realized he had discarded some gold with the dross. "Has your man sent you any other letters?"

"No, Major."

Pinkerton leaned back in his chair, making its legs creak ominously. "Do you think he would be willing to supply us with more information?"

"I'm sure he would, yes." James's greatcoat dripped water on the parlor floor. He was shivering with cold, despite the small fire that spat angrily but gave precious little warmth to the shabby room. A bare patch on the plaster above the fireplace betrayed where a picture had been hastily removed prior to the northern army's arrival; maybe a portrait of Jeff Davis or perhaps of Beauregard, who was the victor of Manassas and the South's favorite general.

Pinkerton peered closely at the letter again, wondering why he had not taken it seriously before. He noted that the writing paper was of high quality, plainly from a stock left over from before the war and of much better manufacture than the discolored, fibrous, and paltry stuff the South now made. The writer had used capital letters, thus disguising his handwriting, but the grammar and vocabulary betrayed him to be a well-educated man, and the information revealed him to be a man at the very heart of the rebel army. Pinkerton knew he had made a mistake when he had first ignored this letter, yet he consoled himself that some nuggets were bound to be lost in the chaos. "Remind me how your man got this letter to you?" Pinkerton demanded.

James had explained the circumstances in a covering letter that he had attached to Adam's long screed, but apparently that explanation had long disappeared. "He gave it to me in Richmond, Major, when I was exchanged."

"And how would you communicate with him now?"

"He said letters should be left in the vestibule of St. Paul's Church in Richmond. There's a bulletin board in that vestibule, crisscrossed with tape, and if a letter is placed under the tapes addressed to the Honorary Secretary of the Confederate Army Bible Supply Society, then he will collect it. I don't think there is any such society," James said, then paused. "And I have to confess I wouldn't know how to get a letter to Richmond." He added the admission humbly.

"Nothing to it, man. We do it almost every day," Pinkerton said heartily, then he pulled open a leather valise and took out a traveling writing case. "We're going to need your friend's help, Major, in these coming weeks." He took a sheet of paper from the case, added an ink bottle and pen, and pushed them all across the table. "Sit yourself down."

"You want me to write to him now, Major?" James asked in astonishment.

"No time like the present, Starbuck! Strike while the iron's still steaming, isn't that what they say? Tarry not! Tell your friend that his intelligence is of the greatest value, and that it was appreciated at the very highest levels of the Federal army." Pinkerton had discovered that a little flattery went a long way with secret agents. He paused as James pulled a candle near his paper and began to write in a swift, efficient hand. The pen had a split nib that spattered small droplets of ink as it scratched fast across the paper. "Write something personal," Pinkerton went on, "so he'll know it's you."

"I already have," James said. He had expressed the hope that Adam had found an opportunity to pass on the Bible to Nate.

"Now write that we would be obliged to your friend if he could help us with the enclosed request."

"Enclosed request?" James asked in puzzlement.

"You won't tell me who he is," Pinkerton said, "so I'm hardly going to tell you what we want of him."

James rested the pen on the edge of the table. He frowned. "Will he be at risk, sir?"

"Risk? Of course he'll be at risk! There's a war on! Risk is the very air we breathe!" Pinkerton scowled and sucked his tobacco pipe at the candle's flame again. "Is your man doing this for money?"

James stiffened at the implication. "He's a patriot, Major. And a Christian."

"Then the reward of heaven is surely all the more reason for him to run a risk?" Pinkerton demanded. "But do you think I want to lose your man? Of course not! I promise you I'll not ask him to do anything which I would not expect my own son to do, of that you can be sure, Major. But let me tell you something else." Pinkerton, as though demonstrating how important his next words were, removed the pipe from his mouth and cuffed the spittle from his lips. "What I'll be asking of your man could well win us this war. That's how important it is, Major."

James dutifully took up the pen. "You simply want me to ask him to fulfill the enclosed request."

"Aye, Major, that's what I want. Then I'll bother you to address the envelope for me." Pinkerton leaned back and sucked on his pipe. He would be asking Adam for information about the rebel defenses to the east of Richmond, for it was in that damp and empty landscape, any day now, that General McClellan planned to spring his surprise attack on the rebel capital. This present slow advance toward the ruins of Manassas had only ever been intended to keep the Confederate army pinned north of their capital while McClellan secretly launched the greatest fleet of history to carry his real attack force around to the rebels' eastern flank. Richmond by May, Pinkerton told himself, peace by July, and the rewards of victory for the rest of his life.

He took the letter and envelope from James. The envelope was made of lumpy brown paper that one of Pinkerton's agents had brought back from a secret visit to the Confederacy and James had addressed it to the Honorable Secretary of the Confederate Army Bible Supply Society care of St. Paul's, Grace Street, Richmond. Pinkerton found one of the cheap-looking green five-cent stamps showing Jefferson Davis's sunken face and gummed it onto the envelope. "This informant, I suppose, will only trust you?" Pinkerton asked.

"Indeed," James confirmed.

Pinkerton nodded. If this strange spy would only trust James, then Pinkerton wanted to make certain James was always close at hand. "And before the war, Major," he asked, "what was your trade?"

"It was a profession," James corrected Pinkerton sternly. "I was a lawyer in Boston."

"A lawyer, eh?" Pinkerton stood and went close to the feeble fire. "It was my dear mother's wish that I should be a lawyer, what in Scotland they call a writer to the signet, but alas, there was never the money for the schooling. But I like to think I would have made a fine attorney had I been given the chance."

"I'm sure you would," James said, sure of no such thing.

"And as a lawyer, Major, you're accustomed to sifting evidence? To winnowing truth from falsehood?"

"Indeed," James said.

"I ask you," Pinkerton explained, "because of late this bureau has been suffering from lack of good order. We've been too busy to keep our files as neat as I'd like, and I need a chief of staff, Major, someone who can make judgments and marshal evidence. I assure you that General McClellan will authorize the move instantly, so there'll be no problems with your present commanding officer. Is it presumptuous of me to offer you such a job?"

"It's most generous, sir, most generous," James said, quite forgetting his sturdy resolve not to call this man "sir." "I should be honored to join you," he went on hurriedly, hardly daring to believe that he was truly being rescued from the echoing, damp store sheds of the commissary department.

"In that case, welcome aboard, Major." Pinkerton held out a hand of welcome. "We don't stand on ceremony here," he said when he had given James's hand a sturdy grip and a vigorous pumping, "so from now on you can call me Bulldog."

"Bulldog?" James stuttered the word.

"Just a nickname, Major," Pinkerton assured James.

"Very good," James hesitated, "Bulldog. And I should be honored if you were to know me as James."

"I intended to, Jimmy, I intended to! We'll start work in the morning, so we shall. You'll want to fetch your traps tonight? You can sleep in the scullery here if you don't mind a rat or two?"

"I became accustomed to rats while in prison," James said, "and worse."

"Then be on your way, Major! We need to start work early in the morning," Pinkerton said, and then, once James had gone, the head of the Secret Service sat and wrote a brief letter that would go south inside James's covering note. The letter asked for detailed information on the rebel defenses east of Richmond, and particularly asked how many troops manned those defenses. Pinkerton then requested that this information be delivered to a Mr. Timothy Webster, care of the Ballard House Hotel on Richmond's Franklin Street.

Timothy Webster was Pinkerton's most brilliant spy, a man who had already made three forays into the Confederacy and was now in the middle of his fourth. This time Webster had established himself as a blockade-running merchant seeking business in Richmond, while in truth he was using the Secret Service's funds to make friends with indiscreet rebel officers and politicians. Webster's mission was to discover and betray the defenses of Richmond, a job that involved horrible risks, but now, with the advent of James Starbuck's informant, Pinkerton felt certain of Webster's success. He sealed the two sheets of paper into the envelope, uncorked a bottle of his precious Scotch whiskey and offered himself a toast. To victory.

COLONEL GRIFFIN SWYNYARD WAS GREEDILY EATING A plate of fried cabbage and potato when Bird and Starbuck reached his tent. It had begun to rain and the heavy clouds had brought a premature dusk so that the Colonel's tent needed to be lit with two lanterns that hung from the ridge pole. The newly promoted Colonel sat beneath the twin lamps wearing a voluminous gown of gray wool over uniform trousers and a dirty shirt. He flinched whenever a bite provoked a twinge of agony from one of his yellowed, decayed teeth. His servant, a cowed slave, had announced Major Bird and Captain Starbuck and then scuttled back into the night where the rearguard's fires struggled against the wind and rain. "So you're Bird," Swynyard said, pointedly ignoring Starbuck.

"And you're Swynyard," Bird responded with a matching curtness.

"Colonel Swynyard. West Point, class of twenty-nine, late U.S. Army, 4th Infantry." Swynyard's bloodshot eyes had a sickly yellow cast in the lamplight. He chewed a spoonful of his dinner, then helped it down with a mouthful of whiskey. "Now appointed second-in-command to the Faulconer Brigade." He pointed his spoon at Bird. "Which makes me your superior officer."

Bird acknowledged the relationship with a curt nod, but refused to call Swynyard "sir," which was presumably what the Colonel wanted. Swynyard did not press the point; instead he scored across his supper plate with a sharp knife, then spooned up another mouthful of the unappetizing mixture. His tent had a newly sawn pinewood floor, a folding table, a chair, a camp bed, and a sawhorse that was being used as a stand for his saddle. The furniture, like the saddle and the tent, was all brand-new. It would have been expensive before the war, but what such equipment must have cost in this time of shortage, Bird did not like to guess. There was a wagon parked just outside the tent that Bird guessed was being used to transport Swynyard's comforts and was yet more evidence of the money that had been expended on the Colonel's accoutrements.

Swynyard bolted down his mouthful of food, then took another pull of his whiskey. Rain pattered on the tent's tight-stretched canvas, while in the dark a horse whinnied and a dog howled. "You are now in the Faulconer Brigade," Swynyard announced formally, "which consists of this Legion, the Izard County Volunteer Battalion from Arkansas, the 12th and 13th Florida Regiments, and the 65th Virginia. All of which are now under the orders of Brigadier General Washington Faulconer, God bless him, who is awaiting our arrival on the Rappahannock tomorrow. Questions?"

"How is my brother-in-law?" Bird asked politely.

"Military questions, Bird. Military."

"Is my brother-in-law's wound recovered sufficiently to allow him to fulfill his military duties at last?" Bird asked sweetly.

Swynyard ignored the mocking question. A tic throbbed in his right cheek as he used his maimed left hand to claw at his gray-streaked beard where a scatter of cabbage scraps had lodged. The Colonel had placed a wad of damp chewing tobacco to one side of his plate, and now he put the tobacco back into his mouth and sucked hard on it as he stood and edged around the sawhorse that served as his saddle stand. "Ever taken a scalp?" he challenged Bird.

"Not that I can recall, no." Bird managed to hide his surprise and distaste at the sudden question.

"There's a knack to it! Like any other skill, Bird, there's a knack! The trouble with young soldiers is that they always try to cut them off and that won't do. That won't do at all. No, you have to peel them off, peel them! Help the peel with a knife, if you must, but only to trim the edges, that way you get something fine and furry! Something like this!" Swynyard had taken a hank of black hair from the pocket of his gown and he waved it to and fro in front of Bird's face. "I've taken more savages' hairpieces than any white man alive," Swynyard went on, "and I'm proud of that, proud of it. I served my country well, Bird, none served it better, I daresay, yet my reward was to watch it elect that black-assed chimpanzee Lincoln, so now we must fight for a new country." Swynyard made this speech emotionally, leaning close enough so that Bird could smell a mix of cabbage, tobacco, and whiskey on his breath. "We shall get on, Bird, you and I. Man to man, eh? How is the regiment? Tell me that."

"They're well," Bird answered curtly.

"Let's hope it is well, Bird. Good and well! The General's not sure it should be commanded by a major, you understand me?" Swynyard held his face close to Bird's as he spoke. "So you and I had better get along, Major, if you want my good opinion to help sway the General's mind."

"What are you suggesting?" Bird asked quietly.

"I don't make suggestions, Major. I ain't clever enough to make suggestions. I'm just a blunt soldier who was weaned on the gun's black muzzle." Swynyard breathed a gust of hoarse laughter over Bird, then dragged the woolen gown tight around his thin chest before going unsteadily back to his chair. "All that matters to me," Swynyard continued after he had sat down, "is that the Legion is ready to fight and knows exactly why it is fighting. Do the men know that, Bird?"

"I'm sure they do," Bird said.

"You don't sound sure, Bird. You don't sound sure at all." Swynyard paused to take some more whiskey. "Soldiers are simple folk," he went on. "There ain't nothing complicated about a soldier, Bird. Point a soldier in the right direction, boot his backside, and tell him to kill, that's all a soldier needs, Bird! Soldiers are nothing more than white niggers, that's what I say, but even a nigger does better if he knows why he's doing it. Which is why, tonight, you will distribute these booklets to the men. I want them to know the nobility of the cause." Swynyard tried to lift a wooden box filled with pamphlets onto the table, but the box's weight defeated him, and so he used his foot to nudge the crate toward Bird instead.

Bird stooped for one of the booklets, then read the title page aloud. " 'The Nigger Question,' by John Daniels." Bird's voice betrayed his distaste for John Daniels's virulent opinions. "You really want me to give this to the men?" he asked.

"You must!" Swynyard declared. "Johnny's my cousin, you see, and he sold those pamphlets to General Faulconer just so the men would read them."

"How generous of my brother-in-law," Bird said acidly.

"And how useful these pamphlets will be." Starbuck spoke for the first time since entering the tent.

Swynyard stared suspiciously at Starbuck. "Useful?" he asked in a dangerous voice after a long silence.

"Fires are terrible hard things to get started in this wet weather," Starbuck said blandly.

The tic in Swynyard's cheek began to flutter. He said nothing for a long while, but just fidgeted with his bone-handled knife as he contemplated the young officer.

"Daniels is your cousin?" Bird broke the silence suddenly.

"Yes." Swynyard took his eyes off Starbuck and laid the knife back on the table.

"And your cousin, I presume," Bird said slowly as the light dawned on him, "wrote the editorial encouraging the army to promote Washington Faulconer?"

"What of it?" Swynyard asked.

"Nothing, nothing," Bird said, though he could hardly hide his amusement as he realized just what price his brother-in-law had paid for Daniels's support.

"You find something comical?" Swynyard demanded malevolently.

Bird sighed. "Colonel," he said, "we have marched a long way today, and I possess neither the energy nor the desire to stand here and explain my amusements. Is there anything else you want of me? Or might Captain Starbuck and I get some sleep?"

Swynyard stared at Byrd for a few seconds, then pointed with his ravaged left hand at the tent's flap. "Go, Major. Send a man for the pamphlets. You stay here." The last three words were directed at Starbuck.

Bird did not move. "If you have business with one of my officers, Colonel," he said to Swynyard, "then you have business with me. I shall stay."

Swynyard shrugged as if to suggest he did not care if Bird stayed or went, then looked at Starbuck again. "How is your father, Starbuck?" Swynyard asked suddenly. "Still preaching brotherly love for the niggers, is he? Still expecting us to marry our daughters to the sons of Africa?" He paused for Starbuck's reply. One of the lamps flared suddenly, then its flame settled again. The sound of men's singing came from the rainy darkness. "Well, Starbuck?" Swynyard demanded. "Is your father still wanting us to give our daughters to the niggers?"

"My father never preached marriage between the races," Starbuck said mildly. He had no love for his father, but in the face of Swynyard's mockery he felt driven to defend the Reverend Elial.

The tic in Swynyard's cheek quivered, then he shot out his wounded left hand and pointed at the two stars that decorated the collar of his brand-new uniform jacket that hung from a nail hammered into one of the tent poles. "What does that insignia mean, Starbuck?"

"It means, I believe, that the jacket belongs to a lieutenant colonel," Starbuck said.

"It belongs to me!" Swynyard said in a rising voice.

Starbuck shrugged as though the jacket's ownership were of small consequence.

"And I outrank you!" Swynyard screamed the words, spewing a mist of spittle and tobacco juice across the remains of his cabbage and potato, "So you will call me 'sir'! Won't you!"

Starbuck still said nothing. The Colonel glared at him, his maimed hand scratching at the table's edge. The silence stretched. The singing in the near darkness had checked when the men first heard the Colonel screaming at Starbuck, and Major Bird guessed that half the Legion was now listening to the confrontation that was taking place inside the yellow-lit tent.

Colonel Swynyard was oblivious of that silent, unseen audience. He was losing his temper, goaded to the loss by the look of amusement on Starbuck's handsome face. The Colonel suddenly seized a short-handled riding whip that lay on his camp bed and snapped its woven thong toward the Bostonian. "You're a northern bastard, Starbuck, a nigger-loving piece of black Republican trash, and there's no place for you in this brigade." The Colonel lurched to his feet and cracked the whip again, this time flicking the tip just inches from Starbuck's cheek. "You are hereby dismissed from the regiment, now and forever, you hear me? Those are the Brigadier General's orders, signed, sealed, and entrusted to me." Swynyard used his left hand to fumble through the papers on his folding table, but the dismissal order eluded him and he abandoned the search. "You will remove yourself now, this minute!" Swynyard flicked the whip's lash toward Starbuck a third time. "Get out!"

Starbuck caught the lash. He had planned to do nothing but ward the blow off, but as the whip's thong curled around his hand a more devilish course suggested itself. He half smiled, then tugged, thus pulling Swynyard off-balance. The Colonel clawed at the table for support, then Starbuck pulled harder and the folding table collapsed beneath Swynyard's weight. The Colonel sprawled on the floor in a splintering mess of broken wood and spilt cabbage. "Guard!" Swynyard screamed as he fell. "Guard!"

A bemused Sergeant Tolliver of A Company pushed his head through the tent's flaps. "Sir?" He looked down at the Colonel, who was lying amid the wreckage of the broken camp table, then shot a despairing look at Bird. "What do I do, sir?" Tolliver asked Bird.

Swynyard struggled to his feet. "You will place this piece of northern scum under arrest," he shouted at Tolliver, "and you will hand him to the provost marshals and order him sent to Richmond, there to be interred as an enemy of the state. You understand me?"

Tolliver hesitated.

"Do you understand?" Swynyard screamed at the hapless Sergeant.

"He understands you," Major Bird intervened.

"You are dismissed from the army," Swynyard shouted at Starbuck. "Your commission is ended, you are finished, you are dismissed!" Spittle landed on Starbuck's face. The Colonel's self-control was gone utterly, eroded by alcohol and Starbuck's subtle goading. He lurched toward Starbuck, fumbling suddenly at the strap of his holster, which hung with his jacket on the tent pole. "You are under arrest!" Swynyard hiccupped, still trying to pull the revolver free.

Bird took hold of Starbuck's elbow and pulled him out of the tent before any murder took place. "I think he's mad," Bird said as he hurried Starbuck away from Swynyard's tent. "Stark, plain mad. Addled. Demented. Moon-touched." Bird stopped a safe distance from the tent and stared back as though he could not really credit what he had just witnessed. "He's drunk too, of course. But he lost his wits long before he ever drowned his tonsils in rotgut. My God, Nate, and he's our new second-in-command?"

"Sir?" Sergeant Tolliver had followed the two officers out of the Colonel's tent. "Am I to arrest Mr. Starbuck, sir?"

"Don't be ridiculous, Dan. I'll look after Starbuck. You just forget about all this." Bird shook his head. "Crazed!" he said in wonderment. There was no movement in the Colonel's tent now, just the glow of the lamplit canvas showing through the rain. "I'm sorry,

Nate," Bird said. He still held Daniels's pamphlet, which he now tore into scraps.

Starbuck swore bitterly. He had expected Faulconer's revenge, but somehow he had still hoped he could stay with K Company. That was his home now, the place where he had friends and purpose. Without K Company he was a lost soul. "I should have stayed with Shanks." Starbuck said. "Shanks" was Nathan Evans, whose depleted brigade had long gone south.

Bird gave Starbuck a cigar, then plucked a brand from a nearby fire to light the tobacco. "We have to get you out of here, Nate, before that lunatic decides to have you arrested properly."

"Arrested for what?" Starbuck asked bitterly.

"For being an enemy of the state," Bird spoke softly. "You heard what the befuddled idiot said. I suspect Faulconer put that idea into his head."

Starbuck stared at the Colonel's tent. "Where the hell did Faulconer find that son of a bitch?"

"From John Daniels, of course," Bird said. "My brother-in-law has just bought himself a brigade, and the price of it was whatever Daniels demanded. Which presumably included a job for that drunken maniac."

"I'm sorry, Pecker," Starbuck said, ashamed of his self-pity. "The bastard threatened you too."

"I shall survive," Bird said confidently. He knew well enough that Washington Faulconer despised him and would like to demote him, but Thaddeus Bird also knew he had the Legion's respect and affection and just how hard it would be for his brother-in-law to fight that attachment. Starbuck was a much easier target for Faulconer. "It's more important, Nate," Bird went on, "to get you safely away from here. What do you want to do?"

"Do?" Starbuck echoed. "What can I do?"

"You want to go back north?"

"Christ, no." Going back north meant facing his father's bitter wrath. It meant betraying his friends in the Legion. It meant crawling home as a penitent failure, and his pride would not let him do it.

"Then go to Richmond," Bird said, "find Adam. He'll help you."

"His father won't let him help me." Starbuck sounded bitter again. He had heard nothing from Adam all winter, and he suspected his erstwhile friend had abandoned him.

"Adam can be his own man," Bird said. "Go tonight, Nate. Murphy will take you to Fredericksburg and you can take a train from there. I'll give you a furlough pass that should see you through to Richmond." No one could travel in the Confederacy without a passport issued by the authorities, but soldiers were allowed to go on leave using furlough slips issued by their regiments.

The news of Starbuck's dismissal had spread like gunsmoke through the Legion. K Company wanted to protest, but Bird persuaded them that this argument could not be won by appealing to Swynyard's sense of justice. Ned Hunt, who regarded himself as the company's jester, wanted to saw through the spokes of Swynyard's wagon or else burn down the Colonel's tent, but Bird would entertain no such nonsense and even placed a guard over the Colonel's tent to stop it. The important thing, Bird maintained, was to get Starbuck safely away from Swynyard's malice.

"So what will you do?" Truslow asked Starbuck while Captain Murphy readied two horses.

"See if Adam can help."

"In Richmond? So you'll see my Sally?" Truslow asked.

"I hope so." Starbuck, despite the night's disasters, felt a small pang of anticipation.

"Tell her I think about her," Truslow said gruffly. It was as close to an admission of love and forgiveness as he was able to make. "If she lacks for anything," Truslow went on, then shrugged because he doubted that his daughter could possibly lack for money. "I wish," Truslow began, then faltered into silence again, and Starbuck supposed that the Sergeant was wishing that his only child was not earning her living as a whore, but then Truslow surprised him. "You and she," he explained, "I'd like to see that."

Starbuck blushed in the dark. "Your Sally needs someone with better prospects than me," he said.

"She could do a lot worse," Truslow said loyally.

"I don't see how." Starbuck let the self-pity well up inside him again. "I'm homeless, penniless, jobless."

"But not for long," Truslow said. "You won't let that son of a bitch Faulconer beat you."

"No," Starbuck said, though in truth he suspected he was already beaten. He was a stranger in a strange land, and his enemies were wealthy, influential, and implacable.

"So you'll be back," Truslow said. "Till then I'll keep the company good and smart."

"You don't need me to do that," Starbuck said. "You never needed me to do that."

"You're a fool, boy," Truslow growled. "I ain't got your brains, and you're a fool not to see that." A curb chain jingled as Captain Murphy led two saddled horses through the rain. "Say your farewells," Truslow ordered Starbuck, "and promise the boys you'll come back. They'll need that promise."

Starbuck said his farewells. The men of the company possessed nothing but what they could carry, yet still they tried to press gifts on him. George Finney had plundered a silver Phi Beta Kappa key from a dead officer's watch chain at Ball's Bluff and wanted Starbuck to take the seal. Starbuck refused, just as he would not accept an offer of cash from Sergeant Hutton's squad. He just took his furlough pass and then strapped his blanket onto the back of his borrowed saddle. He pulled Oliver Wendell Holmes's scarlet-lined greatcoat around his shoulders and hauled himself onto the horse's back. "I'll see you all soon," he said as though he believed it and then rammed back his heels so that none of the Legion would see how close he was to despair.

Starbuck and Murphy rode into the night, passing Colonel Swynyard's darkened tent. Nothing moved there. The Colonel's three slaves crouched under the wagon and watched the horsemen ride into the black rain. The hooves faded into the darkness.

It was still raining when morning came. Bird had slept badly and felt older than his years as he crawled out of his turf-covered shelter and tried to warm his bones beside a feeble fire. He noted that Colonel Swynyard's tent had already been struck and that the three slaves were roping the load onto the Colonel's wagon ready for the day's journey to Fredericksburg. A half mile north, on the far ridge, two Yankee horsemen were watching the rebel encampment through the rain. Hiram Ketley, Bird's half-witted but willing orderly, brought the Major a mug of coffee adulterated with dried sweet potato, then tried to agitate the fire into stronger life. A handful of officers shivered about the miserable fire, and it was when those officers looked past Bird with alarm on their faces that he was aware of someone approaching him. He turned and saw the ragged beard and bloodshot eyes of Colonel Swynyard, who, astonishingly, smiled a yellow smile and held out a hand for Bird to shake. "Morning! You're Bird, yes?" Swynyard asked in an energetic voice.

Bird nodded cautiously but did not accept the hand.

"Swynyard." The Colonel appeared not to recognize Bird. "Meant to talk to you last night, sorry I was unwell." He took his hand back awkwardly.

"We did talk," Bird said.

"We talked?" Swynyard frowned.

"Last night. In your tent."

"Malaria, that's the trouble," Swynyard explained. The tic throbbed in his cheek, making his right eye appear to wink constantly. The Colonel's beard was damp from washing, his uniform was brushed, and his hair had been slicked down with oil. He had retrieved his whip and now held it in his maimed hand. "The fever comes and goes, Bird," he explained, "but it generally strikes at night. Knocks me flat, you see. So if we did talk last night, then I won't remember a thing. Fever, see?"

"You were feverish, yes," Bird said faintly.

"But I'm all right now. Nothing like some sleep to drive off the fever. I'm Washington Faulconer's second-in-command."

"I know," Bird said.

"And you're now in his brigade," Swynyard went on blithely. "There's you, some ragamuffins from Arkansas, the 12th and 13th

Florida Regiments, and the 65th Virginia. General Faulconer sent me to introduce myself and to give you the new orders. You won't be manning the Fredericksburg defenses, but joining the rest of the brigade farther west. It's all written down." He gave Bird a folded piece of paper that had been sealed with Washington Faulconer's signet ring.

Bird tore open the paper and saw it was a simple movement order directing the Legion to march from Fredericksburg to Locust Grove.

"We're in reserve there," Swynyard said. "With any luck we'll have a few days to pull ourselves into shape, but there is one delicate matter we have to deal with first." He took Bird's elbow and moved the startled Major away from the inquisitive ears of the other officers. "Something very delicate," Swynyard said.

"Starbuck?" Bird ventured.

"How did you guess?" Swynyard sounded astonished, but also impressed by Bird's acuity. "Starbuck indeed, Bird. A bad business. I hate to disappoint a man, Bird, it ain't my style. We Swynyards have always been forthright, to a fault I sometimes think, but we're too long in the tooth to change now. Starbuck exactly. The General won't abide him, you know, and we have to get rid of him. I promised I'd do it tactfully, and thought you might know best how to do that?"

"We've done it already," Bird said bitterly. "He went last night."

"He did?" Swynyard blinked at Bird. "He did? Good! First chop! Your doing, I assume? Well done! Then there's no more to be said, is there? Good to meet you, Bird." He raised the whip in a farewell salute, then suddenly turned back. "There was one other thing, Bird."

"Colonel?"

"I've some reading matter for your men. Something to cheer them up." Swynyard gave Bird a yellow grin. "They look a bit sullen, as if they need something to enthuse them. Send a man to collect the booklets, will you? And order any man who can't read to have a friend read it aloud. Good! Well done! Carry on!"

Bird watched the Colonel walk away, then closed his eyes and shook his head as if verifying that the damp morning was not an awful dream. It seemed it was not and that the world really was quite irretrievably insane. "Maybe," he said to no one in particular, "the Yankees have got one just like him. Let's hope so."

Over the valley the mounted Yankee pickets turned and vanished into the damp woods. The southern artillery limbered its guns and followed Colonel Swynyard's wagon south, leaving the Legion to extinguish its fires and pull on its damp boots.

The retreat went on, and it felt like defeat.

The great mass of the Army of the Potomac did not advance beyond Manassas. Instead, in a maneuver designed to throw the rebel forces off balance, the troops returned to Alexandria, just across the river from Washington, where a fleet waited to carry them down the Potomac and out into the Chesapeake Bay and so south to the Union stronghold of Fort Monroe. The fleet had been chartered by the U.S. government and the masts of the waiting ships made a forest above the river. There were sidewheelers from as far north as Boston, ferryboats from the Delaware, schooners from a score of ports on the Atlantic seaboard, and even transatlantic passenger boats with needle-sharp bows and elegant gilt scrollwork handsome about their poops. The steam from a hundred engines hissed into the air while the scream of a hundred whistles frightened the horses that waited to be loaded into the bowels of the vessels. Steam derricks lifted nets of cargo aboard as lines of soldiers climbed the sloping gangplanks. Guns and caissons, limbers and portable forges were tied down on the steamers' decks. McClellan's staff reckoned it would take twenty days for the whole expedition to be transported, all one hundred and twenty-one thousand men with their three hundred cannons, and eleven hundred wagons, and fifteen thousand horses, and ten thousand beef cattle, and the seemingly endless bales of forage and pontoon boats and drums of telegraph wire and barrels of powder, all of which needed to be protected during the voyage by the battleships and frigates and gunboats of the U.S. Navy. The fleet of the Army of the Potomac was the largest ever assembled, proof of the Union's resolve to end the rebellion with one massive stroke. Those mudsills who had complained of McClellan's supine nature would now see how the Young Napoleon could fight! He would take his army to the lightly guarded tongue of land that stretched seventy miles southeastward from Richmond and like a thunderbolt, strike west to capture the rebels' capital and destroy their resolve.

"I have held you back that you might give the deathblow to the rebellion that has distracted our once happy country," McClellan's printed proclamation explained to his troops, then it promised that their General would look over his soldiers "as a parent over his children; and you know that your General loves you from the depths of his heart." The proclamation warned the troops that there would be desperate combats, but also assured them that when they carried their victory home they would regard their membership in the Army of the Potomac as the greatest honor of their lives.

"Fine sentiments," James Starbuck said when he read the proclamation that had been produced on the printing press that traveled with the army headquarters, and he was not alone in admiring the fine words and noble feelings. The northern newspapers might call McClellan the Young Napoleon, but the soldiers of the Army of the Potomac knew their general as "Little Mac" and declared there was no finer soldier in all the world. If any man could bring swift victory it was Little Mac, who had persuaded the Army of the Potomac that they were the best-equipped, best-drilled, and best-trained soldiers in the Republic's history, if not in all the world's history, and though Little Mac's political enemies might complain of his caution and sing sarcastically that all was quiet on the Potomac, the soldiers knew their General had just been waiting for the perfect moment to strike. That moment had now come as hundreds of paddlewheels and propellers churned the Potomac white and hundreds of smokestacks vented coalsmoke to a blue spring sky. The first ships dropped downriver, bands playing, to dip their ensigns as they steamed past George Washington's home at Mount Vernon.

"They'll need more than sentiments," Allen Pinkerton remarked darkly to James. General McClellan's Secret Service Bureau was waiting in a commandeered house close to the Alexandria quays until the General himself was ready to sail, and this morning, as James and his chief stared across the rail lines to the busy quays, Pinkerton was waiting for the arrival of visitors. The rest of the bureau was employed collating the latest scraps of information that had arrived from the South. Every day brought an indigestible mass of such information from deserters or from escaping slaves or in letters from northern sympathizers that were smuggled across the Rappahannock, yet Pinkerton trusted none of it. He wanted to hear from his best agent, Timothy Webster, and through Webster from James's mysterious friend, but for weeks now there had been an ominous silence from Richmond. The good news in that silence was that there had been no mention in the Richmond newspapers of any arrests and no gossip had come north about high-placed southern officers being accused of treason, but Webster's silence worried Pinkerton. "We need to give the General the best intelligence possible," he told James repeatedly. Pinkerton never referred to General McClellan as Little Mac, not even as the Young Napoleon, but always as the General.

"We can certainly reassure the General that the peninsula is lightly defended?" James remarked. He was working at a small camp table that he had set up on the verandah.

"Ah, ha! But that's precisely what the southerners want us to believe," Pinkerton said, turning excitedly to see if a clatter of hooves presaged the arrival of his visitors. A horseman rode past and Pinkerton subsided. "But until I hear further news from your friend, then I'll believe nothing!"

Adam had already sent one reply through the good offices of Timothy Webster, and that one reply had been astonishingly detailed. Except in guns, Adam had written, the defenses facing Fort Monroe were very lightly held. Major General Magruder was screening the fort with four weak brigades, comprising just twenty under-strength battalions. In infantry, at the last count, those battalions had contained just ten thousand men, most of whom Magruder had concentrated in earth-walled forts on Mulberry Island on the southern side of the peninsula and in similar fortifications at Yorktown on the northern side. Some of the Yorktown defenses, Adam had added pedantically, were relics from the unsuccessful British defense of 1783. The fourteen miles between Yorktown and Mulberry Island were guarded by a mere four thousand men and a scatter of dirt forts. Magruder's weakness in numbers was partly compensated by a concentration of artillery, and Adam reported ominously that no fewer than eighty-five pieces of heavy artillery and fifty-five lighter field guns were incorporated in the rebels' defenses. Nevertheless, Adam stressed, even all those guns could not cover every path or track on the peninsula.

Ten miles behind the Yorktown line, Adam reported, close to the small college town of Williamsburg, Magruder had prepared some more earth forts, but these were presently unmanned. Otherwise, Adam said, there were no defenses between Fort Monroe and the new trenches and redoubts being dug around Richmond by General Robert E. Lee. Adam had added apologetically that his information was a week or so out of date and that he understood some further reinforcements were soon to be sent to General Magruder, and he promised to send details of those reinforcements just as soon as he learned of them.

Those further details had never come; indeed no news of any kind had come either from Adam or from Timothy Webster. Their sudden silence was worrying, though James did not believe the silence had any military significance, for every single report that came out of rebel Virginia served to confirm the accuracy of Adam's first detailed account of the peninsula's defenses. The consensus of those reports suggested that Magruder's lines were very thinly held and the last thing the rebels expected was a massive attack from the sea, and James could not understand why Pinkerton was not reassured by that intelligence. Now, waiting on the porch of the Alexandria house, James pleaded with his chief to trust the news coming from beyond the rebel lines. "Magruder, even with his reinforcements, can't have more than fourteen thousand men," James said firmly. He had read every scrap of intelligence coming from the South, and only a handful of the reports contradicted Adam's figures, and that handful James suspected were planted reports intended to mislead the Federal high command. Every instinct in his soul told James that the Young Napoleon would brush the enemy aside with a contemptuous ease. The one hundred and ten thousand men shipping out of the Alexandria quays would meet just fourteen or fifteen thousand rebels, and James, for the life of him, did not understand Pinkerton's qualms.

"They just want us to think they're weak, Jimmy!" Pinkerton now explained his worries. "They want to suck us in before they hit us!" He feinted like a man playing fisticuffs. "Think about your figures!"

James had been thinking about precious little else for two weeks now, but still he humored the small Scotsman. "You know something I don't, Major?"

"In war, James, not every man fights." Pinkerton had been sorting through newspapers at another table on the verandah, but now, after weighting the papers against the day's small wind, he began to stride up and down the wooden deck. On the river, in a pale sunlight, a great transatlantic steamer was maneuvering herself into the wharf where three New Jersey regiments waited. The ship's massive paddle-wheels churned mightily and a small tugboat thumped angry puffs of black smoke as it butted its padded bow against the steamer's elegant bows. One of the regimental bands was playing "Rally Round the Flag, Boys!" and Pinkerton was beating time to the music as he paced the porch. "In war, Jimmy, only a handful of men actually carry a rifle and bayonet to the enemy, yet thousands more serve, and serve nobly! You and I are fighting for the union, yet we do not march in the mud like common rankers. You'll grant me the point?"

"Of course," James said cautiously. He could not bring himself to call Pinkerton "Bulldog," though other members of the department cheerfully used the small Scotsman's nickname.

"So!" Pinkerton turned at the end of the verandah. "We agree that not every man is counted in the ranks, only those who actually carry a rifle, you grasp my point? Yet behind those weapon-carrying heroes, Jimmy, are a host of cooks and clerks, of signalmen and teamsters, of staff men and generals, of bandsmen and doctors, of orderlies and provosts, of engineers and commissary clerks." Pinkerton accompanied this catalog of men by expansive gestures which summoned an imaginary host from the air. "My point, Jimmy, is that behind the fighting men are thousands of other souls who are feeding and supplying, supporting and directing, and all pushing forward to make the fighting possible. You grasp my argument?"

"Up to a point, yes," James said cautiously, his tone suggesting that while he grasped his chief's argument, he was not yet persuaded by it.

"Your friend himself said that reinforcements were being sent to Magruder's lines," Pinkerton declared vigorously. "How many men? We don't know! Where are they? We don't know! And how many are uncounted? We don't know!" Pinkerton stopped beside James's table and seized a pencil and sheet of paper. "We don't know, James, but let us make some educated estimates. You reckon that Magruder has fourteen thousand men? Very good, let us start with that figure." He scribbled the number at the top of the sheet of paper. "Those, of course, are only the men present at roll call, so we have to add in those at sick call and those on furlough, and you can be sure that those fellows will rally round their filthy flag as soon as the fighting begins. So how many would that be? Six thousand? Seven? Call it seven." He scribbled the new number beneath the first. "So now we have deduced that General Magruder has at least twenty-one thousand men, and those twenty-one thousand need feeding and supplying, and those duties must add at least another ten thousand troops, and we should not forget the bandsmen and hospital men and all the ancillaries who make an army work, and they must surely total a further ten thousand men." Pinkerton added that figure to his column. "And then we must reckon that the enemy are almost certainly trying to mislead us by undercounting their numbers, so a prudent man would add fifty percent to our final figure to compensate for their lying deceptions, and what do we have?" He spent a few seconds scribbling his calculations. "There! Sixty-one thousand, five hundred men! Some of the spies give a figure close to that, don't they?" Pinkerton leafed through the piles of paper, looking for some of the reports

James had discarded as being too carefully contrived. "There!" He flourished one such letter. "And that's just at Yorktown, James! Who knows how many are garrisoned in the towns behind Yorktown?"

James rather thought the number was zero, but he did not like to contradict the small Scotsman who was so energetically sure of himself.

"My report to the General," Pinkerton proclaimed, "will say that he can expect to fight at least sixty thousand men in the Yorktown entrenchments. Where, remember, even the great General Washington chose to starve his enemies rather than attack them, even though he did outnumber them by two to one. And we face at least the same odds, Jimmy, and who knows how many more rebels will swarm out of Richmond to support Magruder's lines? It's a desperate task, desperate! You see now why we need another report from your friend?" Pinkerton still did not know Adam's identity and had abandoned his attempts to prise the name out of James. Not that James's reticence in any way disappointed Pinkerton, who regarded James's appointment as a brilliant success, for the lawyer had brought the Secret Service Bureau some desperately needed organization.

James sat unhappily at his table. He was unconvinced by Pinkerton's mathematics and knew that had this been a Massachusetts courtroom and Pinkerton a hostile witness, he would have enjoyed picking at that farrago of dubious assumptions and unlikely arithmetic, but now he forced himself to suppress his doubts. War made all things different, and Pinkerton, after all, was Major General McClellan's personal choice as Secret Service chief and presumably understood these matters in a way that was impossible for James to comprehend. James still felt himself to be a military amateur and so patriotically hushed his doubts.

Pinkerton turned as a buggy came rattling over the rail lines that lay between the house and the Alexandria quays. The buggy's horses pricked their ears and showed the whites of their eyes as a locomotive hissed a sudden gust of steam, but the driver calmed the beasts down as he hauled on the reins. Pinkerton recognized the buggy's driver and passenger and waved a hand in greeting. "It's time," he told James mysteriously, "for desperate measures."

The two men climbed down from the buggy. They were young men, both clean-shaven, both dressed in civilian clothes, but otherwise as different as chalk and cheese. One was tall with lank fair hair falling over a thin and rather melancholy face, while the other was short and rubicund, with tightly curled black hair and a cheerful expression. "Bulldog!" the smaller man exclaimed as he ran up the verandah steps. "It's grand to see you again, so it is!"

"Mr. Scully!" Pinkerton was equally delighted to greet his visitors. He embraced Scully, then shook the other man's hand before introducing both to James. "Be pleased to meet John Scully, Major, and Price Lewis. This is Major Starbuck, my chief of staff."

"It's a grand day, Major!" John Scully said. He had an Irish accent and a quick smile. His companion, altogether more reserved, offered James a limp handshake and a reserved, almost suspicious nod.

"Mr. Scully and Mr. Lewis," Pinkerton declared with palpable pride, "have volunteered to travel south."

"To Richmond!" Scully responded happily. "I hear it's a grand wee city."

"It smells of tobacco," James said, really for want of anything else to say.

"Like myself, eh, Bulldog?" Scully laughed. "A right wee tobacco stinker I am too, Major. The last woman I took to bed said she didn't know whether to make love to me or smoke me!" Scully laughed at this display of his own wit, Price Lewis looked bored, Pinkerton beamed with delight, and James struggled not to show his shocked disapproval. These men, after all, were about to attempt something extraordinarily brave, and he felt he should endure their coarseness.

"Major Starbuck is a God-fearing churchman." Pinkerton had detected James's embarrassment and offered the explanation to John Scully.

"As I am myself, Major," Scully assured James hurriedly, and matched action to words by making the sign of the cross. "And if I made a confession, doubtless I'd be told what a wicked boy I've been, but what the hell? You have to make a laugh or two, don't you, or else you'll end up with a face as miserable as this Englishman here." He grinned good-naturedly at Price Lewis, who pointedly ignored the jibe and watched the New Jersey soldiers file on board the transatlantic steamer instead.

"Europeans," Pinkerton explained to James, "can travel the Confederacy more easily than Yankees. Mr. Lewis and Mr. Scully will pose as blockade runners seeking business."

"And it will all be dandy as long as no one recognizes us," Scully said cheerfully.

"Would that be possible?" James asked worriedly.

"A wee chance, but hardly one to fret over," Scully said. "Price and I spent some time ferreting out southern sympathizers in Washington and throwing the rascals back across the border, but we're about as certain as a man could ever be that none of those bastards are in Richmond. Isn't that a fact, Price?"

Price bowed his head in grave acknowledgment.

"It seems you put yourselves in great danger," James said in fervent tribute to the two men.

"Bulldog pays us to endanger ourselves, don't you now?" Scully said cheerfully. "And I hear the women of Richmond are as beautiful as they are desperate for real Yankee money. And Price and I do love obliging the ladies, ain't that God's honest truth, Price?"

"If you say so, John, if you say so," Lewis said airily, still gazing loftily at the activity at the quay.

"I can't wait to get my hands on one of those southern girls," Scully said lasciviously. "All airs and graces, eh? All frills and furbelows. Too good for the likes of us until we chink a few good northern coins, and then we'll watch the skirt hoops roll away, eh, Price?"

"If you say so, John, if you say so," Price Lewis said, then put a hand to his mouth as though disguising a yawn.

Pinkerton moved to end the small talk, explaining to James that Lewis and Scully were traveling south to discover what had happened to Timothy Webster. "He's not been a well man," Pinkerton said, "and there's always the risk that he could be in his sickbed or worse, in which case Mr. Lewis and Mr. Scully will need to get the information direct from your friend. Which means, Jimmy, that they need a letter from you claiming they can be trusted."

"Which we can be, Major," John Scully said happily. "Except with the ladies, isn't that a fact, Price?"

"If you say so, John, if you say so."

James sat at the table and wrote the requisite letter. It would be used, he was assured, only if Timothy Webster had disappeared, otherwise the letter would stay securely hidden inside John Scully's clothing. James, writing at Pinkerton's dictation, assured Adam that the need for information about the defenses on the peninsula behind Fort Monroe was as urgent as ever, and that he should trust whatever instructions accompanied this covering letter, which came with prayerful good wishes from his brother in Christ Jesus, James Starbuck. He then addressed the envelope to the Honorary Secretary of the Confederate Army Bible Supply Society, and Pinkerton sealed the envelope with a common gummed seal before handing it with a flourish to Scully. "There's a message board in the vestibule of St. Paul's Church, and that's where you put it."

"St. Paul's now, would that be a prominent church?" Scully asked.

"In the very center of the city," Pinkerton assured him.

Scully kissed the envelope, then put it in a pocket. "We'll have your news within the week, Bulldog!"

"You'll cross tonight?"

"And why not?" The Irishman grinned. "The weather looks fine, and there's a good wee wind for us."

James had learned enough to know that Pinkerton's preferred method of infiltrating the Confederacy was for his men to travel across the wide mouth of the Potomac by night, leaving from one of the deserted lonely creeks on the Maryland shore and running silent under a dark sail to the Virginia coast. There, somewhere in King George County, a northern sympathizer provided the agents with horses and papers. "Allow me to wish you well," James said very formally.

"Just pray the women are glad to see us, Major!" Scully said happily.

"And send us news as soon as you can!" Pinkerton added sternly. "We need numbers, John, numbers! How many thousands of troops are stationed in the peninsula? How many guns? How many troops in Richmond stand ready to support Magruder?"

"Worry not, Major, you'll have your numbers," John Scully answered cheerfully as the two agents went back to their waiting buggy. "Two days to Richmond!" John Scully cried happily. "Maybe we'll wait for you there, Bulldog! Celebrate victory in Jeff Davis's wine cellar, eh?" He laughed. Price Lewis raised a hand in solemn farewell, then clicked his tongue at the horse. The buggy rattled back across the rail tracks.

"Brave men," Pinkerton said with a hint of a sniff. "Very brave men, Jimmy."

"Yes, indeed," James said.

On the quays the steam derricks lifted boxes and bales of artillery ammunition: cannonballs and bolts, canister rounds and case shot, shells, and grape. Another great ship was turning in the river, its spadelike paddles slapping the water white as it fought against the Potomac's swift current. More men arrived on the quay, pouring out of a newly stopped train to form in ranks and wait their turn on the river. Their regimental band began to play while the Stars and Stripes, hanging from a dozen jackstaffs, cracked like whips in the fresh spring wind. The army of the North, the greatest army in all American history, was on the move.

To where just ten thousand rebels guarded a peninsula.

Belvedere Delaney arranged for Nate Starbuck to work in the Confederate Passport Bureau. Starbuck's first reaction had been disgust. "I'm a soldier," he told the lawyer, "not a bureaucrat."

"You're a pauper," Delaney had responded icily, "and people are willing to pay very large bribes for a passport."

The passports were required not just to travel beyond Richmond, but even to be on the city's streets after dark. Civilians and soldiers alike needed to make applications for passports at the filthy, crowded office which stood on the corner of Ninth and Broad Street. Starbuck, arriving with Delaney's patronage, was given a room to himself on the third floor, but his presence was as superfluous as it was tedious. A Sergeant Crow did all the real work, leaving Starbuck to stare out of the window or else read a novel by Anthony Trollope that some former occupant of the dusty office had used to prop up the broken leg of the table. He also wrote letters to Adam Faulconer at the army headquarters at Culpeper Court House, begging his friend to use his influence to get him restored to Company K of the Faulconer Legion. Starbuck knew that Washington Faulconer had never been able to resist his son's entreaties, and for a few days he let his hopes stay high, but no reply came from Adam, and Starbuck, after two more importunate appeals, abandoned his attempts.

It was a full three weeks before Starbuck realized that no one expected him to be in the office, and that as long as he paid his respects to Sergeant Crow once or twice a week, he was free to enjoy whatever pleasures Richmond offered. Those pleasures were given a dangerous air by the continuing arrival of northern troops at Fort Monroe. A small panic had swept through the city at the first news of those landings, but when the Yankees made no attempt to break out of their lines, the received opinion became that the northerners were merely pausing on their way to reinforce the Federal garrison at Roanoke. Belvedere Delaney, with whom Starbuck lunched often, scorned that idea. "Why land them at Fort Monroe?" Delaney asked at one such luncheon. "No, my dear Starbuck, they'll be marching on Richmond soon. One battle and the whole fuss will be over. We shall all be prisoners!" He sounded rather pleased at the prospect. "At least the food can't be worse. I'm learning that the worst thing about war is its effect on luxuries. Half the things that make life worth living are unobtainable, and the other half are ruinously expensive. Isn't this beef awful?"

"It tastes better than salt pork."

"I keep forgetting you have served in the field. Maybe I should hear the sound of a bullet once before the war ends? It will make my war memoirs so much more convincing, don't you think?" Delaney smiled, showing off his teeth. He was a vain man and proud of his teeth, which were all his own, unchipped and clean, almost unnatural in their whiteness. Starbuck had met Delaney the year before, when he had first been stranded in Richmond, and the two had struck up a cautious friendship. Delaney was amused that the Reverend Elial Starbuck's prodigal son was in Richmond, though his liking for Starbuck ran deeper than that of mere curiosity, while Starbuck's affection for Delaney arose partly because the lawyer was so ready to be helpful, and partly because Starbuck needed the friendship of men like Delaney and Bird who would not judge his actions by the standards of his father's unforgiving faith. Such men, Starbuck thought, had traveled a mental road he wanted to follow himself, though sometimes, in Delaney's company, he wondered if he was clever enough to free himself of guilt. Starbuck knew that Delaney, for all his carefully cultivated exterior of Pickwickian affability, was both clever and ruthless; qualities the lawyer was presently using to amass a fortune from the sale of what Delaney liked to describe as the twin necessities of warriors: women and weapons. Now the lawyer took off his glasses and polished their lenses on his napkin. "People say bullets whistle, is that true?"

"Yes."

"In what key?"

"I've never noticed."

"Maybe different bullets sound different notes? A skilled marksman might be able to play a tune," Delaney suggested, then happily sang the opening line of a song that had been popular in Richmond all winter long: " 'What are you waiting for, Tardy George?' though he's not waiting any longer, is he? Do you think the war's climacteric shall be reached on the peninsula?"

"If it is," Starbuck said, "I want to be there."

"You are foolishly bloodthirsty, Nate." Delaney grimaced, then held aloft a gruesome morsel of gristle for Starbuck's inspection. "Is this food, do you think? Or something that died in the kitchen? No matter, I shall have something at home instead." He pushed his plate to one side. They were lunching in the Spotswood House Hotel, and when his own meal was done Starbuck produced a sheaf of blank passports that he pushed across the table. "Well done," Delaney said, pocketing the passes. "I owe you four hundred dollars."

"How much?" Starbuck was shocked.

"Passports are valuable, my dear Starbuck!" the small sly lawyer said with delight. "Northern spies pay a fortune for these scraps of paper." Delaney laughed to show that he was teasing. "And it is only right and proper that you should share in my ill-gotten gains. Believe me, I sell these for a rare fortune. I assume you would like payment in northern money?"

"I don't care."

"You do, believe me you do. A northern dollar is worth at least three of our southern ones." Delaney, careless of the stares of other diners, counted out a stack of the newfangled dollar bills that were replacing much of the North's coinage. Southern money was supposed to be of equal value, but the whole system of value and price seemed to have gone mad. Butter was fifty cents a pound in Richmond, firewood eight dollars a cord, coffee unobtainable at almost any price, while even cotton, the supposed staple of southern prosperity, had doubled in price. A room which a year before would not have rented for fifty cents a week was now fetching ten dollars a week.

Not that Starbuck cared. He had a room in the stable block of the huge house on Franklin Street where Sally Truslow and her two companions now lived with their servants, cooks, and dressmaker. The house was one of the finest residences in the city and had belonged to a tobacco merchant whose fortunes had been hard-hit by the northern blockade. The man had been forced to sell, and Belvedere Delaney had then transformed the house into Richmond's most exclusive and expensive place of assignation. The furniture, pictures, and ornaments were, if not of the very highest quality, at least fine enough to pass a candlelit inspection, while the food, liquor, and entertainment were as lavish and elegant as wartime privations allowed. The ladies held receptions in the evening, and by day were at home to callers, though only those visitors who had made arrangements beforehand were allowed beyond the sculpted newel post at the foot of the grand staircase. Money changed hands, but so discreetly that the rector of St. James's had visited the house three times before discovering the nature of its business, after which he never visited again, though the same knowledge did not deter three of his fellow clergymen. Delaney's rule was that no officer below the rank of major was to be admitted and no civilian whose clothes betrayed a vulgar taste. The clientele, in consequence, was wealthy and on the whole civilized, though the necessary admission of members of the Confederate Congress depressed the house's sophistication far below Delaney's extravagant hopes.

Starbuck had a small, damp stable room that lay at the end of a dank and abandoned garden. In lieu of rent he provided Delaney with passes, while to the women his presence was a deterrent to the crime which preyed on Richmond. Burglaries were so common as to go almost unremarked while street robberies were flagrant and frequent. Which made Starbuck an even more welcome guest in the house, for he was always happy to escort one of the women to Ducquesne's, the Parisian hairdresser on Main Street, or else to one of the dress shops that somehow discovered enough material to go on manufacturing luxury goods.

He was idling outside Ducquesne's one morning, waiting for Sally and reading one of the *Examiner*'s usual demands for the Confederacy to abandon its supine stance and end the war by invading the north. It was a sunny morning, the first in almost three weeks, and the taste of spring warmth had given the city a jaunty air. The two veterans of Bull Run who guarded Ducquesne's salon were teasing Starbuck about the state of his uniform. "With a girl like that, Captain, you shouldn't be wearing rags," one of the two said.

"Who needs clothes with a girl like that?" Starbuck asked.

The men laughed. One had lost a leg, the other an arm; now they stood guard over a hairdresser's shop with a pair of shotguns. "Say anything in that paper about the Young Napoleon?" the one-armed man asked.

"Not a word, Jimmy."

"So he ain't at Fort Monroe?"

"If he is then the *Examiner* hasn't heard about it," Starbuck said.

Jimmy spat a long stream of tobacco juice into the gutter. "If he ain't there, they ain't comin' here, and we'll know they're comin' here when he gets there." He sounded gloomy. The Virginia newspapers might mock McClellan's pretensions, but there was nevertheless a feeling that the North had found its military genius and the South had no one who would prove his equal. At the war's beginning the name of Robert Lee had filled Virginia with optimism, but Lee's bright reputation had been dulled in the early fighting in western Virginia, and now he spent his time digging endless trenches around Richmond, earning himself the nickname "King of Spades." He still had his supporters, chief among them Sally Truslow, who reckoned Lee to be the greatest general since Alexander, but that opinion was based solely on the fact that the courtly Lee had once raised his hat to Sally in the street.

Starbuck gave the newspaper to Jimmy, then glanced at a clock in a shop window to gauge how much longer Sally would fuss with her hair. He reckoned she would be at least another quarter hour and so he tipped his hat back, lit a cigar, and leaned against one of the gilded pillars that framed Ducquesne's entrance. It was then that the voice hailed him.

"Nate!" The call came from across the street, and for a second Starbuck could not see who had shouted because a wagon team rolled past with a load of cut timber, and after the wagon a smart buggy with painted wheels and fringed cushions rattled by, then Starbuck saw it was Adam who was now hurrying between the traffic with an outstretched hand. "Nate! I'm sorry, I should have written. How are you?"

Starbuck had been feeling bitter about his friend, but there was such a wealth of affection and remorse in Adam's voice that the bitterness vanished immediately. "I'm well," he said lamely. "And you?"

"Busy, horribly busy. I spend half my time here and half at the army headquarters. I have to liaise with the government and it isn't easy. Johnston doesn't like the President overmuch, and Davis ain't the biggest admirer of the General, so I tend to get bitten by both sides equally."

"Whereas I just got bitten by your father," Starbuck said, some of his bitterness returning.

Adam frowned. "I'm sorry, Nate, truly." He paused, plainly embarrassed, then shook his head. "I can't help, Nate. I wish I could, but father's set against you and he won't listen to me."

"Have you asked him?" Starbuck asked.

Adam paused, then his innate honesty conquered his temptation to prevaricate. "No, I haven't. I haven't seen him for a month, and I know it won't do any good writing to him. Maybe he'll soften if I ask him directly? To his face? Can you wait till then?"

Starbuck shrugged. "I'll wait," he said, knowing how little choice he had in the matter. If Adam could not change his father's mind, no one could. "You look well," he said to Adam, changing the subject. The last time Starbuck had seen his friend was at Ball's Bluff, where Adam had been hag-ridden with the horrors of battle, but now he had regained all his good looks and enthusiasm. His uniform was clean, his saber scabbard shone in the sun, and his spurred boots gleamed.

"I am well," Adam said very emphatically. "I'm with Julia."

"The fiancee?" Starbuck asked teasingly.

"Unofficial fiancee," Adam offered the correction. "I wish it was official." He smiled shyly. "But we all agree it would be better to wait until hostilities are concluded. Wartime is no time for marriage." He gestured across the road. "You'll come and meet her? She's with her mother in Sewell's."

"Sewell's?" Starbuck thought he knew every dress shop and milliner in Richmond, but he had not heard of Sewell's.

"The Scripture shop, Nate!" Adam chided his friend, then explained that Julia's mother, Mrs. Gordon, had opened a Bible teaching class for the free blacks who had come to find work in Richmond's wartime economy. "They're looking for simple testaments," Adam explained, "maybe a child's version of Luke's Gospel? Which reminds me, I have a Bible for you."

"A Bible?"

"Your brother left it here for you. I've been meaning to send it to you for months. Now come and meet Mrs. Gordon and Julia."

Starbuck hung back. "I'm with a friend," he explained, and gestured at Ducquesne's window with its elaborate display of lotions and tortoiseshell combs and beribboned wigs, and just as he made the gesture the door opened and Sally walked out. She offered her arm to Starbuck and smiled prettily at Adam. She knew Adam from Faulconer County, but it was evident that Adam did not recognize Sally. The last time he had seen her she had been a ragged girl in a faded cotton shift who had been lugging water and herding animals on her father's smallholding, whereas now she was in a hooped silk skirt and wore her hair looped and curled beneath a beribboned bonnet.

"Ma'am," Adam acknowledged her with a bow.

"Adam, you know . . ." Starbuck began.

Sally interrupted him. "My name is Victoria Royall, sir." That was her professional name, bestowed on Sally in the brothel on Marshall Street.

"Miss Royall," Adam said.

"Major Adam Faulconer," Starbuck completed the introduction. He could see the delight that Sally was taking in Adam's ignorance and resigned himself to endure her mischief. "Major Faulconer is a very old friend of mine," he told Sally as if she did not know.

"Mr. Starbuck has mentioned your name to me, Major Faulconer," Sally said, behaving in her most demure fashion. She looked demure too, for her dress was of a very dark gray and the red, white, and blue ribbons in her bonnet were more a patriotic gesture than a display of luxuries. No one flaunted jewels or finery on Richmond's streets, not when crime was so prevalent.

"And you, Miss Royall, you come from Richmond?" Adam asked, but before Sally could offer any answer Adam saw Julia and her mother emerge from the Scripture shop on the opposite side of the road, and he insisted that Starbuck and Sally come and be introduced.

Sally had her arm in Starbuck's. She giggled as they trailed Adam over the road. "He didn't know me!" she whispered.

"How could he? Now, for God's sake, be careful. These are church people." Starbuck offered the warning and then composed his face into a stern respectability. He handed Sally up the curb, politely throwing away what was left of his cigar, then turned to face Mrs. Gordon and her daughter.

Adam made the introductions and Starbuck lightly touched the gloved fingers of the ladies' outstretched hands. Mrs. Gordon proved to be a thin, shrewish woman with a pinched nose and eyes as sharp as a hungry hawk, but her daughter was altogether more surprising. Starbuck had expected a mousy church girl, timid and pious, yet Julia Gordon had a forthright air that immediately destroyed his misconception. She was black-haired and dark-eyed and had a face that was almost defiant in its strength. She was not beautiful, Starbuck thought, but she was certainly handsome. She carried character, strength, and intelligence in her looks, and Starbuck, meeting her gaze, felt oddly jealous of Adam.

Sally was introduced, but Mrs. Gordon immediately turned back to Starbuck, wanting to know if he was related to the famous Reverend Elial Starbuck of Boston. Starbuck confessed the famous abolitionist was his father.

"We know him," Mrs. Gordon said disapprovingly.

"You do, ma'am?" Starbuck asked, holding his scruffy hat in his hand.

"Gordon"—Mrs. Gordon spoke of her husband—"is a missioner of the ASPGP."

"Indeed, ma'am," Starbuck said respectfully. Starbuck's father was one of the trustees of the American Society for the Propagation of the Gospel to the Poor, a mission that carried salvation into the darkest corners of America's cities.

Mrs. Gordon gave Starbuck's poor uniform a glance. "Your father cannot be pleased that you are wearing a Confederate uniform, Mr. Starbuck?"

"I'm sure he's not, ma'am," Starbuck said.

"Mother has judged you before she knows the facts," Julia intervened with a light touch that made Starbuck smile, "but you shall be given a chance to make a plea of mitigation before her sentence is passed."

"It's a very long story, ma'am," Starbuck said respectfully, knowing he dared not describe how he had fallen in hopeless and unrewarded love with an actress for whose sake he had abandoned the North, his family, his studies, and his respectability.

"Too long to be heard now, I daresay," Mrs. Gordon said in a voice made brusque by years of chivvying reluctant churchgoers into some semblance of enthusiasm. "But nevertheless I am delighted to see you defending states' rights, Mr. Starbuck. Our cause is noble and just. And you, Miss Royall"—she turned to Sally—"you are from Richmond?"

"From Greenbrier County, ma'am," Sally lied, naming a county in the far western part of the state. "My father didn't want me staying on there with all the fighting going on, so he sent me to a relative here." She was doing her best to smooth out the country roughness of her speech, but an echo of it remained. "An aunt," she explained, "on Franklin Street."

"Would we know her, perhaps?" Mrs. Gordon was appraising the fineness of Sally's dress and the expense of her parasol and the delicacy of the lace collar that made a distinct contrast to the darned, simple clothes that mother and daughter wore. Mrs. Gordon must also have noted that Sally was wearing powder and paint, accoutrements that would never have been allowed in Mrs. Gordon's house, but there was an innocence about Sally's youth that maybe softened Mrs. Gordon's disapproval.

"She's real sick." Sally tried to evade further inquiry about her notional aunt.

"Then I'm sure she would like a visit." Mrs. Gordon responded to the mention of a sickbed like a vigorous old warhorse hearing the trumpet. "And where does your aunt worship, Miss Royall?"

Starbuck sensed that Sally had run out of invention. "I was introduced to Miss Royall at the Grace Street Baptist Church," he said, deliberately naming one of the city's lesser-known congregations. Starbuck was aware of Julia Gordon's grave gaze, and aware too of trying to make a good impression on her.

"Then I'm sure we must know your aunt," Mrs. Gordon persisted to Sally. "I think Gordon and I are familiar with all the evangelical families in Richmond. Is that not so, Julia?"

"I'm sure that is so, Mother," Julia said.

"Your aunt's name, Miss Royall?" Mrs. Gordon insisted upon an answer.

"Miss Ginny Richardson, ma'am," Sally said, using the name of the madame of the brothel on Marshall Street.

"I'm not sure I know any Virginia Richardson." Mrs. Gordon frowned as she tried to place the name. "Of Grace Street Baptist, you say? Not that we are Baptists, Miss Royall." Mrs. Gordon made the disclaimer in much the same tone with which she might have assured Sally that she was not a cannibal or a Papist, "But of course we know of the church. Perhaps sometime you would like to hear my husband preach?" The invitation was made to both Starbuck and Sally.

"I most surely would," Sally said with an enthusiasm that stemmed from her relief at not having to invent any more details about her imaginary aunt.

"You could take tea with us?" Mrs. Gordon suggested to Sally. "Come on a Friday. We offer divine service to the wounded in Chimborazo Hospital on Fridays." The hospital was the largest army hospital in Richmond.

"I would like that," Sally said sweetly and eagerly, as though Mrs. Gordon's proposal would enliven her otherwise dull evenings.

"And you too, Mr. Starbuck," Mrs. Gordon said. "We always need healthy hands to assist in the wards. Some of the men cannot hold their Scriptures."

"Of course, ma'am. It would be a privilege."

"Adam shall arrange it. No crinolines, Miss Royall, there's not enough room between the cots for such frills. Now come, Julia." Mrs. Gordon, having got in her lick against Sally's costume, bestowed a smile on Sally and a nod to Starbuck, then swept away down the street. Adam hastily promised he would leave a letter for Starbuck at the Passport Bureau, then, after touching his hat to Sally, ran to catch up with the Gordons.

Sally laughed. "I was watching you, Nate Starbuck. You like that Bible girl, don't you?"

"Nonsense," Starbuck said, but in truth he had been wondering just what it was about the plain-dressed Julia Gordon that had attracted him. Was it, he wondered, because the missioner's daughter represented a world of piety, intelligence, and innocence that he had forever lost by his backsliding?

"She looked a bit like a school miss to me," Sally said, putting her hand through his arm.

"Which is probably what Adam needs," Starbuck said.

"Hell, no. She's much too strong for him," Sally said scathingly. "Adam was always a ditherer. Never could make up his mind to jump one way or the other. But he never recognized me, did he?"

Starbuck smiled at the pleasure in her voice. "No, he didn't."

"He was looking at me real strange, like he thought he should know me, but he never did manage to place me!" Sally was delighted. "You reckon they'll invite us for tea?"

"Probably, but we won't go."

"Whyever not?" Sally asked as they began walking toward Franklin Street.

"Because I spent my whole damn life in respectable evangelical houses and I'm trying to get away from them."

Sally laughed. "You wouldn't go for your Bible girl?" she teased Starbuck. "But I'd like to go."

"Of course you wouldn't."

"I would too. I like to see how folks live and how they do things proper. I ain't never been invited to a respectable house. Or are you ashamed of me?"

"Of course I'm not!"

Sally stopped and made Starbuck turn to face her. There were tears in her eyes. "Nate Starbuck! Are you ashamed to take me into a proper house?"

"No!"

"Because I earn a living on my back? Is that it?"

He took her hand and kissed it. "I am not ashamed of you, Sally Truslow. I just think you'll be bored. It's a dull world. A world without crinolines."

"I want to see it. I want to see how to be respectable." She spoke with a pathetic obstinacy.

Starbuck guessed this perverse ambition of Sally's would pass, and thus he decided there was small need to oppose it. "Sure," he said, "if they ask us, we'll go. I promise you."

"I don't get asked anywhere," Sally said, still close to tears as they walked on. "I want to be asked somewhere. I can take a night off."

"Then we'll go," Starbuck said soothingly, and he wondered what would happen if the missioner discovered that his wife had invited a whore to take tea, and that thought made him laugh aloud. "We'll surely go," he promised. "We surely will."

Julia teased Adam about Sally. "Was she not a little gaudy?"

"Decidedly. Indeed."

"But you seemed fascinated by her?"

Adam was too blunt a character to detect Julia's teasing. Instead he blushed. "I assure you . . ."

"Adam!" Julia interrupted him. "I think Miss Royall is a remarkable beauty! A man would have to be made of granite to remain unaware of her."

"It was not that," Adam said truthfully, "but the feeling I'd seen her somewhere before." He was standing in the parlor of the Reverend Mr. Gordon's small house on Baker Street. It was a dark room, heavy with the smell of furniture wax. The glass-fronted bookshelves held commentaries on the Bible and tales of mission life in heathen countries while the room's one window looked out across the pious headstones of Shockoe Cemetery. The house was in a very humble area of Richmond, built in close proximity to an almshouse, a charity hospital, the city poorhouse, and the cemetery. Nor could the Reverend Mr. Gordon afford a better house, for it was the rule of the

American Society for the Propagation of the Gospel to the Poor that its missioners live among their flock, and to ensure that the rule was followed, the society's trustees kept their missioners' salaries at a pitiably low level. Those trustees were all northerners, and it was their parsimony which explained Mrs. Gordon's avid adhesion to the southern cause. "I'm sure I know Miss Royall." Adam frowned. "But for the life of me I can't place her!" He was annoyed with himself.

"Any man who can misplace a beauty like Miss Royall must be hard-hearted," Julia said, then laughed at Adam's evident confusion. "Dear Adam, I know you are not hard-hearted. Tell me about your friend Starbuck. He looks interesting."

"Interesting enough to need our prayers," Adam said and explained as best he could how Starbuck had been studying for the ministry, but had been tempted away. Adam did not describe the nature of the temptation and Julia was too clever to ask. "He took refuge here in the South," Adam explained, "and I fear that it is not just his political allegiances that have changed."

"You mean he's a backslider?" Julia asked gravely.

"I fear so."

"Then we shall certainly pray for him," Julia said. "Has he back-slid so far that we should not invite him to tea?"

"I hope not," Adam said, frowning.

"Then do we invite him or not?"

Adam was not entirely sure, then he remembered how his friend had been attending prayer meetings at Leesburg, and he decided that Starbuck must have retained enough respectability to earn an invitation from the missioner's family. "I think you may," Adam said gravely.

"Then you shall write and invite them both for this Friday. I have a feeling that Miss Royall needs a friend. Now, will you stay for luncheon? I fear it is a poor soup only, but you are welcome. Father would like it if you stayed."

"I have business. But thank you."

Adam walked back into town. Miss Royall's identity still nagged at him, but the more he thought about it, the more elusive the identification became. He finally managed to dismiss the puzzle from his mind as he climbed the steps of the War Department.

His duties meant that Adam spent one or two days each week in Richmond, from where he kept General Johnston informed of political opinion and professional gossip. He also acted as Johnston's liaison with the headquarters of the Confederate Commissary Department which requisitioned supplies and directed where they should be sent.

It was that duty which gave Adam an intimate knowledge of where the army's brigades and battalions were posted, which knowledge he had been so careful to pass to Timothy Webster. Adam assumed that his two recent letters had long ago been forwarded to McClellan's headquarters and he often wondered why the northern troops were taking so long to take advantage of the peninsula's weak defenses. The North was pouring men into Fort Monroe, yet only a handful of rebels opposed them and still the North made no move to destroy that handful. At times Adam wondered whether Webster had forwarded his letters, then he would suffer an attack of sheer terror at the thought that maybe Webster had been secretly arrested, and Adam would only regain his composure after reminding himself that Webster did not know and could not possibly discover the identity of his mysterious correspondent.

Adam now settled in his office and wrote his daily dispatch to Johnston. It was a dull document listing the numbers of men released from the hospital fever wards in Richmond and describing what supplies were newly available in the capital's armories and storehouses. He finished with a summary of the latest intelligence, which reported that Major General McClellan was still in Alexandria and that the forces in Fort Monroe were showing no signs of aggression, then he bundled the latest editions of the newspapers to make one large packet that a dispatch rider would carry to Culpeper Court House. He sent the package downstairs, then opened the letter from his father that had been waiting on his desk. The letter, as Adam expected, was yet another plea that Adam should leave Johnston's staff and join the Faulconer Brigade. "I think you should take command of the Legion from Pecker," Washington Faulconer had written, "or, if you'd prefer, you could be my chief of staff. Swynyard is difficult, doubtless he will show his finer qualities in battle, but till then he is overfond of the bottle. I need your help." Adam crumpled the letter, then walked to the window and stared uphill to where the fine white pillars of the noble Capitol Building were touched by the afternoon sun. He turned as his office door opened suddenly. "You might have to add some news to your dispatch, Faulconer," a shirt-sleeved officer called to Adam.

Adam had to hide his sudden excitement. "They're moving from Fort Monroe?" he asked.

"Oh Lord, no. The damn Yankees have taken root there. Maybe they never plan to move! You'd like some coffee? It's the real thing, fetched from Liverpool on a blockade runner."

"Please."

The officer, a captain called Meredith from the Signal Department, shouted for his orderly to bring the coffee, then came into the room. "The Yankees are idiots, Faulconer. Plumb crazy! Fools!"

"What have they done?"

"They are half-wits! Rattleheads, numskulls!" Meredith sat in Adam's swivel chair and put his mud-stained boots up on the leather-topped desk. He lit a cigar, chucking the match into a spittoon. "They are know-nothings, dunderheads, blockheaded lubberlouts. In brief they are northerners. You know who Allen Pinkerton is?"

"Of course I know."

"Harken then, and I shall amuse you. Over here!" This last was to the orderly who had edged into the room with the two mugs of coffee. Meredith waited till the orderly was gone, then took up his tale. "It seems that Pinkerton wished to send some secret agents to spy on us. They were sent to discover our darkest desires and innermost secrets, and who does he send? Does he send some secretive fellow plucked from obscurity? No, he sends two fools who, not six months ago, were employed as plug-uglies evicting southern sympathizers from Washington! Lo and behold, one of the men they evicted walks into them on Broad Street. 'Hello,' says he, 'I know you two beauties. You're Scully and Lewis!' Our heroes deny it, but the fools are carrying papers with their real names on them. Price Lewis and John Scully, large as life! How feather-brained can you be? So now the North's two finest spies are clapped in irons in Henrico Jail. Isn't that splendid?"

"It's certainly foolish," Adam said. His heart was suddenly racing as fear whipsawed through him. Scully and Lewis? Was Webster using one of those names as a disguise? Was the truth being beaten out of the two men even now? There were terrible rumors about the punishments given to traitors in the secret cells of the Confederate prisons, and Adam almost whimpered as another pang of terror soured his gut. He forced himself to look calm and to take a sip of the hot coffee, all the while reminding himself that he had not signed the two long documents he had sent to Webster, and had taken pains to disguise the handwriting on both detailed reports. Even so, the shadow of the noose suddenly seemed very close. "They'll hang, I suppose?" he asked casually.

"The bastards certainly deserve to, but Lewis is English and the wretched Scully is Irish, and we need London's goodwill more than we need to watch two of the Queen's subjects twitching at the end of a pair of ropes." Meredith sounded disgusted at the leniency. "The bastards won't even get ten kinds of hell beaten out of them in case the British government objects. And they know it, which is why the two bastards aren't admitting anything."

"Maybe they have nothing to admit?" Adam suggested lightly.

"Of course they do. I'd make the clods squeal," Meredith said darkly.

"I won't trouble Johnston with the news," Adam said. "I'll wait till they have something to say."

"I just thought you'd like to know," Meredith said. He clearly felt that Adam's response had been too muted, but Major Faulconer had the reputation of being an odd fish around the headquarters. "Can't tempt you to Screamersville tonight?" Meredith asked. Screamersville was the black section of Richmond and held the city's wildest brothels, gambling houses, and liquor dens. Liquor was officially banned in Richmond in an attempt to cut the crime rate, but no provost patrol would dare go into Screamersville to enforce the law, any more than they would try to confiscate the champagne from the city's expensive *maisons d'assignation*.

"I have other engagements tonight," Adam said stiffly.

"Another prayer meeting?" Meredith asked mockingly.

"Indeed."

"Say one for me, Faulconer. I plan to need a prayer or two tonight." Meredith swung his boots off the desk. "Take your time with the coffee. Just put the mug back in our room when you're done."

"Surely. Thank you."

Adam drank the coffee and watched the shadows lengthen across Capitol Square. Clerks were scurrying with bundled documents from the government offices to the Capitol Building while a patrol of provosts, their bayonets fixed, paced slowly down Ninth Street past the Bell Tower, which rang the alarm for fires and other city emergencies. Two small children walked hand in hand with one of their family's slaves, going uphill toward the statue of George Washington. Two years ago, Adam thought, this city had seemed as homely and friendly as Seven Springs, his family's estate in Faulconer County, but now it reeked of danger and intrigue. Adam shuddered, thinking of the trapdoor falling open beneath his feet and the void swallowing him and the roughness of a rope around his neck and the snatch as the noose jerked taut, then he told himself he had no need to worry, for James Starbuck had given his word never to reveal Adam's name, and James was a Christian and a gentleman, so it was quite impossible for Adam to be betrayed. The arrest of Scully and Lewis, whoever they were, need not concern Adam. Thus reassured, he sat at his desk, drew a piece of notepaper toward him, and wrote an invitation for Captain Nathaniel Starbuck and Miss Victoria Royall to take tea at the Reverend Mr. Gordon's home on Friday.

JOHN SCULLY AND PRICE LEWIS ADMITTED NOTHING, NOT even when documents that might have incriminated a saint were found sewn into their clothing. Lewis, the Englishman, had a map of Richmond on which had been sketched an outline of the new defenses dug by General Lee with hatched marks suggesting where the existence of redoubts and star forts was merely surmised. A memorandum attached to the sketch map demanded confirmation of the assumptions and an assessment of the artillery contained in the new works. John Scully, the small Irishman, carried an unstamped letter addressed to the Honorary Secretary of the Confederate Army Bible Supply Society which had been signed by a Major James Starbuck of the U.S. Army who described himself as "brother in Christ" to the letter's unnamed addressee. The letter said that the enclosed instructions could be trusted, and those instructions begged for a complete and up-to-date enumeration of the Confederate troops under General Magruder's command with especial care taken to report the total number of troops available in the towns, garrisons, and forts between Richmond and Yorktown.

John Scully, confronted with the letter that had been discovered sewn into the lapel of his jacket, swore he had bought his clothes from a sutler outside the city and had no idea what the letter meant. He smiled at the Major conducting the interrogation. "I'm sorry, Major, so I am. I'd help you if I could."

"Damn your help." Major Alexander was a tall fleshy man with bushy sidewhiskers and an expression of perpetual indignation. "If you don't talk," he threatened Scully, "we'll hang you."

"That you won't, Major," Scully said, "seeing as how I'm a citizen of Great Britain."

"Damn Britain."

"And ordinarily I'd agree with you, so I would, but as of this moment, Major, this is one Irishman who would go on his knees and thank the Almighty God for making him British." Scully smiled like a cherub.

"Being British won't protect you. You'll hang!" Alexander threatened, but still Scully would not talk.

Next day came news that the Yankees had at last broken out of their lines at Fort Monroe. General McClellan had arrived on the peninsula, and all Virginia now knew from where the thunderbolt would fall. A mighty army was advancing against the slender defenses strung between Yorktown and Mulberry Island. "Another month," Price Lewis assured John Scully, "and we'll be rescued. We'll be heroes."

"If they don't hang us first," John Scully said, making the sign of the cross.

"They won't. They daren't."

"I'm not so sure." Scully's confidence was weakening.

"They won't!" Price Lewis insisted. But the very next day a military tribunal was summoned to the jail and presented with the map of Richmond's defenses and the letter addressed to the Honorary Secretary of the Confederate Army Bible Supply Society. The evidence overcame whatever scruples the tribunal might have felt for the prisoners' nationality, and less than an hour from the moment when the court had convened, the president sentenced the two prisoners to death. Scully shuddered in fear, but the tall Englishman simply sneered at his judges. "You won't dare do it."

"Take them away!" The Lieutenant Colonel who had presided over the tribunal slammed his hand on the table. "Hanged by the neck, you dogs!"

Scully suddenly felt the wings of death's angel very close above him. "I want a priest!" he pleaded with Major Alexander. "For the love of God, Major, bring me a priest!"

"Shut your face, Scully!" Price Lewis called.

The Englishman was hurried down the corridor to his cell while John Scully was put into a different room where Major Alexander brought him a bottle of rye whiskey. "It's illegal, John. But I thought it might help your last hours on earth."

"You won't dare do it! You can't hang us!"

"Listen!" Alexander said, and in the silence Scully could hear the sound of hammering. "They're building the scaffold ready for the morning, John," Alexander said softly.

"No, Major, please."

"Lynch, his name is," Alexander said. "That should please you, John."

"Please me?" Scully asked, bemused.

"Doesn't it please you to be hanged by another Irishman? Mind you, old Lynch is no craftsman. He bungled his last two. One was a black fellow who took twenty minutes to die and it wasn't a pretty sight. Dear me, no. Twitching he was, and pissing himself, and the breath scraping in his throat like sandpaper. Terrible." Alexander shook his head.

John Scully crossed himself, then closed his eyes and prayed for strength. He would be strong; he would not betray Pinkerton's trust. "All I want is a priest," he insisted.

"If you talk, John, you won't hang in the morning," Alexander tempted him.

"I've nothing to say, Major, except to a priest," Scully insisted bravely.

That night a priest came to John Scully's new cell. The priest was a very old man, though he still had a fine head of long white hair that flowed well below the collar of his soutane. His face was a dark brown, as if his life had been spent in the tropical mission fields. It was an ascetic, kindly face, touched with a hint of abstract intellectualism that suggested his thoughts had already gone to a higher and better world. He settled on Scully's bed and took an old, threadbare scapular from his case. He kissed the embroidered strip of cloth and placed it around his thin neck, then made the sign of the cross toward the prisoner. "My name is Father Mulroney," he introduced himself, "and I'm from Galway. I'm told you want to make a confession, son?"

Scully knelt. "Forgive me, Father, for I have sinned." He crossed himself.

"Go on, my son." Father Mulroney's voice was deep and fine, the voice of a man who has preached sad things to great halls. "Go on," Mulroney said again, his marvelous voice low and comforting.

"It must be ten years since my last confession," Scully began, and then the dam broke and he poured out the list of all his transgressions. Father Mulroney closed his eyes as he listened, the only sign of wakefulness being the slight beat of one of his long, bony fingers on a delicate ivory crucifix that hung on a simple iron chain about his neck. He nodded once or twice as Scully listed his pathetic sins: the whores cheated, the oaths made, the trifles stolen, the lies told, the religious duties ignored. "My mother always said I'd come to a bad end, so she did." The small Irishman was almost weeping as he finished.

"Peace, my son, peace." The priest's voice was dry and whispery, yet very comforting. "You repent of these sins, my son?"

"I do, Father, oh God, I do." Scully had begun to weep. He had fallen forward so that his head rested on his hands, which, in turn, were supported by the old man's knees. Father Mulroney's face showed no reaction to Scully's terror and remorse; instead he lightly stroked the Irishman's head with long fingers and stared around the white-painted cell with its lantern and its grim barred window. The tears ran down Scully's face to make a damp patch on Mulroney's faded and threadbare soutane. "I don't deserve to die, Father," Scully said.

"Then why are they hanging you, my son?" Mulroney asked, and went on stroking Scully's short black hair. "What have you done that's so bad?" the priest asked in his sad, kind voice, and Scully told how Allen Pinkerton had asked Lewis and Scully to travel south to look for the missing agent, the best agent the North possessed, and how Pinkerton had assured them that as British subjects they would be safe from any rebel recriminations, yet how, despite that assurance, they had been condemned to hang by the military tribunal.

"Of course you don't deserve to die, my son," Mulroney said with indignation in his voice, "for all you ever did was try to help your fellowman. Isn't that the truth of it?" His fingers still soothed Scully's fears. "And did you ever find your man?" Father Mulroney's own Irish accent seemed to have grown stronger during the confession.

"We did, Father, and the reason he disappeared is that he's ill. Sick as a dog, he is. He's got the rheumatism fever. He was supposed to be in the Ballard House Hotel, only he moved, and it took us a day or so to find him, but the poor man's in the Monumental Hotel now, and one of Pinkerton's ladies is looking after him there."

Mulroney calmed Scully, who was gabbling the words desperately. "The poor man," Mulroney said. "You say he's ill?"

"He can hardly move. He's terrible sick, so he is."

"Give me his name, my son, so I can pray for him," Mulroney said softly, then the priest sensed a hesitation in Scully, and so he tapped his fingers in very mild reproof. "This is a confession you're making, my son, and the secrets of the confessional go to the grave with a priest. What you say here, my son, is a secret between you, me, and God Almighty. So tell me the name so I can pray for the poor man."

"Webster, Father, Timothy Webster. And he was always the real spy, not us. Price and I are just doing a favor for Pinkerton by coming to look for him! Webster's the real spy. He's the best one there is!"

"I shall pray for him," Mulroney said. "And the woman who's looking after the poor man, what would her name be, my son?"

"Hattie, Father, Hattie Lawton."

"I shall pray for her too," Mulroney said. "But the Major in the prison here, what was his name? Alexander? He said you were carrying a letter?"

"We were only to deliver the letter if we never found Webster, Father," Scully said, then described the bulletin board in the vestibule of St. Paul's where the letter would have been tucked beneath the criss-crossed tape. "What's the harm in delivering a letter to a church, Father?"

"None at all, my son, none at all," Mulroney said, then assured the frightened man that it had been a good confession. He gently lifted Scully's head and told the Irishman he must make a good contrition and say four Hail Marys, then he absolved him in solemn Latin, and afterward he promised that he would seek mercy for Scully from the Confederate authorities. "But you know, my son, how little they listen to us Catholics. Or to us Irishmen, indeed. These southerners are as bad as the English, so they are. They've small love for us."

"But you'll try?" Scully looked desperately up into the kindly eyes of the priest.

"I shall try, my son," Mulroney said, then gave the blessing and made the sign of the cross above Scully's head.

Father Mulroney walked slowly back to the jail's main office where Major Alexander waited with a thin, bespectacled lieutenant. Neither of the officers spoke as Father Mulroney took off the scapular, then lifted the soutane over his head to reveal an old but finely cut black suit. There was a bowl of water on the table, and the old man began washing his hands as though he wanted to rid his fingers of the lingering touch of Scully's hair. "The person you want," the man who had called himself Mulroney now said in an accent that had nothing of Ireland in it at all, but only Virginia, "is a Timothy Webster. You'll find him in the Monumental Hotel. He's sick, so he shouldn't give you any trouble. He has a female attendant called Hattie Lawton. She's another of the scum, so take her as well." The old man took a silver case from his pocket and extracted a slender, fragrant cigar. The bespectacled Lieutenant leaped forward and snatched up a candle from the table and offered it to the cigar. The old man sucked on the flame and then offered the Lieutenant a jaundiced look. "You're Gillespie?"

"Yes, sir, indeed, sir."

"What's in the bag, Gillespie?" The old man nodded at a leather bag that hung from the Lieutenant's shoulder. Gillespie opened the bag to reveal a brass funnel and a six-sided bottle made of dark blue glass.

"My father's oil," Gillespie said proudly.

The old man's mouth twisted. "You were planning on administering the oil to the prisoners, perhaps?"

"It works wonders with lunatics," Gillespie said defensively.

"I don't care about your damn lunatics," the old man snapped. "You can try it on another prisoner, one who doesn't matter to anyone. But Lewis and Scully have to be spared." His thin, ascetic face twitched with a spasm of disgust, then he smoothed his long silver hair back over his collar and looked at Alexander. "I fear political considerations dictate that the scum will have to live, just in case their deaths dissuade the British from helping us. But even the British won't expect us to keep them in any comfort. Put them in the Negro section, let them break stone for a few months." He drew on the cigar, frowning, then gave orders that the letter addressed to the Honorary Secretary of the Confederate Army Bible Supply Society was to be put in the vestibule of St. Paul's where it was to be watched night and day in case the spy came to collect it. "But arrest Webster first."

"Of course, sir," Alexander said.

The old man took a fine gold ring from his pocket. It was engraved with an ancient coat of arms, testimony to the man's long pedigree. "Is it still raining?" he asked as he slipped the ring on a finger.

"It is, sir, yes," Alexander said.

"That will obstruct the Yankees' approach, will it not?" the old man said grimly. The northerners' advance on Yorktown was being slowed by mud and rain, but even so the old man knew what terrible danger the Confederacy faced. So little time, but at least this night's work had uncovered one more spy and might even yield the traitor who skulked behind the mask of being the Honorary Secretary of the Confederate Army Bible Supply Society. The old man looked forward to finding that man and watching him swing on a rope's looped end. He took a derringer pistol from his jacket pocket and checked that it was loaded, then picked up his cloak and hat. "I shall come in the morning to see this Webster for myself. Good day, gentlemen." He crammed the hat on his long hair, then went out to where an antique carriage with varnished panels and gilded axle bosses waited in the slashing rain. A slave opened the door and folded down the carriage steps.

Alexander let out a breath when the old man was gone, almost as though he sensed that a sinister presence had passed from the prison. Then he drew his revolver and checked that its percussion caps were firmly in place. "To work," he told Gillespie. "To work! Let's go and find Mr. Webster! To work!"

The rain turned the roads leading inland from Fort Monroe into strips of slick yellow dirt. The pale strips looked firm enough, but as soon as a horse put a hoof to the surface the sandy crust broke to expose a quagmire of glutinous red mud beneath.

A troop of northern cavalry abandoned the road to ride southward under a low, gray sky and a spitting rain. It was April, and the trees were in bud and the meadows a lovely green, yet the wind was cold and the troopers rode with their collars turned up and their hats pulled low. Their commander, a captain, peered through the rain in case the enemy cavalry should suddenly appear like gray-clad devils in the murk, but to his relief the land seemed empty.

A half hour after they had left the road the patrol emerged from the shelter of some skinny pine trees to see the red scars of freshly turned earth marking the line of rebel fortifications that stretched from Yorktown to Mulberry Island. The earthworks were not continuous, but consisted rather of earthen forts with heavy guns that enfiladed the intervening stretches of flooded water meadow. The Captain led his patrol southward, stopping every few hundred yards to examine the enemy works with a small telescope. The Colonel had been particular in his demand that all his cavalry patrols should attempt to determine whether the enemy cannons were real or made of wood, and the Captain sourly wondered how in the name of God he was supposed to attempt that piece of research. "You want to ride up to the rampart and give one of those guns a rap with your knuckles, Sergeant?" the Captain asked the man riding beside him.

The Sergeant chuckled, then disappeared beneath his greatcoat to light a cigar.

"The guns look real to me, Captain!" one of the men called.

"So did the guns at Manassas," the Captain said, then jumped with astonishment as one of the distant cannons suddenly fired. The smoke from the gun jetted thirty yards out from the embrasure to shroud the tongue of fire in the smoke's heart. The missile, evidently a solid ball or a shaped bolt of iron, crashed through the newly green trees just behind the patrol.

"Bastards," the Sergeant said, and rammed his spurs back. None of the cavalry had been hurt, but their sudden acceleration provoked a jeer from the distant rebel gunners.

A half mile farther on the Captain came upon a small knoll that protruded a few feet above the flat, water-laced landscape. He led his men to the knoll's summit where they dismounted and where the Captain discovered a tree that had a convenient crutch in which he could rest his telescope's barrel. From here he had a view between two of the rebel redoubts, a view across a stretch of marshland where hyacinths grew bright and deep into the rebel rear where he could just make out a road running among some shadowed pine trees. There were troops marching on the road, or at least struggling along the muddy road's verges. He counted them, company by company, and realized he was seeing a whole rebel battalion marching south.

"Listen, sir." The Sergeant had come to stand beside the Captain.

"Can you hear it, sir?" The Captain turned down his collar and, by lis-tening hard, caught the sound of distant trumpets carried on the cold wind. The sound was thin and far away. One trumpet sounded, another answered the call, and now that the Captain had turned his ears to those elfin noises it seemed as though the whole of this damp land was filled with the calls. "There are enough of the bastards," the Sergeant said with a shudder, as though the ghostly noise presaged a mysterious enemy.

"We've only seen the one battalion," the Captain said, but then another column of gray-clad troops appeared on the far road. He watched through the telescope and counted another eight compa-nies. "Two battalions," he said, and no sooner had he spoken than a third regiment came into view.

The cavalry stayed on the knoll for two hours, and in that time the Captain saw eight rebel regiments marching south. One hopeful rumor had claimed that the rebels only had twenty battalions to guard all the Yorktown defenses, yet here, five miles south of the famous town, the Captain had watched regiment after regiment march by. The enemy was plainly in far greater strength than the optimists had hoped.

The cavalry remounted their horses in midafternoon. The Cap-tain was the last to leave the knoll. He turned at the last moment and saw yet another rebel regiment appearing in the far trees. He did not stay to count heads, but instead carried his news eastward through the waterlogged meadows of rich clover and past sullen farmhouses where unsmiling people watched their enemy pass.

The northern cavalry patrols all returned to tell identical stories of massive troop movements behind the rebel lines, of hidden units signaling with trumpets, and of real guns packed in newly dug earth-works. McClellan listened to the reports and shuddered. "You were right," he told Pinkerton. "We're facing at least seventy thousand men, maybe a hundred thousand!" The General had taken over the commandant's comfortable quarters in Fort Monroe from where he had a view of the massed shipping that had brought his army south from Alexandria. That army was ready for action now and McClellan had hoped to use it in a lightning-fast lunge toward Richmond, a maneuver that would have cracked through the eggshell defenses anchored on Yorktown, but today's cavalry reconnaissances meant there could be no sudden lunge after all. The capture of Yorktown and Richmond would have to be done the old-fashioned way, the hard way, with siege guns and patience and counter-trenching. His one hundred and twenty-one thousand men would have to wait while the besieging redoubts were constructed and the massive siege guns were dragged from Fort Monroe along the nightmare roads. The delay was a pity, but Pinkerton had cautioned him that the rebel defenses were manned in far greater strength than anyone supposed, and now the General thanked the head of his Secret Service Bureau for that timely and accurate intelligence.

Meanwhile, behind the rebel earthworks, the single battalion of Georgia troops that had marched nine times along the same stretch of muddy road, and had doubled back nine times through the trees before trudging the road again, shivered in the dusk and grumbled that their time was being wasted. They had joined the army to beat the living hell out of Yankees, not to march around and around in damn circles listening to scattered buglers serenade the empty trees. Now, in the lonely woods, they lit fires and wondered if the rain would ever stop. They felt very lonely, and no wonder, for there were no other infantry battalions within three miles. Indeed, there were only thirteen thousand men stretched across the whole damp peninsula, and those thirteen thousand troops were supposed to stop the largest army ever assembled in America. It was no wonder that the Georgia men shivered and grumbled about having played the damn fool all day in the rain.

In the twilight the trees were filled with the screeching call of birds. The sound was subtly different from the call of the same bird in Georgia, but the men who had marched around in circles all day were country boys and knew well enough what bird made such a racket in the evening trees.

General Magruder knew too, and he at least smiled at the sound because he had spent these days trying to fool the Yankees into thinking that they faced a host when in truth the defensive line was pitiably manned. Magruder had marched and countermarched his men all day, putting on a show of force, and now in the evening rain he prayed that the birdsong was for McClellan and not for him.

Because in the dusk the mockingbirds sang.

It seemed it would never cease raining. Water poured down the gutters of Richmond to where the river frothed white with the effluents pumped from the ironworks and the tobacco factories and the tanyards and the slaughteryards. The few people in the streets hurried beneath somber black umbrellas. Even at midday coal-gas lamps were lit in the chamber where the Confederate Congress debated a measure that would encourage the development of a synthetic saltpeter for the manufacture of gunpowder. The voices in the chamber had to fight against the sound of rain outside. A handful of the Congressmen listened, some slept, while others sipped whiskey that had been sold by pharmacies as medicine and was thus free of the liquor ban imposed on the city. One or two of the Congressmen worried that the Yankee army closing on Yorktown would make all these discussions futile, but no one dared articulate such a thought. There had been too much defeatism lately, and too many good reasons for it; too many coastal forts captured by the U.S. Navy and too many hints that the Confederacy was encompassed by an implacable enemy.

Sally Truslow, arm in arm with Nate Starbuck, did not care about the Yankees seventy miles away, or about the rain. Sally was elated at the thought of taking tea in a respectable house, to which end she had dressed in a dark, high-necked dress with long sleeves and a skirt barely plumped by a mere two petticoats. She had forsworn all cosmetics other than a brushing of powder and a hint of black about her eyes.

Sally and Starbuck ran down Franklin Street, half protected by the umbrella Starbuck held, then sheltered in the doorway of a bakery on the corner of Second Street until a horsecar came into sight. They crowded aboard and paid the fare to Shockoe Cemetery. "Maybe they won't go to the hospital in this weather?" Sally said. She pushed close against Starbuck in the damp, crowded bus and peered through a filthy glass window at the rain.

"Bad weather doesn't stop good works," Starbuck said dourly. He was not looking forward to the afternoon or evening, for not even Sally's ebullient company could reconcile him to this encounter with a world he thought he had left far behind in Boston. Yet he could not deny Sally her happiness, and so he had decided to endure whatever discomfort the day presented even though he still did not understand why Sally had been so pleased when Adam's invitation arrived.

Sally herself hardly knew, though she did understand that the Gordons were a family and she dimly perceived that in all her life she had never been a member of a family, at least not of an ordinary, unexciting, simple, plain family. She had been the daughter of a horse thief and his woman, two fugitives who farmed a hard patch in the high mountains, and now she was a whore and shrewd enough to know she could climb as high as any ambition desired if she just understood the true value of the services she offered, but she also knew she could never have the satisfactions of belonging to plain, ordinary, straightforward folk. Sally, unlike Starbuck, had a sentimental idea that the commonplace was the reward of success. She had grown up an outcast and yearned for respectability, while Starbuck had grown up respectable and reveled in being a rebel.

Julia and Mrs. Gordon greeted them in the narrow hallway where there was scarcely room to take off the wet cloak and coat and pile them on a mirrored hallstand around which Sally and Starbuck edged to enter the parlor. The spring day was cold enough to justify a fire in the small cast-iron hearth, though the pile of glowing coals was so small that the heat barely reached beyond the plain iron fender. The floor was covered in strips of painted cotton-canvas, poor man's carpet, but everything was scrupulously clean, smelling of lye and polish, and suggesting to Starbuck just why Adam would be attracted to a daughter of this house with its suggestion of honest poverty and simple values. Adam himself stood by a piano, a second young man was standing in the window, while the Reverend John Gordon, the missioner, warmed himself before his tiny heap of smoking coals.

"Miss Royall!" he greeted Sally, though with a mouth obstructed by cake. "Excuse me, my dear." He wiped one hand on the skirt of his frock coat, placed the cup and saucer on the mantel, and at last held out a welcoming hand. "It is a pleasure to meet you."

"Sir," Sally said, and dropped a flustered curtsey instead of shaking the offered hand. In her own house she knew how to greet generals and senators, she could tease the city's most eminent doctors and scorn the witticisms of its lawyers, but here, faced with respectability, she lost all her assurance.

"It is a pleasure to meet you," the Reverend John Gordon repeated with what seemed to be a genuine affability. "I believe you know Major Faulconer? So allow me to introduce Mr. Caleb Samworth. This is Miss Victoria Royall." Sally smiled, curtseyed again, then moved aside to make room for Starbuck, Mrs. Gordon, and Julia. More introductions were made, and then a pale and timid maid brought in another tray of teacups and Mrs. Gordon busied herself with the pot and strainer. Everyone agreed the weather was terrible, quite the worst springtime in Richmond's memory, and no one mentioned the northern army that was somewhere out on the city's eastern flank.

The Reverend John Gordon was a small, thin man with a very pink face and a scalp rimmed with wispy white hair. He had a weak chin that another man might have disguised with a full beard, but the missioner was clean-shaven, suggesting that his wife did not like beards. Indeed, the missioner looked so small and defenseless, while Mrs. Gordon appeared so very formidable, that Starbuck concluded that it was she and not he who ruled this deliberately cramped roost. Mrs. Gordon handed out the tea and inquired after the health of Miss Royall's aunt. Sally replied that her aunt was neither better nor worse, and there, much to Sally's relief, the matter of her aunt's sickness rested.

Mrs. Gordon explained Caleb Samworth's presence by revealing that he was the possessor of a wagon in which they would all travel to Chimborazo Hospital. Samworth smiled when his name was mentioned, then stared at Sally like a man dying of thirst might gaze on a distant but unreachable stream of cool water. The wagon, he explained haltingly, belonged to his father. "You may have heard of us? Samworth and Son, Embalmers and Undertakers?"

"Alas, no," Starbuck said.

Adam and the wilting Samworth invited Sally to sit with them in the window. Adam moved a great heap of empty cloth bags that the ladies of the house, like almost all the ladies in Richmond, were stitching out of whatever scraps of old material they could spare. The bags were being taken to Granny Lee's new earthworks to be filled with sand, though how much good such ramparts would prove against the northern horde that pressed forward from Fort Monroe no one could tell. "You sit here, Mr. Starbuck," the Reverend John Gordon said, drawing up a chair beside his own, then he launched into a long lamentation for the problems secession imposed on the American Society for the Propagation of the Gospel to the Poor. "Our headquarters, you understand, are in Boston."

"Mr. Starbuck knows well enough where the Society's headquarters are, Gordon," Mrs. Gordon interjected from her throne behind the tea tray. "He is a Bostonian. Indeed his father is a trustee of the Society, is that not so, Mr. Starbuck?"

"Indeed he is," Starbuck said.

"One of the trustees," Mrs. Gordon added pointedly, "who has depressed the missioners' emoluments these many years."

"Mother," the Reverend John Gordon chided his wife timidly.

"No, Gordon!" Mrs. Gordon would not be deflected. "While God gives me tongue I shall speak, indeed I shall. One of the blessings of the South's secession has been to free us of our northern trustees! God clearly intended it to be so."

"We have heard nothing from headquarters in nine months!" the Reverend John Gordon explained in a worried voice to Starbuck. "Fortunately the mission's expenses are being met locally, praise God, but it is worrying, Mr. Starbuck, most worrying. There are accounts missing, reports half finished, and visitations undone. It is irregular!"

"It is a providence, Gordon," Mrs. Gordon corrected her husband.

"Let us pray so, Mother, let us pray so." The Reverend John Gordon sighed and took a bite from his slice of dry and mealy fruitcake. "Your father, then, is the Reverend Elial Starbuck?"

"Yes, sir, he is." Starbuck sipped his tea and managed to stop himself from grimacing at the bitter taste.

"A great man of God," Gordon said rather glumly. "Strong in the Lord."

"But blind to the needs of the Society's missioners!" Mrs. Gordon observed tartly.

"I find it strange, forgive me, that you should be wearing southern uniform, Mr. Starbuck?" the Reverend John Gordon inquired diffidently.

"I'm sure Mr. Starbuck is doing the Lord's work, Gordon." Mrs. Gordon, who had found Starbuck's loyalty equally inexplicable when she had met him outside the Scripture shop, now chose to defend her guest against her husband's quieter curiosity.

"Indeed, indeed," the missioner said hurriedly. "Even so, it is tragic."

"What is tragic, sir?" Starbuck asked.

The Reverend John Gordon waved his hands in a helpless gesture. "Families divided, a nation divided. So sad."

"It would not be sad if the North would simply withdraw its troops and allow us to live in peace," Mrs. Gordon said. "Don't you agree, Miss Royall?"

Sally smiled and nodded. "Yes, ma'am."

"They won't withdraw," Adam said gloomily.

"Then we'll just have to beat the hell out of them," Sally said unthinkingly.

"I was wondering"—Julia played a tinny note on the pianoforte to cut across the sudden surprise that had filled the room after Sally's words—"that perhaps we should not use such mournful hymns in the ward tonight, Father?"

"To be sure, my dear, to be sure," her father said. He explained to Sally and Starbuck that he began his ward services with a selection of hymns and a prayer, and afterward one of the party would give a reading from God's word. "Perhaps Miss Royall would like to read the Scriptures?" he suggested.

"Oh no, sir, no." Sally, aware that she had blundered once already, blushed as she declined the offer. She was learning to read and, in the last year, had progressed so far that she could actually open a book for pleasure, but she had no faith in her ability to read aloud.

"You are saved, Miss Royall?" Mrs. Gordon asked suspiciously as she peered hard at her guest.

"Saved, ma'am?"

"You have been washed in the blood of the Lamb? You have accepted Jesus into your heart? Your aunt, surely, has introduced you to your Savior?"

"Yes, ma'am," Sally said timidly, not having a clue as to what Mrs. Gordon meant.

"I should be happy to read for you," Starbuck interjected to the Reverend John Gordon.

"Mr. Samworth reads Scripture very well," Mrs. Gordon said.

"Perhaps, Caleb, you would read from God's word?" the Reverend John Gordon asked, "and after that"—he turned to his guests again to explain the form of service—"we have a time for prayer and testimony. I encourage the men to witness to the power of God's saving grace in their lives, and then we sing another hymn and I make a few remarks before we close our worship with a last hymn and a blessing. We then give the patients some time for private conversation or prayer. Sometimes they need us to write letters for them. Your assistance"—he smiled first at Sally, then at Starbuck—"will be very greatly appreciated, I'm sure."

"And we shall need help distributing the hymnals," Mrs. Gordon said.

"It'll be a pleasure," Sally said warmly, and to Starbuck's amazement she really did seem to be enjoying herself, for when the conversation became general once more her laughter sounded clear and often across the small room. Mrs. Gordon frowned at the sound, but Julia was plainly enjoying Sally's company.

At five o'clock the sallow maid collected the tea plates, and afterward the Reverend John Gordon said a word of prayer in which he begged Almighty God to shower blessing upon their worship this evening, and then Caleb Samworth fetched the wagon which was kept in a yard just around the corner in Charity Street. The wagon was painted black and had a black canvas cover supported by hoops. Two benches ran on either side of the wagon's bed, while a pair of shining steel rails were fixed down its center. "Is that where they put the casket?" Sally asked as Caleb helped her up the steps built into the folded-down backboard.

"Indeed, Miss Royall," he said.

Sally and Julia shared a bench with Adam, Starbuck sat with the Reverend and Mrs. Gordon, while Caleb Samworth perched on the driver's box swathed in an oilskin cape. It took the hearse twenty minutes to reach the hill where the newly constructed hospital sheds spread across the grass of Chimborazo Park. It was dusk and a dim yellow lamplight was showing through scores of tiny windows. A haze of coalsmoke lingered in the rain over the shed's tarred roofs. The mission party alighted outside the ward chosen for this night's service, then Caleb and Adam took the wagon to fetch the hospital's harmonium while Julia and Sally distributed copies of the mission's hymnal.

Starbuck went with Adam. "I wanted a word in private," he confided to his friend as the undertaker's cart jolted over the wet ground. "Have you spoken to your father?"

"I haven't had a chance," Adam said. He did not look at Starbuck but stared into the wet night.

"All I want is to be back with my company!" Starbuck appealed.

"I know."

"Adam!"

"I'll try! But it's difficult. I have to choose the right moment. Father's touchy, you know that." Adam shook his head. "Why are you so keen to fight? Why don't you just sit the war out here?"

"Because I'm a soldier."

"A fool, you mean," Adam said with a touch of exasperation,

then the wagon lurched to a halt, and it was time to carry the harmonium back to the ward.

There were sixty sick men in the wooden shed. Twenty of their cots were arranged against each long wall while another twenty cots were set in a double row in the hut's center. A potbellied stove occupied a central position, its hot plate crowded with coffeepots. The nurse's table was pushed aside to make room for the harmonium. Julia pumped the carpeted pedals, then played a few wheezy chords as though clearing the cobwebs out of the instrument's reeds.

The Reverend and Mrs. Gordon went around the cots shaking hands and saying words of comfort. Sally did the same, and Starbuck noted how her presence cheered the wounded men. Her laughter filled the shed with brightness and Starbuck thought that he had never seen Sally so happy. Water buckets were placed about the ward so that the patients' wound dressings could be kept damp, and Sally found a sponge and gently moistened the dark-stained bandages. The ward stank of decaying flesh and human waste. It was cold and damp despite the stove, and dark despite the half-dozen lanterns that hung from the rough-sawn rafters. Some of the men were unconscious, most were fevered, only a few had battle wounds. "Once the fighting starts proper again," a sergeant who had lost an arm told Starbuck, "that's when you'll see the wounded arrive." The Sergeant had come for the service with a score of other patients from neighboring sheds, bringing chairs and extra lanterns. The Sergeant had been injured in a train accident. "Fell onto the rails," he told Starbuck, "when I was drunk. My own fault." He looked appreciatively at Sally. "There's a rare-looking girl, Captain, a girl to make a man's life worth living."

The sound of the hymn singing brought yet more patients to the ward, together with some unwounded officers who had been visiting friends and who now crowded at the back of the shed. Some of the wounded were Yankees, but all the voices swelled in melody, filling the shed with a sentimental comradeship that made Starbuck suddenly yearn for the company of his soldiers. One man alone seemed unaffected by the singing; a bearded, pale, gaunt creature who had been sleeping, but who suddenly woke and began to scream in terror.

The voices faltered, then Sally crossed to the man's side and pulled his head into her arms and stroked his cheek, and Starbuck saw the man's fluttering hands calm down on the threadbare gray blanket that was his cot's covering.

The gaunt man stayed silent as the voices sang on. Starbuck watched Julia at the harmonium, then suddenly felt the pull of his old faith tug at him. Maybe it was the yellow light, or the faces of the wounded who looked so pathetically pleased to have God's word brought to them, or maybe it was Julia's absorbed beauty, but Starbuck was suddenly assailed with a sinner's guilt as he listened to the Reverend John Gordon pray that God's blessings would shower upon these wounded souls. The missioner proved to have a gentle and effective manner that seemed far more suitable than the strong rant that Starbuck's father would have employed. The Scripture was from Ecclesiastes chapter twelve and Samworth read it in a high, nervous voice. Starbuck followed the passage in his brother's Bible, which Adam had sent with the invitation to take tea.

The words of Scripture struck sharp at Starbuck's soul. "Remember now thy Creator in the days of thy youth," the passage began, and James had written beside it in his tiny handwriting, "Easier to be a Christian in later life? Years bring wisdom? Pray for grace now," and Starbuck knew he had fallen from grace, that he was a sinner, that the doors of hell gaped as wide as the flaming maw of the blast furnaces down by Richmond's river, and he felt the trembling terror of a sinner come face to face with God. " 'Because man goeth to his long home,' " Samworth read, " 'and the mourners go about the street. Or ever the silver cord be loosed, or the golden bowl be broken, or the pitcher be broken at the fountain, or the wheel broken at the cistern,' " and the words filled Starbuck with the sudden premonition that he would die an untimely death: flensed by a Yankee shot, disemboweled by a vengeful, righteous shell, a sinner gone to his long and fiery home.

He did not hear much of the sermon, or many of the testimonies in which the wounded men gave praise to God for His blessings on their lives. Instead Starbuck was lost in the dark pit of remorse. After the service, he decided, he would seek a word with the Reverend John Gordon. He would lay his sins before God and, with the missioner's help, seek to return his soul to its proper place. But how could he ever take his proper place? He had quarreled with Ethan Ridley because of Sally, and he had killed Ethan Ridley because of the quarrel, and that one act alone would surely damn his soul forever. He told himself the killing had been self-defense, but his conscience knew it was murder. Starbuck blinked back tears. All was vanity, but what use was vanity in the face of eternal damnation?

It was well past eight o'clock when the Reverend John Gordon pronounced his blessing on the patients, and then the missioner moved from bed to bed, praying and offering encouragement. The wounded seemed so young; even to Starbuck they seemed like mere boys.

One of the hospital's senior surgeons arrived, still in his bloody apron, to thank the Reverend John Gordon. With the surgeon was a clergyman, the Reverend Doctor Peterkin, who was the hospital's honorary chaplain as well as one of the city's more fashionable ministers. He recognized Adam and went to talk with him, while Julia, her music put away, crossed to Starbuck. "How did you find our little service, Mr. Starbuck?"

"I was moved, Miss Gordon."

"Father is good, isn't he? His sincerity shines." She was worried by Starbuck's expression, mistaking his sinner's guilt as a distaste for the ward's horrors. "Does it deter you from soldiering?" Julia asked.

"I don't know. I hadn't thought about it." He looked at Sally, who was now devoting herself to the ragged, frightened man who gripped her hands as though she alone could keep him alive. "Soldiers don't think they'll end up in places like this."

"Or worse," Julia said drily. "There are wards here for the dying, for men who can never be helped. Though I'd like to help them." She spoke wistfully.

"I'm sure you do," Starbuck said gallantly.

"I don't mean by visiting and playing hymns, Mr. Starbuck, I mean by nursing them. But mother won't hear of it. She says I will contract a fever, or worse. Nor will Adam permit it. He wants to protect me from the war. You know he disapproves of it?"

"I know," Starbuck said, then glanced at Julia. "And you?"

"There's nothing here to merit approval," Julia said. "Yet I confess I am too proud to want the North to triumph over us. So maybe I am a warmonger. Is that what makes men fight? Mere pride?"

"Mere pride," Starbuck said. "On the battlefield you want to prove you're better than the other side." He recalled the joy of hitting the Yankees' open flank at Ball's Bluff, the panic in the blue ranks, the screams as the enemy were tumbled off the crest and down to the bloody, bullet-lashed river. Then he felt guilty at that remembered pleasure. The gates of hell, he thought, would surely gape especially wide for him.

"Mr. Starbuck?" Julia asked, concerned for the horror that showed on his face, but before he could respond and before Julia could say another word, Sally suddenly hurried across the ward and took Starbuck's elbow.

"Take me away, please." Her voice was low and urgent.

"Sal—" Starbuck checked himself, realizing that Julia knew Sally as Victoria. "What is it?"

"That man," Sally just breathed the words, not even bothering to indicate which man she spoke of, "recognizes me. Please, Nate. Take me away."

"I'm sure it doesn't matter," Starbuck said softly.

"Please!" Sally hissed. "Just take me out of here!"

"Might I help?" Julia asked, puzzled.

"I think we should go," Starbuck said, though the trouble was that Sally's cloak and his coat were piled at the end of the shed where the bloody-aproned surgeon was standing, and it was the surgeon who had recognized Sally and spoken with the Reverend Doctor Peterkin, who, in turn, now talked to Mrs. Gordon. "Come," Starbuck said, and he pulled Sally by the hand. He would abandon the coats, even though he regretted losing the fine gray coat that had belonged to Oliver Wendell Holmes. "You will forgive me?" he asked Julia as he edged past her.

"Mr. Starbuck!" Mrs. Gordon called imperiously. "Miss Royall!"

"Ignore her," Starbuck said to Sally.

"Miss Royall! Come here!" Mrs. Gordon called and Sally, stung by the tone, turned toward her. Adam hurried down the ward to see what was the matter while the Reverend John Gordon looked up from where he knelt beside a fevered man's cot.

"I will speak with you outside," Mrs. Gordon declared, and she turned onto the small porch where, on fine days, the patients could take the air under the shelter of a sloping roof.

Sally plucked up her cloak. The surgeon smirked and offered her a bow. "Son of a bitch," Sally hissed at him. Starbuck extricated his coat and went onto the porch.

"Words fail me," Mrs. Gordon greeted Sally and Starbuck in the rainy darkness.

"You wanted words with me?" Sally confronted her.

"I cannot believe it of you, Mr. Starbuck." Mrs. Gordon ignored the defiant Sally and looked at Starbuck instead. "That you, raised in a godly home, should have the ill manners to introduce a woman like this into my house."

"A woman like what?" Sally demanded. The Reverend John Gordon had come onto the porch and, in obedience to his wife's sharp command, closed the door, though not before Adam and Julia had crowded onto the small porch.

"You will go inside, Julia," her mother insisted.

"Let her stay!" Sally said. "A woman like what?"

"Julia!" Mrs. Gordon glared at her daughter.

"Mother, dear," the Reverend John Gordon said, "might you tell us what this is all about?"

"Doctor Peterkin," Mrs. Gordon said indignantly, "has just informed me that this, this, woman is a . . ." She paused, unable to find a word she could decently use in front of her daughter. "Julia! Inside this instant!"

"My dear!" the Reverend John Gordon said. "What is she?"

"A Magdalen!" Mrs. Gordon shouted the word.

"She means I'm a whore, Reverend," Sally said sourly.

"And you brought her to my house!" Mrs. Gordon shrieked at Starbuck.

"Mrs. Gordon," Starbuck began, but he could not interrupt the tirade that now poured on his head like the rain that was drumming on the porch's tarpaper roof. Mrs. Gordon wondered if the Reverend Elial Starbuck knew to what depths of iniquity his son had sunk, and how far from God's grace he had fallen, and how evil was his choice of companions. "She is a fallen woman!" Mrs. Gordon screamed, "and you brought her to my house!"

"Our Lord consorted with sinners," the Reverend John Gordon said feebly.

"But He didn't give them tea!" Mrs. Gordon was beyond argument. She turned on Adam. "And you, Mr. Faulconer, I am shocked by your friendships. There is no other word. I am shocked."

Adam looked remorsefully at Starbuck. "Is it true?"

"Sally is a friend," Starbuck said. "A good friend. I'm proud to know her."

"Sally Truslow!" Adam said, the identity of Miss Royall at last yielding to his memory.

"Are you saying you know this woman?" Mrs. Gordon challenged Adam.

"He don't know me," Sally said tiredly.

"I am forced to wonder if you are a fit companion for my daughter, Mr. Faulconer." Mrs. Gordon pressed her advantage on Adam. "This night has been a providence of God; maybe it has revealed your true self!"

"I said he don't know me!" Sally insisted.

"Do you know her?" the Reverend John Gordon asked Adam.

Adam shrugged. "Her father was one of my family's tenants once. A long time ago. Beyond that I don't know her."

"But you do know Mr. Starbuck." Mrs. Gordon had not wrung a full measure of remorse from Adam yet. "Are you telling me you approve of the company he keeps?"

Adam looked at his friend. "I'm sure Nate didn't know Miss Truslow's nature."

"I knew it," Starbuck said, "and as I said, she is a friend." He put an arm around Sally's shoulder.

"And you approve of your friend's choice of companion?" Mrs. Gordon demanded of Adam. "Do you, Mr. Faulconer? For I cannot have my daughter attached, however respectably, to a man who consorts with the friends of scarlet women."

"No," Adam said, "I don't approve."

"You're just like your father," Sally said. "Rotten to the core. If you Faulconers didn't have money you'd be lower than dogs." She pulled herself free of Starbuck's arm and ran into the rain.

Starbuck turned to follow Sally, but was checked by Mrs. Gordon. "You're making a choice!" she warned him. "This is the night you choose between God and the devil, Mr. Starbuck!"

"Nate!" Adam added his voice to Mrs. Gordon's warning. "Let her go."

"Why? Because she's a whore?" Starbuck felt the rage rise in him, a filthy rage of hatred for these sanctimonious prigs. "I told you, Adam, she's a friend, and you don't abandon friends. God damn you all." He ran after Sally, catching up with her at the edge of the sheds where the muddy slope of Chimborazo Park fell steeply down into the Bloody Run, where the city's dueling ground was set beside a stream. "I'm sorry," he told Sally, taking her arm again.

She sniffed. The rain made her hair dank and straggling. She was crying and Starbuck pulled her into his body, covering her with the scarlet lining of his coat. The rain stung his face. "You were right," Sally said, her voice muffled. "We shouldn't have gone."

"They shouldn't have behaved like that," Starbuck said.

Sally cried softly. "I sometimes just want to be ordinary." She managed to speak through the tears. "I just want a house and babies and a rug on the floor and an apple tree. I don't want to live like my father and I don't want to be what I am now. Not forever. I just want to be plain. Do you know what I mean, Nate?" She looked up at him, her face lit by the fires of the forges that burned day and night beside the river on the far side of the run.

He stroked her rain-dampened face. "I know," he said.

"Don't you want to be ordinary?" she asked.

"Sometimes, yes."

"Jesus," Sally swore. She pulled away from him, cuffed her nose, and pushed her wet hair off her forehead. "I thought if the war ends I'd have enough money to buy a small store. Nothing fancy, Nate. Dry goods, maybe? I'm saving my money, you see, so I can be ordinary. No one special. Not Royall anymore, just plain ordinary. But my father's right," she said with a new note of vengeance, "there are two kinds of folk in this world. There are sheep and wolves, Nate, sheep and wolves, and you can't change your nature. And they're all sheep." She jerked a contemptuous thumb toward the hospital sheds. "Including your friend. He's like his father. He's frightened of women." It was a scathing judgment.

Starbuck held her close again and stared across the shadows of Bloody Run to where the ironwork fires shimmered their reflections on the rain-pocked river. He had not understood till this moment just how alone in the world he was, an outcast, a wolf running alone. Sally was the same, rejected by polite society because in her desperation for escape and independence she had broken its rules, and for that she would never be forgiven, any more than Starbuck would be forgiven. Which meant he must make it alone, he would spit on these people for rejecting him, and he would do it by being the best soldier he could be. He had always known that his salvation in the South lay in the army, for there no man cared what he was as long as he proved a fighter.

"You know what, Nate?" Sally said. "I was thinking in there that maybe I had a chance. Like a real chance? That I could be good." She said the last word fervently. "But they don't want me in their world, do they?"

"You don't need their approval to be a good person, Sally."

"I don't care anymore. One day I'll have the likes of them begging to stand on my carpet, just you watch and see."

Starbuck smiled in the dark. They were a whore and a failed soldier, declaring war on the world. He stooped and kissed Sally's rain-wet cheek. "I must take you home," he said.

"To your room," Sally said. "I don't feel like working."

Beneath them a train pulled out of the city, the light of its fire-box throwing a lurid glow along the damp grass beside the stream. The locomotive was hauling cars of ammunition bound for the peninsula where a thin line of playacting rebels was holding off a horde.

Starbuck walked Sally home, then took her to his bed. He was a sinner and this night, after all, was not for repentance.

Sally left Starbuck just after one o'clock in the morning, so he was alone in the narrow bed when the troops came. He was sleeping soundly, and the first he knew of the incursion was the splintering sound of the outside stable door being broken down. There was no light in the room. He fumbled for his revolver as feet pounded on the stairs and he had just succeeded in pulling the ivory-handled weapon out of its holster when the door crashed open and a wash of lantern light flared bright in the small dingy attic room. "Put the gun down, lad! Down!" The men were all in uniforms and carried rifles with fixed bayonets. Throughout Richmond a fixed bayonet was the mark of "plug-ugly," a provost of General Winder's martial police force, and Starbuck sensibly let the revolver fall back onto the floor. "Your name's Starbuck?" the man who had ordered him to lay the gun down now asked.

"Who are you?" Starbuck shielded his eyes. Three lanterns were in the room now and what seemed to be a whole platoon of soldiers.

"Answer the question!" the voice roared. "Is your name Star-buck?"

"Yes."

"Take him! Quick now!"

"Let me dress, for God's sake!"

"Hurry, lads!"

Two men seized Starbuck, dragged him naked from the bed, and thumped him hard and painfully against the flaking plaster wall.

"Put a blanket round him, boys. We don't want to frighten the horses. Manacle him first, Corporal!" Starbuck's eyes had adjusted and he could see that the commanding officer was a broad-chested, brown-bearded captain.

"What the hell . . ." Starbuck began to protest as the Corporal produced chains and wristbands, but the soldier holding Starbuck pushed him hard against the wall.

"Silence!" the Captain roared. "Take everything, lads, everything! I'll take that bottle as evidence, thank you, Perkins. All papers to be cased up properly; that's your responsibility, Sergeant. And that bottle too, Perkins, to me." The Captain put the whiskey bottles in his uniform's capacious pockets, then led the way down the stairs. Starbuck, his wrists chained and his body loosely swathed in a rough gray blanket, stumbled after the Captain through the empty coach house and out into Sixth Street where a black carriage with four horses waited under the streetlight. It was still raining, and the horses' breath steamed in the gaslight. A church clock struck four and a window at the back of the main house rattled up. "What's going on?" a woman's voice cried. Starbuck thought it might be Sally, but he could not tell.

"Nothing, ma'am! Back to your bed!" the Captain called, then he pushed Starbuck up the carriage steps. The Captain and three soldiers followed. The rest of the party were still searching Starbuck's lodgings.

"Where are we going?" Starbuck asked as the carriage jolted away from the sidewalk.

"You are now a prisoner of the Provost Guard," the Captain responded very formally. "You will speak when you are spoken to and at no other time."

"You're speaking to me now," Starbuck said, "so where are we going?"

It was dark in the carriage so Starbuck did not see the fist that suddenly smacked him hard across the eyes and banged his head against the carriage's backboard. "Shut the hell up, you Yankee bastard," a voice said, and Starbuck, his eyes involuntarily streaming with the effects of the blow, did as the man suggested.

The journey was short, no more than half a mile, and then the iron-rimmed wheels screeched in protest as the carriage slewed around a tight corner before jolting to a stop. The door was thrown open and Starbuck saw the torchlit gates of Lumpkin's Jail, known now as Castle Godwin. "Move!" the Corporal shouted, and Starbuck was pushed down the carriage steps and through a wicket entrance cut into Castle Godwin's larger gates.

"Number fourteen!" a turnkey bawled as the arresting party came through the gate. A uniformed guard led the way through a brick arch and down a stone-flagged corridor lit by two oil lamps until he reached a stout wooden door marked with a stenciled "14." He opened the door with a heavy key made from gleaming steel. The Corporal unlocked the manacles from Starbuck's wrists.

"In there, cuffee," the guard said, and Starbuck was pushed inside the cell. He saw a wooden bed, a metal pail, and a large puddle. The room stank of sewage. "Shit in the bucket, sleep on the bed, or the other way round, cuffee." The guard laughed, then the door crashed shut with an echoing din and the cell was plunged into an absolute darkness. Starbuck, exhausted, lay on the wooden bed and shivered.

They gave him a pair of coarse gray trousers, square leather brogans, and a shirt from which the bloodstains of its last owner had not been removed. Breakfast was a cup of water and the heel of a stale loaf. The city's clocks were striking nine when two guards came and ordered him to sit on the bed and extend his feet toward them. They chained a pair of iron anklets on his feet. "They stay till you leave," one of the guards said, "or till they hang you." He stuck out his tongue and contorted his face into the grotesque leer of a hanged man.

"On your feet!" the second guard said. "Move!"

Starbuck was pushed into the corridor. The chains on his feet forced him into an awkward shuffle, but the guards were evidently used to the slow pace for they did not try to hurry him, indeed they encouraged him to linger as they passed through a courtyard that reminded Starbuck of the lurid tales he had heard of medieval torture chambers. Chains hung from the wall, while in the yard's center was a wooden horse that consisted of a plank mounted sideways on a pair of trestles. The punishment was to sit a man on the plank's edge and weight his feet so that the wood would drive into his groin. "This ain't for your kind, cuffee," one of the two guards said. "They're trying something new on you. Keep walking."

Starbuck was taken to a room with brick walls, a flagged floor with a drain in its center, a table, and a chair. A barred window looked east toward the open sewer of Shockoe Creek, which flowed through the city. One of the small panes was open and the smell of the creek soured the room. The guards, whom Starbuck could observe properly now, stacked their muskets against the wall. They were both big men, as tall as Starbuck, with pale, coarse, clean-shaven faces and the vacant expressions of men who asked and received little of life. One spat a viscous stream of tobacco juice toward the open drain. The discolored spittle landed dead center. "Good one, Abe," the other guard said.

The door opened and a thin, pale man entered. He had a leather bag hanging from one shoulder and a small fair beard that merely fringed his chin. His cheeks and upper lip still gleamed from his morning shave and his lieutenant's uniform was immaculate, brushed spotless and pressed to knife-crease edges. "Good morning," he said in a diffident voice.

"Answer the officer, you Yankee scum," the guard called Abe said.

"Good morning," Starbuck said.

The Lieutenant brushed the seat of the chair, sat down, took a pair of spectacles from a pocket, and hooked them over his ears. He had a very thin and rather earnest face, like a new minister coming to an old congregation. "Starbuck, isn't it?"

"Yes."

"Call the officer 'sir,' scum!"

"Peace, Harding, peace." The Lieutenant frowned in evident disapproval of Harding's rudeness. He had placed the leather bag on the table and now he took a folder from it. He untied the folder's green ribbons, opened its covers, and examined the papers inside. "Nathaniel Joseph Starbuck, yes?"

"Yes."

"Presently residing at Franklin Street, the old Burrell house, yes?"

"I don't know who lived there."

"Josiah Burrell, a tobacco factor. The family fell on hard times, like so many these days. Now, let me see." The Lieutenant leaned back, making his chair creak ominously, then took off his glasses and tiredly rubbed his eyes. "I'm going to ask you some questions, Starbuck, and your role, as you might surmise, is to answer those questions. Normally, of course, these things are subject to law, but there's a war on and I fear the necessity of eliciting the truth cannot wait upon the rigmarole of lawyers. Do you understand?"

"Not really. I'd like to know what the hell I'm doing here."

The guards behind Starbuck growled a warning for his truculence, but the Lieutenant held up a placatory hand. "You shall find out, Starbuck, I do promise you." He fixed the glasses back on his nose. "I forgot to introduce myself. How remiss. My name is Lieutenant Gillespie, Lieutenant Walton Gillespie." He spoke the name as though he expected Starbuck to recognize it, but Starbuck merely shrugged. Gillespie took a pencil from his uniform pocket. "Shall we begin? You were born where?" Gillespie asked.

"Boston," Starbuck said.

"Where exactly, please?"

"Milk Street."

"Your parents' home, yes?"

"Grandparents. My mother's people."

Gillespie made a note. "And your parents live where now?"

"Walnut Street."

"Do they now? How very pleasant for them! I was in Boston two years ago and had the privilege of hearing your father expound the gospel." Gillespie smiled in evident pleasure at the memory. "On we go," he said, and he took Starbuck through a series of questions about his schooling and Yale Theological College and how he had come to be in the South when the war started and what service he had seen in the Faulconer Legion.

"So far, so good," Gillespie said when he had finished hearing about Ball's Bluff. He turned a page and frowned at whatever was written there. "When did you first meet John Scully?"

"Never heard of him."

"Price Lewis?"

Starbuck shook his head.

"Timothy Webster?"

Starbuck simply shrugged to show his ignorance.

"I see," Gillespie said in a tone which suggested that Starbuck's denial was particularly puzzling. He made a pencil mark, still frowning, then took off his spectacles and massaged the bridge of his nose momentarily. "Your brother's name is what?"

"I've got three brothers. James, Frederick, and Sam."

"Their ages?"

Starbuck had to think. "Twenty-six or -seven, seventeen, and thirteen."

"The oldest. His name is?"

"James."

"James." Gillespie repeated the name as though he had never heard it before. In the courtyard a man suddenly screamed and Starbuck heard the distinct sound of a whip slashing through the air, then the crack of the lash slapping home. "Did I shut the door, Harding?" Gillespie asked.

"Tight shut, sir."

"So noisy, so noisy. Tell me, Starbuck, when you last saw James?"

Starbuck shook his head. "It has to be long before the war."

"Before the war," Gillespie said as he wrote it down. "And the last time you received a letter from him?"

"Again, before the war."

"Before the war," Gillespie repeated again slowly, then took a small penknife from his pocket. He opened the blade and sharpened the point of his pencil, fussily brushing the shards of wood and lead into a neat pile at the table's edge. "What does the Confederate Army Bible Supply Society mean to you?"

"Nothing."

"I see." Gillespie laid his pencil down and leaned back in the rickety chair. "And just what information did you send to your brother about the disposition of our forces?"

"None!" Starbuck protested, at last beginning to understand what this whole farrago was about.

Gillespie once again took off his spectacles and rubbed them against his sleeve. "I mentioned to you earlier, Mr. Starbuck, that we are forced, regrettably forced, to extreme measures in our attempts to elicit the truth. Usually, as I said, we would have recourse to a process of law, but extreme times demand extreme measures. Do you understand?"

"No."

"Then let me ask you again. Do you know John Scully and Lewis Price?"

"No."

"Have you been in communication with your brother?"

"No."

"Have you received letters care of the Confederate Army Bible Supply Society?"

"No."

"And did you deliver a letter care of Mr. Timothy Webster at the Monumental Hotel?"

"No," Starbuck protested.

Gillespie shook his head sadly. When Major Alexander had arrested Timothy Webster and Hattie Lawton he had also discovered a letter written in tight block capitals that described the entire disposition of Richmond's defenders. The letter was addressed to Major James Starbuck, the same name that appeared on the communication taken from John Scully. The letter would have been a disaster to the South's cause for it had even offered a description of the playacting with which General Magruder had been attempting to deceive McClellan's patrols. All that had prevented Webster from delivering the letter was a terrible rheumatic fever that had kept the man in bed for weeks.

Starbuck, questioned again about the letter, shook his head. "I've never heard of a Timothy Webster."

Gillespie grimaced. "And you insist upon those answers?"

"They're the truth!"

"Alas," Gillespie said, and he pulled open the leather bag and took out a funnel of bright brass and a bottle made of blue-colored glass. He unstoppered the bottle, letting a thin, sour smell fill the room. "My father, Starbuck, like yours, is a man of some eminence. He is the medical superintendent of the Chesterfield Lunacy Asylum. You know it?"

"No." Starbuck gazed at the bottle apprehensively.

"There are two schools of opinion governing the treatment of lunacy," Gillespie said. "One theory claims that madness can be coddled out of patients by fresh air, good food, and kindness, but the second opinion, to which my father adheres, insists that lunacy can be shocked out of the sufferer's system. In essence, Starbuck"—Gillespie looked up at the prisoner and his eyes seemed oddly bright—"we must punish the lunatic for his aberrant behavior and so drive him back into the company of civilized men. This"—he held up the blue-glass bottle—"has been declared the finest coercive substance known to science. Tell me about Timothy Webster."

"There's nothing to tell!"

Gillespie paused, then nodded at the two guards. Starbuck turned to resist the nearest man, but he was too slow. He was hit from behind and thrown down to the floor, and before he could twist around he was pinned onto the stone. The chains around his ankle clanked as his hands were pinioned behind his back. He swore at the two guards, but they were big men accustomed to subduing prisoners and they ignored his oaths, instead turning him onto his back. One of them took the brass funnel and rammed it into Starbuck's mouth. When he resisted by gritting his teeth the man threatened to hammer the funnel down and so break his teeth, and Starbuck, knowing when he was beaten, released his jaw.

Gillespie knelt beside him with the blue bottle. "This is croton oil," he told Starbuck, "you know of it?"

Starbuck could not speak, so he shook his head.

"Croton oil is drawn from the seeds of the *Croton tiglium* plant.

It's a purgative, Mr. Starbuck, and a very violent one. My father employs it whenever a patient exhibits offensive behavior. No madman can be violent or perverse, you see, when he is having a score of bowel movements every ten minutes." Gillespie smiled. "What do you know about Timothy Webster?"

Starbuck shook his head, then tried to twist his way out of the guards' grip, but the two men were far too strong for him. One of them pushed Starbuck's head hard back onto the flagstones while Gillespie poised the bottle over the funnel. "In times past the treatment of lunacy depended upon simple physical punishments," Gillespie explained, "but my father's contribution to medicine was the discovery that an application of this cathartic is far more efficient than any amount of whipping. A small taste first, I think." He poured a thin stream of the oil into the funnel. It tasted fatty and rank in Starbuck's mouth. He choked on it, but one of the guards clamped a hand around his jaw and Starbuck had no choice but to swallow the oil. It left a burning sensation in his mouth.

Gillespie eased the bottle away and motioned for the guards to free Starbuck. Starbuck gasped for breath. His mouth burned and his gullet seemed raw. He sensed the thick oil hitting his stomach as he struggled to his knees.

Then the purgative hit. He doubled over, spewing vomit onto the floor. The spasm left him breathless, but before he could recover, another spasm ripped up from his belly, then his bowels opened uncontrollably and the room filled with his terrible stink. He could not stop himself. He groaned and rolled on the floor, then jerked as another spasm of vomit tore up his body.

The guards grinned and stepped back from him. Gillespie, careless of the awful smell, watched avidly through his spectacles and made an occasional note in a small book. Still the spasms racked Starbuck. Even when there was nothing left in his belly or bowels he kept on gasping and twitching as the awful oil scoured through his guts.

"Let us talk again," Gillespie said after a few minutes, when Starbuck was calmer.

"Bastard," Starbuck said. He was filthy, lying in filth, his clothes smeared with filth; he was humiliated and helpless and degraded by the filth.

"Do you know a Mr. John Scully or a Mr. Lewis Price?" Gillespie asked in his precise voice.

"No. And to hell with you."

"Have you been in communication with your brother?"

"No. Damn you."

"Have you received letters care of the Confederate Army Bible Supply Society?"

"No!"

"And did you deliver information to Timothy Webster at the Monumental Hotel?"

"I'll tell you what I did, you bastard!" Starbuck raised his face and spat a dribble of vomit toward Gillespie. "I carried a gun into battle for this country, which is more than you ever did, you shit-faced son of a bitch!"

Gillespie shook his head as though Starbuck was peculiarly recalcitrant. "Again," he said to the guards and lifted the bottle from the table.

"No!" Starbuck said, but one of the guards threw him down and both men pinioned him to the floor. Gillespie brought the croton oil.

"I'm curious to discover just how much oil one person can endure," Gillespie said. "Move him this way, I don't want to kneel in his droppings."

"No!" Starbuck moaned, but the funnel was thrust into his mouth once more and Gillespie, half smiling, poured another stream of the viscous yellowish liquid into the brass maw.

The spasms hit again. The pain was much worse this time, a terrible flaying raw agony that burned in Starbuck's belly and spread outward as he twisted in his own filth. Twice more Gillespie poured the purgative down his throat, but the extra liquid yielded no more information. Starbuck still insisted he knew no one called Scully or Lewis or Webster.

At midday the guards threw buckets of cold water over him. Gillespie watched expressionless as the inert and stinking body of the northerner was carried out of the room to be dumped in his cell and then, annoyed with himself for being late, he hurried away to the regular Bible class that met at lunchtime in the nearby Universalist church.

While Starbuck lay in the damp and whimpered.

Reluctantly, like a heavy beast rousing itself from a long sleep, the rebel army took itself away from its positions around Culpeper Court House. It moved slowly and cautiously, for General Johnston could not yet be certain that the North was not attempting a giant piece of deception. Maybe the much-advertised voyage of the great ships from Alexandria to Fort Monroe was merely an elaborate charade to make him move his troops to Richmond's blind side? Such a ruse would open the roads of northern Virginia to the real Federal attack and, fearing just such a deception, Johnston sent cavalry patrols deep into Fauquier and Prince William counties, then still farther north into Loudoun County. The men of the partisan brigades, the ragged riders whose job was to stay behind and harass any northern invaders, crossed the Potomac into Maryland, yet all the patrols came back with the same news. The Yankees were gone. The defenses around Washington were fully manned, and the forts that guarded the northern enclave in Virginia's Fairfax County were strongly garrisoned, but the North's field army had vanished. The Young Napoleon was attacking in the peninsula.

The Faulconer Brigade was among the first to be ordered to the outskirts of Richmond. Washington Faulconer summoned Major Bird to receive the orders. "Isn't Swynyard supposed to be your errand boy?" Bird demanded of Washington Faulconer.

"He's resting."

"You mean he's drunk."

"Nonsense, Pecker." Washington Faulconer wore his new uniform jacket that bore the wreathed stars of a brigadier general on its collars. "He's bored. He's fretting for action. Man's a warrior."

"Man's a dipsomaniac lunatic," Bird said. "He tried to arrest Tony Murphy yesterday for not saluting him."

"Captain Murphy has a rebellious streak," Faulconer said.

"I thought we were all supposed to have a rebellious streak," Bird observed. "I tell you, Faulconer, the man's a souse. You've been cheated."

But Washington Faulconer was not about to admit a mistake. He knew as well as anyone that Griffin Swynyard was a liquor-sodden disaster, but the disaster would need to be endured until the Faulconer Brigade had made its reputation in battle and thus provided its commander with the freedom to defy the power of the Richmond *Examiner*. Which paper was now open on Faulconer's camp table. "You see the news about Starbuck?"

Bird had not even seen the paper, let alone heard any news of Starbuck.

"He's been arrested. It is believed he traded information with the enemy. Ha!" Faulconer made the explanation with evident satisfaction. "He never was any good, Pecker. God only knows why you champion him."

Bird knew his brother-in-law was looking for an argument so he refused to offer him the satisfaction. "Anything else, Faulconer?" he asked coldly instead.

"One other thing, Pecker." Faulconer, his coat buttoned and belt buckled, drew his curved saber and cut it through the air with a deliberately casual motion. "The elections," Faulconer said vaguely, as if he had only just thought of the topic.

"I've arranged for them."

"I don't want any nonsense, Pecker." Faulconer pointed the saber's tip at Bird. "No nonsense, you hear me?"

In two weeks the Legion was required to hold new elections for company officers. The requirement had been imposed by the Confederate government, which had just introduced conscription and, at the same time, had extended the terms of service of those men who had originally volunteered one year's service. From now on the one-year men must serve till death, disability, or peace discharged them from the ranks, but thinking that the bitter pill needed a candy coating, the government had also ruled that the one-year regiments be given another chance to select their own officers. "What nonsense could there be?" Thaddeus Bird asked innocently.

"You know, Pecker, you know," Faulconer warned.

"I have not the first, the faintest, the slightest idea what you mean," Bird said.

The saber tip slashed around to quiver just inches from Bird's ragged beard. "I don't want Starbuck's name on the ballot."

"Then I shall make sure it isn't there," Bird said in all innocence.

"And I don't want the men writing his name in."

"That, Faulconer, is beyond my control. It's called democracy. I believe your grandfather and mine fought a war to establish it."

"Nonsense, Pecker." Faulconer felt the usual frustrations of dealing with his brother-in-law, and his usual regret that Adam so mulishly refused to leave Johnston and take over the Legion's command. Faulconer could think of no other man whom the Legion would accept as a replacement for Pecker, and even Adam, Faulconer conceded, would have a difficult time replacing his uncle. Which meant, Faulconer privately conceded to himself, that Bird would probably have to be given the colonelcy of the regiment, in which case why could he not demonstrate just a hint of gratitude or cooperation? Washington Faulconer believed himself to be a man of charitable and kind instincts, and all he really wanted was to be liked in return, yet so often he seemed to engender resentment instead. "The men certainly wouldn't be tempted to vote for Starbuck if there was a good officer leading K Company," Faulconer now suggested.

"Who, pray?"

"Moxey."

Bird rolled his eyes. "Truslow would eat him alive."

"Then discipline Truslow!"

"Why? He's the best soldier in the Legion."

"Nonsense," Faulconer said, but he had no other candidate to suggest. He sheathed his saber, the blade hissing against the scabbard's wooden throat. "Tell the men that Starbuck's a traitor. That should cool their enthusiasm. Tell them he'll be hanged before the month's out, and tell them that's exactly what the son of a bitch deserves. And he does deserve it! You know damn well he murdered poor Ethan."

In Bird's opinion the killing of Ethan Ridley had been the best day's work Starbuck had ever done, but he kept that opinion to himself. "Have you any other orders, Faulconer?" he asked instead.

"Be ready to leave in an hour. I want the men to look smart. We'll be marching through Richmond, remember, so let's put on a show!"

Bird stepped outside the tent and lit a cheroot. Poor Starbuck, he thought. He did not believe in Starbuck's guilt for a single instance, but there was nothing Bird could do about it, and the schoolmaster turned soldier had long decided that what he could not affect he should not allow to affect him. Still, he thought, it was sad about Starbuck.

Yet, Bird reflected, Starbuck's tragedy was doubtless about to be swallowed in the greater disaster posed by McClellan's invasion. When Richmond fell the Confederacy would stagger on for a few defiant months, but bereft of its capital, and shorn of the Tredegar Iron Works which were the largest and most efficient in all the South, the rebellion could hardly be expected to survive. It was odd, Bird thought as he strolled along the brigade's camp lines, but it was just about one year to the day since the rebellion had begun with the guns firing on Fort Sumter. One year, and now the North was curling around Richmond like a great mailed fist about to crack tight shut.

Drums beat, and the shouted orders of the drill sergeants echoed back across the damp campground as the brigade got ready to march. The sun actually appeared from behind the clouds for the first time in weeks as the Faulconer Legion left, marching south and east to where America's fate would be decided in battle.

On one point only did Lieutenant Walton Gillespie trap Starbuck into some kind of admission of wrongdoing, and having found that weakness Gillespie worked on it with a desperate enthusiasm. Starbuck had admitted selling passports for gain and Gillespie pounced on the admission. "You admit signing passports without verifying their validity?"

"We all do."

"Why?"

"For money, of course."

Gillespie, already pale, actually seemed to blanch at this confession of moral turpitude. "You mean you accepted bribes?"

"Of course I did," Starbuck said. He was as weak as a kitten, his gullet and belly a mass of raw pain while his face had erupted into weeping pustules wherever the croton oil had splashed on his skin. The weather was warming, but he shivered all the time and feared he was catching a fever. Day after day he had been questioned, and day after day he had ingested the filthy oil until now he no longer knew how long he had been in jail. The questions seemed unending, while the vomit and the dysentery racked him day and night. It hurt him to swallow water, it hurt him to breathe, it hurt him to be alive.

"Who bribes you?" Gillespie asked, then grimaced as Starbuck spat a bloody scrap of dribble onto the floor. Starbuck was sitting slumped in a chair for he was too weak to stand and Gillespie did not like to interview men crumpled on the floor. The two guards leaned on the wall. They were bored. In their own private opinions, which they accepted counted for nothing, this damn northerner was innocent, but Gillespie still kept at him. "Who?" Gillespie insisted.

"All kinds of damn people." Starbuck was so weary, so hurt. "Major Bridgford came once with a stack of forms, so did—"

"Nonsense!" Gillespie snapped. "Bridgford wouldn't do such a thing."

Starbuck shrugged as though he did not care one way or the other. Bridgford was the Provost Marshal of the army, and he had indeed brought Starbuck a sheaf of blank passports for signature and afterward had dropped a bottle of rye whiskey on Starbuck's desk as payment for the favor. A score of other senior officers and at least a dozen Congressmen had done the same, usually paying more than an illegal bottle of liquor, and Starbuck, at Gillespie's bidding, named them all. The only man he did not name was Belvedere Delaney. The lawyer was a friend and a benefactor and the least Starbuck could do in return was to protect him.

"What did you do with the money?" Gillespie asked.

"Lost it at Johnny Worsham's," Starbuck answered. Johnny Worsham's was the city's largest gambling den, a riotous place of women and music guarded by two black men so tall and powerful that even the armed provosts dared not tangle with them. Starbuck had lost some of the money there, but most of it was safely locked away in Sally's room. He dared not reveal that hiding place for fear that Gillespie would go after Sally. "Played poker," he added. "No damn good at poker." He gave a dry heave, then groaned as he tried to restore his breath. Gillespie had abandoned the croton oil these last few days, yet still Starbuck was half bent double because of the pains in his belly.

The next day Gillespie reported to Major Alexander, who grimaced when he saw how little had been learned from Starbuck. "Maybe he's innocent?" Alexander suggested.

"He's a Yankee," Gillespie said.

"He's guilty of that, certainly, but is he guilty of writing to Webster?"

"Who else could it be?" Gillespie demanded.

"That, Lieutenant, is what we are supposed to determine. I thought your father's scientific methods were infallible? And if they are infallible, then Starbuck must be innocent."

"He takes bribes."

Alexander sighed. "We might as well arrest half the Congress for that crime, Lieutenant." He leafed through the reports of Gillespie's interrogation, noting with distaste the huge amounts of oil that had been forced down the prisoner's throat. "I have a suspicion we're wasting our time," Alexander concluded.

"Another few days, sir!" Gillespie said urgently. "I'm sure that he's ready to break, sir. I know he is!"

"You said that last week."

"I've withheld the oil these last few days," Gillespie said enthusiastically. "I'm giving him a chance to recover, then I plan to double the dose next time."

Alexander closed Starbuck's file. "If he had anything to tell us, Lieutenant, he'd have confessed it by now. He's not our man."

Gillespie bridled at the implication that his interrogation had failed. "You do know," he asked Alexander, "that Starbuck had quarters in a brothel?"

"You'd condemn a man for being lucky?" Alexander asked.

Gillespie blushed. "One of the women has been asking for him, sir. She visited the prison twice."

"Is she the pretty whore? The one called Royall?"

Gillespie's blush deepened. In truth Victoria Royall had been more beautiful than his dreams, but he dared not admit that to Alexander. "She was called Royall, certainly. And she was royally insolent. She wouldn't tell me what her interest in the prisoner was, and I think she should be questioned."

Alexander shook his head wearily. "Her interest in the prisoner, Lieutenant, is that her father served in his infantry company, and she probably served in Starbuck's bed. I talked to the girl and she knows nothing, so there's no need for you to question her further. Unless you had a different entertainment in mind?"

"Of course not, sir." Gillespie bridled at the suggestion, though in truth he had been hoping that Major Alexander would deputize him to question Miss Victoria Royall.

"Because if you did have something different in mind," Alexander went on, "then you should know that the *nymphs du monde* in that house are the most expensive in all the Confederacy. You might find the ladies in the establishment opposite the YMCA more to your purse's taste."

"Sir! I have to protest . . ."

"Be quiet, Lieutenant," Alexander said tiredly. "And in case you have a mind to visit Miss Royall privately, then do reflect on just how many high-ranking officers are among her clients. She can probably make a great deal more trouble for you than you can for her." Some of those clients had already protested Starbuck's imprisonment, which Alexander himself was finding increasingly hard to justify. God in his heaven, the Major thought, but this case was proving difficult. Starbuck had seemed the obvious candidate, but he was admitting nothing. Timothy Webster, bedridden in his cell, had yielded no information in his interrogations, while the man set to watch the notice board in St. Paul's was patently wasting his time. A false letter had been placed under the tapes of the message board in the church vestibule, but no one had appeared to collect it.

"If you'd just let me administer my father's purgatives to Webster," Gillespie suggested eagerly.

Alexander cut off the suggestion. "We have other plans for Mr. Webster." Alexander also doubted whether the ailing Webster knew the identity of the man who had written to Major James Starbuck. Maybe only James Starbuck knew.

"The woman captured with Webster?" Gillespie suggested.

"We are not going to have the northern newspapers claiming that we purge women," Alexander said. "She'll be sent back north unharmed." The sound of a military band prompted Alexander to cross to his office window and stare down at a battalion of infantry that was marching eastward on Franklin Street. Johnston's army, stirred at last from its positions around Culpeper Court House, was arriving to defend the Confederacy's capital. The very first regiments to arrive had already gone to thicken Magruder's defenses at Yorktown, while the later arrivals were now making their encampments east and north of Richmond.

The infantry band was playing "Dixie." Children with sticks instead of muskets swaggered beside the troops who all wore daffodils in their hats. Even from the third floor Alexander could see how ragged and ill-uniformed the soldiers were, but they marched steadily enough and their morale seemed high. They tossed daffodils to the prettier girls. A mulatto girl standing among the spectators on the far pavement had a whole armful of the flowers and laughed as the soldiers piled on yet more blooms. The infantry was being deliberately routed through the city so that Richmonders would know an army had come to their defense, though the soldiers themselves needed defending from the city, or rather from its diseased whores, and so the marching column was escorted by lines of provosts with fixed bayonets who made sure that no man slipped away into the crowds.

"We can't just release Starbuck," Gillespie complained. He had gone to stand at the second window.

"We can accuse him of bribery, I suppose," Alexander conceded, "but we can't haul him in front of a court-martial looking like he's on his deathbed. Clean him up, let him recover, then we'll decide whether to put him on trial for taking bribes."

"So how do we find our real traitor?" Gillespie asked.

Alexander thought of an old man with long hair and gave an involuntary shudder. "I guess we'll have to sup with the devil, Gillespie." Alexander turned from the window and stared morosely at a map of Virginia that hung on his office wall. Once past Yorktown, he thought, there was nothing to stop the Yankees. They would burst against the defenses of Richmond like a spring tide pushed by an onshore gale. They would surround the city, then strangle it, and what of the Confederacy then? In the west, despite the southern newspapers' attempts to paint a victory, Beauregard had retreated after taking massive casualties at a place called Shiloh. The North was claiming victory there and Alexander feared their claims would prove true. How soon before the North claimed victory here in Virginia as well? "Have you ever thought," he asked Gillespie, "that maybe this is all a waste of effort?"

"How can it be?" Gillespie was puzzled by the question. "We have the moral right. God won't desert us."

"I was forgetting God," Alexander said, then put on his hat and went to find the devil.

T WO SOLDIERS FETCHED STARBUCK FROM HIS CELL. They woke him in the darkness, making him cry aloud in sudden fear as they pulled the blanket off his cot. He was still not properly awake as they hurried him into the corridor. Expecting another interrogation, Starbuck instinctively turned to his right, but one of the soldiers pushed him in the other direction. The prison was sleeping, its corridors smoky from the small flames of the tallow candles that burned every few paces. Starbuck shivered despite the palpable warmth in the spring air. It had been days since Gillespie had last administered croton oil to him, but he was still painfully thin and cemetery-pale. He was no longer retching and he had even managed to eat some prison gruel without his stomach immediately voiding the coarse food, but he felt kitten-weak and hog-filthy, though the ending of his interrogation had at least given him a sliver of hope.

Starbuck was taken to the prison guardroom where a slave was ordered to knock the anklets off his feet. On the guardroom table was a perpetual calendar made of pasteboard cards in a wooden frame.

The cards recorded that it was Monday, April 29, 1862. "How are you feeling, boy?" the sergeant behind the table asked. He was cradling a tin mug in his big hands. "How's your stomach?"

"Empty, raw," Starbuck said.

"Best thing for it today." The sergeant laughed and sipped at the cup before making a wry face. "Parched goober-pea coffee. Tastes like Yankee shit."

The soldiers ordered Starbuck into the prison yard. The absence of the leg chains caused him to lift his feet unnaturally high, making his gait grotesque and clumsy. A black-painted prison coach waited in the yard with its single rear door open and a swaybacked, blinkered horse in the shafts. Starbuck was pushed into the vehicle. "Where am I going?" he asked.

There was no answer. Instead the coach door was slammed on him. There was no handle inside the door and there were no windows in the coach. It was just a felon's van; a wooden box on wheels with a slatted bench on which he sat and groaned. He heard the guards climbing onto the back step of the vehicle as the driver cracked his whip.

The coach lurched forward. Starbuck heard the prison gates creak open, then the clumsy vehicle jolted over the gutter and into the street. He shivered in the lonely darkness, wondering what new indignities were about to be heaped on him.

It was a half hour before the coach stopped and the door was pulled open. "Out, cuffee," one of the guards said, and Starbuck stepped down into the crepuscular dawn and saw he had been fetched to Camp Lee, Richmond's old Central Fair Grounds that lay west of the city. The camp was now the biggest troop depot in the capital. "That way," the guard said and pointed toward the rear of the coach.

Starbuck turned and for a second or two he could not move. At first it was incomprehension that kept him motionless, then, as he realized just what he looked at it in this dawn, a wave of terror froze him.

For there, in the ghost light, was a scaffold.

The gibbet was newly built of raw, clean wood. It was a monstrous thing, gaunt in the gray remnants of night, with a platform twelve feet above the ground. Two posts on the platform supported a square beam ten feet higher still. A rope hung from the beam, its noosed end presumably coiled on the trapdoor. A ladder led from the grass to the platform on which there waited a bearded man in black shirt, black trousers, and stained white jacket. He leaned on one of the posts, smoking a pipe.

A small crowd of uniformed men waited at the foot of the scaffold. They smoked cigars and made small talk, but when Starbuck appeared they fell silent as one by one they turned to watch him. Some of them grimaced, and no wonder, for Starbuck was dressed in a filthy shirt, dirty ragged trousers held up with a frayed piece of knotted string, and clumsy leather brogans that flapped on his feet like butter boxes. His ankles had been worn to bloody scabs by the irons, his hair was matted and filthy, and his new beard was a mess. He stank.

"You're Starbuck?" a mustachioed major barked at him.

"Yes."

"Stand and wait there," the Major said, pointing to a space apart from the small crowd. Starbuck obeyed, then turned in alarm as the coach that had fetched him from the city suddenly lurched away. Was he to leave here in the pine coffin that waited beside the ladder? The Major saw the terror on Starbuck's face and frowned. "It ain't for you, you fool." Relief coursed through Starbuck. It made him feel shaky, almost wanting to cry.

A second carriage arrived as the prison coach pulled away. The newly arrived carriage was an elegant, old-fashioned vehicle with dark varnished panels, gilded axle bosses, and four matching horses. The coach's Negro driver reined in on the far side of the scaffold, pulled on the brake, then climbed down to open the carriage's door. An old man appeared. He was tall and thin, with a great mane of white hair that framed a darkly tanned and deeply lined face. He was not in uniform, but was instead dressed in an elegant black suit. The dawn's light reflected from the man's watch chain and its pendant seals, and from the silver head of his cane. It also glittered from his eyes, which seemed to be staring straight at Starbuck in a fixed gaze that was oddly disturbing. Starbuck stared back, fighting the discomfort of the old man's inspection, and just when it seemed that he was locked into a childish competition to discover who would look away first, a commotion behind Starbuck announced the arrival of the scaffold's victim.

Camp Lee's commandant led the small procession, and after him came the Episcopal chaplain who read aloud from the Twenty-third Psalm. The prisoner followed, helped along by two soldiers.

The prisoner was a big man, fine-looking, with a strong mustache, a clean-shaven chin, and a head of thick dark hair. He was dressed in shirt, trousers, and shoes. His hands were tied in front of him, his legs bore no chains or ropes, yet even so he seemed to be having trouble walking. He limped, and each step was plainly an agony. The crowd fell silent again.

The embarrassment and pain of watching a crippled man walk to his death was made worse when the prisoner tried to climb the ladder. His pinioned hands would have made the climb difficult at the best of times, but the pain in his legs made the ascent almost impossible. The two soldiers helped him as best they could, and the white-jacketed executioner tapped the sparks from his pipe, then leaned down to help the prisoner up the last few rungs. The prisoner had made small noises of agony with each step. Now he limped forward to the trapdoor, and Starbuck saw the executioner duck down to pinion the victim's feet.

The chaplain and the commandant had followed the prisoner to the platform. The sun's first rays were touching the scaffold's crossbeam with a lavish golden light as the commandant unfolded the warrant of execution. " 'In accordance with the sentence passed on you by the Court-Martial lawfully assembled here in Richmond on the sixteenth day of April . . . ' " In the camp's commandant began to read.

"There is no law by which you may do this," the prisoner interrupted the commandant. "I am an American citizen, a patriot, a servant of this country's lawful government!" The prisoner's protest was given in a husky voice that still managed to generate a startling power.

" 'You, Timothy Webster, were sentenced to death for the crime of espionage, carried on unlawfully within the borders of the sovereign Confederate States of America . . . ' "

"I am a citizen of the United States!" Webster roared his defiance, "which alone has authority over this place!"

" 'Which sentence shall now be carried out according to the provisions of law.' " The commandant finished in a hurry, then stepped away from the trapdoor. "Have you anything to say?"

"God bless the United States of America!" Timothy Webster said in his harsh, deep voice. Some of the watching officers had taken off their hats, others half looked away. The hangman had to stand on tiptoe to put the black hood over Webster's head and the noose around his neck. The chaplain's voice was a murmur as he began to recite the Psalm again. The sunlight crept down the upright posts toward the condemned man's hood.

"God save the United States of America!" Webster cried aloud, his voice muffled by the hood, and then the hangman kicked back the bolt that held the trapdoor in its place and there was a gasp from the spectators as the pinewood hatch swung hard away and the prisoner hurtled downward.

It all happened so quickly that Starbuck did not recall the details until later, and even then he was not certain that his mind had not embellished the events. The rope seemed to tighten, the prisoner even checked momentarily, but then the noose seemed to ride up over his hooded face and suddenly, with hands and feet tied like a hog, Webster fell to the ground to leave the hanging rope swinging in the dawn with the black hood caught in its empty noose. Webster screamed with pain as he landed on his fragile, rheumatic ankles. Starbuck shuddered at the sound of the man's pain, while the old white-haired man with the silver-topped cane just stared fixedly at Starbuck.

One of the watching officers turned away, a hand to his mouth. Another braced himself by leaning on a tree. Two or three pulled on flasks. One man crossed himself. The hangman just gaped down through the open hatch.

"Again! Do it again!" the commandant called. "Hurry. Pick him up! Leave him, Doctor." A man, evidently a doctor, had knelt beside Webster, but now backed away uncertainly as two soldiers ran to pick up the fallen man. Webster was sobbing, not from fear, but because of the awful pain in his joints.

"Hurry!" the commandant shouted again. One of the watching officers vomited.

"You will kill me twice!" Webster protested in a voice made tremulous with agony.

"Hurry!" The commandant seemed close to panic.

The soldiers pulled Webster to the ladder. They had to untie his feet and place them one by one on the rungs. Webster inched up, still sobbing with the pain, as the hangman retrieved the noose. One of the spectators reached up with a drawn sword to push the trapdoor shut once more.

The hood had fallen off the noose and the hangman was complaining he could not do his job without the black bag. "It doesn't matter!" the commandant snapped. "Get on with it, for Christ's sake!"

The chaplain was shaking so hard that he could not hold the Bible still. The hangman retied the prisoner's feet, placed the noose back about his neck, then grunted as he tightened the knot beneath the victim's left ear. The chaplain began to say the Lord's Prayer, gabbling the words as though he feared he might forget them if he said the prayer too slowly.

"God bless the United States!" Webster called aloud, though in a voice that was a sob of hurt. He was bent over in pain, but then, in the full wash of the morning sun, he made a supreme effort to beat the agony and to show his killers that he was stronger than they. Inch by inch he forced his crippled, hurt body until he at last stood upright. "God bless the United—"

"Do it!" the commandant screamed.

The hangman hit the bolt and once again the trapdoor banged open and once again the prisoner shot through, only this time the rope snapped taut and the body danced for a second as the neck stretched and snapped. One of the watching officers gasped in shock as the body bounced on the rope's end. Webster had been killed instantly this time, his neck snapped clean so that his canted face seemed to gaze up at the swinging trapdoor that creaked in the early light. Dust sifted down from the platform. The dead man's tongue showed between his lips and then a liquid began to drip from his right shoe.

"Get him down!" the commandant shouted.

The officers turned away, all but a doctor who hurried under the platform to certify the spy's death. Starbuck, wondering why he had been fetched through the city to witness the barbarous execution, turned to stare at the rising sun. He had not seen an open sky for so long. The air felt fresh and clean. A cockerel called in the camp, its cry counterpointing the sound of hammer and nails as soldiers coffined the spy's broken body.

A bony hand fell hard on Starbuck's shoulder. "Come with me, Starbuck, come with me." It was the old white-haired man who had spoken and who now led Starbuck toward his carriage. "Now that our appetite is whetted," the old man said happily, "let us go for breakfast."

A few yards from the gibbet a grave had been dug. The coach rattled by the empty hole, then jolted south across the parade ground and headed toward the city. The old man, hands clasped on his silver cane, smiled all the way. His day, at least, had started well.

Hyde House, where the old man lived, occupied a triangular lot where Brook Avenue cut diagonally across Richmond's grid of streets. The lot was hemmed in by a tall brick wall that was capped with a course of white pitted stone above which a profusion of trees and blossoms showed. Deep inside the unkempt trees, and approached through a metal gate topped with spikes, was a three-story house, grand once, railed around with verandahs on every floor and fronted with an ornate carriage porch. It was not raining, but in the early morning air everything about the house seemed damp. Even the fine blossomed creepers that were draped from the verandah rails drooped disconsolately, while the verandahs themselves had peeling paint and broken balustrades. The wooden front steps up which the old man led Starbuck seemed green and rotted. A slave snatched the varnished front door open an instant before the old man would have walked straight into its heavy panels.

"This is Captain Starbuck," the old man snarled at the pretty young woman who had opened the door. "Show him to his room. His bath is drawn?"

"Yes, massa."

The old man pulled out his watch. "Breakfast in forty-five minutes. Martha will show you where. Go!"

"Sir?" Martha said to Starbuck and beckoned him toward the stairs.

Starbuck had not uttered a single word during the journey, but now, surrounded by the sudden and fading luxuries of this old mansion, he felt his self-assurance drain away. "Sir?" he said to the old man's back.

"Breakfast in forty-four minutes!" the old man said angrily, then disappeared through a door.

"Sir?" Martha said again, and Starbuck let the girl lead him upstairs to a wide and lavish bedroom. The room had been elegant once, but now its fine wallpaper had been spotted and stained by damp, and its lavish carpet was moth-eaten and faded. The bed was draped with threadbare tapestries on which, laid out as carefully as though they were a suit of the finest evening clothes, Starbuck's own Confederate uniform lay. The coat had been laundered and darned, the belt was polished, and his boots, which stood fitted with trees at the bed's foot, had been mended and waxed. Even Oliver Wendell Holmes's overcoat was there. The slave threw open a door that led to a small dressing room where a hip bath stood steaming in front of a coal fire. "You want me to stay, massa?" Martha asked timidly.

"No. No." Starbuck could scarcely believe what was happening to him. He walked into the dressing room and put a tentative hand into the water. It was so hot he could scarcely bear its touch. A pile of white towels waited on a cane chair, while a straight razor, soap, and a shaving brush stood beside a white china bowl on a washstand.

"If you leave your old clothes outside the door . . ." Martha said, but did not finish the sentence.

"You'll burn them?" Starbuck suggested.

"I'll come back for you in forty minutes, massa," she said, and dropped a curtsey before backing through the door and closing it behind her.

One hour later Starbuck was shaved, scrubbed, dressed, and filled with eggs, ham, and good white bread. Even the coffee had been real, while the cigar that he smoked after the meal was fragrant and mild. The richness of the food had threatened to provoke another spasm of sickness, but he had taken the meal slowly at first, then ravenously when his stomach did not rebel. The old man had scarcely spoken throughout breakfast, except to mock and deride paragraphs in the morning newspapers. He was, to Starbuck's curious gaze, a creature as extraordinary as he seemed malevolent. His house slaves were plainly frightened of him. Two girls served the meal, both as light-skinned and attractive as Martha. Starbuck wondered whether he was just in a state to find all women desirable, but the old man saw him look at one of the two slaves and confirmed his judgment. "I can't abide ugly things round the house, Starbuck. If a man has to own women, he might as well possess the prettiest, and I can afford them. I sell them when they're twenty-five. Keep a woman too long and she fancies she knows your life better than you do yourself. Buy them young, keep them docile, sell them sharp. There lies happiness. Come into the library."

The old man led the way through double doors into a room that was pure magnificence, though a magnificence that had been allowed to decay horribly. Beautifully carved bookcases reached from the hardwood floor to the decorated plaster ceiling twelve feet above, but the plaster was crumbling and the gold leaf on the bookcases was worn away, and the leather-bound books had spines hanging loose. Old tables were littered with books swollen with moisture and the whole sad room reeked of damp. "My name is death," the old man said in his beguiling voice.

"Death?" Starbuck could not hide his surprise.

"Small D, E, apostrophe, A, T, H. French origin: de'Ath. My father came here with Lafayette, never went home. Nothing to go back to. He was a bastard, Starbuck, born to the wrong side of an aristocratic whore's blanket. Whole family got what they deserved in the

French terror. Heads chopped off by Doctor Guillotine's splendid device. Ha!" De'Ath settled behind the largest table, which was a mess of books, papers, inkwells, and pens. "The excellent Doctor Guillotine's machine made me the Marquis of something or other, except under the wisdom of our former country we are not allowed to use titles. Do you believe in that Jeffersonian nonsense that all men are created equal, Starbuck?"

"I was brought up to believe it, sir.".

"I am not interested in what nonsenses were thrust into your infant head, but rather what nonsenses are lodged there. Do you believe all men are created equal?"

"Yes, sir."

"Then you are a fool. It is obvious to the meanest intelligence that some men are created wiser than others, some stronger, and a fortunate few more ruthless than the rest, from which we might fairly deduce that our Creator intended us to live within the comfortable confines of a hierarchy. Make all men equal, Starbuck, and you elevate foolishness into wisdom and lose the ability to tell the one from the other. I told Jefferson that often enough, but he never listened to other men's sense. Sit down. Tap your ash onto the floor. When I die it will all rot away." He waved a thin hand to show that he was talking about the house and its glorious but decaying contents. "I don't believe in inherited wealth. If a man can't make his own money, then he should not have the disposition of another man's fortune. You have been ill-treated."

"Yes, I have."

"It was your misfortune to be considered a Confederate. If we capture a northerner and think him a spy we don't beat him in case the northerners beat our spies. We don't mind hanging them, but we won't beat them. Foreigners we treat according to what we desire from their countries, but our own people we treat abominably. Major Alexander is a fool."

"Alexander?"

"Of course, you did not meet Alexander. Who questioned you?"

"A little bastard called Gillespie."

De'Ath grunted. "A pale limpid thing who learned his techniques from his father's lunatics. He still believes you're guilty."

"Of taking bribes?" Starbuck asked scornfully.

"I should hope you did take bribes. How else can anything ever get achieved in a republic of equals? No, Gillespie thinks you're a spy."

"He's a fool."

"For once I agree with you. Did you enjoy the hanging? I did. They botched the job, didn't they? That's what happens when you entrust responsibility to cretins. They're supposed to be our equals, but they can't even hang a man properly! How difficult can it be? I daresay you or I would get it right first time, Starbuck, but you and I were endowed by our Creator with brains, and not with a skullful of stale semolina. Webster suffered from rheumatic fever. The worst punishment would have been to let him live in a damp place, but we were merciful and strung him up. He was reputed to have been the North's best and brightest spy, but he can't have been very bright if we managed to catch him and bodge him to death, eh? Now we have to catch another one and bodge him to death as well." De'Ath climbed to his feet and walked to a grimy window through which he stared at the thick damp vegetation that screened the house. "President Davis has appointed me, *ex officio*, to be his witch-finder general or rather to be the man who rids our country of traitors. You think the task is possible?"

"I wouldn't know, sir."

"Of course it isn't possible. You can't draw a line on the map and say henceforth everyone on this side of the line will be loyal to a new country! We must have hundreds of people who secretly wish for the North to win. Hundreds of thousands if you count the blacks. Most of the white ones are women and preachers, that kind of harmless fool, but a few of them are dangerous. My job is to cull the truly dangerous and use the rest to send false messages to Washington. Read this." De'Ath crossed the room and tossed a piece of paper into Starbuck's lap.

The paper was very thin and covered with block capitals that had been written very small, but with a huge ambition to betray. Even

Starbuck, who knew nothing of the army's dispositions, realized that if this message reached McClellan's headquarters it would be of immense use. He said as much.

"If McClellan believes it, yes," de'Ath allowed, "but our job is to make sure he doesn't get the chance. You see who it's addressed to?"

Starbuck turned the page over and read his brother's name. For a few seconds he stared at the ascription in sheer disbelief, then he cursed softly as he understood just why he had spent the last few weeks in jail. "Gillespie believed I wrote this?"

"He wants to believe it, but he's a fool," de'Ath said. "Your brother was a prisoner here in Richmond, was he not?"

"Yes."

"Did you see him when he was here?"

"No," Starbuck said, but he was thinking that Adam had seen James during his imprisonment, and he lifted the letter again and looked closely at the handwriting. It was disguised, but even so he felt a sinking fear that this was his friend's writing.

"What are you thinking?" De'Ath sensed something in Starbuck's manner.

"I was thinking, sir, that James is ill-suited for matters of deception and guile," Starbuck lied smoothly. In truth he had been wondering if Adam was his friend anymore. Adam could surely have visited him in jail, could even have stopped Gillespie's torture, yet as far as Starbuck knew Adam had not tried to do either of those things. Was Adam so horrified by Starbuck introducing Sally into a respectable home that he had cut off his friendship? Then Starbuck imagined Adam being pushed up the scaffold's ladder and standing on the trapdoor while the hangman clumsily pinioned his ankles and tugged the hood over his head and, however strained the friendship, Starbuck knew he could not countenance that sight. He told himself that just because Adam had talked to James did not make Adam a traitor. A score of Confederate officers must have visited the prisoners in Castle Lightning.

"Who does your brother know here in Richmond?" De'Ath's voice was still suspicious.

"I don't know, sir. James was a prominent lawyer in Boston before the war, so I guess he must have met plenty of southern attorneys?" Starbuck made his voice sound innocent and speculative. He dared not reveal Adam's name, else his friend would be taken to the damp cells at Castle Godwin and stuffed with Gillespie's croton oil.

De'Ath glowered silently at Starbuck for a few seconds, then lit a cigar, tossing the spill into the dirt that littered the grate. "Let me tell you what is about to happen, Starbuck. Let me tell you the war's grim news. McClellan pours men and guns into his siege works at Yorktown. Within a day or two we shall retreat. We have no choice. That means the northern army will be free to advance on Richmond. Johnston believes he can stop them at the Chickahominy River. We shall see." De'Ath sounded dubious. "By this time next week"— de'Ath blew a plume of smoke toward an oil painting so darkly varnished that Starbuck could hardly see the picture beneath—"Richmond may well be abandoned."

That made Starbuck sit up straight. "Abandoned!"

"You think we're winning this war? My God, man, do you believe those tales of victory at Shiloh? We lost that battle. Thousands of men dead. New Orleans has surrendered, Fort Macon is taken, Savannah is threatened." De'Ath growled the list of Confederate reverses, astonishing and dispiriting Starbuck. "The North has even closed its recruiting offices, Starbuck, and sent their recruiters back to their battalions. You know why? Because they know the war is won. The rebellion is over. All that remains for the North to do now is to take Richmond and mop up the pieces. That's what they think and maybe they're right. How long do you think the South will survive without Richmond's factories?"

Starbuck did not reply. There was nothing to say. He had not dreamed that the Confederacy was so precarious. In prison he had heard rumors of defeats at the southern and western extremities of the Confederate States, but he had never guessed that the North was now so close to victory that it had closed its recruiting offices and returned the recruiting officers to their regiments. All the North needed to do now was capture Richmond's hellish tangle of blast fur-

naces and molten metal, of slave quarters and coal dumps, of shrieking whistles and crashing steam hammers, and the rebellion was history.

"But maybe we can yet win." De'Ath broke into Starbuck's
gloomy thoughts. "Though not if spies like that bastard are betraying
us." He gestured toward the letter on Starbuck's lap. "We found that
letter hidden in Webster's hotel room. He never had a chance to send
it north, but sooner or later another man will get the news across the
lines."

"So what do you want of me?" Starbuck asked. Not a name, he
prayed, anything but a name.

"Why are you fighting?" de'Ath suddenly asked.

Starbuck, taken aback by the question, just shrugged.

"Do you believe in slavery as an institution?" de'Ath challenged
him.

It was a question Starbuck had never really considered because
growing up in the Reverend Elial Starbuck's house meant that he had
never needed to consider it. Slavery was plain evil and that was the
end of the matter, and that attitude was so deeply ingrained in Starbuck that even after a year in the Confederacy he felt uncomfortable
in the company of slaves. They made him feel guilty. Yet he was also
sure that the real argument was not about whether slavery was right
or wrong; most people knew it was wrong, but just what the hell
could be done about it, and that dilemma had baffled the best and
most benign minds of America for years. The question was simply
too deep for a glib answer and, once again, Starbuck merely
shrugged.

"Were you unhappy with the government of the United States?"

Before the war Starbuck had never given the government of the
United States a moment's thought. "Not particularly," he said.

"Do you believe there are vital constitutional principles at stake?"

"No."

"So why are you fighting?"

Again Starbuck just shrugged. It was not that he did not have an
answer, but rather that his answer seemed so very inadequate. He

had begun fighting for the South as a gesture of his own independence from an overpowering father, but in time it had become something more than mere rebellion. The outcast had found a home, and that was enough for Starbuck. "I've fought well enough," he answered belligerently, "not to need to say why I fight."

"And you still want to fight for the South?" de'Ath asked in a skeptical voice. "Even after what Gillespie did to you?"

"I'll fight for K Company, the Faulconer Legion."

"Maybe you won't get a chance to. Maybe it's all too late." De'Ath drew on his cigar. A nub of ash fell from its tip to smear his coat. "Maybe this war is over, Starbuck, but on the chance that we might yet see these bastards off our land, then will you help?"

Starbuck nodded cautiously.

De'Ath blew smoke across the room. "Tomorrow's newspapers will report that the charges against you are dropped and that you have been released from prison. You need that in print so that your brother believes your story."

"My brother?" Starbuck was confused.

"Think about it, Starbuck." De'Ath lowered himself into a porter's chair that stood beside the hearth. The chair's capacious hood shrouded his face in shadows. "There is a spy, a very capable spy, who has been in contact with your brother. He has been sending intelligence through Webster, but Webster's illness cut the flow of information and so the North sent two fools called Lewis and Scully to restore it. Lewis and Scully are now captured, Webster is bodged to death, and the North must be wondering just how in the name of God they are to get in touch with their man again. Then, out of the blue, you turn up in their lines carrying the spy's message. Or rather you turn up with a false message that I shall concoct. You will tell your brother that you are disenchanted with the South, that your experiences in jail have disabused whatever romantic notions you once had about supporting the rebellion. You will tell him that you allowed your disenchantment to be known in Richmond, which is why some person unknown passed you a letter in the hope that you would deliver it to your brother. You will then volunteer to return to

Richmond to serve as a messenger for any further communications. You will convince your brother that your newfound passion for the North has persuaded you to take Webster's place. It's my belief that your brother will believe you and that he will tell you how you may get in touch with this spy, and you, if you are truthful about serving the Confederacy and not your native North, will then tell me. Thus we shall set a trap, Mr. Starbuck, and give ourselves the exquisite pleasure of watching a fool bodge another spy to death."

Starbuck thought of Adam hanging, his golden head canted at the rope's stark angle, his tongue swollen between parted teeth, his urine dripping from his swinging boots. "Suppose my brother doesn't trust me?" Starbuck asked.

"Then you will still have delivered some false information that will help our cause and you can slip back here in your own good time. Conversely you can betray us, of course, by persuading your brother's superiors that we are a beaten force reduced to cavilling tricks of intelligence in an effort to survive. I must confess, Mr. Starbuck, that the North so outnumbers us at present that we shall probably not survive, but I would like to think we shall play our hand to the very last card." De'Ath paused, drawing on his cigar so that its tip glowed bright in the dark of the chair's hood. "If we are to be beaten," he went on softly, "then let us at least give the bastards a mauling that will give them nightmares for years to come."

"How do I cross the lines?"

"There are men called pilots who escort travelers through the lines. I'll provide you with one of the best, and all you have to do is deliver to your brother a letter I shall write. It will be in the same disguised handwriting as the letter Webster was carrying, only this letter will be a tissue of lies. We shall weave fantasies of imaginary regiments, of cavalry sprung like seeded dragons' teeth from the soil, of guns innumerable. We shall convince McClellan that he faces a vengeful horde of serried thousands. We shall, in brief, attempt a deception. So will you be my deceiver, Mr. Starbuck?" De'Ath's eyes glittered from under the hood of the porter's chair as he waited for Starbuck's answer.

"When will you want me to go?" Starbuck asked.

"Tonight." De'Ath offered Starbuck a skull smile. "You may enjoy the amenities of this house till then."

"Tonight!" Starbuck had somehow imagined he would have a few days to prepare.

"Tonight," de'Ath insisted. "It will take two or three days to get you safely through the lines, so the quicker you leave the better."

"There's something I want first," Starbuck said.

"Of me?" De'Ath sounded dangerous, like a man unaccustomed to making bargains. "Gillespie? Is that it? You want revenge on that pathetic creature?"

"I'll work my revenge on him in my own time," Starbuck said. "No, I need to make some visits in the city."

"Who?" de'Ath demanded.

Starbuck offered the ghost of a smile. "Women."

De'Ath grimaced. "You don't like Martha?" He gestured irritably toward the back of the house where, presumably, his slaves were quartered. Starbuck said nothing and de'Ath scowled. "And if I let you make your visits, will you carry my message to your brother?"

"Yes, sir."

"Then you may see your doxies tonight," de'Ath said sourly, "and afterward ride eastward. Agreed?"

"Agreed," Starbuck said, though in truth he intended to play a much more difficult game, a game he did not intend should lead to a dawn gibbet with a friend twitching at the rope's end. "Agreed," he lied again, then waited for the night.

It had taken the northern troops four weeks to build the siege works needed to destroy the rebel earthworks at Yorktown. Major General McClellan was an engineer by training and a siege enthusiast by avocation, and he planned to use the siege as a demonstration of his country's implacable efficiency. The eyes of the world were on his campaign; newspapermen from Europe and America were attached to his army while military observers from all the great powers rode with his headquarters. At Yorktown, where the United States had first made itself free, the world would witness the flowering of a continent's military prowess. It would see a siege of ruthless ferocity, engineered by the world's new Napoleon.

First the roads from Fort Monroe to Yorktown had needed to be corduroyed so that the army's vast train of wagons could reach the siege ground opposite the Yorktown defenses. Hundreds of axemen felled and trimmed thousands of trees. Teamsters then dragged the trunks out of the woods to where the logs were laid lengthwise on the treacherous mud roads. A second layer of logs was laid crosswise to form the roadway itself. In some places the new log roads still sank beneath the glutinous red mud and yet more layers of newly cut trunks needed to be added until at last the guns and ammunition could be dragged forward.

Fifteen artillery batteries were built. The early part of the work was done at night when the laborers were safe from rebel sharpshooters. At each of the fifteen sites the workmen threw up an earth bank six feet high, then faced its steep sides with mats of woven wood that would stop the earth sliding away in the incessant rain. The walls of each battery were fifteen feet thick, a depth necessary to stop and smother an exploding rebel shell. Protecting the front of each battery was a ditch from which the material for the massive wall had been excavated, and in front of each ditch the engineers laid abatis of tangled branches. Any rebel attack trying to assault a battery would first have to force a way through the chest-high, thorn-infested tangles, then wade through the quagmire in the bed of the flooded ditch before climbing the wall's slick face to where a line of sandbags formed the parapet, and all that time the attackers would be under the fire of the battery's guns and enfiladed by the cannon fire from the flanking batteries north and south.

Once the walls, ditches, and abatis were finished the batteries were readied for the guns. The smaller guns, the twelve-pounders and four-inch rifles, merely needed a timber-faced ramp up which they could recoil after each shot, but the large guns, the great cannons that would blast the rebel defenses into bloody ruin, needed more careful work. Foundations were dug behind the embrasures, then filled with rubble stone brought from Fort Monroe in heavy wagons. The engineers then laid an aggregate of stone, sand, and cement that was leveled to make a rock-hard platform, though before the concrete could set hard a great curve of metal rail was sunk into its surface. The rail formed a semicircle, its open side facing the enemy. Just inside the embrasure a metal post was sunk into the gun platform so that the curved rail described an arc like a compass line around the post's protruding stud.

The post's stud and the curved rail were now ready to take a gun carriage. The base of the carriage was simply a pair of cast-iron beams that sloped upward from front to back. Beneath the rear of the twin beams was a pair of metal wheels which fitted into the curved rail, while at the front was the socket that slid over the post's greased stud, so that now the whole gun carriage could be swung around on the hinge of the post. Mounted on top of the beams was the gun carriage itself which, when the gun was fired, slid back along the beams. The friction of the tons of metal crashing back along the twin beams was sufficient to soak up the massive recoil. Last of all the huge guns themselves were brought to the batteries. The biggest guns were too heavy for the corduroyed roads and had to be fetched from Fort Monroe on flat-bottomed boats that crept up the peninsula's creeks at the top of the spring tides. The guns were transferred from the barges onto sling carts that consisted of little more than a pair of wheels so vast that the heavy gun barrels could be suspended from their axle. The weird, gaunt vehicles rolled up to the batteries and the mighty cannon were winched carefully down until their trunnions dropped into the sockets of the waiting carriages. The job had to be done at night, yet even so the rebels detected the activity and sent shell after shell screaming across the waterlogged ground in an effort to frustrate the Yankee progress.

The biggest guns were monsters more than thirteen feet long and over eight tons in weight. They fired a shell that was eight inches in width and weighed two hundred pounds. A dozen more guns fired shells a hundred pounds in weight, and even those smaller guns were larger than any of the cannon concealed behind the rebel embrasures.

Yet still McClellan was not satisfied and he decreed that the siege bombardment could not commence until he had brought up the North's largest mortars, the largest over ten tons in weight. The mortars were short-barreled, wide-mouthed guns that squatted on their wide wooden bases like monstrous cooking pots and could blast shells weighing two hundred and twenty pounds into a high looping trajectory that would drop the tumbling missiles almost vertically into the Confederate lines. The big guns on their traversing carriages were designed to batter down the rebel ramparts with direct fire while the mortar bombs exploded behind the crumbling walls to fill the rebel bastions with high-explosive death. McClellan planned to keep up the bombardment for twelve terrible hours, and only when the great guns had finished their awful work would the northern infantry be asked to cross the spring grass that grew between the lines.

The guns were at last emplaced. Each of the batteries had been equipped with stone-lined underground chambers and day by day those magazines were filled with six hundred wagonloads of ammunition brought from the ships at Fort Monroe. Other engineers sapped forward to dig the parallel, a trench placed ahead of the fifteen batteries that would serve as the launching point for the infantry attack. None of this was achieved without loss. Rebel sharpshooters sniped from their lines, mortar fire sometimes fell among the diggers, cannon fire might rip away the thin wicker shield protecting a working party from the enemy's sight, yet inch by inch and yard by yard the Federal siege lines took shape. Bombproof shelters were dug for the gunners so that they might survive the Confederate counterbattery fire, ranges were measured precisely and the heavy guns laid with a mathematical exactitude. If all the guns fired together, and McClellan was determined that they should, then each northern volley would throw more than three tons of explosive shells into the rebel lines. "We shall keep that weight of fire going for twelve hours, gentlemen," McClellan informed the eager foreign observers on the night before the bombardment. McClellan reckoned he could soak the rebel lines with more than two thousand tons of fiery metal and that at the end of that skyborne slaughter the surviving rebel defenders would be reeling and dizzy, easy meat for the northern infantry. "We shall give the seceshers a half day's medicine, gentlemen," McClellan boasted, "then see what kind of defiance they can show. We shall see them beaten by tomorrow afternoon!"

That night, almost as if they knew what fate was being planned for them in the morning, the rebel guns opened fire on the completed northern lines. Shot after shot screamed through the rainy darkness, the burning fuses scratching red lines of fire against the night. Most of the shells exploded harmlessly in the waterlogged ground, but a few found targets. A tethered mule team screamed in pain, a tent in the lines of the 20th Massachusetts was hit and two of its occupants were killed, the first men of the battalion to die in action since their disastrous baptism of fire on Ball's Bluff. And still the rebel shells whipped through the night until, as suddenly as the bombardment had begun, the guns fell silent and left the darkness to barking dogs, whinnying horses, and the calls of the mockingbirds.

The next day dawned clear. There were clouds in the north and the local farmers swore that rain would come soon, yet the early sun shone bright. Smoke from ten thousand cooking fires rose from the tented encampments of the northern infantry. The men were cheerful, anticipating an easy victory. The gunners would wreck the enemy defenses, then the infantry would stroll across the intervening ground to dig the survivors out of the smoking rubble. It would be a textbook assault, proof that an American general and an American army could achieve in twelve hours what Europeans had bungled in as many weeks in the Crimea. McClellan had been an observer of the Crimean sieges and was determined that the French and British officers with his army would be taught a quiet but unmistakable lesson this day.

Deep in the brand-new gun emplacements the Yankee gunners made their last preparations. The big cannon were loaded, friction primers were pushed into touchholes, and artillery officers examined their targets through telescopes. Over a hundred heavy guns waited for the signal to launch their terrible destruction on the Confederate defenses. A month's hard work had been invested in this moment, and to many northerners waiting in their bastions it seemed as if the world held its breath. In the York River the gunboats edged nearer the shore, ready to add their own cannon fire to the slaughtering weight of the army's bombardment. A small wind lifted the ships' ensigns and carried the smoke of their steam engines east across the water.

A half mile behind the Yankee gun emplacement, hidden by a grove of pine trees that had somehow escaped the axes of the road builders, a curious yellow form took monstrous shape. Men struggled to pour carboys of sulfuric acid into vats half filled with iron turnings and still more men worked the giant pumps that pushed the hydrogen formed in those vats along rubberized canvas hoses that led to the great, yellow-skinned balloon that slowly swelled to its full bulbous shape above the trees. The balloon's inflation had begun in the dark so that it would be ready soon after sunrise, and by dawn the huge device needed a crew of thirty men to keep it earthbound. Two men climbed into the balloon's wicker basket. One was Professor Lowe, the famous aeronaut and balloonist whose skills had made the vehicle possible, the other was General Heintzelman, who was being carried aloft so that his seasoned military eye could spy on the destruction wrought by the guns. Heintzelman was looking forward to the experience. He would watch the guns work, then he would telegraph to McClellan when he saw the rebel lines break apart and flee westward in panic. Professor Lowe tested the telegraph equipment, then shouted for the crew to let the vehicle go.

Slowly, like a stately yellow moon rising above the trees, the balloon lifted. Fifteen hundred feet of cable tethered the vehicle to a massive winch that slowly unwound as the aeronauts climbed higher and higher into the clear patch of sky. The sight of the balloon normally provoked a flurry of long-range cannon fire from the rebel lines, but this morning there was only silence. "Saying their prayers, maybe?" Professor Lowe suggested happily.

"They need to," General Heintzelman answered. He drummed his fingers on the edge of the balloon's basket. He had made a wager with his chief of staff that the rebel defenders would break in six hours, not twelve. The basket swayed and creaked, but it was not, Heintzelman decided, an unpleasant sensation. Better than most sea voyages, that was certain. As the balloon passed eight hundred feet the General trained his telescope on the western horizon where he could see the dark smoky smear that was the rebel capital. He could even see the scars of earth where fresh defenses had been carved into the hills around the city. "The serpents' lair, Professor!" Heintzelman proclaimed.

"Indeed, General, and we shall scour the vipers soon enough!"

Heintzelman abandoned his sightseeing and instead stared down at the enemy lines that lay so clear beneath him. He felt hugely powerful, granted a godlike view of his enemies' secrets. He could see their batteries, and the trenches leading from their bombproof shelters, and the tents hidden behind earth walls. War would never be the same again, Heintzelman thought, not when there was no hiding place left. He trained his telescope on one of the bigger enemy gun batteries. None of the Yankee guns would open fire until Heintzelman was ready to report on the effects of their fire and that moment, he decided, had now come. "I think we're ready to communicate, Professor," the General said.

"Not many cooking fires, General," Lowe said, nodding toward the rebel encampments where a handful of shabby tents showed among the ragged, turf-covered shelters. A few fires smoked in the lines, but very few, and no smoke at all showed from the tin chimneys sticking out of the earth shelters by the batteries.

Heintzelman stared into the gun battery. A rebel flag stirred on its flagstaff, but no gunners were visible. Were they expecting the bombardment and already under shelter? He raised the telescope to search the encampment. He could see where horses had been tethered and where limbers had left the imprint of their wheels on the grass, but he could see no men.

"What shall we tell them?" Lowe asked. The Professor had a hand poised over the balloon's telegraph machine which communicated to the ground by a wire that ran down the tethering cable. A second telegraph machine waited at the balloon's earthbound station to relay the aeronauts' news to General McClellan's headquarters. McClellan himself had stayed in bed, content to let his gunners do their work without his presence.

An aide woke the Young Napoleon two hours after sunrise. "We have a report, sir, from the balloon."

"So?" The General resented being woken.

"The enemy, sir, is gone."

McClellan peered at his watch on the bedside table, then leaned over and pulled back a shutter. He flinched from the bright sunlight, then turned again to the aide. "What did you say?"

"The enemy lines, sir, they are deserted." The aide was Louis Philippe Albert d'Orleans, the Count of Paris, come to America in the spirit of Lafayette to help restore America's unity, and for a moment he wondered whether his English was at fault. "The rebels have retreated, sir," he said as clearly as he could. "The lines are empty."

"Who says?" McClellan asked angrily.

"General Heintzelman is in the balloon's gondola, sir, with Professor Lowe."

"They're dreaming. Dreaming!" The General could not abide such stupidity. How could the rebels have retreated? Only last night they had lit up the sky with their cannonade! The gun flashes had flickered like summer lighting on the western horizon, the fuses had seared the sky with lines of airborne fire, and the explosions had echoed dark across the waterlogged fields. The General slammed the shutter hard against the light and waved his aristocratic aide back toward the door. Downstairs the telegraph machine clattered with more news from the balloonists, but the General did not want to know. He wanted another hour's sleep. "Wake me at eight o'clock," he ordered. "And tell the guns to open fire!"

"Yes, sir, of course, sir." The Count of Paris backed quietly from the room, closed the door, then allowed himself to sigh in disbelief at the General's obtuseness.

The gunners waited. Behind them, high in the sky, the yellow balloon tugged at its tether. The sun went behind cloud and the first spots of rain pattered on the balloon's rubberized skin. A dozen foreign military attaches and a score of newspapermen waited in the largest Federal batteries for the order to open fire, but though the guns were laid and loaded and the primers ready, no order came from the balloon.

Instead a small cavalry picket rode forward from the Federal lines. The dozen horsemen were spread out in a long skirmish line in case an enemy gun crammed with grapeshot or canister was fired at them. They advanced very cautiously, stopping every few paces while their officer gazed at the enemy works through his telescope. The horses lowered their heads to crop at the luscious long grass that had grown undisturbed in the space between the two armies.

The cavalry moved on again. Here and there a sentry was visible on the enemy redoubts, but the sentries did not move even when hit by the bullets of northern sharpshooters. The sentries were men of straw, guarding abandoned earthworks, for in the night General Johnston had ordered Magruder's defenders to retreat toward Richmond. The rebels had gone silently, abandoning their guns, their tents, their fires, abandoning whatever could not be carried on their backs.

General McClellan, awake at last to the truth of the day, ordered a pursuit, but no one in the northern army was prepared for sudden action. The cavalry horses were grazing, while the cavalrymen were playing cards and listening to the rain drum on the sides of their tents. The only troops ready for action were the artillerymen, and their targets had melted away in the night.

The rain fell harder as the northern infantry took possession of the abandoned lines. The cavalry at last saddled their horses, but the detailed orders for the pursuit were lacking and so the horsemen did not move. McClellan, meanwhile, was composing his dispatch to the northern capital. Yorktown, the General told Washington, had fallen in a brilliant display of northern soldiering. He claimed that a hundred thousand rebels with five hundred guns had been evicted from their lines, enabling the march upon the enemy capital to be resumed. There would be more desperate battles, he warned, but for this day at least, God had smiled upon the North.

Magruder's men, unpursued and unmolested, marched west while the Young Napoleon sat down to his belated lunch. "We have a victory," he told his aides. "Thank God Almighty, we have a victory."

De'Ath gave Starbuck his last instructions in the hallway of the decaying Richmond house. Rain streamed from broken gutters and cascaded off the porch roof; it dripped from the thick foliage in the garden and puddled on the sandy driveway where de'Ath's ancient carriage waited. The coach's gilded axle bosses reflected the dim light cast by the flickering lanterns on the porch. "The coach will take you to your ladies," de'Ath said with a sour twist on the last word, "but you will not keep the coachman waiting beyond midnight. At that time he will take you to a rendezvous with a man named Tyler. Tyler is the pilot who will take you through the lines. This is the pass to get you out of the city." De'Ath handed Starbuck one of the familiar brown paper passports. "Tyler's the man to pilot you back too. If you come back."

"I shall come back, sir."

"If there's anything to come back to. Listen!" The old man gestured toward the road which lay beyond his garden's high, stone-capped wall, and Starbuck heard the sound of wheels and hooves. The traffic had been thick ever since the news of Yorktown's abandonment had reached the city and plunged Richmond into panicked flight. Those who had the money had hired carts or carriages, piled them with their luggage, and set off for the state's southern counties, while those people unable to carry their treasures to safety were burying them in their back yards. The hallways of the government offices were stacked high with boxes of official papers addressed to Columbia, South Carolina, which would be the next capital of the Confederacy should Richmond fall, while in the Byrd Street depot of the Richmond and Petersburg Railway there was a locomotive waiting with a full head of steam and a train of armored boxcars, ready to evacuate the Confederacy's stack of gold. Even the President's wife, it was rumored, was readying to take her children away from the advancing Yankees. "Thought she would," de'Ath had commented sourly when that news was brought to Hyde House. "The woman has the breeding of a fishwife."

Now, in the rainy darkness, de'Ath made certain that Starbuck had the false letter which the old man had concocted that afternoon. The letter, in a handwriting that imitated the block capitals of the document found in Webster's hotel room, reported a massive concentration of rebel troops in Richmond. The letter was sewn into a waterproof oilcloth pouch that was concealed in the waistband of Starbuck's trousers. "I have it, sir," Starbuck said.

"Then God be with you," de'Ath said abruptly, and turned away.

Starbuck guessed he would get no other farewell than that brief benediction and so he pulled Oliver Wendell Holmes's coat around his shoulders, crammed on his slouch hat, and ran through the rain to the waiting carriage. He wore no weapons. He had abandoned carrying a sword after his first battle, he had left his rifle with Sergeant Truslow, and the fine ivory-handled revolver which he had taken from Ethan Ridley's corpse at Manassas had been stolen while he was in prison. Starbuck would have liked to carry a revolver, but de'Ath had advised against it. "Your object is to get through the lines, not to be mistaken for an infiltrator. Go unarmed, keep your hands held high, and tell lies like a good lawyer."

"How does a lawyer lie?"

"With passion, Mr. Starbuck, and with a self-inflicted belief, albeit temporary, that the facts he is reciting are the very stuff of God's own truth. You have to believe in a lie, and the way to believe is to convince yourself that the lie is a shortcut to the good. If telling the truth will not help a client, then don't tell the truth. The good is the client's survival, the lie is the servant of the good. Your lies are the servants of the Confederacy's survival, and I pray God you desire that survival as much as I do myself."

De'Ath's Negro driver was on the coach's box, swathed there in a multiplicity of coats and with his head covered by a canvas hood. "Where to, massa?" the man called.

"Just go down Marshall. I'll tell you when to stop," Starbuck said, then climbed inside as the great vehicle lurched forward. The coach's seats were of cracked hide and were leaking horsehair. Starbuck lit himself a cigar from the shielded lantern that dimly illuminated the coach's interior, then he eased up one of the leather roller blinds. The coach's progress was slow, for the coming of night had scarcely diminished the evacuation traffic. Starbuck waited till they had passed Thirteenth Street and then he pulled down the window and shouted at the driver to stop outside the Medical College of Virginia. He had deliberately stopped a good distance away from his destination so that the driver could not report to de'Ath which house he had visited.

"Just wait here," he ordered, then jumped down to the roadway and hurried two blocks down Marshall before turning up Twelfth Street. The house he wanted lay on the far side of Clay Street, a big house, one of the most lavish in all Richmond, and Starbuck slowed down as he approached the house for he was uncertain how best to approach this business.

He understood well enough the trap that de'Ath was laying, but he was unwilling to let Adam walk into that trap. If indeed the traitor was Adam. Starbuck had no proof, only a suspicion that his erstwhile friend's distaste for the war could easily have been transformed into betrayal, and that Adam's friendship with James could easily have provided a means for that betrayal to be carried out.

If, indeed, "betrayal" was the right word. Because if the spy was Adam, then he was only being loyal to the country of his birth, just as Starbuck was now being loyal to a friendship. That friendship might have been tested, it might even have been broken, but even so Starbuck could not cold-bloodedly allow the trap to be sprung. He would give Adam his warning.

And so he crossed the street and climbed the steps of the Faulconer town house. He pulled the big brass handle and heard the house bell jangle deep in the servants' quarters. Starbuck had lived in this house once, back when he had first come to Richmond and when Washington Faulconer had been his ally and not his enemy.

The door opened. Polly, one of the maids, gaped at the soaking wet figure on the top step. "Mr. Starbuck?"

"Hello, Polly. I was hoping young Mr. Faulconer was at home."

"He's not here, massa," Polly said, and then, as Starbuck moved to step in out of the rain, she raised a frightened hand to stop him.

"It's all right, Polly," Starbuck tried to soothe her fears. "I just want to write a note and leave it here for Mr. Adam."

"No, massa." Polly obstinately shook her head. "You're not to be let in. Mr. Adam's orders."

"Adam said that?" Starbuck would have believed it if the prohibition had come from Washington Faulconer, but not of Adam.

"If you ever come, you're to be turned away. Mr. Adam said so," Polly insisted. "I'm sorry."

"It's all right, Polly," Starbuck said. He looked past her to see that the pictures which had graced the famous curving staircase had all been taken down. There had been a fine portrait of Adam's sister Anna on the wall facing the door, but now there was just a square of lighter-colored wallpaper. "Can you tell me where Mr. Adam is, Polly? I only want to talk with him. Nothing else."

"He's not here, massa." Polly tried to close the door, but then a new voice spoke from behind her.

"Adam has been ordered back to the army," the voice said. It was a woman's voice and Starbuck peered into the shadowy recesses of the hall to see a dark, tall figure standing silhouetted in the doorway of the downstairs parlor.

"I'm obliged to you, ma'am," Starbuck said. "Is he with his father's troops? Or with General Johnston?"

"With General Johnston." The speaker came out of the shadows and Starbuck saw it was Julia Gordon. He pulled off his hat. "It seems," Julia went on, "that since Yorktown's abandonment, it is a case of all hands to the pumps. Do you think we are about to be over-run by vengeful northerners, Mr. Starbuck?"

"I'm sure I don't know, Miss Gordon." The rain beat on his head and trickled down his cheeks.

"Nor do I know. And Adam does not write to tell me, so it is all a great mystery. Why don't you come in out of the rain?"

"Because I've been forbidden to enter the house, Miss Gordon."

"Oh, stuff and nonsense. Let him in, Polly. I won't tell anyone if you don't."

Polly hesitated, then grinned and opened the door wide. Starbuck stepped over the threshold, dripping water onto the plain dust-sheet that protected the hardwood floor by the front door. He let Polly take his coat and hat, which she draped over a stepladder that had been used to lift down the paintings. Almost everything was gone from the hall: the fine European furniture, the pictures, the Turkish rugs, even the splendid gilded chandelier that had hung in the staircase well from fifty feet of chain. "All of it sent packing to Faulconer Court House," Julia said, seeing Starbuck gaze about the room. "General Faulconer believed his belongings would be safer in the country. Things must be truly desperate, don't you think?"

"The North has stopped recruiting soldiers," Starbuck said, "if that denotes anything."

"Surely it denotes that we have lost?"

Starbuck smiled. "Maybe we haven't even begun to fight?"

Julia liked the bravado and beckoned toward the lit parlor. "Come into the parlor so Polly doesn't have to be terrified that some-one will see you and report her to the General." Julia led him into the downstairs parlor that was lit by two overhead gasoliers. Most of the furniture was gone, though the bookshelves were still crammed with volumes and a plain kitchen table stood next to some open crates. As Starbuck entered the familiar room he thought how odd it was to hear Washington Faulconer described as the General, yet so he was, and an even more powerful enemy because of it. "I'm sorting out the family's books," Julia said. "The General didn't want to send all his volumes to the country, only the valuable ones, and he trusts me to tell him which those are."

"Aren't they all valuable?"

Julia shrugged. "Some nice bindings, perhaps, but most of the books are fairly commonplace." She plucked one at random. "Motley's *Rise of the Dutch Republic*? Hardly a rare volume, Mr. Starbuck. No, I'm putting aside the very best bindings, the books with espe-cially fine plates, and a handful of others."

"You know about books?" Starbuck asked.

"I know more about books than General Faulconer does," Julia said with a hint of amusement. She was wearing a dress of dark blue cotton with a high collar and looped panniers at her waist. The arms of the dress were protected by a pair of white linen dust sleeves. Her black hair was piled high and pinned, though some strands had come loose to hang over her forehead. She looked, Starbuck thought, oddly attractive, and he felt guilty for that thought. This was Adam's fiancee.

"You're not removing yourself to safety, Miss Gordon?" Starbuck asked her.

"Where could we go? My mother's people live in Petersburg, but if Richmond falls then Petersburg cannot be far behind. The General murmured an invitation for us to take ourselves to Faulconer Court House, but he made no provisions for our furniture and poor Mr. Samworth's hearses have been taken for the army's use, which means our belongings must stay here. And where Mother's furniture is, there is Mother, so it seems that for the lack of a cart we must stay in Richmond and endure the Yankee invasion. If it happens." She glanced at a plain tin-cased clock that looked as if it had been borrowed from the servants' quarters. "I don't have long, Mr. Starbuck, as my father is coming to escort me home in a few moments, but I did want to apologize to you."

"To me?" Starbuck asked in surprise.

Julia offered him a solemn look. "About the night at the hospital," she explained.

"I doubt if you have anything to apologize for," Starbuck said.

"I think we do," Julia insisted. "You would have thought, would you not, that a mission to the poor would be accustomed to dealing with girls like your friend?"

Starbuck smiled. "Sally's not very poor."

Julia liked that remark and smiled back. "But she is your friend?"

"Yes, she is."

Julia turned back to the table and began sorting through the books as she spoke. "We are enjoined, are we not, to imitate Christ in all things? Yet on that night I think our Savior would have been more pleased with your behavior than with ours."

"Oh, no," Starbuck said awkwardly.

"I think so. Adam has forbidden me to mention that night ever again. Forbidden me, Mr. Starbuck!" She had plainly been piqued by the order. "Adam is very embarrassed by it. He is afraid of offending my mother, you see? More afraid of that, I think, than of offending me." She wiped dust from the spine of a book. "Macauley's *Essays*? I think not. Was your friend very hurt?"

"Not for long."

"Baynes's *Christian Life*. I doubt that would have been of much guidance to us that night. Look, the pages aren't even cut, but even so it's not of any value. Except for its spiritual advice, but I doubt the General would thank me for that." She tossed the book back onto the table. "Would your friend be offended if I called on her?"

The request startled Starbuck, but he managed to conceal his surprise. "I think she would be pleased, yes."

"I ventured to suggest as much to Adam, but he was very definitely not pleased at the idea. He informed me that pitch defiles, and I'm sure I was grateful for the information but I could not resist thinking that such pitch is more likely to defile a man than a woman. Wouldn't you agree?"

"I think that may well be true, Miss Gordon," Starbuck said with a straight face.

"Mother would disapprove if she thought I was contemplating such a visit, and her disapproval I can understand. But why should Adam mind so very much?"

"Shouldn't Caesar's wife be above suspicion?"

Julia laughed. She had a very quick laugh that animated her face and stung Starbuck's heart. "You think Adam is Caesar?" she asked mockingly.

"I think he wants what is best for you," Starbuck said tactfully.

"Do you think he knows?" Julia asked vehemently. "I'm sure I don't know what's best for me. I would like to be a nurse, but mother says that isn't a suitable occupation and Adam agrees with her." She threw a book onto the table, then seemed to regret the violence of the throw. "I am not entirely sure Adam knows what is best for himself," Julia added, half to herself, then picked up a slim book bound in dark red leather. "Lambarde's *Eirenarcha*. Over two hundred years old and well worth keeping. Do you think Adam knows what is best for me, Mr. Starbuck?"

Starbuck was obscurely aware of deep, dark waters that might be best unplumbed. "I should hope he does, if you're to marry."

"Are we to marry?" Her dark eyes were defiant. "Adam wants to wait."

"Till the war's over?"

Julia laughed, breaking the odd intimacy that had existed for a few seconds. "That's what he says and I'm sure he must be right." She blew dust off a book, peered at the title, and tossed it into one of the open crates. The gaslights suddenly dimmed, then brightened again. Julia grimaced. "They keep doing that. Is it a sign of civilization's ending? Did I hear you tell Polly that you wanted to see Adam?"

"Yes. Rather urgently."

"I wish I could help you. General Johnston demanded his presence and Adam flew to obey. But where General Johnston is, I cannot tell, though I suppose if you were to march toward the sound of the guns you would find him. Might I pass on a message? I'm sure he'll be back in the city soon and if not, then I can always send him a letter."

Starbuck thought for a few seconds. He could not simply go to the army and search for Adam. His pass was only good for this one journey out of the city and the provosts would never let him roam the army's back areas searching for a headquarters aide. He had planned on leaving a message here for Adam, but then he decided that the message might just as easily be delivered by Julia. "But not," he begged her, "by letter."

"No?" Julia was intrigued.

Letters, Starbuck knew, could be opened and read, and this message, with its implication of a traitorous correspondence, must not be read by men like Gillespie. "When you next see him," he asked Julia, "would you tell him that he would be well advised to suspend his correspondence with my family?" He almost said "brother," but decided he did not need to be specific. "And if he finds that advice mysterious, then I will explain it as soon as I can."

Julia gazed very gravely at Starbuck for a few seconds. "I find it mysterious," she said after a while.

"I fear it must remain a mystery."

Julia picked up a book and glanced at its spine. "Adam said you were in jail?"

"I was released today."

"An innocent man."

"As driven snow."

"Really?" Julia laughed, evidently unable to be stern for long. "The newspaper said you took bribes. I'm glad you didn't."

"I did, though. Everyone does."

Julia put the book down and gave Starbuck a speculative look. "You are at least honest about your dishonesty. But not about your friendships. Adam tells us we are not to talk to you or to your friend, and you say he is not to talk to your family? We are all to take vows of silence? Well, despite all, I shall talk to your friend Miss Royall. What would be the best time to call?"

"Late morning, I think."

"And what name does she prefer?"

"I suspect you had better ask for Miss Royall, though her real name is Sally Truslow."

"Truslow. With a W?" Julia wrote it down, then copied out the address on Franklin Street. She glanced at the clock again. "I must see you out before my father arrives and worries that I am being defiled by the touch of pitch. Maybe, one day, we shall have the pleasure of meeting again?"

"I would like that, Miss Gordon."

In the hallway Starbuck pulled on his coat. "You have the message, Miss Gordon?" he asked.

"Adam is not to correspond with your family."

"And please don't tell anyone else. Just Adam. And not by letter, please."

"I ceased needing to be told everything twice when I was an infant, Mr. Starbuck."

Starbuck smiled at the reproof. "My apologies, Miss Gordon. I'm used to dealing with men, not women." With those words he left her smiling, and was smiling himself as he walked into the rain. He carried a memory of her face that was so strong that he almost walked into the path of a wagon carrying another fugitive's furniture eastward. The Negro driving the team shouted a protest, then flicked his whip over the heads of the skittish horses. The wagon was heaped high with furniture that was half protected from the rain by an inadequate tarpaulin.

Starbuck walked on from one pool of gaslight to another, assailed by a sense of sudden loss. He had been defiant to Julia, claiming that the South had yet to begin fighting, but the truth was surely otherwise. The war was over, the rebellion lost, the North triumphant, and Starbuck, his wagon hitched to a dying star, knew he had to turn his life about and strike off anew. He stopped to turn and stare at the Faulconer House. It was, he thought, a moment of farewell. A portion of his life that had begun with a friendship at Yale was ending in a night of panicked defeat, but at least in its ending Starbuck could afford a feeling of self-denying nobility. His friend had rejected him, but he had been true to his friend. He had delivered Adam the warning, and thus snatched his friend from the gallows at Camp Lee. Adam would survive, would marry, would doubtless prosper.

Starbuck turned away from the house and walked on toward de'Ath's waiting coach. The streets echoed with iron-shod wheels and the shouts of teamsters. Lights burned late. Down in the valley a train banged and clashed, its steam whistle mournful in the long rain. Slaves and servants heaped cabin trunks and carpetbags onto wagons; children cried. Somewhere to the east, cloaked by the night, a vengeful army came to claim back a city and Starbuck went to save himself.

He went in through the back door, going into the kitchen where Grace and Charity were broiling venison on the black-leaded stove. The two slaves screamed when Starbuck came through the door, then greeted him with a chorus of questions about where he had sprung from and exclamations at the state of his clothes and health. "You've gone skinny!" Grace said. "Look at you!"

"I missed your cooking," Starbuck said, then managed to tell them that he needed to see Miss Truslow. "Is she busy?"

"Busy? Busy with the dead!" Grace said ominously, but would not explain more. Instead she took off her apron, patted her hair into a rough order, then climbed the stairs. She came back five minutes later and told Starbuck to use the back staircase to Sally's room.

The bedroom was on the third floor and looked across the wet, tangled garden toward the stable block where the window of his old room showed as a black rectangle. The walls of the bedroom were papered in an elegant pale green stripe and her bed was canopied in green cloth. Dried flowers stood in a gilded vase on the mantel and landscapes hung in lacquered frames on the walls. The room was lit by two gas mantles, but candles stood on a table in case the city's gas supply should fail. The furniture was waxed and polished, the draperies were clean, the rugs well beaten and aired. It was a room that suggested solid American virtue, clean and prosperous, a room of which Starbuck's mother would have been proud.

The door clicked open and Sally hurried in. "Nate!" She ran across the room and threw her arms around his neck. "Oh, God! I was so fretting for you!" She kissed him, then brushed at his coat. "I tried to find you. I went to the city jail, then down to Lumpkin's, and I asked people to help, but it was no good! I couldn't get to you. I wanted to, but . . ."

"It's all right. I'm fine," he told her. "I'm really fine."

"You're thin."

"I'll grow back," he said, smiling, then cocked his head toward the open door through which the sound of laughter came from downstairs.

"They're raising the dead," Sally said wearily. She took the chignon from her hair and laid it carefully on her dressing table. Without the false curls she looked younger. "They're having a fake seance," she explained. "All of them drunk as Indians and trying to get advice off General Washington. It's because the Yankees are coming, so everyone's high on whiskey."

"But not you?"

"Honey, you want to make money in this business, you stay cold stone sober." She crossed the room and was about to push the door shut, but paused. "Or did you want to go downstairs? Join in?"

"No. I'm going away."

She sensed the portentousness in his voice. "Where?"

He showed her the pass. "I'm going across the lines. Back to the Yankees."

Sally frowned. "You going to fight for them, Nate?"

"No. There'll be no more fighting soon. It's going to be over, Sally. The bastards have won. They're so damn cocky that they've even closed their recruiting stations. Think what that means!"

"It means they're confident," Sally said scornfully, then banged the door shut. "And so what? Have you ever known a Yankee who wasn't confident? Hell, that's why they're Yankees. All strut and flurry, Nate, and showing the rest of the world how to suck eggs, but I don't see any of them marching down Franklin Street yet. It's like my pa says. It ain't over till the hog stops squealing." She crossed to a table and took two cigars from a humidor. She lit both from a gaslight and brought one to Starbuck, then crouched opposite him on the hearthrug. Her hooped skirts rustled as she crouched. She was dressed in an elaborate white silk dress, wide-skirted and narrow-waisted, with bare shoulders beneath a shawl of pearl-studded lace. There were more pearls at her neck and on her ears. "Did you come to say good-bye?" she asked him.

"No."

"For what then? That?" She jerked her head toward the bed.

"No." He paused. The sound of a bottle breaking came from downstairs, followed by an ironic cheer. "Some seance," he said with a smile. Spiritualism was rife in Richmond, condemned from the city's pulpits, but succored by the families of men killed on the battle-field who wanted reassurance that their sons and husbands were safe on the far side of death.

"It ain't a proper seance. They're just sitting around the table kicking its legs." Sally paused and offered Starbuck a cautious smile. "So what is it, Nate?"

He took the plunge. Adam was safe, now it was his turn. "Do

you remember that night at the hospital?" he asked her. "How you told me you wanted to be ordinary? Just to be plain ordinary. Maybe to run a store? So come with me. This pass will get us both across the lines." He was not entirely sure of that, but he was quite certain that he would not go without Sally if she agreed to accompany him. "I've got permission to go," he told her, "because I'm doing something for the government."

Sally frowned. "For our government?"

"I have to deliver a letter," Starbuck said, and he saw that she still suspected he was going back to fight for the North, and so he explained more. "There's a spy here in Richmond," he told her, "a dangerous one, and they want me to trap him, see? And to do it I have to take this letter to the Yankees."

"And they don't expect you to come back?" Sally asked.

"They want me to come back," Starbuck admitted, but he did not explain any further. He had already revealed as much as he dared, and he did not know how to tell her the rest; how he believed Adam was the spy and how by coming back to Richmond he would entrap his friend. Instead he had planned to carry the false letter and let that undo the damage Adam had already caused, and then he would go away with Sally and leave the armies to fight out the ragged end of the war. At best, he reckoned, there could only be a month or two's fight left in the Confederacy and it would be better to strike out of the wreckage now than be destroyed in the final catastrophe. "Bring your money," he urged Sally, "and we'll go north. Maybe to Canada? Maybe Maine? We'll start your dry goods store. Maybe we'll go west?" He frowned, knowing he was expressing himself badly. "I'm saying you can start again. I'm saying come with me, I'll look after you."

"On my money?" Sally smiled.

"You've got some money of mine. I know it isn't much, but between us we can manage. Hell, Sally, we can settle wherever we want! Just you and me."

She drew on the cigar, watching him. "Are you offering to marry me, Nate Starbuck?" Sally asked after a while.

"Of course!" Had she not understood that?

"Oh, Nate." Sally smiled. "You're a great one for running away."

"I'm not doing that," he said, nettled by the accusation.

She did not notice his hurt. "Sometimes I want to marry, Nate, and sometimes I don't. And when I do, honey, God knows I'd marry you before anyone else." She smiled sadly at him. "But you'd tire of me."

"No!"

"Sh!" She put a finger to his lips. "I saw you look at that Bible girl at the hospital. You'd always want to know what it would be like to marry your own kind."

"That's not fair," Starbuck protested.

"But it's true, honey." She drew on the cigar. "You and me are friends, but we'd make a rotten marriage."

"Sally!" Starbuck protested.

She shushed him. "I'll see this war through, Nate. If the Yankees come I'll spit on them, then make money out of the bastards. I don't know what else I'll do, but I do know I won't run away."

"I'm not running away," he protested, but too weakly.

She thought for a second. "You haven't had things hard, Nate. I know lots of boys like you. You like your comforts." This time she saw she had hurt him and so she reached out a hand and touched his cheek. "Maybe I'm wrong. I keep forgetting this ain't your country, but it is mine." She fell silent for a while, thinking, then she gave him a swift smile. "There comes a time when you have to stand on your own feet, not on your father's shoulders. That's what my pa taught me. I ain't a quitter, Nate."

"I'm not . . ."

"Sh!" She touched his lips again. "I do know that the Yankees ain't won yet, and you told me yourself that it takes five of them to beat one of our boys."

"I was boasting."

"Just like a man." She smiled. "But the hog's still squealing, honey. We ain't beat yet."

Starbuck sucked on the cigar. He had convinced himself that

Sally would come with him. He had never for one moment imagined that she would prefer to stay and risk the Yankee victory. He had thought they would run away together and make a small refuge far from the world's troubles. Her refusal left him confused.

"Nate?" Sally asked. "What is it you want?"

He thought about the question. "I was happy last winter," he said. "When I was with the company. I like being a soldier."

"Then if you want something, honey, go get it. Like my pa says, the world don't owe no one a damn thing, which means you have to go out there and grow it, make it, buy it, or steal it." She smiled at him. "You being honest about this spy business?"

He looked up at her. "Yes. I promise."

"Go catch the bastard, honey. You promised to deliver that letter, so do it. And if you want to run away after that, that's your business, but you do it on your own feet, not mine." She leaned forward and kissed him. "But if you do come back here, honey, I'll still be here. I owe you still." It was for Sally's sake that Starbuck had murdered Ethan Ridley, and Sally's gratitude for that act was heartfelt and deep. Now she threw what remained of her cigar onto the tiles of the hearth. "You want me to give you the money that's yours?"

He shook his head. "No." His certainties were vanishing, leaving him confused again. "Would you do something for me?" he asked Sally.

"If I can, sure."

"Write to your father."

"My pa!" She sounded alarmed. "He doesn't want a letter from me!"

"I think he does."

"But I can't write proper!" She was blushing, suddenly ashamed of her lack of education.

"He doesn't read too good either," Starbuck said. "Just write to him and tell him I'm coming back. Tell him I'll be with the company before the spring finishes. Promise him that."

"I thought that bastard Faulconer wouldn't have you in the Legion?"

"I can beat Faulconer."

Sally laughed. "A minute ago, Nate, you were all for running away and hiding yourself in Canada, now you're taking on General Faulconer? Sure, I'll write my pa. You certain about your money?"

"Keep it for me."

"So you are coming back?"

He smiled. "Hog's still squealing, honey."

She kissed him, then climbed to her feet and crossed to her dressing table where she carefully fixed the chignon on her brushed-back hair. She made sure the curls fell naturally, then gave him a smile. "I'll see you, Nate."

"You will, too." He watched her walk to the door. "The Bible girl," he suddenly remembered.

"What about her?" Sally paused with her hand on the door's edge.

"She wants to come and talk to you."

"To me?" Sally grinned. "What about? Jesus?"

"Maybe. Do you mind?"

"If Jesus don't mind, why the hell should I?"

"She feels bad about that night."

"I'd forgotten it," Sally said, then shrugged. "No, I didn't forget. I kind of hoped to forget. But maybe I can teach her a thing or two."

"Such as?"

"What a real man is, honey." She grinned at him.

"Don't upset her," Starbuck said and was surprised by that sudden impulse of protection toward Julia, but Sally had not heard him. She had already gone out of the door. He finished his cigar. It seemed there was no easy way out, which meant he had a promise to keep and a spy to betray. Somewhere in the night a clock struck the hour and Starbuck went into the dark.

W HAT IS THIS?" BELVEDERE DELANEY HELD A BANK
note between his finger and thumb as though the crumpled thing held a contagion. " 'Parish of Point Coupee,' " he read
aloud from the note's inscription, " 'two dollars.' My dear Sally, I do
hope that isn't what you charge for your services?"

"Real funny, ain't you," Sally said, then took the note from the
lawyer's hand and added it to one of the piles on the cherrywood
table. "Gambling winnings," she explained.

"But what am I to do with it?" Delaney inquired fastidiously, taking up the offending bank note again. "Am I to travel to Louisiana and
demand that the Parish Clerk of Point Coupee pay me two dollars?"

"You know well enough that they'll discount it at the Exchange
Bank," Sally said briskly, taking back the note and adding it to the
week's takings. "That's four hundred and ninety-two dollars and
sixty-three cents from downstairs." "Downstairs" meant the tables
where poker and euchre were played, and where the house took a
straight percentage of the winnings. The policy was that any kind of

money agreeable to the players could be used at the tables, but upstairs the only acceptable currencies were the newfangled northern dollar bills, gold and silver coinage, and Virginia Treasury Notes.

"And how much of the four hundred and ninety-two dollars is in useful money?" Delaney asked.

"Half," Sally admitted. The rest was in fancy bills issued by a variety of southern banks, merchants, and municipal governments who had harnessed their printing presses to replace the dearth of northern money.

"The Bank of Chattanooga," Delaney said derisively, riffling through the bank notes. "And what in the name of Jehovah is this?" He dangled a scrap of faded paper. "A twenty-five-cent note from the Inferior Court of Butts County, Jackson, Georgia? My God, Sally, we're rich! A whole quarter!" He tossed the note onto the table. "Why don't we just print up some notes for ourselves?"

"Why don't we?" Sally asked. "It'd be a damn sight easier than the work I do upstairs."

"We could invent whole parishes! Whole counties! We could devise our own banks!" Delaney was quite taken with the idea. Anything that sabotaged the Confederacy appealed to Belvedere Delaney, and destroying the currency would certainly hasten the demise of the rebellion. Not that the South's currency needed much debasement; prices were rising every day and the whole financial system was based upon loose promises that depended for their fulfillment on final Confederate victory. Even the government's official bank notes admitted as much, promising to pay the bearer the face value of the note but only six months after peace had been declared between the warring sides. "We could put a printing press in the coach house," Delaney suggested. "Who's to know?"

"The printer?" Sally suggested sourly. "You'd need too many people, Delaney, and sure as eggs they'd end up blackmailing you. Besides, I've got a better idea for the coach house."

"Tell me."

"Black it out, carpet it, put in a table and a dozen chairs, and I'll

guarantee you a bigger profit than you can ever make out of my bedroom."

Delaney shook his head, not understanding. "You're going to
serve meals?"

"Hell no. Seances. Set me up as Richmond's best medium, feed
me gossip, charge five bucks a general session and fifty bucks for a private consultation." The idea had come to Sally the previous night
when the house's clients had conducted their fake seance in the darkened parlor. It had been a game, but Sally had noted how some of the
participants had still expected a supernatural intervention, and she
reckoned that superstition could be harnessed to profit. "I'll need a
helper to rap on walls and wave around the cheesecloth," she told a
fascinated Delaney, "and we'll have to develop some other tricks."

Delaney liked the idea. He waved a vague hand toward the
upper floors. "And you'd leave the bedroom business?"

"So long as I'm making more money, hell yes. But I'll need you
to invest some cash first. We can't gammon the city with a cheap
room. It's got to be done proper."

"You're brilliant, Sally. Quite brilliant." Delaney's praise was
genuine. He enjoyed his weekly meetings with Sally, whose business
acumen impressed him and whose sturdy good sense amused him. It
was Sally who ran the financial side of the house, doing it with a brisk
efficiency and a tough honesty. The whorehouse, with its luxuries
and air of exclusivity, was a gold mine to the lawyer, but it was also a
place where he picked up gossip about southern politicians and military commanders, and all that gossip was passed on to Delaney's contact in Washington. How much of the information was true or useful
Delaney did not always know, nor did he particularly care. It was
enough that he was siding with the North and could thus anticipate
profiting from that allegiance when, as he saw it, the inevitable northern victory occurred. Now, still mulling over Sally's proposal to turn
the house's back premises into a spiritualist shrine, Delaney took his
share of the week's money. "So tell me the news?"

Sally gestured through the window to where refugees' carts and coaches still jammed the street. "That's the news, ain't it? We'll soon have no customers left."

"Or a new set arriving?" Delaney suggested delicately.

"And we'll charge them double," Sally sniffed, then asked if it was true that the northern recruiting offices had been closed down.

"I'd not heard as much," Delaney said, taking care not to show how elated he was by the news.

"The Yankees must be pretty cock-a-hoop," Sally said with a grimace.

And with good reason, Delaney thought, for the northern army was just a day's march from the city now. "Which client told you about the recruiting offices?" he asked Sally.

"Wasn't no customer," Sally said. "It was Nate."

"Starbuck?" Delaney asked in surprise. "He was here?"

"Last night. They'd just let him out of jail."

"I saw he'd been released," Delaney said. The news had been in both the *Examiner* and the *Sentinel*. "Is he in his old room? I should say hello."

"Silly bastard's being a damn fool." Sally lit herself a cigar. "God knows where he is."

"Meaning what?" Delaney asked. Sally had been trying to disguise the anxiety in her voice, but Delaney was far too acute to miss her tone and he knew just how fond of Starbuck she was.

"Because he's risking his damn life," Sally said, "that's what. He's taking a letter across the lines and he wanted me to go with him."

Delaney scented a rich morsel here, but he dared not be too eager in his questioning lest he rouse Sally's suspicions. "He wanted you to go to the Yankees? How odd."

"He wanted me to marry him," Sally corrected her employer.

Delaney smiled at her. "What sophisticated taste our friend Starbuck has," he said gallantly. "And yet you turned him down?" He teased her very gently with the question.

Sally grimaced. "He reckoned we could set up a dry goods store in Maine."

Delaney laughed. "My dear Sally, you would be wasted! And

you'd hate Maine. They live in icehouses, suck on salt fish for their subsistence, and sing Psalms for entertainment." Delaney gave a rueful shake of his head. "Poor Nate. I shall miss him."

"He says he's coming back," Sally said. "He didn't want to come back, not if I'd run off with him, but since I ain't moving he says he'll deliver his letter, then get himself back here."

Delaney pretended to hide a yawn. "What sort of letter?" he asked innocently.

"He never said. Just a letter from the government here." Sally paused, but then her worry for Starbuck drove her to explain further and she never once suspected that her explanations might endanger Starbuck. Sally trusted Delaney wholly. The lawyer was a friend, a uniformed Confederate officer, and a man of gentle kindness. Other whores put up with beatings and scorn, yet Belvedere Delaney always behaved with consideration and courtesy to the women he employed; indeed he seemed as concerned for the happiness and health of his employees as for the profits they made him, and so Sally felt free to pour her worries into his sympathetic ear. "Nate reckons there's a spy," she said, "a real dangerous one who's telling the Yankees everything our army plans on doing, and if he can deliver the letter safe then that'll finish off the spy. He didn't tell me more than that, but it's enough. He's an idiot. He don't want to be mixed up in that nonsense, Delaney. He'll end up hanging like that man they strung up at Camp Lee." Webster's end had made a rich story for the newspapers, which had depicted the hanging as the deserved fate of a spy.

"We certainly don't want poor Nate to hang," Delaney said gravely, and he saw that his right hand was trembling slightly, just enough to make the smoke from his cigar shiver as it rose toward the molded ceiling. His first reaction was that Starbuck was on a mission to entrap him, then he dismissed that fear as self-indulgent nonsense. Richmond was full of spies, ranging from the open and eccentric like the rich and crazy Betty Van Lew, who stumped about the city muttering treason and carrying gifts to northern prisoners, to the subtle and secretive like Delaney himself. Yet Delaney was privy to remarkably few military secrets, and Sally's words suggested that the spy

Starbuck was hunting was a military man and one who had access to all the Confederacy's secrets. "So what do you want me to do?" Delaney asked Sally.

Sally shrugged. "I reckon Nate'll only be happy if he can get back into the Legion. He likes being there. Can't you fix it? If he gets back from seeing the Yankees, of course."

"And if there's still a Confederacy," Delaney said dubiously.

"Of course there'll be a Confederacy. We ain't whipped yet. So can't you talk to General Faulconer?"

"Me!" Delaney shuddered. "Faulconer doesn't like me, my dear, and he positively hates Nate. I can tell you now that Faulconer won't let Nate back into his precious Legion."

"Then can you get Nate into another regiment? He likes being a soldier."

More fool him, Delaney thought, but kept that opinion to himself. "I can try," he said, then he glanced at an ormolu clock that graced the mantel. "I think I should be going, my dear."

"You ain't staying for breakfast?" Sally sounded surprised.

Delaney stood. "Even lawyers have to do some work from time to time, my dear," he said. Delaney was a legal adviser to the War Department, an appointment that entailed less than an hour's work a month, but which paid Delaney an annual salary of $1,560, though admittedly the dollars were in southern scrip. He pulled his jacket straight. "I'll do my best for Nate, I do promise."

Sally smiled. "You're a good man."

"Is that not an astonishing truth?" Delaney kissed Sally's hand with his customary politeness, put his cash into a leather case, and hurried out into the street. It had begun to rain again; the drops brought on an unseasonably chill wind.

Delaney hurried one block north to his apartment on Grace Street, where he unlocked his rolltop desk. There were times when the lawyer suspected that the hundreds of northern informants in Richmond were all competing to provide the best intelligence, and that the winner of that secret competition would reap the biggest rewards when the North took over the city. His pen scratched swifly across the notepaper and he reflected that this small nugget of gossip should garner a top prize when that victory came. He wrote down all that Sally had told him. He wrote swiftly, warning the North that Nathaniel Starbuck was a traitor, and then he sealed his letter inside an envelope that he addressed to Lieutenant Colonel Thorne in the Inspector General's Department in Washington, D.C. He sealed that envelope within another which he addressed to the Reverend Ashley M. Winslow in Canal Street, Richmond, then he handed the packet and three northern dollars to his house slave. "This is urgent, George. It is for our mutual friends."

George knew and shared his master's loyalty. He carried the letter to Canal Street and gave it to a man named Ashley who was owned by a supervisor on the Central Virginia Railroad. George gave Ashley two dollars. By nightfall a train had carried the letter and one of the two-dollar coins to Catlett's Station in northern Virginia, where a free black who owned a small cobbler's shop took charge of the envelope.

While in Richmond, meanwhile, the exodus went on. The President's wife took her children away from the city. The price of haulage tripled. When the wind was in the east there was sometimes an odd muffled percussion in the air, barely detectable, but there all the same. It was the sound of guns. Belvedere Delaney heard the distant gunfire and laid a northern flag in his parlor ready to hang from the window as a greeting to the victorious Yankees. He wondered if his letter would reach Washington in time, or if the war would end before Starbuck's treachery was uncovered. In some ways he hoped the young northerner would live, for Starbuck was an attractive rascal, but a rascal all the same, which probably meant he was doomed to the noose anyway. It would be a death Delaney would regret, but in this season of death one more corpse could not make that much difference. It would be a pity, but scarcely more. The lawyer listened to the sound of faraway guns and prayed it signified rebellion's defeat.

The first Yankees to take notice of Starbuck were men of the 5th New Hampshire Infantry, who mistook him for a rebel straggler and marched him at bayonet point to their adjutant, a gaunt, wild-bearded captain with pebble-lensed spectacles who sat astride a piebald horse and peered through the rain at the bedraggled prisoner. "Have you searched the miserable bastard?" the Captain asked.

"He's got nothing," one of Starbuck's captors answered. "Poor as an honest lawyer."

"Take him to brigade," the Captain ordered. "Or if that's too much trouble just shoot the bastard when no one's looking. That's what deserters deserve, a bullet." He gave Starbuck a crooked grin as if daring him to object to the verdict.

"I'm not a deserter," Starbuck said.

"Never thought you were, reb. I just reckon you're a foot-sore bastard who couldn't keep up. Reckon I'd be doing the seceshers a favor just by killing you, which is maybe why I'll let you live." The Captain gathered his reins and gave a dismissive jerk of his head. "Take the bastard away."

"I'm carrying a message," Starbuck said desperately. "I'm not a deserter and I'm no straggler. I'm carrying a message for Major James Starbuck of the Secret Service. I brought it from Richmond two nights ago!"

The Captain gave Starbuck a long jaundiced look. "Son," he said at last, "I'm bone-weary, I'm dog-hungry, I'm wet through, and I just want to be home in Manchester, so if you're wasting my time I might just get so goddamn tired of you that I'll bury your miserable carcass without even wasting a bullet on it first. So convince me, son."

"I need to borrow a knife."

The Captain looked at the two burly men who had captured Starbuck and grinned as he thought of the prisoner trying to fight them. "You feeling heroic, reb, or just plain lucky?"

"A small knife," Starbuck said tiredly.

The Captain fumbled through layers of damp clothing. Behind him the New Hampshire infantry trudged along the muddy road, rain dripping from greatcoats worn like capes over their haversacks. Some gave Starbuck an inquiring look, trying to see in this captured rebel's frayed gray jacket and patched baggy pants the lineaments of devilry that the northern preachers had described.

The Captain produced a small scrimshaw penknife which Starbuck used to pick at the stitches of his waistband. He brought out the oilcloth pouch, which he handed up to the horseman. "It shouldn't get wet, sir," Starbuck said.

The Captain unfolded the pouch, then slit its stitching to reveal the sheets of onionskin paper. He swore as a raindrop splashed on the top page to dissolve a word into instant oblivion, then hunched forward to shelter the papers from the weather. He pulled the rain-smeared spectacles down on his nose and peered close over their rims at the tight handwriting, and what he read plainly convinced him of Starbuck's truthfulness, for he carefully folded the papers back inside their oilcloth pouch, which he handed back to Starbuck. "You're putting me to a world of trouble, son, but I reckon Uncle Sam would want me to exert myself. You need anything?"

"A cigar."

"Give the man a cigar, Jenks, and take your bayonet out of the poor bastard's ribs. Looks like he's on our side after all."

Horses were found, and an escort formed of two lieutenants who welcomed a chance to ride to Williamsburg. No one was entirely sure where the Army of the Potomac's headquarters was, but Williamsburg seemed the obvious place, and one of the lieutenants had seen a girl there the previous day whom he swore was the prettiest thing he could ever hope to see this side of paradise, and so to Williamsburg they rode. The Lieutenant wanted to know if the girls of Richmond were just as pretty, and Starbuck assured him this was so. "I sure can't wait to get there," the Lieutenant said, but his companion, a much less optimistic man, asked Starbuck how formidable the rebel defenses around the city were.

"Pretty formidable," Starbuck said.

"Well I guess our cannon boys can't wait to chew 'em up. Not since the secseshers skedaddled from Yorktown without waiting to be killed first."

The lieutenants assumed, and Starbuck did not disillusion them, that he was a northern patriot who had risked his life for his country and they were naturally curious about him. They wanted to know where he came from, and when Starbuck told them he was a Bostonian they said they had gone through Boston on their way to the war and what a fine city it was, better than Washington, which was all windy avenues and half-finished buildings and scalpers trying to make a buck or two out of honest country soldiers. They had met President Lincoln there, and he was a good kind of man, plain and straight, but for the rest of the city, they said, there were hardly words bad enough.

The lieutenants were in no particular hurry and stopped at a tavern where they asked for beer. The tavern keeper, a surly man, said he had been drunk dry of beer and offered instead a bottle of peach wine. It was sweet and thick, sickly to the tongue. Starbuck, sitting on the tavern's back porch, saw hatred for the invaders on the tavern keeper's face. In turn the two lieutenants derided the tavern keeper as a long-haired ignoramus in desperate need of northern enlightenment. "It isn't a bad-looking country!" The more cheerful of the two lieutenants gestured at the scenery. "If it was drained proper and cultivated scientifically, a man could make money here."

In truth the rainy landscape looked desperately uninviting. The tavern was built in a clearing of trees just north of the swamps which edged the Chickahominy River. The river itself was no wider than Richmond's Main Street, but it was fringed by broad strips of dank and flooded marshland that gave off a heavy, rank smell. "Looks a sick kind of place to me," the more pessimistic Lieutenant observed. "That kind of swamp breeds illness. It isn't a land for white men."

The lieutenants, disappointed in the thick sweet wine, decided to ride on. Their journey took the three horsemen against a tide of oncoming infantry and Starbuck noted how well the northern soldiers were equipped. None of these men had shoe soles held to uppers with lengths of string, none wore frayed rope belts, none carried flintlock smoothbore muskets like those that had been used by George Washington's men when they had marched these same roads to pin the

British against the sea at Yorktown. These troops did not have uniforms patched with butternut, nor did they need to grind roasted goober peas and smoke-dried apples to make a substitute coffee. These northerners looked well-fed, cheerful, and confident, an army trained and equipped and determined to end a sad business swiftly.

A mile or two short of their destination they passed an artillery park where Starbuck paused to gape in sheer amazement. He had not imagined there were so many guns in all the world, let alone in one small Virginia field. The cannon were lined wheel to wheel, all with newly varnished limbers, all polished, and beyond them were lines of brand-new covered wagons which held the gunners' supplies and spare ammunition. He tried to count the guns, but it was dusk and he could not see clearly enough to make even a rough estimate. There were rows of workmanlike twelve-pounder Napoleons, and lines of Parrott guns with their bulbous breeches, and acres of three-inch rifles with their slender barrels. Some of the guns had blackened muzzles, reminders that the rebels had fought a brisk and bloody delaying action in Williamsburg to slow the Federal advance. Groups of artillerymen gathered around cooking fires among the parked guns, and the smell of roasting meat made the three riders urge their horses on toward the comforts of the nearby town.

The first lantern lights were showing through windows as they trotted into Williamsburg with its fine spread of ancient college buildings. They approached the college along a street of shingled houses. Some of the houses were pristine and neat, but others, presumably those abandoned by their owners, had been rifled by the Yankees. Torn curtains hung at broken windows and smashed china littered the yards. A doll lay in the mud of one yard, and a torn mattress was draped over the splintered remains of a cherry tree. One house had burned to the ground so that all that remained were two gaunt and blackened brick chimney stacks and some twisted, half-melted bed frames. Troops were billeted in all the houses.

The College of William and Mary had suffered just as much as the town itself. The lieutenants tied their horses to a hitching post in the main yard and explored the Wren Building in search of the Secret

Service headquarters. A sentry on the college gate had assured them that the bureau was in residence, but he was not certain just where, and so the three men wandered lantern-lit corridors littered with broken books and torn papers. To Starbuck it looked as if a barbarian horde had come to destroy learning. Every bookshelf had been emptied and the books tipped into piles, or burned in grates or simply kicked aside. Paintings had been slashed and old documents taken from chests that had been broken up for firewood. In one room the linenfold paneling had been prised from the plaster walls by bayonets and splintered into so much matchwood that was now just ash in a wide grate. The corridors stank of urine. A crude effigy of Jefferson Davis with a devil's horns and forked tail had been painted in limewash on a lecture-room wall. Troops were encamped in the high-ceilinged rooms. Some had found professors' gowns hanging in a cupboard and now swooped up and down the corridors swathed in the black silk robes.

"You're looking for headquarters?" A New York captain, his breath stinking of whiskey, pointed the three men toward some houses that lay a short distance away in the darkness. "Faculty houses." He hiccupped, then grinned when a woman's laughter sounded from the room behind him. Someone had chalked "Amalgamation Hall" over the room's doorway. "We have captured the college's liquor and are presently amalgamating its liberated kitchen girls," the Captain announced. "Come and join us."

A New York sergeant offered to escort Starbuck to the house where he believed the Secret Service had its quarters while the two New Hampshire lieutenants, their duty discharged, went to join the New Yorkers' celebrations. The Sergeant was angry. "They've no notion of duty," he said of his officers. "We're on a righteous crusade, not a drunken debauch! They're just kitchen maids, scarce out of childhood! What do we want those poor innocent blacks to think? That we're no better than southerners?"

But Starbuck could spare no sympathy for the Sergeant's unhappiness. He was too consumed by nervous apprehension as he walked down a puddled path toward the row of elegant, lamplit houses. He was just seconds away from meeting his brother and discovering for certain whether his erstwhile friend was a traitor. Starbuck also had to play a deceiver's game and he was not sure he could continue to play it. Maybe, seeing James's face, he would lose his resolve? Maybe this whole deception was God's way of restoring him to righteousness? His heart felt flabby and loud in his chest; his belly, still soured by Gillespie's mistreatment, felt raw. Unto thine own self be true, he told himself, but that just threw up Pilate's question. What is truth? Did God want him to betray the South? For a pittance he would have turned and fled from this confrontation, but instead the Sergeant gestured at a house that was brightly lit by candles and guarded by two blue-coated sentries who huddled from the wind against the red brick wall. "That's the house," the Sergeant said, then called to the two sentries. "He's got business inside."

The house door was marked in chalk. "Major E. J. Allen and Staff, KEEP OUT." Starbuck half expected the sentries to bar him entry, but instead they unquestioningly let him into the entrance hall that was hung with etchings of European cathedrals. A hallstand made from stag antlers was thickly draped with blue coats and sword belts. Men's voices and the sound of cutlery scraping on china came from a room that opened off the hall to Starbuck's left. "Is someone there?" a voice shouted from the dining room.

"I'm looking for . . ." Starbuck began, but his voice was slightly cracked and he needed to start again. "I'm looking for Major Starbuck," he called again.

"And who in the name of holy hell are you?" A short, bearded man with a hard voice appeared in the open doorway. He had a napkin tucked into his collar and a piece of chicken speared onto a fork in his right hand. He gave Starbuck's bedraggled uniform a scornful look. "Are you a miserable rebel? Eh? Is that what you are? Come to beg a decent meal, have you, now that your miserable rebellion has collapsed? Well? Speak up, you fool."

"I'm Major Starbuck's brother," Starbuck said, "and I have a letter from Richmond for him."

The belligerent man stared at him for a few seconds. "Christ on

His cross," he said at last in astonished blasphemy. "You're the brother from Richmond?"

"Yes."

"Then come in, come in!" He gestured with his speared chicken morsel. "Come in!"

Starbuck walked into a room where a dozen men sat around a well-laden table. Candles burned in three candelabras along the polished board, a score of plates held fresh bread, green vegetables, and roasted meat, while red wine and heavy silverware glinted in the flamelight. Starbuck, hungry though he was, noticed none of it; instead he saw only the bearded man on the table's far side who had begun to stand up, but who now seemed frozen motionless halfway up from his chair. He stared at Starbuck, his eyes showing incredulity.

"Jimmy!" the man who had accosted Starbuck in the hallway said. "He says he's your brother."

"Nate," James, still crouched half in and half out of his chair, said in a faint voice.

"James." Starbuck suddenly felt a great rush of affection for his brother.

"Oh, thank God," James said, and he collapsed backward onto his chair as if the moment were too much for him. "Oh, thank God," he said again, touching a napkin to his closed eyes as he prayed his thanks for his brother's return. The other men about the table stared at Starbuck in a still silence.

"I've brought you a message," Starbuck interrupted his brother's silent prayer.

"From?" James said in a tone of eager hope, almost adding the name, but then remembering his promise to keep Adam's identity a secret. He checked his question and even placed a finger to his lips as though warning his brother not to say the name aloud.

And Starbuck knew then. His brother's warning motion intimated that he would indeed know the spy's identity, and that could only mean that the traitor was Adam. It had always had to be Adam, though that inevitability had not stopped Starbuck from hoping and praying that the spy might turn out to be some total stranger. He felt a sudden and immense sadness for Adam, and a despair because he would now need to use this new certainty. James was still waiting for an answer and Starbuck nodded. "Yes," he said, "from him."

"Thank God for that too," James said. "I feared he might be captured."

"Jimmy's at his prayers again," the short, bearded man broke cheerfully into the brothers' conversation, "so you'd better sit and eat something, Mr. Starbuck. You look fair famished. You have the message on you?"

"That is Mr. Pinkerton," James introduced the short man. "The chief of the Secret Service Bureau."

"And honored to meet you," Pinkerton said, thrusting out a hand.

Starbuck shook hands, then gave Pinkerton the square of oilcloth. "I guess you've been waiting for this, sir," he said.

Pinkerton unfolded the sheets and looked at the carefully disguised handwriting. "It's the real thing, Jimmy! From your friend! He's not let us down! I knew he wouldn't!" He stamped a foot on the rug as a sign of happiness. "Sit down, Mr. Starbuck! Sit! Eat! Make room for him! Next to your brother, yes?"

James stood as Nate approached. Nate was so happy to see James again that for a second he was tempted to offer an embrace, but the family had never been demonstrative and so the brothers merely shook hands. "Sit," James said. "I'll trouble Lieutenant Bentley for some chicken? Thank you. And some bread sauce. You always liked bread sauce, Nate. Sweet potato? Sit, sit. Some lemonade?"

"Wine, please," Starbuck said.

James looked horrified. "You drink ardent spirits?" Then, unable to spoil this moment with pious disapproval, he smiled. "Some wine, then, of course. For your stomach's sake, I'm sure, and why not? Sit, Nate, sit!"

Starbuck sat and was assailed by questions. It seemed that every man about the table knew who he was, and all had seen the reports in the Richmond newspapers announcing his release. Those papers had made the journey to Williamsburg a good deal faster than Starbuck, who now assured his brother's colleagues that his imprisonment had all been a mistake. "You were accused of taking bribes?" James scorned the suggestion. "What nonsense!"

"A trumped-up charge," Starbuck said through a mouthful of chicken and bread sauce, "and merely an excuse to hold me while they tried to make me confess to espionage." Someone poured him more wine and wanted to know exactly how he had escaped from Richmond, so Starbuck told of journeying north to Mechanicsville and there turning east into the tangle of small roads that lay above the Chickahominy. He made it sound as though he had made the journey alone, though in truth he would never have reached the northern lines without de'Ath's pilot who had led him safely through quiet back lanes and ghostly forests. They had traveled by night, first to Mechanicsville, then to a farm just east of Cold Harbor, and on the last night through the rebel picket line by the York and Richmond Railroad and so down to a pine wood close to St. Peter's Church where George Washington had married. It was there that the taciturn Tyler had left Starbuck. "You walk from here," Tyler had said.

"Where are the Yankees?"

"We passed them two mile back. But from here on, boy, the bastards are everywhere."

"How do I get back?"

"Go to Barker's Mill and ask for Tom Woody. Tom knows how to find me, and if Tom's not there, you're on your own. Go on, now."

Starbuck had stayed under the cover of the pines for most of the morning, then had walked south until he reached the road where the New Hampshire regiment had captured him. Now, satiated with a meal richer than any he had eaten in months, he pushed his chair back from the table and accepted the gift of a cigar. His brother frowned at his use of tobacco, so Starbuck assured James it was merely to alleviate a bronchial condition caught in the rebel dungeons. He then described his treatment in prison and horrified the company with his graphic account of Webster's hanging. He could give Pinkerton no news of Scully or Lewis, nor of the woman, Hattie Lawton, who had been captured with Webster.

Pinkerton, busy stuffing a pipe with James River tobacco captured along with the faculty house in which they were quartered, frowned at Starbuck. "Why did they let you witness poor Webster's death?"

"I think they expected me to betray myself by recognizing him, sir," Starbuck said.

"They must think we're fools!" Pinkerton said, shaking his head at this evidence of southern stupidity. He lit his pipe, then tapped the sheets of onionskin paper on which de'Ath's false message was written. "Am I to assume you know the man who wrote this?"

"Indeed, sir."

"A family friend, eh?" Pinkerton glanced from the lean Starbuck to the plumper James, then back to Starbuck again. "And I assume, Mr. Starbuck, that if this friend asked you to deliver the letter he must have known of your northern sympathies?"

Starbuck assumed the question was meant as a clumsy test of his loyalty and for a second it actually was, for he understood this was the moment where he must begin telling lies. Either that or confess the truth and see his friends in K Company and in Richmond ground down beneath the northern army. For one blinding instant he felt the temptation to truthfulness, if only for the sake of his soul, but then the thought of Sally made him smile at the expectant Pinkerton. "He knew my sympathies, sir. For some time now I've been helping him collect the information he sends you."

The lie came smoothly. He had even made it sound modest, and for a second or two he was aware of the room's silent admiration, then Pinkerton slapped the table in approbation. "So you did deserve imprisonment, Mr. Starbuck!" He laughed to show it was a jest, then slapped the table again. "You're a brave man, Mr. Starbuck, there's no doubting it." Pinkerton spoke feelingly and the men around the table murmured their approbation of their chief's sentiments.

James touched Starbuck's arm. "I always knew you were on the right side. Well done, Nate!"

"The North owes you a debt of gratitude," Pinkerton said, "and I'll make it my business to see it's paid. Now, if you're through with your victuals, maybe you and I can talk privately? And you, Jimmy, of course. Come. Bring your wine, Mr. Starbuck."

Pinkerton led them into a small and elegantly furnished parlor. Theology books lined the shelves while a sewing machine stood on a walnut table with a half-finished shirt still trapped beneath its foot. Silver-framed family portraits were lined up on a side table. One, a daguerrotype of a small child, had its frame draped with a strip of crepe to signify that the child had died recently. Another showed a young man in Confederate artillery uniform. "Pity that one's not swathed in black, eh, Jimmy?" Pinkerton said as he sat down. "Now, Mr. Starbuck, what are you called? Nathaniel? Nate?"

"Nate, sir."

"You can call me Bulldog. Everyone does. Everyone except Jimmy here because he's too much of a cold Boston fish to use nicknames, ain't that so, Jimmy?"

"Quite so, Chief," James said, gesturing for Starbuck to sit opposite Pinkerton beside the empty fireplace. Wind gusted in the chimney and rattled rain on the curtained windows.

Pinkerton took de'Ath's forged message from his vest pocket. "The news is bad, Jimmy," the detective said gloomily. "It's just as I feared. There must be a hundred and fifty thousand rebels facing us now. See for yourself." James fixed some reading glasses on the bridge of his nose and placed the proffered letter directly under an oil lamp. Starbuck wondered if his brother would spot the counterfeit handwriting, but instead James tutted at the news and shook his head in evident sympathy with his chief's pessimism.

"It's bad, Major, very bad."

"And they're sending reinforcements to Jackson in the Shenandoah, you see that?" Pinkerton pulled on his pipe. "That's how many men they've got! They can afford to send troops away from the Richmond defenses. It's what I've been fearing, Jimmy! For months now the rascals have been trying to convince us their army is small. They want to draw us in, you see? Suck us in. Then they would have hit us with everything!" He shadowboxed two punches. "My God, if it hadn't been for this message, Jimmy, it might have worked too. The

General will be grateful. 'Pon my soul he'll be grateful. I shall visit him in a moment or two." Pinkerton seemed obscurely pleased at the bad news, almost energized by it. "But before I go, Nate, tell me what's happening in Richmond. Don't pull your punches, lad. Tell me the worst, spare us nothing."

Starbuck, thus enjoined, described a rebel capital thronged with soldiers from every part of the Confederacy. He reported that the Tredegar Iron Works had been forging cannon day and night since the war's beginning and that the guns were now pouring from the factory gates toward the newly dug defenses that ringed Richmond. Pinkerton leaned forward as though eager for every word and winced at each new revelation of rebel strength. James, sitting to one side, made notes in a small book. Neither man challenged Starbuck's inventions, but instead swallowed his outrageous inventions whole.

Starbuck finished by saying he had seen trains steam into the Richmond depot of the Petersburg railroad loaded with crates of British rifles that had been smuggled through the U.S. Navy's blockade. "They reckon every rebel soldier has a modern rifle now, sir, and ammunition enough for a dozen battles." Starbuck said.

James frowned. "Half the prisoners we've taken in the last week were armed with old-fashioned smoothbores."

"That's because they're not letting their newest weapons leave Richmond," Starbuck lied smoothly. He was suddenly enjoying himself.

"You see, Jimmy? They're sucking us in! Luring us!" Pinkerton shook his head at this evidence of rebel perfidy. "They'll pull us in, then hit us. My God, but it's clever." He puffed on his pipe, deep in thought. A clock ticked on the mantel, while from the wet darkness came the sound of men's voices singing. Pinkerton finally threw himself back in his chair as though he had been unable to see a way through the thicket of enemies that sprang up around him. "Your friend, now, the fellow who writes these letters," Pinkerton said, pointing his pipe at Starbuck, "how is he planning to send us further letters?"

Starbuck drew on his cigar. "He suggested, sir, that I go back to Richmond and that you use me as you would have used Webster.

Ad—" He stopped himself from saying Adam's name just in time. "Admittedly I'm not ideal, perhaps, but it could be done. No one in Richmond knows I've crossed the line."

Pinkerton stared hard at Starbuck. "What is your status with the rebels, Nate? They let you out of prison, but are they fool enough to expect you back in their army?"

"I asked for some furlough, sir, and they agreed to that, but they'll want me back in the Passport Bureau by the end of the month. That's where I was working when I was arrested, you see."

"My word, but you could be mighty useful to us in that bureau, Nate! My word, but that would be useful!" Pinkerton stood and paced the small room excitedly. "But you're running a fearful risk by going back. Are you really willing to do it?"

"Yes, sir, if it's necessary. I mean if you don't finish the war first."

"You're a brave man, Nate, a brave man," Pinkerton said, and he went on pacing up and down while Starbuck relit his cigar and sucked the smoke deep into his chest. De'Ath, he thought, would have been proud of him. Pinkerton stopped his pacing and stabbed the stem of his pipe toward Starbuck. "The General might want to see you. You'll hold yourself ready?"

Starbuck hid his alarm at the thought of facing the northern commander. "Of course, sir."

"Right!" Pinkerton scooped up the false letter from the table in front of James. "I'm away to see his lordship. I'll leave the two of you to talk." He swept out of the room, shouting for an orderly to bring his coat and hat.

James, suddenly embarrassed, sat in the chair Pinkerton had vacated. He shyly caught his brother's eye, then smiled. "I always knew you weren't a copperhead at heart."

"A what?"

"Copperhead," James said. "It's an insult for northerners who sympathize with the South. Journalists use the word."

"Nasty beasts, copperheads," Starbuck said lightly. One of his men had almost been bitten by a copperhead the previous year and he remembered Truslow barking a warning and then slashing the snake's brown head clean off with his bowie knife. The snake had smelt, Starbuck remembered, of honeysuckle.

"How is Adam?" James asked.

"Earnest. In love, too. She's the daughter of the Reverend John Gordon."

"Of the ASPGP? I've never met him, but I've heard good things of him." James took the reading glasses off his nose and polished them on the skirt of his coat. "You're looking thin. Did they really use purgatives on you?"

"Yes, they did."

"Terrible, terrible." James frowned, then offered his brother a smile of wry sympathy. "Now we've both been in prison, Nate. Who would ever have thought it? I must confess that when I was in Richmond I took great comfort from the Acts of the Apostles. I believed that if the Lord could deliver Paul and Silas from the dungeon then He would surely deliver me. And He did!"

"Me too," Starbuck said, squirming with embarrassment. There was a certain pleasure in deceiving Pinkerton, but none in hoodwinking James.

James smiled. "Adam encouraged me to believe you might come back to our side."

"He did?" Starbuck asked, unable to hide his surprise that his erstwhile friend should have so misunderstood him.

"He told me you'd been attending prayer meetings," James said, "so I knew you must have been laying your burden before the Lord and I thanked God for it. Did Adam give you the Bible?"

"Yes, thank you. It's here," Starbuck said, tapping his breast pocket. The Bible had been waiting with his uniform at de'Ath's house. "Would you like it back?"

"No! No. I would like you to have it, as a gift." James breathed on his glasses and polished their lenses again. "I asked Adam to persuade you to come home. Once I knew his real feelings on the war, of course."

"He did encourage me," Starbuck lied.

James shook his head. "So there really are that many rebel soldiers? I must confess I had my doubts. I thought Pinkerton and McClellan were seeing dangers where none existed, but I was wrong! Well, with God's help we shall prevail, but I admit the fighting will be hard. But at least you have done your duty, Nate, and I shall make it my business to let Father know that."

Starbuck gave a quick embarrassed smile. "I can't see Father forgiving me."

"He's not given to forgiveness," James agreed, "but if I tell him how valuable your services have been, who knows? Maybe he will see his way to restoring his affections?" He busied himself by polishing his spectacles yet again. "He's still angry, I must confess."

"About the girl?" Starbuck asked brutally, referring to the days when he had fled from both Yale and his father's wrath. "And about the money I stole?"

"Yes." James colored, then smiled. "But even Father can't deny the parable of the prodigal son, can he? And I shall tell him that it is time to forgive you." He paused, trapped between his desire to confess an emotion and an upbringing that had taught him to hide all such revelatory feelings. Desire won. "It wasn't till you were gone that I realized how much I missed you. You were always the rebellious one, weren't you? I think I needed your mischief more than I knew. After you'd gone I decided we should have been better friends, and now we can be."

"That's kind of you," Starbuck said, acutely embarrassed.

"Come!" James suddenly slid forward off his chair and knelt on the hooked rug. "Shall we pray?"

"Yes, of course," Starbuck said, and for the first time in months, he went to his knees. His brother prayed aloud, thanking the Lord for the return of this prodigal brother and praying God's blessing on Nate and Nate's future and the North's righteous cause. "Maybe," James finished, "you'd like to add a word of prayer, Nate?"

"Just amen," Starbuck said, wondering what betrayals he would need to make in the next few days if he was to keep the promise he had made to Sally's father. "Just amen."

"Then amen and amen," James said. He smiled, replete with happiness, because righteousness had triumphed, a sinner had come home, and a family disgrace could be ended at last.

The CSS *Virginia*, the ironclad built on the hull of the old USS *Merrimack*, was run aground and burned when Norfolk, her home base, was abandoned. The loss of the rebel ironclad opened the James River to the northern navy, and a flotilla of warships crept upstream toward Richmond. Rebel batteries on the riverbanks were overwhelmed by naval gunfire, the huge missiles of the flask-shaped Dahlgren guns ripping the rain-sodden parapets apart and the screaming hundred-pound shells of the Parrott rifles tearing up the damp-rotted fire platforms and shattering the gun carriages. Mile by mile the northern squadron of three ironclads and two wooden gunboats churned upstream, confident that there was no secessionist ship left afloat on the James capable of challenging them and discovering no shore battery strong enough to stop their inexorable progress.

Six miles south of Richmond, just where the squadron's course turned through a right angle to run straight north toward the heart of the city, one last rebel fort remained. It stood high on Drewry's Bluff, a great hill on the James's southern bank, and its heavy guns pointed east toward the river's mouth. To the north of Drewry's Bluff, where the river ran so invitingly into the heart of rebellion, a barricade of stone-filled barges had been sunk against great pilings. The water heaped above the barricade and flowed white through its sluices, while a tangled mat of driftwood and floating trees was trapped upstream to make the obstacle look even more formidable.

The northern squadron came upon the last fort and its barricade just after dawn one morning. The five warships had been anchored in midstream all night, harassed by rifle fire from the enemy banks, but now, with the rising sun behind them, they cleared their turrets and gundecks for the decisive battle. First they would subdue the fort, then blast a gap through the barricade. "Richmond by nightfall, boys!" an officer on the leading ironclad called to his gun crews. Through his telescope he could see the distant city in the new day's light, could see the sun shining on white spires and on a pillared temple and on the roofs that climbed the city's seven hills. He could see the wretched rebel flags flying and he swore that before this day was through his ship would land a raiding party to take one of those rags from its Richmond staff. First they would destroy this last obstacle, then they would steam upstream into the city's heart and shell its citizens into submission. The army would thus be saved the need to mount a siege. Victory by nightfall.

The five ships loaded their guns, hauled their anchors from the river's mud, and steamed toward battle with their ensigns bright in the rising sun. The rebels fired first, shooting downriver when the leading warship was just six hundred yards away. The rebel shells screamed down from the hill's crest, each missile trailing a whip-thin wisp of fuse-smoke. The first shots plunged into the river, exploding great fountains of water that streamed away into mist. Then the first shells struck home and the rebel gunners cheered. "Save your breath! Reload! Look lively now!" a gun captain shouted.

The ironclad USS *Galena* led the attack, enduring the rebel cannonade as she maneuvered herself into a firing position. First she threw out a stern anchor, then, with her propeller stopped, she let the current swing her around so that the ship's full broadside could be brought against the small fort on its high bluff. The *Galena's* Captain intended to check the current's swing by letting a bow anchor go when he was broadside to the rebel guns, but no sooner had the makeshift ironclad begun to swing than the rebel shells began to tear her armored sides apart. The iron plates bolted over the *Galena's* wooden hull were no match for the fort's big guns. The armor plates buckled and fell, then the enemy shells ripped through the unprotected wooden skin to turn the gundeck into a sudden slaughterhouse of fire and white-hot steel. Screams echoed under low beams, smoke billowed through hatches, and fire exploded out of gunports. The warship cut her anchor cable and, leaking blood from her scuppers, limped downstream to safety.

The *Monitor*, a purpose-built ironclad with a deck and turret of solid metal, thumped up to the point of danger with her nine-foot-wide propeller churning the river brown with bottom mud. The fort's gunners paused to let the smoke from their eight guns dissipate, then turned the quoins and levered their guns' carriages to sharpen their aim. The *Monitor* was an altogether harder target, for she was little more than a flat metal deck flush with the river on which was mounted a circular turret twenty feet across. To the men in the fort she looked like a cake tin afloat on a waterlogged metal tray, then a puff of smoke showed as her auxiliary steam engine engaged the drive that would revolve the ship's gun turret and so bring her two monstrous cannons to bear.

"Fire!" the rebel gun commanders shouted and the flames whipped out of the guns that crashed back on their barbette carriages. The shells and shot cracked down on the ironclad. Some drove great gouts of water from the river, others hit their target square on, but only to bounce off the deck armor and wail above the riverbanks in tumbling flight.

The *Monitor*'s sailors cranked open the gun ports. The whole boat shivered as an enemy shot struck the deck, then again as another shell made the turret reverberate like a giant drum. "Fire!" The turret's officer called the command.

"They won't go high enough!" a gun captain shouted back. "The guns! They can't elevate any higher!" Another enemy shell cracked on the turret, starting dust from every rivet and join in the inner armor. Water splashed across the guns from a near miss, then another shell screamed off the armor plate.

The officer squinted along the gun sights and saw that the weapon's barrel was pointed at the slope below the fort.

"They won't go higher!" the gun captain shouted over the terrible noise of solid shot cracking against the turret's eight layers of one-inch armor plates. The ironclad's main engine thumped in the boat's deep belly, holding her against the current while every few seconds a whipcrack of sound announced the strike of a sharpshooter's bullet fired from the rifle pits that lined the riverbank.

"Fire anyway!" the officer shouted.

The *Monitor* fired, but her huge twin shells merely buried themselves on the damp hill slope and churned a small avalanche of wet dirt away from the rock. Enemy shells banged and bounced off the one-inch armor of her deck and drowned the engines' intake vents with water splashes. The ironclad's helmsman, fighting against the sideways pull of the monstrous propeller, peered through slits in the solid iron blocks of the pilothouse to see nothing but water and gunsmoke. The ironclad fired again, the boat's whole stern momentarily settling a foot lower in the water as the two big guns recoiled, but again the shells fell far short of the earth-walled fort that was built so high above the river. "Go astern!" the ship's captain shouted up to the helmsman. The *Monitor*, its guns unable to hurt the enemy batteries, drifted downstream after the defeated *Galena* and the helmsman listened to the mocking jeers of the rebel infantry on the riverbanks.

The third ironclad, the USS *Naugatuck*, edged past the frustrated *Monitor* to take the lead position in the narrow river. Her first salvo went low, her next broadside screamed above the fort to splinter the tall trees beyond, then her gunners reckoned they had the proper elevation and rammed a one-hundred-pound shell into the twelve-foot barrel of their big Parrott gun. They stood back, the gunner yanked the lanyard to scrape the friction fuse and fire the gun, but instead the whole barrel, over four tons of iron, exploded in a blinding crack. Men whipped away in sprays of blood as jagged fragments of the burst breech whistled across the gundeck. Fire licked the deck, exploding a ready charge at the next gun. That smaller explosion laid open a man's ribs as cleanly as if they'd been cut with a knife and split his intestines like a dribble of butcher's offal across a rope-hauled ammunition hoist. An enemy shell added to the horror, coming through the open gun port to kill two men who were dragging a firehose aft. Flames roared along the gundeck, driving the gun crews up onto the poop where they made easy targets for the rebel sharpshooters on the banks. The ship's pumps brought the fire under control, but not until the *Naugatuck*, like the *Galena* and the *Monitor*, had drifted on the current out of range of the enemy guns. The two smaller gunboats fired on at long range, but neither dared take her fragile wooden hull close to the unscathed heavy guns on Drewry's

Bluff and inch by inch, as though unwilling to admit defeat, the wounded flotilla fell back downstream.

In Richmond the guns sounded like summer thunder, rattling casements and shivering the colored water that filled the long-necked flasks in the windows of Monsieur Ducquesne's hairdressing salon. The twelve hundred slaves who labored in the hellish five acres of the Tredegar Iron Works silently cheered the unseen attackers while their overseers glanced nervously through grimy windows as if they expected to see a monstrous fleet of Yankee ironclads come steaming around the river bend at Rockett's Landing with their smokestacks blackening the sky and their great guns raised to tear the heart from the secessionist capital. But nothing moved on the bend except the wind-stirred water. The guns cracked on, their sound muffled in the long, hot morning.

The sound gave urgency to a meeting of the free citizenry that had been summoned to assemble at the foot of the great steps of the State House. At the top of the steps, framed and given nobility by the soaring columns of Jefferson's architecture, the Mayor of Richmond and the Governor of Virginia both swore that the city would never surrender as long as there was breath in their bodies and pride in their hearts. They vowed to fight street to street, house to house, and promised that the James would run crimson with Yankee blood before Virginia's city yielded to northern tyranny. The crowd, encumbered with weapons, cheered the sentiments.

Julia Gordon, walking home with a pair of skinned rabbits that she had bartered at the Union Street market for a fine damask table-cloth that had formed a part of her mother's wedding goods, paused at the edge of the crowd and listened to the speakers. She noted in the pauses between the cheers how the guns' sound seemed to rise, fall, fade, and echo like some far-off thunderstorm. A famous Confederate congressman had begun speaking, using as his text a copy of the New York *Herald* which told how the citizens of Albany, the capital of New York State, were celebrating the imminent victory of the North over secession. They were dancing in the northern streets, the Congress-man claimed, because the overweening Yankees reckoned their war was won. And why do they reckon thus? the orator asked. Because the great McClellan was marching on Richmond. "And shall McClellan win?" The orator roared the question.

"No!" the crowd roared back.

The Young Napoleon, the speaker said, would meet his Waterloo and the capering in Albany's streets would turn into the shuffle of mourning. The dancing bands would give way to muffled drums and the harlequins to grieving widows. For every brave hero buried in Richmond's Hollywood cemetery, the orator promised, twenty corpses would be interred in the North, and for every teardrop shed by a southern widow, a bucketful would flow in the hated union. Richmond would not surrender, the South would not yield, the war was not lost. The crowd cheered and the far guns echoed.

Julia walked slowly on, the two bloody carcasses dripping from her hand. She skirted the crowd and took the path that led down to the Bell Tower. Crippled beggars sat by the railings that edged the tower, all of them wounded at the battle of Manassas. Beyond the tower, parked beside St. Paul's in Ninth Street, a hearse waited behind a team of horses wearing tall plumes of black feathers. The Negro postilions wore white gloves and black frock coats. Behind the hearse a small military band with black armbands waited for the casket to be brought from the church.

Julia crossed the road in front of the plumed horses, climbed the steps to the War Department, and asked the clerk in the hall office whether Major Adam Faulconer of General Johnston's staff was in the building. The clerk did not even need to examine his book. "All the General's staff are out of the city, miss. We haven't seen Major Faulconer for a month now."

"Did he send a letter for me?" Julia asked. Sometimes staff officers circumvented the postal service by using the army's messengers to carry their private mail into the city. "For Miss Gordon?" Julia said.

The clerk sorted through the letters on his table, but there was nothing for Julia. She thanked him and walked slowly uphill, turning into Franklin Street and trying to decide whether she was disappointed by Adam's silence or whether, in an odd way, it was a relief.

Julia had written to tell Adam she had a message for him, but she had received no reply and was beginning to suspect that Adam's silence was perhaps a symptom of his change of heart.

Julia had been surprised when Adam first courted her, but she had also been flattered, for he was a remarkably handsome man and known to be both honorable and honest. Adam was also—and Julia was not so dishonest to pretend to be blind to the advantage—sole heir to one of Virginia's greatest fortunes, and while Julia constantly told herself that her affection for Adam was in no wise altered by that circumstance, she also knew that the circumstance must have an effect as marked and constant as the unseen pull of the sun on the earth's tides. Julia's mother lived with the constant shame of poverty, which shame made her husband's life a misery, and by marrying into the Faulconer family, Julia knew she could alleviate the unhappinesses of both her parents.

Yet, and Julia fell into a reverie as she walked slowly through the city, there was something which did not ring true about her feelings for Adam. The word "love," she thought, was so imprecise. Did she love Adam? She was sure she did, and she anticipated a married life of good and charitable works that would stretch far ahead, even into the next century, and whenever she thought about that useful good life she saw it in terms of being briskly busy, but never in terms of being happy. Not unhappy, certainly, but not happy either, and then she would chide herself for an un-Christian selfishness in even wanting happiness. Happiness, she told herself, was not a product of pleasurable pursuits, but an effect brought about by being engaged in ceaseless good works.

Yet sometimes, in the middle of the nights when she awoke to the sound of the wind sighing across the roofs and the rain bubbling in the gutters, she felt melancholy because she sensed a lack of joy. Did Adam, she wondered, ever worry about joy? He seemed so gloomy, so full of high purpose and deep troubles. He said it was the war that oppressed his soul, but Julia was not blind to other young people whose love and happiness transcended the fighting.

Julia realized she was walking west on Franklin Street, which meant she must soon pass the house where Sally Truslow lived. Julia had not yet summoned the courage to make that call and was ashamed of that failure. She walked past the house on the far side of the road and felt intimidated by its grandeur. A hazy sun glossed the windows, but could not quite hide the chandeliers that hung in the rooms beyond. The front door gleamed in the unfamiliar sunlight. She had a sudden impulse to cross the road and pull the polished brass bellpull, but then decided that carrying two bloody rabbits into a house, even a house of ill repute, was hardly the best way to save a soul. And that, she assured herself, was why she wanted to visit Sally.

She walked on home, passing houses tightly shuttered and locked because their inhabitants had fled the Yankee approach. The city was safer because of that evacuation for the army had increased the provost patrols in an effort to protect the otherwise unguarded property. Other patrols had searched the city's poorer quarters to root out deserters, while the newspapers also proclaimed that the authorities were hunting down northern spies who sought to betray the Confederacy. The city was full of rumors and fear, and now it shivered to the sound of gunfire. The enemy was at the gates.

Julia reached her parents' house. She stood for an instant and listened to the muffled percussion of the heavy guns firing on the river and she closed her eyes and said a prayer that all the young men would come home safe. Unbidden, she had an image of Starbuck and was so surprised at that incursion that she burst into laughter. Then she carried the rabbits indoors and closed the house against the sound of war.

Belvedere Delaney's letter to Lieutenant Colonel Thorne stayed hidden for a whole week in the cobbler's shop in Catlett's Station. Each day the cobbler added more letters to the hiding place until, at last, he had enough to make his journey worthwhile. Then, with sixteen letters to Colonel Wilde all resealed into one large envelope, he locked his shop and told his friends he was delivering finished shoes to distant customers. Then, carrying a heavy bag of patched shoes with the clandestine mail hidden in its lining, he walked north. Once out of his own district he traveled only at night, taking care to avoid the partisan patrols of horsemen who had been known to string up a free Negro on the nearest hanging tree, passport or no passport.

It took him two nights' travel to reach the Federal lines south of the Potomac, where he simply strolled into a camp of Pennsylvania infantry. "You looking for work, Sambo?" a sergeant challenged him.

"Just the mail clerk, sir." The cobbler pulled off his hat and bobbed his head respectfully.

"There's a mail wagon by the sutler's shed, but I'm watching you! You thieve anything, you black bastard, and I'll have my men use your hide for target practice."

"Yes, sir! I'll behave, sir! Thank you, sir!"

The postal service clerk took the one large envelope, franked it, then pushed the change across the counter and told the cobbler to make himself scarce. Next day the sixteen letters were placed on Lieutenant Colonel Wilde's desk in the Inspector General's Department in Washington, D.C., where they waited with over a hundred other letters that needed the Colonel's attention. The Colonel's office was woefully undermanned, for, in the rapid expansion of the U.S. Army, the Inspector General's Department had perforce become a convenient place to delegate tasks that no other department seemed competent or willing to perform. Among those tasks was the appreciation of intelligence received from the Confederacy, a job which might have been more properly performed by the Secret Service Bureau, but not everyone in the U.S. government shared General McClellan's faith in Detective Pinkerton, and so a separate intelligence service had sprung up in Washington, which, like every other orphaned responsibility, had landed in the Inspector General's Department.

It was that haphazard delegation of responsibility which had first guided Belvedere Delaney's original offer of help to Lieutenant Colonel Thorne's desk. Ever since that day Delaney, like a score of other northern sympathizers in the Confederacy, sent his material to Thorne, who added such correspondence to the great flood of information that threatened to overwhelm an office already overburdened with extraneous duties. Thus, when Delaney's latest letter reached his office, Thorne was nowhere near Washington, but was in Massachusetts conducting an inspection tour of northern seacoast forts, which tour was expected to last for much of the month of May, and so Delaney's letter waited in Washington while Colonel Thorne enumerated Fort Warren's fire buckets and latrines. It was not, Thorne told himself, why he had joined the army, but he still lived in hope that one day he might gallop across a smoke-torn field and save his country from disaster. Colonel Thorne, for all his ramrod-straight back and hardened face and unyielding eye, could still dream a soldier's dreams and pray a soldier's prayer, which prayer was that he would get to fight at least one battle for his country before the Young Napoleon brought America a lasting peace.

And the letter gathered dust.

The land torpedo had been left so that the commander of the Army of the Potomac could see for himself to just what abject depths the rebel forces had sunk. "It's only by the grace of Almighty God we discovered this one before it blew, though God knows too many others have exploded without warning." The speaker was a short, brusque major of the Corps of Engineers who was dressed in shirtsleeves and suspenders and had an air of competent efficiency that reminded Starbuck of Thomas Truslow.

Major General McClellan alighted from his horse and walked stiffly across to examine the land torpedo that had been concealed in a barrel stenciled with the misspelled legend "Dried Oisters, Messrs Moore and Carline, Mt Folly, Va." McClellan, immaculate in a blue frock coat with twin rows of brass buttons and a fine gilded belt, approached the barrel gingerly.

"We've made it safe, sir, as you'll see." The Major must have noticed the General's nervousness. "But it was a most ungodly device, upon my soul it was, sir."

"A disgrace," McClellan said, still keeping his distance from the oyster barrel. "A thorough disgrace."

"We found it on yon house." The Major gestured toward a small farmhouse that stood abandoned a hundred yards from the road. "We brought it down here for you to see, sir."

"And so you should, for all the world to see!" McClellan stood very erect, one hand slipped into an unbuttoned opening of his coat and with a concerned frown on his face. That frown, Starbuck had noted, seemed to be the young General's perpetual expression. "I would not have believed," McClellan said loudly and slowly so that the horsemen gathered beside the road could hear every word, "that men born and raised in the United States of America, even men bitten by the envy of secessionism, should stoop to stratagems so low and devices so evil." Many of the mounted officers nodded gravely while Pinkerton and James, who were accompanying Starbuck on this ride westward with the general, tutted loudly. The foreign newspaper reporters, to whom McClellan was really aiming his remarks, scribbled in their notebooks. The only man who seemed unsurprised and unshocked by the booby-trapped barrel was a scarred, one-eyed French military observer who, Starbuck had noted, seemed roundly amused by much of what he saw, even by this evil device.

The oyster barrel had been half filled with sand in which a three-and-a-half-inch shell had been stood upright. The copper fuse plug had been unscrewed from the shell's nose to leave a narrow shaft running into the missile's explosive belly. That shaft had been filled with gunpowder, but not before a crude, old-fashioned flintlock had been soldered onto the shell's nose. The Major demonstrated how a string attached to the underside of the barrel's lid should have tripped the flintlock so that it would have struck a spark that would have ignited the powder and so exploded the main charge buried deep inside the shell. "It would have killed a man easily," the Major said solemnly. "Two or three men if they'd been close enough."

The retreating Confederates had left scores of such land torpedoes. Some were buried in the roads, some by wells, others in deserted houses; so many that by now the advancing Yankees had learned to search for tripwires or other trigger mechanisms, but every day one or two of the implements still found their victims, and every such victim added to the outrage felt by the northerners. "Tactics," McClellan announced to the newspapermen accompanying his headquarters staff, "that even heathen savages might hesitate before employing. You would think, would you not, that with the preponderance of men enjoyed by the rebels they would scarcely need to use such desperate measures? Yet such devices are, I suppose, a mark of their spiritual and moral degradation."

Murmurs of agreement sounded as the General remounted his horse and spurred away from the lethal barrel. The other horsemen jostled into place behind the army's diminutive commander, struggling to get the great man's attention, but McClellan, seeking a companion for the next portion of his journey, gestured to Pinkerton. "Bring your man, Pinkerton!" McClellan called, and Pinkerton urged Starbuck forward. They had waited days for this meeting with the General, a meeting that Starbuck had no enthusiasm for, but which Pinkerton insisted must happen. "So this is your messenger, Pinkerton?" McClellan said fiercely.

"It is, sir, and a brave man."

McClellan glanced at Starbuck, his face giving nothing away. They were riding through a flat country, past worn-out fields and dark sloughs and dripping pine trees. Hyacinths grew on the margins of the small streams, but little else in the scenery looked attractive or cheerful. "Your name?" McClellan barked at Starbuck.

"Starbuck, sir."

"His brother, sir, is one of my most valuable men," Allen Pinkerton gestured toward James with the stem of his pipe. "He's behind us, sir, if you'd like to greet him?"

"Quite so, good," McClellan said unhelpfully, then went silent again. Starbuck looked surreptitiously at the Yankee commander, seeing a short, stoutly built man with light brown hair, blue eyes, and a fresh complexion. The general was chewing tobacco and every now and then spat a stream of juice onto the road, taking care to lean well out of his saddle so that none of the spittle would soil his uniform or spatter on his highly polished boots. "Did you know what was in the message you delivered?" McClellan suddenly demanded of Starbuck.

"Yes, sir."

"And? And? What of it? You agree with it?"

"Of course, sir."

"It's a bad business," McClellan said, "a bad business." He fell silent again and Starbuck noticed that the sardonic French officer had ridden close so he could listen to their conversation. McClellan also saw the Frenchman. "You see, Colonel Lassan, just what we are fighting?" The General twisted in his saddle to confront the Frenchman.

"Exactly what is that, *mon General?*"

"An overwhelming enemy, that is what! An enemy that can match us two soldiers to one, and what does Washington do? You know what they do? They prevent McDowell's Corps from reinforcing us. In all the annals of warfare, Colonel, in all military history do you know another piece of treachery to match that? And why? Why? To preserve Washington, which is under no attack, none! They are fools! Cowards! Traitors! Apes!" The sudden passion astonished Starbuck, though he was hardly surprised by it. Most of the army knew of Major General McClellan's anger that President Lincoln had prevented the 1st Corps from sailing to reinforce the men on the peninsula. McClellan, the President said, must make do with the hundred and twenty thousand men he already possessed, but McClellan declared that the missing thirty-five thousand were the key to northern victory. "If I just had those men I might achieve something. As it is we can only hope for a miracle. Nothing else will save us now, only a miracle."

"Indeed, *mon General*," Colonel Lassan said, though with what Starbuck took to be an extraordinary lack of conviction.

McClellan turned back to Starbuck and wanted to know what units he had seen marching through the streets of Richmond, and Starbuck, who had by now become accustomed to telling monstrous lies, detailed unit after unit that he had neither seen nor heard of. He invented a whole Florida brigade, made up a cavalry regiment from Louisiana, and described batteries of heavy artillery that he conjured from the warm Virginia air. To his astonishment and amusement McClellan listened as avidly as Pinkerton had done, taking Starbuck's word as proof that a mighty enemy did indeed wait to ambush him in the environs of Richmond. "It's what we feared, Pinkerton!" McClellan said when Starbuck's invention had run its course. "Johnston must have a hundred and fifty thousand men!"

"At least that many, sir."

"We must be cautious. If I lose this army, then the whole war is done," McClellan said. "We need to know the exact deployments of these new rebel brigades." This last requirement was addressed to Pinkerton, who assured the General that Starbuck would be ready to travel back to Richmond just as soon as he was given the list of questions which McClellan wanted answered by the prized, mysterious spy who seemed to lie at the very heart of the Confederate high command. "You'll get your questions," McClellan assured Starbuck, then raised a hand in response to a cheering group of Negroes who stood beside the road. A woman in a ragged dress and torn apron ran forward with a bunch of hyacinths that she offered to the General. McClellan hesitated, plainly hoping that one of his aides would take the flowers for him, but the woman thrust the blossoms up into his hands. He took them with a forced smile. "Poor people," he said when they were out of earshot. "They believe we've come to liberate them."

"You haven't?" Starbuck could not resist the question.

"This is not a war to divest United States citizens of their lawful property, not even those citizens foolish enough to make armed rebellion against their government." The General sounded peeved at having to make the explanation. "This is a conflict about preserving the union, and if I believed for one moment that we were risking white men's blood to free slaves I would resign my commission. Isn't that so, Marcy?" He hurled the request for confirmation over his shoulder and Marcy, a gloomy-looking staff officer, confirmed that was indeed the General's firm opinion. McClellan suddenly scowled at the hyacinths in his hand and tossed them to the side of the road, where the blossoms scattered across a puddle. Starbuck turned in his saddle and saw that the Negroes were still watching the horsemen. He felt a sudden temptation to dismount and gather up the flowers, but just as he twitched his reins Pinkerton's horse trod the blossoms into the mud.

The sight of the Negroes provoked Colonel Lassan, who spoke perfect English, to tell of a slave girl he had met in Williamsburg. "Only nineteen, and a pretty thing. She had four sons already and each one of them whelped off a white man. She reckoned that made her boys more valuable. She was proud of that. She said a good half-breed male infant could sell for five hundred dollars."

"A pretty half-breed girl would fetch a deal more," Pinkerton offered.

"And some are damn near white," a staff officer observed. "Damned if I could tell the difference."

"Buy a white one, Lassan, and take her home," Pinkerton suggested.

"Why just one?" the Frenchman asked with mock innocence. "I could manage a boatload if they were all pretty enough."

"Is it true," McClellan broke into the conversation in a tone which suggested he disapproved of such idle and lascivious talk, "it is true," he repeated as he stared intently at Starbuck, "that Robert Lee is made second-in-command to Johnston?"

"I'd not heard as much, sir," Starbuck said truthfully.

"I pray it is true," McClellan said with a thoughtful frown. "Lee's always been too cautious. A weak man. He doesn't like responsibility. He lacks moral firmness, and men like that prove timid under fire. I've noticed it. What do they call Lee in the South?" he asked Starbuck.

"Granny, sir."

McClellan gave a short bark of a laugh. "I suspect a young Napoleon can manhandle a grandmother, eh, Lassan?"

"Indeed, *mon General*."

"But can he handle a hundred and fifty thousand rebels?" McClellan asked, then fell silent as he pondered that question. They were riding through an area where infantry was encamped and the northern troops, discovering that their General was in the vicinity, ran to the road and began cheering. Starbuck, dropping back from McClellan's side, noted how the small General was immediately encouraged by the troops' adulation and how genuine that adulation was. The men were invigorated by McClellan's presence just as the General was vivified by their cheers. There were even greater cheers when he stopped his horse and begged a soldier to lend him his smoking pipe so he could light himself a cigar. That homely touch seemed especially moving to the infantrymen who crowded around to touch the General's big bay horse.

"Tell us when we're going to beat the rebs, General!" a man shouted.

"In good time! All in good time! You know I won't risk your lives unnecessarily! All in good time!" One of the men offered the General a piece of hardtack and McClellan raised huge cheers by disingenuously inquiring whether you were supposed to eat the thing or use it to shingle a roof.

"He's a wonderful man," James confided to his brother.

"Isn't he?" Starbuck said. In these last few days he had discovered that the best way to handle James was to offer a bland agreement to everything his brother said, yet even that small gesture was sometimes hard. James's relief and pleasure at the prodigal's return were heartfelt and he wanted to make Starbuck happy as a reward for that change of heart, but his attentions could be cloying. James might believe, like his father, that tobacco was the devil's weed, but if Starbuck wanted to smoke then James was happy to buy cigars from the army's sutlers whose wagons acted as trading posts wherever a regiment was encamped. James even pretended to believe Starbuck's claim that he needed wine and whiskey to settle his dyspeptic stomach and used his own money to buy the so-called medicine.

James's tender assiduity only increased Starbuck's guilt, a guilt that was worsened when he saw how much his brother liked having his company. James was proud of his brother, envied him indeed, and took pleasure in spreading the story that his brother, far from having been a copperhead this past year, had in fact been an agent for the North ever since the war's first shots. Starbuck did not deny the story, but James's pleasure in it only made the younger brother's conscience more tender as he contemplated betraying the trust. Though, perversely, the prospect of that betrayal became ever more inviting because it meant returning to Richmond and so escaping James's attentions. All that was delaying Starbuck's return was the list of questions which he was supposed to deliver to Adam. Those questions were being devised by McClellan and Pinkerton, but as each day brought fresh rumors of rebel reinforcements, so each day added more questions and amended those already on the list.

Another rush of eager soldiers came to surround the General, so many that James and Starbuck were driven apart by the press of bodies. Starbuck's horse edged sideways and began cropping at the grass growing between the muddy ruts cut into the road's verge. General McClellan delivered his customary speech about leading his precious boys to victory, but only when the time was right and the circumstances propitious. The men cheered the words as the General rode on westward.

"They will follow him anywhere," a sardonic voice spoke softly from just behind Starbuck. "Unfortunately he never wants to lead them anywhere."

Starbuck turned to see that the speaker was the savage-looking French military attache, Colonel Lassan, whose ruined eye was covered with a mildewed patch. The Frenchman's uniform was one of faded glory, the metallic thread of his tunic tarnished and his epaulettes ragged. He wore a massive, steel-hilted, straight-bladed sword, and had two revolvers holstered on his saddle. He lit a cigar and offered it to Starbuck. The gesture allowed the other staff officers to ride on by, which was evidently what the Frenchman desired. "A hundred and fifty thousand men?" Lassan asked skeptically.

"Maybe more." Starbuck had taken the cigar. "Thank you."

"Seventy thousand?" The Frenchman lit a cigar for himself, then clicked his tongue to make his horse walk obediently on.

"Sir?"

"I'm guessing, monsieur, that General Johnston has seventy thousand men. At the most, and that your mission is to deceive General McClellan." He smiled at Starbuck.

"The suggestion, sir, is outrageous," Starbuck protested hotly.

"Of course it's outrageous," Lassan said in an amused tone, "but also true, yes?" Ahead of them, dimly visible through a squall of rain that was sweeping toward the party of horsemen, the bulbous yellow shape of one of Professor Lowe's balloons swayed in the gray sky. "Let me tell you my position, Mr. Starbuck," Lassan continued suavely. "I am an observer, sent by my government to watch the war and to report to Paris what techniques and weapons might be useful to our own army. I am not here to take sides. I am not like the Count of Paris or the Prince de Joinville"—he gestured at two elegant French staff officers who rode close behind the General—"who have come here to fight for the North. I frankly do not care which side wins. It is not my business to care, only to observe and to write reports, and it seems to me that perhaps it is time I watched the fighting from the southern side."

Starbuck shrugged, as if to suggest that Lassan's decisions were none of his business.

"Because I would very much like to see how seventy thousand men plan to outwit a hundred and twenty thousand," Lassan said.

"The rebels' one hundred and fifty thousand men," Starbuck said doggedly, "will dig in and see the northerners off with cannon fire."

"Not so," Lassan said. "You can't afford to have so many Yankees sitting on your doorstep, nor can you afford to match McClellan at siege warfare. The man may be a bombast, but he knows his engineering. No, you rebels have to outmaneuver him and the battle will be fascinating. My problem, of course, is that I am not allowed to cross the lines. My choices are either to sail to Bermuda and pay a blockade runner to smuggle me into one of the Confederacy's ports, or else to go west and work my way back overland through Missouri. Either way I shall miss this spring's fighting. Unless, that is, you will consent to allow me to accompany you when you go back to the rebel side?"

"If I go back to the rebel side," Starbuck said with as much haughtiness as he could muster, "I shall do so as a servant of the United States."

"Nonsense!" Lassan said equably. "You're a rogue, Mr. Starbuck, and one rogue can always recognize another. And you're an inventive liar. The 2nd Florida Brigade! Very good, Mr. Starbuck, very good. Yet surely there are not enough white men living in Florida to make one brigade, let alone two! Do you know why General McClellan believes you?"

"Because I'm speaking the truth."

"Because he wants to believe you. He desperately needs to be outnumbered. That way, you see, no disgrace attaches to his defeat. So when will you be going back?"

"I cannot say."

"Then let me know when you can say," Lassan said. Somewhere ahead of the horsemen there sounded the bark of artillery fire, the noise dimmed by the damp air. The sound seemed to be coming from the left-hand side of the road beyond a distant belt of trees. "Watch now," Lassan said to Starbuck. "We shall stop our advance at any moment. You see if I'm not right."

The guns cracked again, and suddenly General McClellan raised a hand. "We might pause here," the General announced, "just to rest the horses."

Lassan offered Starbuck an amused look. "Are you a betting man?"

"I've played some poker," Starbuck said.

"So do you think the rebels' pair of deuces will beat the Young Napoleon's royal flush?"

"Nothing can beat a royal flush," Starbuck said.

"It depends on who is holding it, Mr. Starbuck, and whether they dare play it. Maybe the General doesn't want to get his nice new cards dirty?" The Frenchman smiled. "What are they saying in Richmond? That the war is lost?"

"Some are," Starbuck said, and felt himself coloring. He had said that himself, and had tried to persuade Sally of it.

"It isn't," Lassan said, "not as long as the Young Napoleon is the South's enemy. He's frightened of shadows, Mr. Starbuck, and I suspect your job is to make him see shadows where there are none. You're one of the reasons why seventy thousand men might well beat a hundred and twenty."

"I'm just a northerner who has come to his senses," Starbuck retorted.

"And I, monsieur, am the King of Timbuctoo," Lassan said. "Let me know when you want to ride home." He touched his hat and spurred on, and Starbuck, watching the Frenchman ride toward the sound of the guns, suddenly knew he was wrong and Sally was right. The hog was still squealing, and the war was not lost.

"You think the war's lost, you bastard?" Sergeant Truslow grabbed hold of Izard Cobb's ear, ignoring the man's yelp of pain. "If I tell you to hurry, you towheaded piece of shit, you hurry. Now hurry!" He kicked Cobb in the rear. A bullet whistled overhead, making Cobb duck. "And hurry upright!" Truslow shouted, "you goddamn son of a pregnant bitch!"

A burst of smoke showed as a cannon fired from the far tree line. The fuse smoke of the shell traced a tiny gray streak in the air, visible only to the men almost directly in line with the missile's trajectory. Sergeant Truslow, seeing the shell coming, knew there was no time to take cover and so pretended insouciance. The missile slammed into the railroad embankment behind him just a heartbeat before the cannon's noise cracked over the river and marshes.

"Corporal Bailey!" Truslow shouted almost as soon as the dirt thrown up by the striking shell had subsided.

"Sergeant!"

"Dig that shell out!" The shell had failed to explode, which meant there could be a perfectly usable missile buried in the soft dirt of the embankment. If there had been a Confederate artillery battery nearby Truslow would have offered the gunners the salvaged shell to be returned to its senders, but lacking any gunners who might appreciate the gift, he reckoned he would rig it as a land torpedo.

The Legion was on the southern bank of the Chickahominy River, hard by the trestles of the Richmond and York Railroad bridge. The last Confederate locomotive to cross the bridge had steamed by three hours before, dragging behind it all the rolling stock from the depot at White House and the sidings of Tunstall's Station. The engineers had then set charges to the bridge, lit the fuses, and watched as nothing happened. The Faulconer Legion, the nearest infantry unit to the bridge, had then been ordered to hold off the enemy's skirmishers while the engineers determined just what had gone wrong with their explosives.

The bridge was no great piece of engineering. It did not have to fly across a cavernous gorge or carry the rails between two mighty hills; instead it was little more than a low trestled pier that plodded through the marshes, splashed across the river, then went stolidly on for another wet quarter mile until the rails again reached solid ground on the Chickahominy's far bank. It was on that solid ground that the Yankees had unlimbered two field guns beside a dense grove of moss-hung trees, and now the northern artillery fire was crashing across the grassy marsh with its stagnant pools, stunted bushes, and reed beds. Some dismounted northern cavalrymen were also on the far ground, adding their carbine fire to the cannonade, while yet another group of dismounted cavalrymen was advancing along the trestle bridge in the hope of driving the southern engineers away.

"Sergeant Hutton!" Truslow shouted. "Bring your squad! Hurry now!"

Carter Hutton shouted at his men to close on the embankment where Truslow formed them in two ranks. For a few seconds they made a tempting target for the gunners, but Truslow had been timing the cannon fire and knew he had a half minute while the artillerymen reloaded. "Aim at those bastards! Straight down the rails! Sights at three hundred yards." He glanced at the advancing cavalrymen who had not recognized the danger and still advanced along the dry rails instead of using the marshy ground on either side of the trestles. "Fire!" Truslow shouted. "Now get down, off the rails, hurry!"

Five seconds later a shell screamed just above the place where Truslow's twin files had been standing and exploded harmlessly in the trees behind the Legion's position. The smoke from Truslow's volley cleared to show that the advancing cavalrymen had scattered into the rain-filled pools on either side of the bridge. "Keep their heads down!" Truslow shouted, then turned as Andrew Bailey walked up with the excavated shell cradled in his arms. It was a ten-pound shell, just under three inches across, with a zinc plug in its nose. Truslow placed the shell on a rail tie and used the back blade of his bowie knife to unscrew the plug. Two men crouching nearby edged fearfully away, earning a look of scorn from Truslow.

The zinc plug had sealed the shaft sunk into the shell. In the shaft was a sliding plunger tipped with a brass percussion cap that should have been thrown forward by the shell's impact to explode on the underside of the plug. The sliding plunger was held in place by two thin and brittle metal projections that were designed to stop the detonator slipping forward and exploding when the shell was being transported or manhandled. Only the violent impact of a landing shell should have sufficient force to snap the metal projections, but this shell, landing in the soft earth of the embankment, had stayed intact.

Truslow used the knife blade to break the twin projections, then turned the shell upside down to shake the plunger loose. The plunger, topped with its percussion cap, had a narrow hole drilled down its center and filled with explosive. That powder was supposed to carry the fire down to the main charge that was protected from damp by a paper diaphragm. Truslow used a stick to pierce the diaphragm, then half filled the shell's empty fuse shaft with gunpowder taken from rifle cartridges. Lastly he put the plunger back into its tube, but now, instead of dropping to the bottom of the shaft, the plunger protruded an inch above the shell's nosecone. If anyone were to strike the exposed plunger the fire would lance down into the shell, explode the gunpowder Truslow had put in the shaft, and so ignite the main charge.

Now he needed to place the shell. Once the last train had passed the engineers had pulled up the steel rails and loaded them on the train's wagons for transport to Richmond, but they had left the wet wooden ties sunk in the ground. Truslow had two men dig up one of the ties, then excavate a hole in the coffin-shaped space the tie had left imprinted in the railbed. He placed the shell in the hole, its point uppermost, then put a stone next to it and carefully balanced the rail tie on the stone. He very gently rocked the tie, moving it an inch up and down, then stepped back to admire his work. The tie seemed to be raised an inch or so from its position, but with any luck the Yankees would not notice and a man would step on the tie and so bang the wood down onto the percussion cap.

"Enjoying yourself, Sergeant?" Major Bird had walked forward from the tree line where most of the Legion waited.

"Pity to waste a good shell," Truslow said, detecting a slight note of disapproval in Bird's otherwise innocent question.

Bird was not certain that land torpedoes were an entirely sporting method of waging war, yet he also knew that to wage a war on sporting lines was a ridiculous notion, the sort of notion his brother-in-law would entertain. War was about killing, not about obeying arcane rules of chivalry. "A letter's just arrived for you," he told Truslow.

"For me?" Truslow asked, astonished.

"Here." Bird took the letter from his pocket and handed it over, then used his half binocular to see how the engineers were progressing. "What's taking all the time?"

"Damp fuses," Truslow said, then brushed his hands against his coat before opening the delicate pink envelope and taking out the single pink sheet that must have come from a prewar stock of gilded and deckled paper. Truslow peered at the signature first. "It's from my Sally!" He sounded surprised. A bullet whistled past his ear and a shell tumbled overhead, making an eerie wail as it passed.

"Oh good," Major Bird said, not at Truslow's news, but because the engineers were at last scrambling back toward the southern bank.

"Give them cover!" Truslow shouted, and the skirmishers' rifles snapped angrily across the river. "I didn't know my Sally could even write."

Judging from the envelope, Bird thought, she could not. It was a miracle the letter had arrived at all, except the army was good at trying to work that particular miracle. Few things benefited morale as much as letters from home. "What does she say?" Bird asked.

"Can't rightly tell," Truslow growled.

Bird gave the Sergeant a shrewd glance. Truslow was, without doubt, the toughest man in the Legion, indeed he was probably the toughest man Bird had ever met, yet there was a look of embarrassed shame in Truslow's eyes now. "Can I help?" Bird asked casually.

"It's the girl's writing," Truslow said. "I can make out her name, just about, but not much else."

"Let me," Bird said, who knew full well that Truslow was no great reader. He took the letter, then looked up as the engineers ran past him. "Fall back!" Bird shouted at the men of K Company, then he looked down at the letter again. "My God," Bird exclaimed. The handwriting was truly appalling.

"Is she all right?" Truslow immediately asked, his voice full of anxiety.

"It's just her handwriting, Sergeant, nothing else. Let me see now. You'll be surprised to hear from her, she says, but she is indeed well and she reckons that she ought to have written a long time ago, but says she's just as stubborn as you are which is why she didn't write," Bird paraphrased. He and Truslow, left alone on the embankment, were suddenly the target for a flurry of carbine shots. An engineer shouted at the two men to get back before the fuse was lit and so they began walking slowly toward the safety of the trees. "She says she's sorry for what happened," Bird went on reading the letter as the cavalry bullets whistled around them, "but she's not sorry for what she did. Does that make sense?"

"Never could make hide or hair out of what that girl said," Truslow commented gruffly. In truth he missed Sally. She was a stubborn little bitch, but the only kin he had.

Bird hurried on, not wanting to embarrass Truslow by noticing the Sergeant's tears. "She says that she saw Nate Starbuck! This is interesting. He came to her when they let him out of prison and he asked her to write to you and promise that he'll be coming back to the Legion. So that's why she's writing. I must say," Bird said, "that Starbuck has a curious way of announcing his return."

"So where is he?" Truslow demanded.

"She doesn't say." Bird turned the letter over. The engineers had lit the fuse and the spark-spitting trail hissed unnoticed past the two men. Bird frowned as he tried to decipher the second page. "She said that's why she wrote, because Nate asked, but she's glad he asked because it's time you and she became friends. And she also says she has a new job, one you'd approve of, but she doesn't say what it is. There, that's it." Bird handed the letter back to Truslow. "I'm sure you can make it out for yourself now that I've described it."

"Reckon I can," Truslow said, then sniffed again. "So Mr. Starbuck's coming back!"

"According to your daughter, yes." Bird sounded dubious.

"So you won't need to appoint an officer to K Company?"

"I wasn't going to," Bird said.

"Good," Truslow said. "After all, we elected Starbuck, didn't we?"

"I'm afraid you did." And much against General Faulconer's will, Bird reflected happily. Over seven hundred men had placed votes in the election of field officers and Starbuck's name had been written onto more than five hundred of the slips.

"And if elections mean anything," Truslow said, "then Starbuck should be here, shouldn't he now?"

"I suppose he should," Bird said, "but I confess I can't see General Faulconer allowing it. Or Colonel Swynyard." Not that Swynyard was much in evidence these days. So far as Bird could determine the brigade's second-in-command was lost in a perpetual stupor brought on by an unending supply of four-dollar-a-gallon skull-rot whiskey.

"A dollar of my money says that Starbuck can whip the General," Truslow said. "He's a smart one, Starbuck."

"A dollar?" Bird asked. "Done." He shook Truslow's grimy hand just as the bridge exploded behind them. Three hundred pounds of gunpowder shattered the stilts and sent the old timbers spinning into the air. Smoke and noise boiled across the marshes, startling a hundred fowl up from the reed beds. The river water seemed to recoil from the explosions, then washed back with a great rush to send a plume of steam billowing after the smoke. Where there had been a bridge there was now just a line of rotted, blackened stumps in the churning water, while up and downstream the debris splashed into the Chickahominy or else slapped down into the stagnant marsh pools where the cottonmouths and moccasins squirmed away.

One piece of wood flew high into the air and then tumbled down with an unerring aim to smack direct onto the tie that Truslow had balanced with such care on the stone. The impact of the wood banged the tie onto the percussion cap and the shell beneath exploded, biting a small crater into the rain-weakened embankment. "Son of a bitch," Truslow said, evidently speaking of the wasted effort he had expended on the land torpedo, but Major Bird saw that the Sergeant was smiling anyway. Such happiness, he decided, was something to be prized in wartime. Today might be filled with laughter, yet tomorrow could bring what the preachers called the long dark home in the dirt. And the thought of such graves filled Bird with a sudden terror. Suppose Truslow did not live to see his Sally again? Or suppose his own dear Priscilla were widowed? That thought filled Thaddeus Bird with the dread that he was not tough enough to be a soldier. Because war, to Bird, was a game, despite all his caustic preaching to the contrary. War, to Bird, was a game of wits in which the unregarded school-teacher would prove he was wittier and cleverer and faster and better than all the rest. Yet when the wax-skinned dead were lined in sepulchral judgment, and their bruised, dirt-clotted eyes asked clever Bird to explain why they had died, he had no answer.

The two Yankee guns fired a last futile time and their shells skipped and slapped across the marsh. The river's turmoil subsided until the water once again slid slow and gray past the blackened remnants of the bridge to carry its dead cargo of white-bellied fish toward the sea. A mist crept off the wetland to mingle with the gunsmoke. The woods were filled with whippoorwills, and Major Bird, who did not believe in God, suddenly wished to Almighty God that this goddamn war was over.

~ PART THREE ~

T HE ARMIES CAME TO A STOP IN A CURVE WHICH RAN around Richmond's northeastern flank. General Johnston had now retreated so far that the northern soldiers could hear the hours being tolled on Richmond's church bells and, when the wind was in the west, smell the city's rich stench of tobacco and coalsmoke.

Richmond's newspapers grumbled that the Yankees had been allowed too close to the city and the doctors of both armies complained because so many troops were stationed in the disease-ridden marshes of the Chickahominy River. The hospitals filled with men dying of the river's fever, an ailment that, even as the days warmed toward summer's stifling heat, made its victims shake with uncontrollable fits of shivering. Doctors explained that the fever was a natural consequence of the invisible miasma that crept from the river with the sepulchral mists which whitened the marshes at dawn and dusk, and if the armies could but move to higher ground then the fever would disappear, but General Johnston insisted that the fate of Richmond depended on the river and that his men must therefore endure the mist-borne miasma. There was a strategy, Johnston insisted, and in the face of that military word the doctors could do nothing but abandon their arguments and watch their patients die.

At the end of May, on a Friday afternoon that was sultry and still, Johnston assembled his aides and explained that strategy. He had pinned a map to the parlor wall of the house that served as his head-quarters and was using a walnut-handled toasting fork as a pointer. "You see, gentlemen, how I have forced McClellan to straddle the Chickahominy? The northern army is a divided force, gentlemen, a divided force." He emphasized the remark by rapping the map north and south of the river with the toasting fork. "One of the first rules of war is never to divide your force in the face of the enemy, but that is just what McClellan has done!" Johnston was in one of his didactic moods, treating his aides as though they were a group of new cadets at West Point. "And why should a general never divide his force?" he now asked, peering expectantly at his aides.

"Because it can be defeated in detail, sir," one of the aides replied smartly.

"Precisely. And tomorrow morning, gentlemen, at dawn, we shall obliterate this half of the northern army." Johnston tapped the toasting fork on the map. "Obliterate, gentlemen, obliterate."

He had indicated that portion of the map which lay east of Richmond and south of the Chickahominy River. The river's source lay northwest of the city, then, widening swiftly, the watercourse ran slantwise across the city's northern approaches and down through the lowlands that lay to the east of Richmond before it joined the wider flow of the James. Johnston's Confederate army was all south of the river, but McClellan's larger force was divided; half the troops were north of the Chickahominy's malarial swamps and half were south. It was Johnston's intention to crash out of the dawn mists and tear that southern half into bloody ruin before the Yankee troops north of the river could march over their replacement bridges to rescue their beleaguered colleagues. "And we shall do it tomorrow morning, gentlemen, at dawn," Johnston said, and could not resist a satisfied smile when he saw their astonishment.

He was pleased because their surprise was exactly the response he wanted. Johnston had informed no one of his plans; neither his second-in-command, General Smith, nor even his President, Jefferson Davis. There were too many spies in Richmond, and too many men who might be tempted to desert to the enemy with the news, and to prevent that betrayal Johnston had hatched his plans in secret and kept them hidden until now, the afternoon before battle, when his aides must carry his orders to the divisional commanders.

Daniel Hill's division would lead the attack, striking at the center of the enemy lines. "Hill must fight alone for a while," Johnston explained to his aides, "because we want to suck the Yankees in, embroil them, then we'll hit their flanks, here and here." The toaster rapped on the map, tearing it each time and showing how, like the outer tines of a trident, the twin attacks would slam into an enemy who would have conveniently impaled himself on the trident's central spike. "Longstreet strikes their northern flank," Johnston continued, "while General Huger's division hits their southern, and by midday, gentlemen, the Yankees will be dead, prisoners, or fugitives in the White Oak Swamp." Johnston could taste the victory already; he could hear the cheers as he rode into Richmond's Capitol Square and see the envy on the faces of his rival generals like Beauregard and Robert Lee. The plan, he knew, was brilliant. All that lay between this moment and glory was the battle that would begin when his gray-clad troops swarmed out of the dawn mists, and if those troops had surprise on their side, then victory, Johnston believed, was assured.

Three aides were given the sealed orders to carry to the three generals of division. Adam Faulconer was ordered to ride to General Huger's headquarters, which lay on the very edge of Richmond. "One set of orders," Johnston's chief of staff, an affable man called Morton, said as he handed the sealed packet to Adam, "and your signature here, Adam." Colonel Morton held out a receipt which acknowledged that Adam had indeed taken possession of the envelope. "You get Huger to sign the receipt here, see? Old Huger will probably invite you to supper, but be back here by midnight. And for

God's sake, Adam, make sure he knows what he's supposed to be doing tomorrow." That was why Johnston had taken such care to demonstrate his strategy to his aides; so that they, in turn, could answer his generals' questions. Johnston knew that if he had fetched the generals to his headquarters the army would have smelt the imminent excitement and some wretched man would have been bound to slip over to the enemy in the night and warn them that trouble was brewing.

Adam signed the receipt, thus acknowledging that he had taken responsibility for one set of orders, then he put the paper into a leather pouch on his belt. "I'd be on your way," Colonel Morton advised, "before the rain comes. And make sure Huger signs that paper, Adam! Either him or his chief of staff. No one else."

Adam waited on the house verandah as his horse was saddled. The air was motionless and stagnant, heavy and dark, matching his brooding and despondent mood. He fingered the precious order, wondering if the destruction of all his hopes lay inside the sealed envelope. Perhaps, he thought, the envelope was the key to southern victory, and he imagined the northern army fleeing as they had at Bull Run, and in his fears he saw panicked men floundering in the chest-high sloughs of White Oak Swamp and being shot down by malicious, gleeful rebels like the cackling fiends who had fired from the summit of Ball's Bluff. He saw the Chickahominy spilling blood-reddened waters into the James and shuddered at the realism of his imaginings, and for a mad second he was tempted to take his horse and gallop it across the lines, roweling its flanks bloody as he spurred past the astonished Confederate pickets and so to the northern army. Then he thought of the grief that such a desertion would cause his father, and he thought of Julia in Richmond, and all the old turmoil surged up inside Adam. The war was wrong, yet he was a Faulconer and so heir to a family that had ridden into battle beside George Washington. Faulconers did not disgrace their lineage by deserting to the enemy.

Except how could the country founded by Washington be the enemy?

Adam fingered the orders in his belt pouch and wondered for the thousandth time why the Young Napoleon had proved so hesitant. Adam had betrayed the South's weakness on the peninsula and as a consequence had expected McClellan to break out of Fort Monroe like an avenging angel, but instead the northern commander had chosen a stately, cautious approach that had given the rebels ample time to stiffen and thicken the defenses of Richmond. And now, just when the North was within an easy afternoon's walk of Richmond, the rebels were planning an onslaught that could tear the heart from the northern army, and Adam, standing on the verandah and watching clouds black as night heap ominously above the stagnant forests, knew that he was incapable of stopping the disaster. He did not have the courage to desert.

"Young Adam! Don't move!" Colonel Morton pushed his head through the muslin curtains of a window at the verandah's far end. "We've got another letter for you!"

"Very good, sir," Adam acknowledged. An orderly had just brought Adam's horse to the front of the house and Adam told the man to tie the reins to the balustrade. The horse lowered its head and grazed a patch of grass that grew thick by the verandah steps. A slave who belonged to the owner of the commandeered house was digging at the hoof-trampled remains of a vegetable garden. The man was tired and kept pausing, but then he would remember Adam's presence on the verandah and so he would wipe his brow and bend again to his work. Adam, watching the man, felt an impulse of irrational and unfair anger at the whole black race. Why in God's name had anyone imported them to America, for without them the country would surely be the happiest, most peaceful land on earth. That unbidden thought made him feel ashamed of himself. It was not the fault of the slaves, but of the slavocracy. It was not the black race, but his own kind who had disturbed the peace and soured the land's content. "It's too hot to work, isn't it?" he called to the slave, trying to make open amends for his private thoughts.

"Too hot, massa. Certain too hot."

"I'd rest if I were you," Adam said.

"Plenty rest in heaven, Lord Jesus be praised, massa," the slave said and thrust the spade's broad blade back into the reddish, dull soil.

"Here you are, Adam," Colonel Morton strode onto the verandah, his spurs clinking as he walked. "We're lending Pete Longstreet some of Huger's men. Huger won't like it, but Longstreet will be advancing closer to the Yankees, so he needs the extra rifles. For God's sake be politic with Huger."

"Of course, sir." Adam took the proffered envelope. "Will you be requiring . . ." He had begun to ask whether Colonel Morton would want another signature from General Huger acknowledging receipt of this second set of orders, but then Adam checked his words. "Very good, sir."

"Back by midnight, young Adam, we all need our beauty sleep tonight. And be gentle with old Huger. He's a prickly beast."

Adam rode west. Where the road passed through the woods the air seemed even more oppressive. Leaves hung motionless, their stillness oddly threatening. The day felt unnatural, but so much of Adam's world seemed unreal these days, even Julia, and that thought reminded him that he should make an effort to see her soon. She had written with her mysterious summons, and even though she had insisted that her message was not of a personal nature Adam could not shake a suspicion that Julia wanted to end the engagement. Of late Adam had begun to think that he did not really understand Julia, and to apprehend that her desires were altogether more complicated than he had ever supposed. On the surface she was a conventional, pious, and dutifully gracious young lady, but Adam was subtly aware of a quicksilver vivacity that Julia kept hidden, and it was that quicksilver quality that made Adam feel unworthy of her. He suspected his mother had possessed the same quality and that it had been crushed out of her by his father.

Adam stopped his horse in a stretch of woods where no army camps were visible. His journey had taken him through a score of regimental camps, but suddenly he was alone in a heavy, dark, and still forest and able to tease into the light an idea that had been flickering in the back of his mind. He opened his pouch and brought out the two messages. They were wrapped in identical light brown envelopes, sealed with identical blobs of scarlet wax, and addressed in the same spiky black handwriting. The battle orders were thicker than the second set of instructions, but otherwise there was nothing to distinguish one envelope from the other.

He brought out the receipt. It mentioned one set of orders only.

Adam looked back at the envelopes. Suppose, he thought, he simply forgot to deliver the battle orders? Suppose Huger did not march in the morning. Suppose then that the North won tomorrow's battle and took Richmond; who would then care about a missing set of orders? And if, by some outlandish chance, the South won tomorrow without Huger's troops, who would care? And even if his dereliction were discovered—and Adam was not so foolish as to presume that it would not eventually be found out—then it need not be construed as an act of treason, but rather as one of simple forgetfulness or, at worst, of carelessness. The dereliction would doubtless cost him his job on Johnston's staff, but it would not bring disgrace, merely an unfortunate reputation for carelessness. And maybe, he told himself, he should spend this war sheltering beneath his father's wing. Maybe he would be happier as his father's chief of staff where, if nothing else, he could at least try to preserve his father's tenants and neighbors in the Legion from the worst rigors of war. "Oh, dear God," he murmured aloud, and it was really a prayer for his own happiness and not for guidance because he already knew what he was going to do.

Slowly, deliberately, and with due ceremony, Adam tore the battle orders across, and then across again, and then he tore the ragged pieces into further shreds. He tore them as though he were rending the very fabric of history, and when the orders were reduced to a handful of scraps, he scattered the specks of paper into the black waters of a ditch beside the road. And with that act of treacherous destruction there came a sudden leaping happiness. He had sabotaged victory! He had done the Lord's work on a black day and he felt as though a wearisome burden of guilt and indecision had rolled away from him. He spurred his horse westward.

A half hour later Adam came to the small house that served as Huger's headquarters where, with a punctiliousness that verged on insubordination, Adam insisted on receiving the General's signature before he handed over the single remaining envelope. He then stood respectfully aside while Huger opened and read the single sheet of orders. The General, proud of his French ancestry, was a fussy, cautious man who had enjoyed a successful career in the old U.S. Army and now relished making unfavorable comparisons between his old employer and his new. "I don't understand!" he told Adam after reading the order a second time.

"I'm sorry, sir?" Adam was standing with Huger's aides on a verandah that looked down on Gillies Creek. The house was so close to Richmond that Adam could see the sprawl of roofs and chimneys that lay behind Rockett's Landing where the masts and yards of a dozen ships trapped by the barricade at Drewry's Bluff showed in the evening's gloom. Beneath the house, at the end of a long meadow dotted with the wagons and guns belonging to Huger's artillery, the Richmond and York Railroad ran beside the creek, and in the fading light that was made worse by the mass of dark cloud, a train steamed slowly toward the city. The train drew a curious collection of flatcars on which was mounted the Confederacy's balloon unit. The balloon itself was a fine confection made from the best silk dresses donated by Richmond's ladies and was raised and lowered by means of a giant winch that was bolted to one of the flatcars. Other flatcars housed the chemical apparatus that manufactured the hydrogen. The balloon, which had been observing the enemy lines beyond the torn-up railhead at Fair Oak Station, was still being winched down as the train clanked and crashed and puffed beneath General Huger's headquarters. "Am I to understand"—the white-haired Huger now peered over a pair of reading glasses at Adam—"that some of my men are being given over to General Longstreet's command?"

"I believe that is so, sir, yes," Adam said.

Huger gave a series of small snuffling snorts that were evidently intended to denote sarcastic laughter. "I suppose," Huger finally observed, "that General Johnston is aware, even dimly aware, that I am senior to General Longstreet?"

"I am sure he is, sir."

Huger was working his dudgeon into a fine display of wounded vanity. "General Longstreet, I seem to remember, was a paymaster in the old army. A mere major. I don't believe he was ever made more than a major or entrusted with any duty more onerous than distributing the troops' wages. Yet now he is to give men under my command their orders?"

"Only a few of your men, sir," Adam observed tactfully.

"And why?" Huger demanded. "Surely Johnston has his reasons? Has he thought to explain those reasons to you, young man?"

Johnston had, but it would have defeated Adam's purpose to have passed on the explanation, so he contented himself with the lame observation that General Longstreet's division was camped closer to the enemy and that therefore it had been thought prudent to beef up his brigades with the extra men. "I'm sure it's only a temporary expedient, sir," Adam finished, then stared past the unhappy Huger to where the train had come to a complete halt while the balloon was winched down the last few feet. The smoke from the locomotive looked oddly white and bright against the black cloud.

"I am not complaining," Huger said indignantly. "I am above such petty considerations, and in the exigencies of this army such insults are to be expected. But it would have been civil of Johnston to have asked if I minded my troops being yielded to the orders of a mere paymaster. Would it not have been civil?" he inquired of his own aides, who both nodded their eager agreement.

"I am certain General Johnston means you no slight, sir," Adam said.

"You may be certain of what you like, young man, but I am more experienced in these matters." Huger, who reckoned himself to be something of a natural aristocrat, drew himself erect so he could look down his nose at Adam. "Perhaps General Johnston needs my men to guard the army's wages, is that it?" This joke was again signaled by a series of snorting snuffles that caused Huger's aides to smile in companionable appreciation. "There was a time," Huger said, folding the orders into a tight square, "when military matters were performed properly in North America. When such things were done in a soldierly fashion. As in a well-organized army." He tossed the folded orders onto a bench suspended by chains hanging from the verandah's beams. "Very well, young man, tell Johnston I've received his orders, even if I cannot understand them. I'm sure you'll want to return to your master before the rain comes, and so I'll bid you good day." This curt dismissal, delivered without even offering Adam as much as a glass of water, was a deliberate snub, but Adam did not mind. He had taken his huge risk and he had played his part well, but he did not think he could go on parrying the General's questions. My God, Adam thought with a pang of terror, but there would be hell to pay when Johnston discovered what had happened. Then, once again, Adam reassured himself that he was guilty of nothing worse than forgetfulness.

He put the signed receipt into his pouch and went back to his horse. It was a Friday evening and he knew he would find Julia in the nearby Chimborazo Hospital. He was feeling guilty about her letter, and knowing that he had this whole evening free, he rode to meet his fiancee. His route took him past one of General Lee's new star-shaped forts that ringed the city. The earthwork was crowned with rows of freshly filled sandbags donated by the sewing circles of Richmond. The ladies had used every spare scrap of available fabric so that the newly placed ramparts looked like a quilt of flowery chintzes, deep velvets, and gaily patterned cottons, and in the sinister light of the storm-threatening dusk, that patchwork effect was oddly cheerful, a domestic touch in a warlike scene. The air, which had been sultry and still all day, suddenly stirred as an unexpected gust of wind lifted the folds of the Confederate battle flag above the gaily colored bastions. The country to the south, beyond the river, was lit by some last slanting rays of sunshine that reached far beneath the clouds so that the land seemed brighter than the sky. Adam, his new act of treachery completed, tried to read into that distant shaft of golden sunlight an augury of happiness and success.

He had to show his headquarters pass to one of the sentries at the guardpost that barred the road into the city. A far-off rumble of thunder sounded like gunfire coming from the land between the rivers. The sentry grimaced. "Reckon there'll be a storm tonight, Major. Right big one, too."

"It looks bad," Adam agreed.

"Never known a spring like it," the sentry said, then paused as a second clap of thunder rolled ominously over the sky. "Maybe it'll drown a Yankee or two. That'll save us having to kill all the sumbitches."

Adam did not respond, but just took his pass back and spurred onward. Lightning stuttered in the northern sky. He urged the horse into a trot, racing against the rain that began to fall in huge and ominous drops just as he turned into the hospital grounds. An orderly told Adam which ward was having the missioner's service and he galloped the horse through the sudden gusting wind that snatched at the smoke dribbling from the thin metal chimneys jutting from each hut. The rain began to fall harder, drumming on the tin roofs and quivering the taut canvas of the tents which had been erected as supplementary wards. He found the right hut, tied his horse to the porch upright, then plunged inside just as an explosion of thunder seemed to tear the heart out of the skies and trigger a veritable cloudburst of rain that rattled so loud on the ward roof that the Reverend John Gordon's voice was quite drowned out. Julia, seated at the wheezing little harmonium, smiled her pleasure at Adam's unexpected arrival. Adam, closing the door behind him, saw that this was one of the Friday nights when Julia's mother had chosen not to come to the hospital. There were just Julia, her father, and the inevitable Mr. Samworth, who looked nervously up at the roof as another crash of thunder bellowed over the sky.

The service limped on, interrupted by thunder and muted by the noise of the rain. Adam, standing by a window, watched the night fall across Richmond and saw the new darkness punctuated by slivers of lightning that offered a hellish luminosity to the city's spires. The storm seemed to intensify like the echoes of a war in heaven, while the rain pounded the roof with such a malevolent force that the Reverend Mr. Gordon gave up the unequal struggle and called for a hymn. Julia pumped the small instrument and led the ward in "Praise God From Whom All Blessings Flow." Once the singing was done the missioner pronounced an inaudible blessing and so abandoned the storm-racked service.

"This must pass over soon!" The Reverend Mr. Gordon had to shout at Adam to make himself heard, yet the storm seemed fixed above the city and relentless in its fury. The ward's roof leaked in a dozen places and Adam helped move the cots away from the cold streams. Julia wanted to see the storm for herself, and wrapping her coat about her, went to stand on the small verandah at the back of the ward where, under the shelter of the shingled lean-to roof, she and Adam watched the great storm shudder the skies above Virginia. Bolt after bolt of lightning cracked down to earth, and crash after crash of thunder echoed in the clouds. Night had fallen, but it was a night riven by fire and made huge by the sky's explosions. A dog howled somewhere in the hospital, while rivers of water ran and gurgled and poured into the black depths of the Bloody Run.

"Mother has a headache. She can always tell when a storm's coming by her headaches," Julia told Adam in an unsuitably cheerful voice, but Julia had always liked storms. She apprehended something very special in nature's fury, believing that she was witnessing a feeble echo of the chaos out of which God had created the world. She clutched her coat tightly about her and, in the lightning flashes, Adam saw that her eyes were bright with excitement.

"You wanted to see me?" Adam asked her.

"I hope you wanted to see me too!" Julia said teasingly, though inwardly she yearned for him to offer a passionate declaration that he would have ridden through a dozen such storms just to be beside her.

"Of course I did, yes," Adam said. He stood decorously apart from Julia though, like her, he had his back pressed hard against the shed's wall, where he gained most benefit from the verandah's small roof. Water poured off the shingles to make a curtain that was lit by a silver sheen whenever lightning flickered from the clouds. "But you wrote to me," Adam reminded her.

Julia had almost forgotten the letter with its hint of an important message and now, so long after, she suspected that the message had probably lost most of its urgency. "It was about your friend Nate Starbuck," she explained.

"Nate?" Adam, half expecting to be told that his engagement was ended, could not hide his surprise.

"He came to call on you just after he'd been released from prison," Julia said. "I happened to be at your father's house and I know I shouldn't have invited him inside, but it was raining almost as hard as it is now and he seemed so desolate that I took pity on him. You don't mind, do you?" She stared up at Adam.

Adam had almost forgotten the impulse that had made him warn his father's servants to turn Starbuck away from the house. At the time and in the wake of the appalling introduction of a fallen woman into the missioner's house, the ban had seemed a just precaution, but Adam's outrage had cooled since that terrible night. "What did he want?" Adam now asked.

Julia paused as a torrent of thunder cracked and faded above the city. Lightning backlit the clouds, flickering across the hidden sky like misted rivers of airborne silver. One lightning bolt had started a fire somewhere in the town of Manchester across the James River, for there was a dull red stuttering glow that lasted a few seconds before the rain drowned it out. "He had a message for you," Julia said. "I thought it was all very mysterious, but he wouldn't explain it to me. He just said you'd understand. He says you're to stop corresponding with his family."

Adam felt a chill run through him. He said nothing, but just stared into the dark river valley where the rain hammered at the sullen water.

"Adam?" Julia inquired.

Adam was suddenly besieged by the image of a noose hanging from a high beam. "He said what?" he managed to ask.

"He said that you were to cease corresponding with his family. Does that seem strange to you? It seemed very odd to me. After all, the Starbuck family is in Boston, so how can you correspond with them? I'm told people do get letters through to the North, but I'm sure I can't imagine you going to that kind of trouble just to write to the Reverend Elial Starbuck. And Nate also said that he would explain as soon as he was able, but he was equally mysterious about when that might be."

"Oh, dear God," Adam said and shivered as all the terror came whipping back. He thought of the shame if his father were to discover that his son had betrayed Virginia. And how had Starbuck found out? Had James written to him? There could be no other explanation. How else could Starbuck have discovered it? And if Starbuck knew, who else did? "Where is Nate?" he now asked Julia.

"I don't know. How would I know?" In truth Julia had the strangest idea that Starbuck had crossed the lines, but as her source for that belief was Sally Truslow she did not think it wise to make any mention of it. Julia had finally summoned the courage to visit Sally, going to the house armed with a Bible and a bag full of tracts describing the fearsome terrors of hell awaiting all sinners, but the visit had unexpectedly turned into a joyous morning of laughter in which, instead of attempting to lead the younger woman to the Lord, Julia had found herself admiring Sally's collection of gowns and shawls. They had talked of cambric and chambray, and whether tarlatan could replace tulle as a material for veils, and Julia had fingered Sally's silks and satins, and after the city's damp fears, such talk of baubles and frills had been nothing but relief. Julia's religious beliefs had been offended only by Sally's enthusiastic plans to establish a spiritualist shrine in the house's back quarters, but Sally's evident cynicism and her honest description of how she planned to deceive the clients had ended up sparking Julia's amusement rather than her disapproval. Julia had also been touched by the concern Sally had shown for Starbuck and flustered when Sally had claimed how much Starbuck liked Julia. It had all been very odd, much too odd to explain to Adam, who would surely have exploded in righteous anger at the mere thought of his fiancee visiting one of Richmond's courtesans, though in truth Sally's house had outwardly appeared to be as respectable as any in the city and a good deal cleaner than most. Yet Julia could no more tell Adam of that visit than she could have told her mother. "Does it matter where Nate is?" Julia now asked Adam.

"I suppose not." Adam shifted uneasily, his spur chains and scabbard links clinking softly beneath the roar of the rain and the howl of the wind.

"So what does the message mean?" Julia asked directly. Her curiosity had been piqued by Adam's reaction, which, to her mind, looked startlingly like guilt.

Adam shook his head, but then did offer a halting explanation. "It goes back," he said slowly and not altogether articulately. "Back to when Nate first arrived here. I have been trying. Father anyway tried to restore Nate's family connections. It seemed important." Adam was a bad liar, and to cover his embarrassment he pushed away from the hut's wall and rested his hands on the balustrade. "I think Nate resents our efforts," he finished lamely.

"So it isn't so very mysterious after all?" Julia said, not believing a word Adam had said.

"No," Adam said, "not really."

Julia listened to the dogs howling and the horses whinnying and the tent canvas flogging in the wind. "What did Nate do?" she asked after a long pause.

"What do you mean?"

"I mean what did Nate do to lose his family's affections?"

For a long time Adam did not answer, then he shrugged. "He ran away."

"Is that all?"

Adam was certainly not going to tell Julia that there had been a woman involved, an actress who had used Starbuck as her foil, then dropped him in Richmond. "He behaved very badly," Adam said pompously, knowing it to be an inadequate explanation and also an unfair one. "Nate isn't a bad man," he added, but did not know how to finish his qualification.

"Just passionate?" Julia asked.

"Yes," Adam said, "just passionate," then fell silent as a massive explosion of thunder tore the sky apart. A sheet of lightning crashed down on the river's far bank to illuminate the naval yard with a stark white corpse light that was set off with jet-black shadows. "When the Yankees come"—he changed the subject from Nate Starbuck's character—"you should stay at home."

"Did you think I was planning to welcome them to Richmond?" Julia asked tartly.

"You have a flag? I mean a United States flag?" Adam asked.

"No."

"I'm sure there's one in my room in Clay Street. Ask Polly to give it to you. Hang it out of a window at home."

That sounded very supine advice to Julia. "You seem very sure that they will enter Richmond," she said.

"They will," Adam said fervently. "It's God's will."

"It is?" Julia was surprised. "Then why, I wonder, did God allow this war to happen at all?"

"We declared war," Adam said. "Man did that, not God, and it was the South that made the declaration." He fell silent for a while, examining his own conscience and finding it wanting. "I believed everything my father said back then. He told me America just needed a little bloodletting, like a doctor leeching a disease. One sharp battle and we would all learn the wisdom of peaceful negotiations. Now look at it!" He waved a hand out toward the storm and Julia dutifully stared across the valley to where a blue-white splinter of lightning silhouetted the tracery of ships' rigging on the river and spilt white fire along the waterway. The rain drummed the earth and splashed off the ward's roof and poured out of gutters and flooded in the run below the hospital. "We're going to be punished," Adam said.

Julia remembered Starbuck's bravado, quoting John Paul Jones's fine defiance. "I thought we hadn't begun to fight?" She echoed Starbuck's words and rather surprised herself by her belligerence. She had never thought of herself as a supporter of the war party, but she was too engaged in the discussion to realize that she was using a political allegiance as a means of arguing about a personal relationship. "We can't just admit defeat without fighting!" she insisted.

"We're going to be punished," Adam said again. "We unleashed the evil, you see. I saw that today." He fell silent and Julia, thinking he must have witnessed some appalling injury, did not probe, but then Adam offered a quite different explanation, saying how he had found himself blaming a slave for the war. "Don't you see how war brings out the worst in all of us?" he asked her. "All the ropes that bind us to decency and to God are being cut away and we're drifting on a rotten tide of anger."

Julia frowned. "You think the South deserves to lose because you were uncharitable to a slave?"

"I think America is one country," Adam said.

"It sounds to me," Julia said, doing her best to curb a rising anger, "that you're fighting for the wrong side."

"Maybe I am." Adam said quietly, but not so quietly that Julia could not hear him over the seething rain.

"Then you should go north," Julia said coldly.

"Should I?" Adam asked in an oddly meek voice, as if he really did want her advice.

"You must surely fight for what you believe in," Julia said bluntly.

Adam nodded. "And you?" he asked.

Julia remembered something Sally had said, something that had surprised her: that men, for all their boasts and show, were as weak as newborn kittens. "Me?" Julia asked as though she had not immediately understood what Adam was implying.

"Would you abandon the South?"

"Would you want me to?" Julia asked, and in truth it was an invitation for Adam to woo her and to declare that great love deserved extravagant gestures. Julia did not want love to be commonplace, she wanted it to hold the same life-changing mysteries as religion and to be as tempestuous as the storm that now racked its anger across the whole peninsula.

"I would want you to do whatever your heart and soul tells you to do," Adam said stiffly.

"Then my heart tells me to stay in Virginia," Julia responded just as coldly. "It tells me I should work here, in the hospital. Mother doesn't approve, but I might have to insist. Would you object if I were to become a nurse?"

"No," Adam said, but without the slightest conviction. He seemed bereft, like a traveler marooned in a strange land, then he was saved from saying anything more because the door from the ward opened and the Reverend John Gordon peered anxiously onto the verandah.

"I was fearing the two of you had been washed away," Julia's father said in as strong a reproof as he was capable of delivering. His wife would have protested at the impropriety of Adam and Julia being alone in the darkness, but the Reverend Mr. Gordon could not bring himself to discern anything sinful in their behavior.

"We're quite dry, Father," Julia said, deliberately misconstruing her father's gentle reprimand. "We were just watching the storm."

"The winds blew, and beat upon that house; and it fell not: for it was founded upon a rock," the Reverend John Gordon quoted happily from Matthew's gospel.

" 'I came not to send peace,' " Julia quoted from the same gospel, " 'but a sword' ". She was looking at Adam as she spoke, but Adam was unaware of her gaze. He was staring across a dark void split by fire and remembering the scraps of white paper shred in a black ditch. That was a trail of treason that should bring northern victory, and in that victory's blessed wake, peace. And surely, Adam told himself, in peace all would be made whole again.

Tomorrow.

The rain-soaked earth steamed in the morning sun. The attack should have been two hours old by now, it should already have ripped the heart from the Yankee lines and be driving the northerners back toward the White Oak Swamp, but nothing moved on the three roads that led from the rebel lines into the Yankee positions.

General Johnston had planned to use the three roads like a trident. Hill's division would advance in the center first, attacking down the Williamsburg Stage Road to assail the northern troops massed behind Fair Oaks Station. Johnston hoped that the Yankee infantry would then close on Hill's advancing troops like swarming bees, only to be struck from the north by Longstreet's division and from the south by Huger's. All that was needed for Hill's division to begin its attack was a message that Longstreet and Huger's troops had advanced from their camps close to Richmond. Longstreet's men should be on the Nine Mile Road, close to Old Tavern, while Huger's division should be on the Charles City Road near White's Tavern.

Except both roads were empty. They were puddled deep by the night's tempestuous rain, but otherwise deserted. The morning mists cleared away to reveal a waterlogged landscape rippled by a brisk cold wind that was strong enough to keep the Yankees' two observation balloons grounded and to snatch at the smoke of the cooking fires that struggled to consume the rain-soaked wood. "Where the hell are they?" Johnston demanded, and sent his aides splashing through the soaked meadows and along the ominously empty roads in search of the missing divisions. "Find them, just find them!" he shouted. By now, according to his timetable, the attacks should already have broken through the Yankee lines and be driving a mass of panicked refugees toward the treacherous White Oak Swamp. Instead the Yankees were oblivious of their fate and the eastern horizon was misted with the smoke of their cooking fires.

An aide came back from General Huger's headquarters to say that he had discovered the General in bed, fast asleep.

"He was what?" Johnston demanded.

"Asleep, sir. All his staff were asleep too."

"After sunup?"

The aide nodded. "Fast asleep, sir."

"Good God Almighty!" Johnston stared in disbelief at the aide. "Didn't he get any orders?"

The aide, a friend of Adam's, hesitated as he looked for a way to spare his friend.

"Well?" Johnston demanded angrily.

"His chief of staff says not, sir," the aide said, with an apologetic shrug in Adam's direction.

"Goddamn it!" Johnston snapped. "Morton!"

"Sir?"

"Who took Huger his orders?"

"Major Faulconer did, sir, but I can assure you the orders were delivered. I've got the receipt with the General's signature. Here, sir." Colonel Morton produced the receipt and handed it to the General.

Johnston glanced at the paper. "He did get the orders! Which means he just overslept?"

"So it would seem, sir," the aide who had woken General Huger answered.

Johnston seemed to quiver with a suppressed fury that he was quite unable to express in words. "And where the hell is Longstreet?" he asked instead.

"We're still trying to find him, sir," Colonel Morton reported. He had sent an aide to the Nine Mile Road, but the aide had disappeared as thoroughly as Longstreet's division.

"For the love of God!" Johnston shouted, "find me my goddamn army!"

Adam had hoped to spread confusion by his destruction of Huger's orders, but he could never have dared to hope that the confusion would have been so thoroughly compounded by General Longstreet, who had airily decided that he did not want to advance along the Nine Mile Road and instead had elected to use the Charles City Road instead. The decision meant that his division had to march clean through the encampments of General Huger's troops. General Huger, rudely woken with orders that he should have been advancing eastward on the Charles City Road, discovered that it was choked solid with Longstreet's troops. "Damn the paymaster," Huger said and ordered breakfast.

A half hour later the paymaster himself came to Huger's headquarters. "Hope you don't mind me using your road," Longstreet said, "but my road was too wet for marching. Knee-deep in mud."

"You'll take some coffee?" Huger suggested.

"You're damn cool, Huger, for a man facing battle," Longstreet said, glancing at the generous plate of ham and eggs that had just been served to his fellow General.

Huger knew nothing of any battle, but he was certainly not going to reveal his ignorance to a jumped-up paymaster. "So what are your orders today?" he asked, masking his growing alarm that he might have missed something important.

"Same as yours, I imagine. March east till we find the Yankees, then attack. Is that fresh bread?"

"Help yourself," Huger said, wondering if the world had gone mad. "But I can't advance if you're on my road."

"I'll step aside for you," Longstreet offered generously. "I'll get my fellows over the creek, then give them a rest while you march past us. Will that do?"

"Why not have some ham and eggs too?" Huger asked. "I'm not sure I'm hungry." He stood and shouted for his chief of staff. He had a division to move and a battle to fight. Good God, he thought, but these things had been arranged better in the old army! So much better.

Back at the army's headquarters General Johnston opened his watch for the hundredth time. The battle should have been four hours old and still not a shot had been fired. The wind rippled the puddles but did little to stir the day's humidity. The muskets would choke up today, Johnston thought. A dry day meant that gunpowder burned clean while wet weather promised fouled rifle barrels and hard ramming for the men. "Where in God's name are they?" he cried in frustration.

General Hill's division had been ready since daybreak. His men, sheltering in woods where great trees had been split apart by the night's lightning strikes, clutched their rifles and waited for the signal to advance. The foremost ranks could see the Yankee picket posts at the far side of a damp clearing. Those guardposts were rough shelters made from felled branches behind which the northern pickets took what cover they could from the weather. Some of the enemy had hung coats and shirts to dry on their crude windbreaks. One Yankee, not suspecting that the woods across the clearing were crammed with an enemy waiting to attack, took a shovel and walked along the tree line. He waved toward the rebels, assuming that he was merely being observed by the same southern pickets with whom, just the day before, he had exchanged coffee for tobacco and a northern newspaper for a southern.

General Hill opened his watch. "Any news?"

"None, sir." The general's aides had ridden to White's Tavern and Old Tavern and seen nothing.

"Have you heard anything from Johnston?"

"Nothing, sir."

"Goddamn it. This ain't no way to win a war." Hill rammed his watch into his coat pocket. "Give the signal!" he shouted at an artillery battery whose three spaced shots would be the agreed signal for the attack to begin.

"You'll advance unsupported?" an aide asked, aghast at the thought of the division taking on half the northern army without any flanking reinforcements.

"They're only goddamn Yankees. Let's see the bastards run. Fire the signal!"

The dull, harsh, soulless sounds of the three signal shots broke the noontime peace. The first shot splintered through the far woods, scattering droplets and pine needles, the second skipped up from the wet meadow to smack into a tree trunk, while the third and last brought on the battle.

"Johnston won't attack," James Starbuck assured his brother.

"How do we know?"

"McClellan knew him before the war. Knew him well, so he knows his mind," James explained, oblivious of the irony that the United States Secret Service might be expected to discover a slightly more reliable indicator of enemy intentions than the mind-reading abilities of the commanding General. James reached for the plate of bacon and helped himself. He had always been a healthy eater, and though this was lunchtime and the cooks had provided him with a lavish plate of fried chicken, James had demanded that the bacon left over from breakfast be served as well. "Have some bacon," he invited his brother.

"I've eaten enough." Starbuck was leafing through the enormous pile of newspapers that were brought to wherever the Secret Service had its field headquarters. This pile contained the Louisville *Journal*, the Charleston *Mercury*, the Cape *Codman*, the New York *Times*, the New York *Herald*, the *Mississippian*, the *National Era*, *Harper's Weekly*, the Cincinnati *Gazette*, the Jacksonville *Republican*, the Philadelphia *North American*, and the Chicago *Journal*. "Does anyone read all these papers?" Starbuck asked.

"I do. When there's time. There never is enough time. We don't have enough staff, that's the trouble. Just look at that pile!" James looked up from the newspaper he was reading and gestured at the telegraph messages that needed decoding and that lay untranslated for lack of sufficient clerical help. "Maybe you could join us, Nate?" James now suggested. "The chief likes you."

"When I get back from Richmond, you mean?"

"Why not?" James was delighted with the idea. "Sure you don't want some bacon?"

"Very sure."

"You take after Father," James said, cutting a piece of newly baked bread and slathering it with butter, "whereas I've always been fleshy like mother." He turned a page of the newspaper, then looked up as Pinkerton came into the room. "How's the General?" James asked.

"Sick," Pinkerton said. He paused to steal a rasher of bacon from James's plate. "But he'll live. The doctors have wrapped him in flannel and are dosing him with quinine." General McClellan had gone down with the Chickahominy fever and was alternately sweating and shivering in a commandeered bedroom. Pinkerton's Secret Service had taken over a neighboring house, for the General never liked to be far from his best source of information. "But the General's thinking clearly," Pinkerton went on, "and he's agreed it's time you should go back." He pointed what was left of his rasher of bacon at Starbuck.

"Oh, dear God," James said and glanced at his younger brother in consternation.

"You don't have to, Nate," Pinkerton said, "not if you think it's too dangerous." He put the rest of the bacon into his mouth and went to the window to peer up at the sky. "Too damn windy for balloons. Never seen a storm like last night's. Did you sleep?"

"Yes," Starbuck said, hiding the pulse of excitement that fluttered inside him. He had begun to suspect that he would never be given the list of questions and never get back to the southern side and never see Sally or her father again. In truth he was bored, and if he were honest he was most bored with the company of his brother. James was as good a soul as any that walked on earth, but he had no conversation beyond food, family, God, and McClellan. When Starbuck had first come to the Yankee lines he had feared his loyalties would be tested and his reverence for the Stars and Stripes would be resurrected so strongly that it would break his rebel allegiances, but the tedium of James's company had served as a barrier to that renewal of patriotism.

Besides, he had nurtured the image of himself as an outcast, and in the rebel army Starbuck had a reputation as a renegade, a daredevil, a rebel indeed, while in this bigger army with its tighter organization he could only ever be just another young man from Massachusetts who would forever be bounded by his family's expectations. In the South, Starbuck thought, he himself defined what he wanted to be and the only limits to that ambition lay within himself, but in the North he would forever be Elial Starbuck's son. "When?" he asked Pinkerton a little too eagerly.

"Tonight, Nate?" Pinkerton suggested. "You'll say you've been traveling." Pinkerton and James had concocted a story to explain why Starbuck had stayed away from Richmond so long. The story claimed that Starbuck had recovered from his prison experience by traveling through the lower Confederacy where he had been delayed by bad weather and unpunctual trains. Pinkerton, like James, had no idea that such a story was unnecessary, that all Starbuck needed was the paper that Pinkerton now produced and that he would deliver to de'Ath, his powerful protector in Richmond. "Putting the General to bed at least made him concentrate on our business," Pinkerton said happily, "so now you can take these questions to your friend." McClellan's questions, just like the false message that de'Ath had provided Starbuck, were sealed inside a sewn oilcloth pouch.

Starbuck took the packet and thrust it into his pocket. He was wearing one of his brother's cast-off Yankee coats, a voluminous double-breasted blue uniform jacket that hung from Starbuck's lean body in great folds.

"We need to know a lot more about Richmond's defenses," Pinkerton explained. "It's going to become a siege, Nate. Our guns against their earthworks, and we want your friend to tell us which forts are the weakest." Pinkerton looked back to James. "Is that bread fresh, Jimmy?"

"Good God." James ignored his chief's question and instead stared wide-eyed at a newly secured copy of the Richmond *Examiner* that lay beside his plate. "Well, I never," he added.

"Bread, Jimmy?" Pinkerton tried again.

"Henry de'Ath's dead," James said, oblivious of his chief's hunger. "Well, I never."

"Who?" Pinkerton demanded.

"Eighty years old, too! A good age for a bad man. Well, I never."

"Who in the name of hell are you talking about?" Pinkerton demanded.

"Henry de'Ath," James said. "That's the end of an era, and no mistake." He peered closely at the newspaper's smudged ink. "They say he died in his sleep. What a rogue, what a rogue!"

Starbuck felt a shiver pass through him, but he dared not betray his sudden worry. Maybe Henry de'Ath was not the man who had sent Starbuck across the lines, but some other man with the same surname. "What sort of rogue?" he asked.

"He had the principles of a jackal," James said, though not without a note of admiration. As a Christian he had to disapprove of de'Ath's reputation, but as a lawyer he felt envy for the man's effectiveness. "He was the only man Andrew Jackson refused to fight in a duel," James went on, "probably because de'Ath had killed six men by then, maybe more. He was lethal with a sword or pistol. And lethal in a courtroom too. I remember Judge Shaw telling me that de'Ath had once boasted to him of knowingly sending at least a dozen innocent men to the scaffold. Shaw naturally protested, but de'Ath claimed that the tree of liberty was irrigated by blood and told Shaw not to be so particular whether the blood was innocent or guilty." James shook his head in reproof at such wickedness. "He always claimed to be half French, but Shaw was certain he was a natural son of Thomas Jefferson." James actually blushed at retelling this scrap of lawyers' gossip. "I'm sure that wasn't true," he added hastily, "but the man attracted that kind of exaggeration. Now he's gone to his final judgment. Jeff Davis will miss him."

"Why?" Pinkerton demanded.

"They were thick as thieves, sir," James said. "De'Ath was an *eminence grise*. Must have been one of Davis's closest advisers."

"Then thank God the bastard's cold in his bed," Pinkerton said cheerfully. "Now is that bread fresh?"

"It is, Chief," James said, "very fresh."

"Carve me a piece, if you would. And I'll thank you for a leg of chicken too. What I thought we'd do"—Pinkerton turned back to Starbuck when he had secured his luncheon—"is send you over the James River tonight. We'll have to put you two or three hours' walk from Petersburg and you'll have to get yourself north from there. You think you can manage that?"

"I'm sure of it, sir," Starbuck said and was astonished that his voice sounded so normal, because inside he was consumed with a stomach-churning terror. De'Ath dead? Then who in Richmond would speak for Starbuck? Who in the Confederacy could guarantee that he was not a deserter? Starbuck shook suddenly. He could not go back! That realization flooded cold into his consciousness. Only de'Ath could vouch for him, and without de'Ath he was friendless in

Richmond. Without de'Ath he appeared a double turncoat, doubly despicable, and without de'Ath he could surely never return to the South, let alone rejoin the Legion.

"You're looking nervous, Nate!" Pinkerton said robustly. "Are you worried about going back? Is that it?"

"I shall be fine, sir," Starbuck said.

"I'm sure you will. All my best agents are nervous. Only fools don't show a touch of nerves at the thought of going south." The Scotsman turned in puzzlement as a rumble of gunfire sounded in the long distance. "Is that gunfire?" he asked, "or more thunder?" He crossed the room and opened a window wide. The unmistakable sound of gunfire rolled along the horizon, faded, then swelled again as another battery joined in. Pinkerton listened, then shrugged. "Maybe a gun crew exercising?"

"Can I borrow a horse to take a look?" Starbuck asked. He wanted to be alone to decide his future now that his sponsor was dead. He imagined de'Ath lying in the crumbling mansion with a sardonic smile on his dead lips. Would the old man have left a note exonerating Starbuck? Somehow Starbuck doubted it and he shivered again despite the heat.

"Take my horse," James offered.

"But be back here before six!" Pinkerton warned Starbuck. "I have a man coming to take you down to the river at six!"

"Six o'clock," Starbuck promised and then, in a daze of uncertainty and fear, he went to the stables.

Pinkerton took Starbuck's chair and helped himself to more chicken. "He's a fine young man, your brother. But high-strung, Jimmy, very high."

"He always suffered from nervous debility," James said. "And he doesn't help himself by using tobacco and alcohol."

Pinkerton smiled. "I've been known to use those myself, Jimmy."

"But you're a well-set man," James explained, "and my brother's thin. People like you and I, Major, suffer in the belly and bowels, but men like my brother will always suffer in their nerves. He takes after my father in that."

"It must be a great thing to be educated," Pinkerton said, settling himself to his plate. The sound of gunfire increased, but he ignored it. "Now my own dear grandmother, God rest her soul, always claimed there was no disease on God's earth that a wee dram of good whiskey would not cure. I doubt you'll agree with her, Jimmy, but she lived a good long while and scarce knew a day's sickness."

"But she only recommended a wee dram," James said, delighted to have scored the point, "not a hog's bellyful, Major, and no sensible person will dispute whiskey's curative powers, but sadly it is not usually imbibed as a medicine."

"Your brother likes his drop," Pinkerton pointed out wickedly.

"Nate is a sore disappointment," James admitted. "But I look at it this way, Major. He has forsworn his political mistake, so he is well started on the hard road to redemption. He backslid a long way, but with God's grace he'll come back every step of that path and then go on toward full salvation."

"I daresay you're right," Pinkerton grumbled. He was never comfortable when his chief of staff fell into a preaching mode, but he was sensible of James's solid virtues and knew that the odd sermon was well worth the rigorous order that James brought to the affairs of the Secret Service.

"And maybe we can help Nate's salvation," James persisted, "by offering him a post in the Bureau? We're grievously understaffed, Chief. Just look at that!" He gestured at the pile of telegraphs and interrogations.

"When he's back from Richmond," Pinkerton said, "we'll think on it, I promise you." He twisted toward the window, frowning. "Those guns are lively. You think the seceshers are attacking us?"

"We have no intimation of a rebel attack," James said, thus implying that no assault could possibly be happening. Whenever an attack did take place there was always a trickle of deserters bringing news of the enemy's preparations, but the front between the armies had been unusually quiet these last few days.

"You're right, Jimmy, you're right." Pinkerton turned back to the table. "It's probably just a gunboat exercising its crew. And doubtless we'll hear soon enough if it's anything more remarkable." He picked up a one-week-old copy of the Jacksonville *Republican* and began reading a boastful account of how a blockade runner had evaded the northern warships off the South Carolina coast. The ship had been carrying canvas cloth from Genoa, French-made shoes, British percussion caps, gutta-percha from Malaya and eau de cologne. "Why would they want cologne water?" Pinkerton asked. "Why in God's name would they want that?"

James did not answer. He was applying himself to his lunch plate and had just helped himself to another serving of chicken when the door to the parlor was rudely thrown open and a tall, gaunt-faced colonel stepped into the room. The Colonel was wearing riding boots and carried a crop, while his uniform was spattered with red mud, evidence of how hard he had been riding. "Who the devil are you?" Pinkerton looked up from his newspaper.

"Name's Thorne. Lieutenant Colonel Thorne. Inspector General's Department in Washington. Who the devil are you?"

"Pinkerton."

"Well, Pinkerton, where's Starbuck?"

"Sir? I'm Starbuck, sir," James said, plucking the napkin from his neck and standing up.

"You're Nathaniel Starbuck?" Colonel Thorne asked grimly.

James shook his head. "No, sir, I'm his brother."

"Then where the devil is Nathaniel Starbuck? Have you arrested him?"

"Arrested him?" Pinkerton asked.

"I wired you yesterday. Does no one attend to business here?" Thorne asked the question in a bitter voice, conscious that Delaney's letter revealing Starbuck to be a traitor had lain unopened on his own desk for far too long. "So where the devil is he?"

James fluttered a feeble hand toward the back of the house. "In the stables, I believe."

"Then take me there!" Thorne drew a revolver from a holster at his waist and slipped a percussion cap onto one of the chamber's cones.

"Might I ask . . ." James began nervously.

"No you damn well may not ask! Take me to the stables!" Thorne shouted. "I haven't come all the way from Washington to watch you dithering like a virgin in her wedding bed. Now move!"

James ran to the stables.

The door of the stall where his horse had been cribbed swung creaking in the wind. The stall was empty. "He was going to see what the firing was about," James said weakly, frightened of Thorne's savage expression.

"He'll be back here by six," Pinkerton assured Thorne.

"You had better pray he is," Thorne said. "Where's McClellan? He'll have to find me some cavalry and we'll pursue the treacherous bastard."

"But why?" James asked. "Why? What's he done?"

But the Colonel had already gone. The guns cracked on the horizon where now a film of white smoke showed pale above the trees. Nate was gone west, something terrible was adrift in the universe, and James felt his heart sink hard. He prayed his fears were wrong, then went to find a horse.


The Confederate infantry half trotted and half walked across ground that was hard in places and like a morass in others. The Yankee pickets saw the line of gray and brown uniforms emerge from the woods and ran back to warn their comrades that the rebels were advancing.

Bugles sounded the alarm in the Federal encampments spread across the farms south of Fair Oaks Station. General McClellan had trained these men well and would have been proud of the way they stood to their arms. Whole regiments dropped the letters they were writing and the coffee they were brewing, they dropped their baseballs and playing cards, and they snatched up the rifles that were stacked like tepee poles as they ran to form ranks behind the waist-high abatis that protected their camps. The skirmishers ran out to a line of rifle pits that had been dug a hundred paces ahead of the abatis where a slight rise in the ground supposedly kept the soil above the floodline, but the night's storm had flooded the pits anyway and so the skirmishers knelt beside the waterlogged holes and pulled out the muzzle stoppers which had kept the rain from rusting their rifle barrels. The rest of the newly alerted regiments formed two long ranks which now stood in the warm, hard wind and watched the trees from which the pickets had just come running. Men loaded their weapons and placed percussion caps on their rifles' cones.

The abatis in front of the waiting infantry was a tangled barrier of felled trees. It was interrupted by gaps that let the skirmishers through and by the earth ramparts of artillery emplacements. The cannons, mostly twelve-pounder Napoleons but with a handful of ten-pound Parrotts, were already loaded with shell. Gunners pulled tarpaulins off ammunition limbers, rammed friction primers into touch-holes, and ordered rounds of canister stacked in readiness for the second and third shots. Birds were flapping up from the trees, disturbed by the advancing rebels, then a pair of deer bolted from the woods and galloped across the front of a new battalion of unblooded New Yorkers. "Hold your fire!" a sergeant snarled at a man tracking the deer with his rifle. "Aim low when they come, look for their officers! Steady now!" The Sergeant paced along the front of his nervous men. "They're just a bunch of ragged-assed farmboys, no different from you miserable lot. There ain't nothing magical in rebs. They can be killed like anyone else. Aim low when you see them."

One boy was muttering Christ's name over and over again. His hands were shaking. Some of the men had pushed their ramrods into the wet turf so they would be more readily at hand for reloading. "Wait, lads, wait," the Sergeant said, seeing the nervousness on the young faces. The Colonel galloped behind their rear rank, his horse's hooves kicking up sprays of water and dirt.

"Where are they?" a man asked.

"You'll see 'em soon enough," another man said. In the line's center the colors looked bright against the dull sky.

Somewhere off to the right a blast of musketry sounded like a burning canebrake. A cannon fired with a noise that made the men jump. Over on that flank men were screaming like demons and smoke was drifting above the wet ground, but there was still no enemy visible in front of the New York boys. A second cannon fired, spewing a plume of smoke thirty yards along the ground. A shell burst in the air behind the New York regiment, evidence that a rebel battery was in action somewhere in the vicinity. One of the waiting New Yorkers suddenly buckled over and vomited a bellyful of hard-tack and coffee onto the grass. "You'll feel better when you see them," the Sergeant growled. Another deer burst from the trees and galloped north toward the smoke and noise, then reversed itself and ran across the regiment's front. There were shapes moving among the trees now and the flicker of dull light reflecting from weapons and the splash of bright color where a rebel battle flag showed among the pines.

"Ready! Aim!" the Colonel of the New Yorkers shouted, and seven hundred rifles came up into seven hundred shoulders. The skir-mishers had already opened fire from beside the flooded rifle pits, dotting the rough ground with patches of smoke that were whipped northward on the wind.

"Wait for it! Wait for it!" the Sergeant called. A lieutenant slashed at a weed with his sword. He tried to swallow, but his throat was too dry. For days now he had been constipated, but suddenly his bowels felt like water. "Steady now! Wait for it!" The Sergeant stepped back into the front rank.

And then, quite suddenly, they were there; the enemy they had all read about and had been told about and had joked about, and a poor, tattered enemy they looked too, nothing but a scattered line of ragged men in dirt-brown and rat-gray uniforms who emerged from the shadows of the far trees.

"Fire!" The Colonel had drawn his sword and now whipped it down. The New York regiment's front rank vanished behind the gouts of smoke.

"Fire!" the gun captains shouted and the artillery shells screamed into the edge of the woods and exploded in sudden small smoke clouds. Men swabbed out barrels and rammed canisters down onto powder charges.

"You're stopping them, boys! You're holding them!" The New

Yorker's chaplain strode up and down behind the companies, his Bible in one hand and a revolver in the other. "Send their souls to the Lord, boys, translate the rascals to glory. Well done! Praise the Lord, aim low!"

"Fire!" The canisters split apart at the guns' muzzles to fan like duckshot across the rough ground. Rebels were snatched backward, their blood stippling the puddles left by the night's rain. Steel ramrods clattered in rifle barrels as the New Yorkers reloaded. The smoke of their opening volley had thinned and they could see the enemy was still advancing, though now they came forward in small groups of men who stopped, knelt, fired, then came on again, and all the time they made the weird, ululating scream that was the famous rebel yell. Their new battle flag looked bloodred against the trees. "Fire!" the Sergeant shouted and watched as one of the rebel groups was stopped cold. Two men in gray went down. A ramrod, fired in error, wheeled through the smoke. Rebel bullets smacked into the logs at the heart of the abatis while others whistled overhead. The New York skirmishers were falling back, yielding the useless rifle pits to the rebel skirmishers. Smoke was beginning to hide the battlefield and make a patchy screen behind which the rebels were mere shapes punctuated by rifle flames.

The cannon cracked back on their carriages and dug their trails deep into the waterlogged turf. There had been no time to make proper embrasures with hardened floors, only time to erect a rough wall in front of the guns that now choked out the killing blasts of canister. Each twelve-pounder was now being double-shotted with two full canisters rammed on top of a bag containing two-and-a-half pounds of gunpowder so that every barrel fired fifty-four musket balls, each musket ball a full one-and-a-half inches across. The canisters themselves were made from tin that tore apart, and the balls were packed in sawdust that vanished in flame at the cannons' muzzles. The balls cracked on the tree trunks beyond the attacking rebels, splashed into the wet soil, and tore into Confederate bodies. Each time the guns fired they recoiled farther, digging their trails deeper into the soft ground, and the gunners had neither the strength nor the time to haul the heavy weapons out of the sucking mud. Barrels had to be lowered to compensate for the sinking trails, but still the gunfire was doing its job and holding the rebel attack. The unsettling sound of the rebel yell had stopped, replaced by the swishing noise of canister tearing through the far woods.

"You're beating them! You're beating them!" The New York Colonel stood in his stirrups to shout at his men. "You're doing just bully," he said, then gave a stifled gasp as a bullet slapped into his lower throat. The Colonel began to twitch his head in the manner of a man whose stiff collar was too tight. He tried to speak, but no words came, just a mix of blood and spittle. He slumped back hard onto his saddle, a look of astonishment on his bearded face as his sword slipped out of his hand to quiver point first in the mud.

"Boys are doing real well, sir, real well!" A major rode up beside the Colonel, then watched appalled as his commanding officer toppled slowly out of the saddle. The Colonel's horse whinnied and trotted forward, dragging the Colonel by his left foot, which was trapped in its stirrup.

"Oh, Christ," the Major said. "Doctor! Doctor!" Then another cannon crashed its hollow-sounding noise of canister, only this time the canister balls flickered into the New York ranks, crackling in the abatis and sending four men reeling back. Another field gun cracked and the Major saw that the rebels had put two guns on his forward left flank and were unlimbering two more. He turned his horse to ride toward the threatened flank, but already the wing company was edging backward from the rebel threat. There were other northern troops on that flank, but they were too far away to help, and besides, those men were fighting off their own surge of rebel attackers.

"Hold them! Hold them! Hold them!" the Major shouted, but the arrival of the rebel artillery had given heart to the southern attack and now the gray-brown figures were coming closer to the abatis and their musketry was becoming ever more deadly. Wounded men limped and crawled away from the New York ranks, going to find help from the bandsmen who served as medical orderlies. The Yankee dead were pushed out of the ranks and the living closed on the center. Their mouths were dry from the salt in the gunpowder that leaked whenever they bit a cartridge open, and their faces were blackened by the powder. Sweat ran clean lines through the black faces. They rammed and fired, rammed and fired, flinching when the heavy rifles punched back into bruised shoulders, then they rammed and fired again. The ground behind the rebels was heaped with dead and wounded, with groups of the casualties concentrated wherever the canister blasts had cut through the advancing ranks. The new rebel color, with its starred blue cross on a bright red field, had been torn by canister, but a man picked up the staff and ran forward until a Yankee bullet shattered his leg and put the flag down again. Another man plucked it up and a dozen New York riflemen fired at him.

A New York sergeant watched a boy ram a bullet home and saw that the ramrod only went twenty inches into the barrel before being stopped. The Sergeant pushed through the ranks and seized the gun. "You have to fire the goddamn bullet before you shove another one on top." The Sergeant reckoned the boy had put at least four or five charges into the rifle and had forgotten to prime the cone with a percussion cap each time. The Sergeant tossed the rifle aside and picked up a dead man's gun. "That's why God gave you percussion caps, lad, to kill rebels. Now get on with it."

The New York Major turned and galloped past the body of his Colonel back to the nearest Yankee battery, where his horse slid to a stop in a slurry of wet mud. "Can't you bear on those guns?" he asked, pointing with his drawn sword to the rebel artillery that was pumping smoke into the killing ground.

"We can't move the guns!" an artillery lieutenant called back. The northern guns were dug so deep in the mud that the combined strength of men and horses could not unglue them. A shell moaned overhead to explode just beyond the New Yorkers' tents. Two of the Yankee guns fired, but their trails were now dug in so deep that their canister just whistled eerily over the heads of the rebels.

Then the weird screaming began again, the shrill, blood-curdling yelp that somehow suggested insanity as well as a perverse enjoyment of killing, and it was that sound, rather than the musketry or the rebel artillery, that persuaded the New Yorkers that they had done their duty. They stepped back from the abatis, still firing as they went, but eager to escape the hell of canister and rifle fire that ripped through the abatis and drove men down from the ranks. "Steady now, boys, steady!" the Major called as his troops backed away. The wounded begged to be taken with the retreating battalion, but every unwounded man who slung his rifle to help save a casualty was one less gun to help stave off the attack. The rebel fire was growing in intensity while the New York fire slackened, yet even so the green New Yorkers were putting on a brave display. They kept firing as they went and they did not panic.

"Proud of you, boys! Proud of you!" the Major shouted dry-mouthed, then yelped as a pain like a sledgehammer's hit struck his left arm. He stared in disbelief at the blood that suddenly dripped thick from his sleeve. He tried to move his hand from under the drip-ping blood, but only his little finger would move, so he crooked his arm upright, and that stopped the dripping blood. He felt oddly faint, but dismissed the sensation as unworthy. "You're doing well, boys, real well!" His voice lacked conviction and blood was puddling in the elbow of his sleeve.

The rebels were at the abatis now, using it as a breastwork for their rifles. Some men began dragging parts of the barricade aside, while others discovered the gaps left for the pickets and darted through. Puffs of smoke appeared from the rebel lines and were shredded away. The New Yorkers were going back faster now, pan-icked by the sight of the gunners who were abandoning their mired cannon and fleeing on the backs of their team horses. One artillery officer stayed and tried to spike the weapons by hammering soft metal nails into their touchholes, but he was first shot, then bayo-neted by a rebel who eagerly rifled his victim's pockets.

The Major at last managed to put a tourniquet above his left elbow. His horse trotted unguided through the regiment's tents, which were still immaculate from the morning inspection. The tents' side flaps and doors were all properly brailed up, the groundsheets were swept, and the men's bedding was folded neatly. Campfires burned. On one a pot of untended coffee boiled away. Playing cards fluttered in the wind. The rebels were coming on faster now and the New Yorkers began running for the shelter of the tree line behind their camp. Somewhere beyond those trees, around the road junction where seven tall pine trees stood in an isolated clump, there were more northern troops and larger gun redoubts and a sturdier abatis. That was where salvation lay and so the Yankees fled and the Confederates took over their camp with its treasure troves of food and coffee and comforts sent by loving families to men engaged upon the great and sacred business of holding the union together.

Four miles away, on a glutinous mud road that stretched between gloomy woods, General Huger's division waited while its commanding officer tried to determine just where he was supposed to be. Some of his men were entangled with the rear units of General Longstreet's division and were further confused because Longstreet had just ordered his brigades to about turn and march back the way they had come. The muggy warm air played tricks with the sound waves, sometimes muffling them so the battle seemed to be miles away and at other times making it seem as though the conflict had moved farther east. The two divisions that should have closed like steel jaws on the Yankee army milled in bad-tempered confusion while General Johnston, oblivious that his wings had become entangled and ignorant that his center had started an attack without them, waited at the Old Tavern for the arrival of Longstreet's troops. "Do we have any news of Longstreet?" the General asked for the twentieth time that hour.

"None, sir," Morton said unhappily. Longstreet's division had vanished. "But Huger's men are advancing," Morton said, though he did not like to add that they were advancing so slowly that he doubted any of them would reach the battlefield before nightfall.

"There's going to be a full inquiry into this, Morton," Johnston threatened. "I want to know who disobeyed what orders. You'll arrange it."

"Of course, sir," Morton said, though the chief of staff was more concerned by the rumble of gunfire that sounded from the direction of Hill's division. The rumble was not loud, for once again the layers of warm and sultry air were baffling the sound waves so that the battle's nearby clamor was being muted to the timbre of far-off thunder.

Johnston dismissed his chief of staff's fears about the muffled sound. "An artillery duel on the river," he suggested. "Hill wouldn't attack without support. He's not a fool."

Six miles away, in Richmond, the sound of the guns was much clearer, echoing through streets washed clean by the night's cloudburst. People clambered to rooftops and church belfries to get a view of the gunsmoke rising from the eastern woods. The President had not been informed that any battle was imminent and sent plaintive messages to his army's commander demanding to be told what was happening. Were the Yankees attacking? Should the government's reserves of gold be loaded on the waiting train and carried south to Petersburg? General Robert Lee, as ignorant of Johnston's intentions as President Davis, advised the President to be cautious. It would be better to wait for news, he said, before starting another evacuation panic in the capital.

Not everyone waited nervously for news. Julia Gordon distributed New Testaments in Chimborazo Hospital while across town, in Franklin Street, Sally Truslow used the absence of clients to organize a thorough spring cleaning of the whole house. Sheets were scrubbed and hung to dry in the garden, drapes and rugs were beaten free of dust, delicate glass light shades were washed clean of lampblack, wooden floors were waxed, and windows were polished with newspapers soaked in vinegar. In midafternoon a teamster's wagon brought the great round mahogany table that would be the centerpiece of Sally's seance room, and that had to be waxed. The kitchen steamed with vats of hot water and smelt of lye and washing soda. Sally, her arms and hands reddened, her hair pinned up and her face glistening with sweat, sang as she worked. Her father would have been proud of her, but Thomas Truslow was fast asleep. The

Faulconer Brigade was held in reserve, guarding the Chickahominy crossings northeast of the city where the men listened to the noise of distant battle, played cards, pitched horseshoes, and counted their blessings that their presence was not required this day upon the killing ground.

Starbuck rode south and west, following the road that led to the nearest crossing of the Chickahominy. He hardly knew where he was going, or what he could do. De'Ath had been his sponsor, his protector, and now Starbuck was on his own. For days Starbuck had been terrified that a genuine message from Adam might reach James and thus unmask his treachery, but he had never anticipated this danger, that he would be left friendless on the wrong side of the battlelines. He felt like a hunted animal driven from cover, then he remembered the document that Pinkerton had just given him and wondered if there was enough power in that scrap of paper to see him safe home to the Legion. He was sure that was where he wanted to go, but now he would have to prise the Legion's ranks open without de'Ath's help, and that prospect made him feel close to despair again. Perhaps, he thought, he should just volunteer for a northern infantry regiment. Change his name, pick up a rifle, and so disappear into the blue ranks of America's biggest army.

Starbuck's horse ambled along the verge while its rider tried to find some hope in the whirl of fear and fancy that assailed him. The road had been cut and churned into a morass of deep red mud while the ruts left by the wheels of guns and wagons had filled with stormwater that now rippled under the wind. The countryside here was flat farmland interrupted by swaths of forest and stretches of bog amid which slow streams meandered between rushes, though not far ahead there were low hills that promised firmer footing for his borrowed horse.

The cannon fire was incessant now, suggesting that one side or the other was making a determined effort to dislodge its enemy, yet even so there was remarkably little urgency being displayed in the camps that were uncomfortably pitched in these wet meadows. Men idled away the afternoon as though the battle across the river belonged to some other army or some other nation. A line of soldiers waited at a sutler's store to buy what small luxuries the merchant offered, and a still larger line trailed away from a tent that advertised dried oysters. One of the men winked at Starbuck and tapped his canteen, suggesting that the oyster seller was, in truth, offering illicit whiskey. Starbuck shook his head and rode on. Maybe he should run away? Go to the badlands in the west? Then he remembered Sally's scorn and knew he could not just cut and run. He had to fight for what he wanted!

He passed a Baptist church that was being used as a hospital. Parked beside the church was an undertaker's encampment with its owner's slogan painted in raw vermillion letters on the canvas hood of a covered wagon: "Ethan Cornett and Sons, Newark, New Jersey, Embalming, Cheap and Thorough, Warranted Free of Odor and Infection." A second wagon was piled with pine caskets, each one labeled with the address to which it must be delivered. The embalmed corpses would be taken home to Philadelphia and Boston, Newport and Chicago, Buffalo and St. Paul, and there buried to the accompaniment of sobbing families and the high-flown rhetoric of bloodthirsty parsons. Most bodies were buried where they fell, but some men, dying in hospital, paid to have their corpses carried home. Even as Starbuck watched, a body was brought out of the church and laid on a table beside one of the embalmer's tents. The toes of the corpse's stockings had been pinned together and a label was tied to one ankle. A shirtsleeved man wearing a stained canvas apron and carrying a broad-bladed knife came from a tent to inspect the new body.

Starbuck urged the horse on through the rank smell of embalming chemicals, then up a slight gradient that climbed through a thick belt of woodland beyond which was a small poor farm with fields that had once been fenced with snake rails, though all that was left of the fences were zigzag traces in the grass, for the rails had been stolen for cooking fires. A log cabin sat by the road with a homemade Stars and Stripes hanging from the eaves of its sod roof. The stripes had been made of dark and light colored sacking, while the stars were thirty-four limewash blobs daubed onto a faded scrap of pale blue canvas. The log house was evidently home to a family of free blacks, for an old, white-haired Negro came out of the tiny cabin as Starbuck rode past. The man walked toward his vegetable patch carrying a fork that he hefted in salute to Starbuck. "Go give them hell, master!" he called. "Do the Lord's work now, sir, you hear me, sir."

Starbuck raised a hand in silent acknowledgment. Ahead now he could see a sliding shiny stretch of river and beyond it, far beyond it, a great patch of smoke that looked as though a vast area of woodland was afire. That was the mark of a battle, and the sight of it made Starbuck check his horse and think of K Company, and he wondered if Truslow was under that smoke, and if Decker and the Cobb twins and Joseph May and Esau Washbrook and George Finney were fighting there. God, he thought, but if they were fighting he wanted to be with them. He inwardly cursed de'Ath for dying, then looked beyond the smoke, far beyond, to where a smear of darker vapor betrayed where the foundries and mills of Richmond pumped their noxious smoke into the windy sky, and that evidence of the distant city made him homesick for Sally.

He took a cheroot from his pocket and scratched a match alight. He inhaled the smoke greedily. Putting the matches back into his pocket he felt the cigar shape of the oilskin packet that was his only weapon left. The paper inside would have to be his passport to the Legion, yet if the list of damning questions was found by a rebel provost it could mean the noose. Once again Starbuck felt a tremor of fear and the temptation to run away from both armies.

"Do the Lord's work now, master, go give them hell, sir," the old black man said, and Starbuck turned, thinking it was to him that the old man had spoken again, but instead he saw another horseman spurring up the road toward him. A quarter mile behind that new-comer a group of northern cavalry were roweling their horses through the sticky red mud, the first sign of urgency Starbuck had seen this side of the Chickahominy River.

He looked back to the battle smoke as a hard, percussive drum-roll of cannon fire rumbled cruel across the landscape. Then a half-familiar voice hailed him urgently and Starbuck turned back with a panicked start to realize he was in still more trouble.

THE REBEL ATTACK STALLED AMONG THE ABANDONED tents of the New York regiment. It was not northern resistance that held up the advance, but northern affluence, for within the tents, which themselves were made from stout white canvas of a quality forgotten by the southerners, were boxes of food, knapsacks stuffed with good shirts, spare trousers, and proper leather shoes made to fit either the right or the left foot, unlike the square-toed Confederate-issue brogans which were rigid boxes of stiff leather that could be worn on either foot indiscriminately and promised equal damage to both. Then there were the parcels of food sent from loving northern homes: boxes of chestnuts, jars of green-pepper pickles, bottles of apple butter, paper-wrapped slabs of ginger cake, tins of fruitcake, cans of sugarplums, cloth-wrapped cheeses, and best of all, coffee. Real coffee. Not coffee adulterated with dried and ground goober peas, or coffee made from parched corn pounded into powder, or coffee made from desiccated dandelion leaves mixed with dried apple powder, but real fragrant dark coffee beans.

At first the rebel officers tried to keep their troops moving through the snares of enemy wealth, but then the officers themselves became seduced by the easy pickings within the abandoned tents. There were fine hams, smoked fish, dried oysters, new butter, and fresh-baked bread. There were thick blankets and, in some tents, quilts that had been made by womenfolk for their hero sons and husbands. One quilt displayed a union flag on which a legend had been sewn in letters of golden silk. "Avenge Ellsworth!" the quilt read.

"Who the hell's Ellsworth?" a rebel asked his officer.

"A New Yorker who got himself killed."

"That's a habit of Yankees these days, ain't it?"

"He was the first. Got himself shotgunned when he tried to take one of our flags off a hotel roof in Virginia."

"Son of a bitch should have stayed in New York then, shouldn't he?"

In the officers' tents there were fine German field glasses, family photographs framed in silver standing on folding hardwood tables, elegant traveling writing cases filled with engraved notepaper, leather-bound books, hairbrushes backed with polished tortoiseshell, fine steel razors in leather cases, boxes of Roussell's Shaving Cream, well-thumbed stacks of intimate daguerreotypes of undressed ladies, stone jars of good whiskey, and bottles of fine wine stored in sawdust-filled crates. A Confederate major, coming across one such cache of bottles, fired his revolver into the chest so that the liquor could not tempt his men. The crate's sawdust became discolored with wine as the heavy bullets drove down into the bottles. "Keep the men moving!" the Major shouted at his officers, but the officers were like the men and the men were like children in a toy store and would not be shifted on to the day's proper business.

In the battalion's wagon park, behind the headquarters tents, a sergeant discovered a hundred brand-new Enfield Rifles packed in rope-handled crates stenciled with the rifle manufacturer's name, "Ward & Sons, Birmingham, England." The Enfield was a prized gun and a far more accurate and sturdy rifle than the weapon this regiment of rebels was using, and soon a clamor of men jostled about the wagon to get hold of one of the precious guns.

Slowly the chaos was sorted out. Some officers and sergeants slashed the guy ropes of the tents, collapsing the canvas on the contents to persuade the men to abandon the plunder and keep pressing after the defeated Yankees. On either flank, where no campground served to delay the attack, the rebel lines already pushed on through a wide belt of woodland where windflowers, bloodroot, and violets blossomed, and then the attackers emerged into an open stretch of waterlogged grassland where the wind shivered the puddles and lifted the heavy flags of the Yankee troops who were making their stand just west of the junction where the three roads on which the rebel attacks were supposed to be advancing came together. The crossroads was marked by seven tall pines and two gaunt farmhouses, landmarks of this killing ground where Johnston had planned his annihilation of the Yankees south of the river.

The crossroads was also protected by an elaborate earth-walled fort that was studded with cannon and crowned by old Glory on a staff made of a trimmed pine trunk. The approaches to the fort were traversed by abatis and rifle pits. It was here that Johnston had planned to surround the Yankees, first hitting them in the center, then breaking them from north and south and so driving them whimpering into the snake-haunted marshes of the White Oak Swamp, but instead one rebel division alone advanced from the trees. That division had already broken one northern line and now, across the wind-shivered morass, they saw a second line waiting beneath its bright flags and so the gray and brown troops began to scream their shrill, eerie yell of attack.

"Fire!" a northern officer standing on the fort's rampart called. The northern cannon slammed back on their trails. Shells burst in the far air, white smoke lancing scraps of white-hot steel down onto the rebel line. The minie bullets whistled over the marsh, striking home in misty sprays of blood. The colors fell and were lifted again as the rebels waded on through sodden ground.

General Huger heard the renewed cannonade, but refused to translate it as a summons for urgency. "Hill knows his business," he claimed, "and if he needed our help he'd have sent for us." In the meantime he pushed a brigade cautiously down an empty road, claiming it was a reconnaissance in force. The brigade found nothing. Longstreet, meanwhile, frustrated first in one direction and then in the other, ordered his men to countermarch one more time. Both generals cursed the lack of maps and a drifting afternoon fog that was just thick enough to hide the battle's telltale plume of gunsmoke that would otherwise have told them just where the baffling and muffled sound of guns came from.

President Davis, frustrated by his commanding general's silence, rode from Richmond toward the battlefield. He asked every officer he met what news there was, but no one knew what happened in the marshy fields south of the river. Even the President's military adviser could not discover the truth. Robert E. Lee had no standing in the army's affairs and could only surmise that an attack had been launched from the Confederate lines, though with what aim and with what success he could neither say nor guess. The President asked if anyone knew where Johnston's headquarters was, but no one was certain of that either, but the President decided he must find Johnston anyway, and so his party worked its way eastward in search of news about a battle that flared into life again as Hill's unsupported columns crashed into the Yankee's hard-dug defenses around the seven pines.

Where the guns grew hot as, fed by confusion and succored by pride, the killing kept on.

The man who had hailed Starbuck was the French military observer, Colonel Lassan, who now spurred over the brow of the hill and seized the bridle of Starbuck's horse, dragging him on down the road and so out of sight of the Yankee cavalry. "You know you're in trouble?" the Frenchman asked.

Starbuck was trying to jerk his horse's head out of the Frenchman's grasp.

"Don't be such a bloody fool!" Lassan snapped in his perfect English. "And follow me!" He let go of the bridle and pricked his horse's flanks with his spurs, and such was the authority in his voice that Starbuck instinctively followed as the Frenchman swerved sharply right off the road and across a boggy patch of ground into the sudden cover of some broad-leaved trees. The two men forced a path through grasping undergrowth and low, soaking wet branches, at last reaching a clearer patch of woodland where the Frenchman turned his horse and raised a hand ordering Starbuck to silence.

The two men listened. Starbuck could hear the solid, ear-thumping bang of big guns across the river, and the lighter, sharper crackle of musketry, and he could hear the rustle and moan of the wind in the high trees, but he could hear nothing else. Yet the Frenchman still listened and Starbuck looked with renewed curiosity at his rescuer. Lassan was a tall man, maybe in his forties, with a black mustache and a thin face made singular by the scars of war. Starbuck saw the scars where a Russian saber had laid open the Frenchman's right cheek, a Cossack's bullet had taken his left eye, and an Austrian rifle bullet had mangled his left jawbone, yet despite the injuries there remained such an air of confident enjoyment about the Frenchman that it was hard to call the horribly scarred face ugly. Rather it was superbly battered; a face on which life had left a tale of adventure that had been met with panache. Lassan rode his tall black horse with the same innate grace as Washington Faulconer, while his uniform, which had once been gaudy with lace and gold chain and gilt froggings, was now sun-bleached and darned, and its fine metal embellishments were either tarnished or missing altogether. He must once have had a splendid uniform hat, maybe in lustrous fur or shining brass and towering with plumes or a scarlet crest, but now he wore a floppy farm hat that looked as if it had come from a scarecrow. "It's all right." Lassan broke his silence. "They're not following us."

"Who's they?"

"The leader of the pack is a fellow called Thorne. Comes from Washington." Lassan paused to pat his horse's neck. "Claims to have evidence that you were sent across the lines to mislead the Yankees. Worse, that you were sent over to discover who their best spy in

Richmond is." Lassan took a compass from his pocket and let its needle settle before gesturing northwest. "We'll go this way." He turned
his horse and started it at a walk through the trees. "What it boils
down to, my friend, is that they want to measure your neck for a
rope. I got involved because the energetic Thorne came to McClellan
demanding the use of cavalry. I overheard, and here I am. At your
service, monsieur." Lassan offered Starbuck a rakish grin.

"Why?" Starbuck demanded ungraciously.

"Why not?" Lassan responded cheerfully, then went silent as his
horse descended the bank of a small stream and scrambled up the far
side. "All right, I shall tell you why. It's just as I told you before. I need
to get to the rebel side, simple as that, and preferably before this campaign is over, which means I can't spend weeks traveling halfway
around the damn world to get from Yorktown to Richmond. I prefer
to make a run across the lines, and I guessed you'd be doing the same
thing this afternoon and so I thought to myself, why not? Two heads
are better than one, and when we get to the other side you will be my
guarantor so that instead of arresting and shooting me as a spy they
will accept your word that I am, indeed, Patrick Lassan, Chasseur
Colonel of the Imperial Guard." He grinned at Starbuck. "Does that
make sense?"

"Patrick?" Starbuck asked, his curiosity piqued by the name that
did not seem at all French.

"My father was English and his closest friend was Irish, and thus
the name. My mother is French and I took her surname because she
never found time to marry her Englishman, and what that makes me,
*mon ami*, is a mongrel bastard." Lassan had spoken with evident affection for his parents, an affection that made Starbuck envious. "It also
makes me a bored mongrel bastard," Lassan continued. "The Yankees are a fine, hospitable people, but they are increasingly beset by a
Teutonic discipline. They wish to hedge me in with regulation and
rules. They want me to stay a decorous distance from the fighting as
befits an observer and not a participant, but I need to smell the killing,
otherwise I can't tell how this war is being won and lost."

"We have rules and regulations too," Starbuck said.

"Ah, ha!" Lassan twisted in his saddle. "So you are a rebel?"

For a second the ingrained habit of the last weeks tempted Starbuck to a denial, then he shrugged. "Yes."

"Good for you. So maybe your rules and regulations are as bad as those of the Yankees, I shall see. But it will be an adventure, yes? A fine adventure. Come on!" He led Starbuck out of the trees and across a meadow that was being used as an artillery park. Another road lay ahead and beside it were ranks of resting Yankee infantry. Lassan proposed that if anyone challenged their presence he would explain that he was an official observer riding to the battle and that Starbuck was his orderly. "But our biggest obstacle is crossing the river. Your pursuers will stay on the road behind us, but there's a chance they've telegraphed to all the bridges warning the sentries to keep a lookout for you."

Starbuck felt the sour pulse of fear in his belly. If the Yankees caught him they would hang him, and if the rebel provosts found Pinkerton's paper then they would do the same. Yet by crossing the lines there was still a chance that he could bluff his way back into the Legion. "You're taking a risk, aren't you?" he asked Lassan.

"Not at all. If they apprehend us I shall disclaim all knowledge of your criminal soul. I shall say you tricked and deceived me, then I shall smoke a cigar while you hang. Though don't worry, I shall say a prayer for your soul."

The thought of his damned soul made Starbuck think of all his brother's wasted prayers. "Did you see my brother?" Starbuck asked as he and the Colonel threaded the parked guns toward the infantrymen who rested by the road.

"He was proclaiming your innocence. Your brother, I think, is not a born soldier." It was a delicately kind judgment. "I spent most of the battle at Bull Run in your brother's company. He's a man who likes the confinement of rules and regulations. Not a rogue, I think. Armies could not survive without such careful men, but they need rogues even more."

"James is a good lawyer," Starbuck said in his brother's defense.

"Why do you Americans take such pride in your attorneys? Lawyers are merely the symptoms of a quarrelsome society and every cent given to a lawyer is a sip less champagne, a woman unconquered, or a cigar unsmoked. Damn the bloodsucking lot of them, I say, though I'm sure your brother is a very angel compared to the rest. Sergeant!" Lassan shouted at one of the infantrymen, "what unit are you?"

The Sergeant, persuaded by Lassan's obvious authority, said that his unit was the 1st Minnesota in General Gorman's brigade. "You know what's happening, sir?" the Sergeant asked.

"Damned rebels are twitching, Sergeant. You'll be marching to give them a hiding soon enough. Good luck to you!" Lassan rode on, trotting between the road's deep muddied ruts and the waiting infantry. "This is General Sumner's Corps," he told Starbuck. "Sumner must have closed up to the bridge, which means he's waiting for orders to attack, but I doubt he'll get them very quickly. Our Young Napoleon doesn't seem entirely seized of the day's urgency. He's ill, but even so he should be slightly animated."

"You don't like McClellan?" Starbuck asked.

"Like him?" The Frenchman considered the question for a moment. "No, not much. He's a drill sergeant, not a general. Nothing but a pompous little man with too high an opinion of himself. It wouldn't matter if he could win battles, but he doesn't seem capable of fighting them, let alone winning them. So far all he's done in this campaign is lean on the rebels, using his weight to push them back, but he hasn't fought them. He's scared of them! He believes you've got two hundred thousand men!" Lassan gave a bark of laughter, then pointed up to a shiny telegraph wire that had been strung on makeshift poles alongside the road. "That's our problem, Starbuck. Suppose our friend Thorne has telegraphed ahead, eh? They might be waiting for you at the bridge. They'll probably hang you on the gallows in Fort Monroe. Last cup of coffee, a cigar, a quick trot through the Twenty-third Psalm, then they'll put on the hood and wallop you down through the hatch. A quick way to go, they say. Much better than shooting. Have you ever seen a firing squad?"

"No."

"You will. I'm always astonished how often a firing squad misses. You line the dumb buggers up at ten paces, pin a piece of paper over the poor man's heart, and still they'll pepper his liver and elbows and bladder; anywhere, in fact, that won't put the poor bastard out of his misery, which means that the officer then has to go and give the quivering wretch a coup de grace in the skull. I'll never forget my first. I had a hand shaking like a leaf and the poor bastard twitching like a landed fish. It took me three pistol bullets and a whole fortnight to get his blood out of the stitching in my boots. Messy business, firing squads. You feeling all right?"

"I'm fine," Starbuck said, and in truth Lassan's conversation was diverting him from his worries about de'Ath's death.

Lassan laughed at Starbuck's aplomb. The road had entered a gloomy, dank stretch of forest where creepers trailed from trees and sour pools of water stretched under the branches. The road had been corduroyed, which made the going hard for the horses, so hard that after a while Lassan suggested they dismount and lead the horses by the reins. He talked of the Crimea and of the idiocy of generals, then of the days when he had joined the French army as an officer cadet in 1832. "My father wanted me to join the British army. Be a rifleman, he told me, best of the best, and my mother wanted me to be a French cavalryman. I chose the French."

"Why?"

"Because I was in love with a girl whose parents lived in Paris and I thought if I went to St. Cyr I'd be able to seduce her, while if I moved to England I should never see her again."

Starbuck thought of Mademoiselle Dominique Demarest of New Orleans, cheap actress and cheaper whore, who had tempted him to leave Yale and run away with a traveling band of showmen. He wondered where Dominique was now and whether they would ever meet to settle accounts with her. Then, quite suddenly, he realized he had no grudge against Dominique. She had only made him do what he had wanted to do, which was to flee from his family's stultifying bonds. "What happened to the girl?" Starbuck asked.

"She married a draper in Soissons," Lassan said. "And now I can hardly remember what she looked like."

"Was your father angry?"

"Only about my taste in women. He said he'd seen a prettier face on a bullock." Lassan laughed again. "But I made my choice for love, you see, and I don't regret it. And maybe if I'd chosen the other way I wouldn't have regretted that either. There isn't an optimum of life, just one hell of a good time waiting for those who have the courage to take it. And courage is what we must now have, *mon ami*." Lassan gestured at the bridge that had just come into view. "Cross this bridge and we only have the bullets and shells of two armies to survive."

The bridge was a miserable-looking contraption. The mud-covered corduroy road led straight through a stagnant marsh, then seemed to elevate itself a foot or two above the mephitic, rank river before sliding down to another distasteful stretch of bog on the water's southern bank. The slight elevation was caused by four pontoons, tin-covered wooden punts that carried the corduroyed roadway across the river. The pontoons were held in place by enormously long ropes that had been carried back to the forests and tied to trees, but it was evident that there was a problem with the complicated arrangement of ropes, pontoons, pulleys, and roadway. The storm of the previous night had raised the river's level and brought down a mass of floating debris that had become trapped against the bridge, so stretching the mooring lines that the road now bulged dangerously downstream. There was plainly a danger that the pressure of water and flotsam would snap the lines and destroy the bridge, to prevent which disaster a score of unhappy engineer troops were standing up to their chests in the swirling, muddy water as they tried to clear the bridge and secure new mooring lines.

"You can't cross!" A shirtsleeved engineer accosted Lassan and

Starbuck as the two men led their horses out from the cover of the forest. The engineer was middle-aged, his pants were smeared with mud, and his whiskered face dripped with sweat that had also turned his white shirt dark with damp. "I'm Colonel Ellis, Engineer Corps," he introduced himself to Lassan. "The bridge isn't safe. The storm gave it a hell of a beating." Ellis gave Starbuck a glance, but showed no other interest in him. "There's another bridge a mile upriver."

Lassan grimaced. "How do we reach this other bridge?"

"Go back the way you've come. After half a mile there's a turning to the left, take it. Another half mile there's a T junction, turn left again." Ellis slapped at a mosquito. Out in the river a line of men hauled on a cable and Starbuck saw the fragile bridge dip and quiver as the big rope tightened. The line came up from the water, looped with dripping vegetation, then one of the men in the river screamed as he saw a snake clinging to the newly tautened rope. He let go of the line and the panic spread to his fellows, who all released their grip and fled toward the bank. The bridge creaked as it surged downstream again.

A sergeant bellowed at the troops, cursing them for chicken-livered bastards. "It's only a goddamn moccasin! It won't kill you! Now take hold! Haul, you bastards, haul!"

"You know there's a corps waiting to cross this bridge?" Lassan asked Colonel Ellis sternly, as though the Engineer Colonel was personally responsible for delaying the advance of the corps. "They're waiting on the far side of the woods."

"They're not crossing anything till the bridge is repaired," Ellis said bad-temperedly.

"I think we should discover for ourselves whether the bridge is safe," Lassan said airily. "The future of the union might depend on it. In war, Colonel, there are risks that should be taken which would be unthinkable in peace, and if a fragile bridge is the only route to victory then it must be risked." He declaimed this nonsense as he marched resolutely on toward the bridge, which was quivering under the force of the water's onslaught. Starbuck could see how the stormwater had tugged two of the pontoons out of their alignment and as a result the corduroy road had fanned apart to reveal ankle-wide gaps between its top layer of logs.

"Who are you?" The mud-spattered Engineer Colonel hurried after the Frenchman. Lassan ignored him, instead glancing into a small tent that was precariously pitched close to a stagnant pool and inside which a telegraph machine chattered unattended. "I demand to know who you are!" the Colonel, red-faced, insisted.

"I am General Lassan, Viscount Seleglise of the Duchy of Normandy and a Chasseur of the Emperor's Imperial Guard, presently attached to Major General George McClellan's staff." Lassan strode on with Starbuck beside him.

"I don't care if you're the King of Siam," Ellis insisted. "You still can't cross."

"Maybe not, which means I shall die trying," Lassan said very grandly. "If my body is recovered, Colonel, pray have it sent back to Normandy. My companion, on the other hand, is from Boston, so you may allow his body to rot in whatever noxious swamp it comes to rest. Come on, boy!" This last encouragement was to his horse, which was bridling nervously at the uncertain footing of the bridge's approach. The corduroyed logs sank beneath the weight of the horses and a bubbling ooze of watery mud seeped up between the chinks.

"Get the hell back!" the Sergeant, standing to his waist in water and with the bitter end of a rope in his hands, shouted at Lassan and Starbuck.

"I'm going on. My risk, not yours!" Lassan called back to the Sergeant, then he gave Starbuck a mischievous grin. "Onward, ever onward!"

"Colonel! Please?" Colonel Ellis tried a last appeal, but Lassan simply ignored the engineers and paced resolutely out across the logs to where the damaged bridge inched up above the river's swirling, swollen, hard-running waters. The roadway creaked and dipped as they ventured onto the ramp. Starbuck, passing the first pontoon, saw that it was half flooded with rainwater, then he encountered the bridge's inadvertent bend and his horse tried to shy away from the seethe of the water where it swirled against the driftwood and the pontoons. Starbuck dragged the horse on, but painfully slowly, for the beast needed time to place its hooves on the shaking logs. "Stay on the upstream side," Lassan advised. "The logs are closer together." The second pontoon was almost awash, and under the weight of Lassan's horse the roadway dipped perilously close to the red muddy swirl of the river. "Colonel Ellis!" Lassan shouted back to the working party.

"What is it?"

"You'd find the work easier if you pumped the pontoons out."

"Why don't you mind your own damn business!"

"A good question," Lassan said happily to himself. He and Starbuck were halfway across now, their weight depressing the heavy roadway to within inches of the river's surface. "You have very good engineers in this country," the Frenchman told Starbuck. "Better than ours. The French love being cavalrymen, at worst they will accept being turned into light infantrymen, but anything else is believed demeaning. Yet I have a horrible suspicion that future wars will be decided by the artillerymen and engineers, the mathematical drudges of warfare, while we splendid horsemen will be reduced to mere errand boys. Still, I can't imagine good women falling in love with engineers, can you? That's the good thing about being a cavalryman, it does make the important conquests of life somewhat easier."

Starbuck laughed, then gasped as one boot slid out from beneath him on a greasy patch of log. He managed to keep his balance, though the sudden movement seemed to stretch the nearest pontoon's guy ropes so that the whole bridge lurched under the assault of the river water that bubbled and surged between a crack in the logs. Starbuck and his horse both stood motionless until the worst of the bridge's shaking subsided and they could step cautiously on. "Are you really a viscount?" Starbuck asked the Frenchman, and he remembered that de'Ath too had claimed a French title, though if James's gossip was right, then de'Ath's parentage was even more distinguished.

"I'm never sure," Lassan answered carelessly. "It's an old title, officially abolished at the Revolution, but my grandfather used it and I'm his only direct male descendant. I suppose I lost any right to membership in the nobility when my mother and father made love on the wrong side of the blanket, but every now and then I resurrect the title to astonish the local peasantry."

"And you said you were a general?"

"Brevet only. Once the Austrian wars were over I reverted to being a plain and humble colonel."

"And your government sent you here to see how we fight?" Starbuck asked, astonished that such a man would have been ordered to America.

"Oh, no. They wanted me to command a recruiting depot, nothing but lumpish plowboys, spavined remounts, and drunken sergeants. They sent some bores from the academy and a couple of dull infantrymen to be their official observers here, but I wanted to look for myself so I took an indefinite leave of absence, and the government reluctantly accredited me once they realized I couldn't be stopped. I think of myself as being on holiday, Starbuck." Lassan tugged his horse onward. "Nearly there. I don't know what those silly bastards are fretting over. I could have waltzed a blindfolded division of galloping whores over this bridge."

Starbuck smiled at the outrageous claim, then twisted around as a stern voice hailed them from the river's northern bank. It was Colonel Ellis who called from beside the telegraph tent. "Stop!" Ellis shouted. "Right where you are! Stop!"

Starbuck waved as though he had misunderstood Ellis's order, then kept walking. He was almost off the bridge now and approaching the soggy, uncertain footing of the approach road. He began to hurry, dragging the horse behind him.

"Stop!" Ellis shouted again, and this time he reinforced the order by pulling out his revolver and firing a shot well above Starbuck's head. The bullet ripped into the leaves of the trees that now lay some fifty yards ahead.

"Turn the horse toward him," Lassan said softly, "so he thinks you're obeying. Mount up at the same time, then keep the horse swinging around and ride like hell. Understand?"

"I understand," Starbuck said, and he waved again at the Engineer Colonel and he pulled the horse around to make it clear he was not trying to run away, and at the same time he put his muddy left boot into the stirrup. He gripped the saddle's pommel with his left hand and with a quick effort swung himself up into his brother's saddle. Lassan also mounted.

Colonel Ellis was hurrying toward the bridge, beckoning to the two fugitives. "Come back!"

"Good-bye, *mon Colonel*," Lassan said softly and turned his horse away. "Now ride with me!" the Frenchman shouted and Starbuck slashed back with his heels and his horse took off after the Frenchman's mount. The corduroy road was slippery and treacherous, but somehow the two horses kept their footing. "Ride!" Lassan encouraged Starbuck, and Colonel Ellis offered yet more encouragement by firing his revolver, only this time he was not aiming over the fugitives' heads, but at their horses. Yet the two men were already over a hundred yards away and revolvers were uncertain weapons at anything over forty or fifty yards. The Colonel fired his first two bullets much too fast and his aim was lamentably wide. Then he checked himself to take more careful aim, but Lassan was already in the shadow of the trees where he turned the black horse, drew his own revolver, and fired back past Starbuck. Lassan's shots splashed into the marsh or drove wet splinters up from the road. The Frenchman was not shooting to kill, but rather to throw off the engineer's aim, then Starbuck spurred past him and turned a bend and so rode out of Ellis's sight.

Lassan caught up with Starbuck and the two men rode between woods as dank and overgrown as those on the river's northern bank. "They know where we are now," Lassan said. "Ellis will telegraph them." He was reloading his revolver, ramming the bullets down on the powder with the lever attached to the underside of the weapon's barrel. The sound of battle was louder now, filling the sultry land ahead with the menace of death. Lassan spotted a path in the woods and veered off the road, galloping along an open ride that widened into a field behind a sprawling house. Starbuck followed, tensing himself as the Frenchman jumped a rail fence. Starbuck gripped the reins, closed his eyes, and let the horse bump him up and over. Somehow he clung to the beast's back and when he opened his eyes again he saw they were trotting on a path that ran between a field and more woods. A drill barrow had been abandoned beside the path, a reminder of more peaceful times, while at the far side of the field there was an artillery park where the horses, limbers, and cannon of a northern battery waited for orders. "Best not to look in too much of a hurry," Lassan advised Starbuck. "There's nothing so suspicious on a battlefield as a man in a hurry. Have you noticed that? Soldiers do most things at half speed. The only people in a hurry are staff officers and fugitives."

He turned farther eastward, going into the open field and trotting casually behind the waiting guns. Starbuck rode beside him. A half mile to their left was another belt of timber, beyond which lay a range of low wooded hills that concealed the killing ground. A huge smear of smoke rose into the clouds beyond those hills, and Lassan was heading for the edge of that smoke. "No point in getting into the thick of things, Starbuck. We'll go for the flank."

"You're enjoying this, aren't you?" Starbuck said, content to let the more experienced Frenchman be his guide.

"It's better than sitting in McClellan's headquarters reading the New York *World* for the eighty-ninth time."

"But what about your belongings?" Starbuck asked, realizing suddenly that the Frenchman was proposing to move from the Federal to the Confederate lines with no apparent baggage.

"My belongings are in France. Here in America I have one cloak," Lassan patted the garment that was rolled at the cantle of his saddle. "Some money here." He patted a saddlebag. "Enough to make it worth your while to murder me, but I'd advise you not to try." He smiled happily. "A spare shirt, some tobacco, revolver cartridges, spare underclothes, a copy of Montaigne's essays, one tooth-

brush, three notebooks, two pencils, two razors, a steel, one compass, field glasses, one comb, one watch, one flute, letters of credit,
and my official papers." He patted whatever pocket or saddlebag held
these various possessions. "Once I'm safe with the rebels I'll buy a
spare horse, and once again I will have possessions enough for all my
needs. A soldier shouldn't carry more, and if I grew a beard I
wouldn't even need the razors."

"What about the flute?"

"A man should possess some civilizing talent, *mon ami*, or else
he's just a brute. God, I wouldn't like to fight in this country." He
voiced this opinion as the two horsemen breasted a small rise to see a
tangle of small fields and woods ahead. "This is no place for cavalry,"
Lassan said.

"Why not?"

"Because cavalry hates trees. Trees can hide guns and muskets
and we cavalry like the long rolling plains. First you break the enemy
infantry with artillery, then you loose the cavalry on them, and afterward you bury them. That's the old world's prescription for battle,
but you can only do that in open country. And I tell you, my friend,
that God gives no finer thrill than the experience of riding down a
broken enemy. Hoofbeats, trumpets, the sun above, the enemy
beneath, my God, but war is a wicked thrill." They trotted on, going
past the first evidence of this day's battle. There was a casualty station
in the field where ambulances were bringing the wounded and where
nurses in a uniform of long skirts and men's shirts helped carry the
bloody bodies out of the wagons and into the tents. Beside the casualty station was a small group of sullen men with powder-blackened
faces, fugitives who had run from the rebel's first attacks and who
had now been rounded up by northern provosts. Mules loaded with
panniers of rifle ammunition were being led along a road toward the
smoke plume.

Lassan and Starbuck trotted past the mules and into another belt
of trees where northern infantry waited in the shadows. The men's
faces were unstained with powder, evidence that they had not yet
fought this day.

Beyond the trees the road dropped gently down to where the Richmond and York Railroad ran on its embankment through the damp meadows. The rebels had stripped the road of its rails and blown up the bridge across the Chickahominy, but the efficient northern engineers had restored both and a balloon train had stopped just to the right of the place where the road crossed the tracks. A locomotive puffed smoke into the air while the balloon's crew winched their ungainly vehicle up from a flatbed car. The wind had dropped in the wake of the storm, but even so the balloon's crew was having a hard struggle with the burgeoning envelope of gas.

"Trouble," Lassan grunted.

Starbuck had been gazing at the balloon, but now he looked in the other direction and saw that a cavalry patrol was advancing along the railroad embankment.

"Maybe they're just hunting for skulkers," Lassan guessed. "We must risk it. Once we're in the far woods we'll be safe enough." He pointed to a thick belt of trees that lay on the far side of the railroad. "Just let the horse walk."

Lassan and Starbuck went slowly down the road. The Frenchman lit a cigar that he offered to Starbuck, then took one himself. The patrol was still a long way off and Starbuck felt his confidence rise as he drew nearer and nearer to the steel rails. The road climbed gently to the embankment's level between verges dotted with patches of burned grass where sparks from locomotives had started small fires. Two soldiers carried a reel mounted on a stick from which they unrolled a telegraph wire that would connect the balloon's basket with the wire that had been newly strung along the rail embankment. One of the men shimmied up a pole with a pair of pliers in his teeth. "I hate modern war," Lassan said as he and Starbuck reached the rail crossing. "War should be drumbeats and trumpets, not electric engineers and steam engines." Two ambulances were hurrying north along the road and Lassan drew his horse aside to let them pass. The wheels of the two white-painted wagons clattered over the boards that raised the roadbed to the level of the rails. The ambulances left a trail of fine blood drops on the road. Lassan grimaced at the sight of the ambulances' cargo of moaning, cursing, bleeding passengers, then took out his field glasses to examine the country south of the railroad. Off to the left were rows of tents and a line of earthworks where a battery of guns was emplaced, though the day's fighting all seemed to be a mile or so farther on beyond the trees. Two wig-wag men, their signal flags a blur of motion, stood on the redoubt's parapet to pass a message southward. Nearer at hand the cavalry patrol turned off the embankment and spurred onto the meadows.

"They've seen us," Starbuck warned the Frenchman, who looked leftward to see that the northern horsemen were angling across the fields in a maneuver that seemed designed to head off the two fugitives.

Lassan gazed for a second through his binoculars. "Your brother's there. And Pinkerton. I think we should become fugitives, yes?" He grinned at Starbuck, then trotted down the sloping road that led off the embankment's southern side. At the foot of the slope he looked again at the pursuers and evidently did not like what he saw for he took his heavy metal scabbard with its big, ugly sword and rammed it between his left thigh and the saddle so it would not bounce and bruise him. "Gallop!" he told Starbuck.

Both men rammed back their heels, and their horses threw up their heads and thumped their hooves into the road's red mud. A cavalry bugle sounded the charge and Starbuck twisted awkwardly in his saddle to see the blue-coated horsemen spreading across the field. The closest cavalry were still three hundred yards away and their horses were tired, but suddenly a pistol or carbine banged and Starbuck saw the puff of smoke snatched away behind the horsemen. He was not sure, but he thought he saw James, then another weapon cracked and Starbuck just ducked his head and rode hell-for-leather after Lassan. The Frenchman's horse pounded into the trees where Lassan swerved off the road into the tangled woodland. Starbuck followed, riding desperately around the denser patches of brush and ducking under the low branches until at last Lassan slowed to a trot

and looked behind to make sure the pursuit had been avoided. Starbuck, his heart pounding, tried to calm his sweating horse. "I hate riding," he said.

Lassan held a finger to his lips, then pointed in the direction he
wanted to go. He let the horses walk. Starbuck could smell the rank
sweet stench of powder smoke while the sound of the guns was now
so close that each gunshot gave a percussive thump to the ears, yet
the trees still hid all sight of the battle. Lassan paused again. The
Frenchman's face was alight with happiness. For him this was all a
glorious adventure, a spree in the new world. "Onward," he said,
"ever onward."

The two men emerged from the wood into a small, irregular
meadow where a battalion of northern infantry waited. The officer
leading the battalion's color party whirled his horse around eagerly as
Lassan appeared. "Orders?" he asked.

"Not from us, good luck though," Lassan shouted in answer as
he spurred past the color party. To Starbuck's left the country opened
out and he could see wagons and gun limbers parked at a crossroads,
and jets of smoke showing where the guns fired. There were a group
of pine trees there and two gaunt houses that seemed to lie right
beneath the plume of smoke. A Union flag lifted its scarlet and white
stripes in the smoky breeze, then Starbuck lost sight of the crossroads
as he followed Lassan into another belt of timber.

Lassan led him through a tangle of briers, over a fallen and fungi-
ridden log, then they were in another clearing, and this time Starbuck
could see the rail embankment to his right. There were no soldiers
visible. "We've lost those cavalry," Starbuck said to the Frenchman.

"They're not so far away," Lassan cautioned. "We threw them
off for a moment, but they'll be back. This way."

Their path led into trees again, then into another patch of open
ground which proved to be so swampy that they had to dismount
and lead their horses through the glutinous, sucking turf. Beyond the
swamp was a patch of low scrub oak, then a stand of pines. The noise
of the battle went on incessantly, but somehow, oddly, every evidence of soldiers had disappeared; indeed the woodland was so undis-

turbed that Lassan suddenly pointed to his right and Starbuck saw three wild turkeys in a small clearing. "Good eating?" Lassan asked.

"Very."

"Not today, though," Lassan said and turned to look ahead as an outbreak of rifle fire splintered the humid air. Then, over that fusillade, came the peculiar and chilling noise of the rebel's battle yell, and the sound of that defiant yelp gave Starbuck's heart a leap of excitement. "If I were you," Lassan said, "I'd take off that blue coat."

Starbuck was still wearing his brother's jacket. Now he hurriedly searched the pockets, taking out the Bible that James had left him in Richmond, then his handful of cheap cigars, the box of matches, the penknife, and the oilskin packet of papers. He pushed them all into a saddlebag, then peeled off his brother's coat and let it fall to the ground. Now he just wore his old gray rebel trousers, red suspenders, new shoes his brother had bought him from the sutler of a Pennsylvania regiment, and a broad-brimmed hat as ragged and stained as Lassan's eccentric headgear.

The Frenchman led him on through the trees. From time to time Starbuck would catch a glimpse of the rail embankment to their right, but he still could not see the troops who were giving the rebel yell. Every few seconds a stray rifle bullet tore through the leaves overhead, but it was hard to determine just where the fire was coming from. Lassan was picking his way carefully, as alert as a hunter edging toward a trapped prey. "We may have to cross the rails again," the Frenchman said, then there was no time for deliberation or thought, only for escape as a shout to their rear betrayed that the cavalry had found them again. Both men instinctively kicked their horses into a gallop.

A bullet slapped overhead, another cracked into a tree. Lassan whooped and ducked under a branch. Starbuck followed, gripping the pommel of his saddle as his horse thumped up a muddy path, across a small crest, and down to a road where a double file of Yankee infantry waited. "Make way! Make way!" Lassan shouted in his authoritative voice and the infantry moved magically aside to let the two horsemen pound past. They jumped a low hedge, crossed a field of arable, then once again the bullets came from behind and Starbuck feared that the whole infantry battalion would open fire, but suddenly he was in the woods again and could see soldiers to his left, only these soldiers were in full flight, running from some enemy ahead, and he let his hopes rise in anticipation. The fugitives were northerners, so surely there were rebels close by.

Lassan saw the running men and swerved away from them. Starbuck could hear hooves behind him now and he dared to snatch a glance over his shoulder to see a bearded horseman some twenty paces away. The man had a drawn saber, its blade wickedly bright in the day's cloudy gloom. There were infantry fusillades ahead, a rebel shout again, and more northerners running. Lassan looked over his shoulder and saw the cavalryman closing on Starbuck. The Frenchman pulled his horse left, slowed, and dragged his big sword from its scabbard. He let Starbuck overtake him, then he cut hard across the northerner's path and slammed the sword brutally down onto the skull of the man's horse. The blade drove into the horse's forehead and the beast screamed as it went down onto its knees. It was thrashing its head, spraying blood, then it collapsed and its rider went flying, cursing as he slid into a tangle of thorns beside the track. Lassan had already cut back to his left and was catching Starbuck again. "Always go for the horse, never the man," he shouted as he galloped to catch up with Starbuck.

The Frenchman sheathed his sword as he and Starbuck burst into a wide stretch of open country. To their right the rail embankment was topped by small groups of Yankees who were watching helplessly as a single rebel infantry brigade advanced boldly across the open heath. The brigade was composed of four battalions, three of which were flying the Confederacy's new battle flag while the fourth still carried the old three-striped flag. The brigade was advancing in two lines without either artillery or cavalry support, yet nothing seemed able to stop their progress. In front of them was a chaotic mass of fugitives and behind them a litter of dead and dying men. No other rebels were in sight. It was as if this one brigade had found a gap in the Yankee line and had decided to win the battle on its own.

Starbuck swerved toward the rebel brigade. "Virginia!" he shouted like a battle cry. "Virginia!" He waved to show he was unarmed. Lassan followed him, while sixty yards behind Lassan the northern cavalry burst out from beneath the trees.

The rebel brigade had been the first of General Longstreet's units to reach the battlefield, and its commander, Colonel Micah Jenkins, was just twenty-six years old. He had three battalions of South Carolinians and one of Georgians, and the four southern regiments had already torn through three Yankee positions. Jenkins had been ordered to attack, and no one had ordered him to stop, and so he was marching on deep into the Yankee rear. With a born soldier's luck his brigade had struck the Yankee defenses where there were few guns and only scattered units of infantry, and one by one the northern positions had been overwhelmed and put to panicked flight. Now his men were threatened by a handful of blue-coated cavalry who had appeared on their left flank. A South Carolina captain wheeled his company a half turn to the left. "Make sure you're loaded!" he called. "Aim for the horses!"

Some of the Yankees knew what was coming and sawed on their reins. One horse, turning too quickly, lost its footing in the wet soil and spilled over. Another reared up, whinnying, tipping its rider back over his saddle's cantle. But most of the Yankees whooped and galloped on, consumed with the fine frenzy of cavalrymen in full attack. Thirty horsemen had their sabers drawn, others carried revolvers. A bearded sergeant carried the guidon, a small triangular flag mounted on a lance shaft, and now he lowered the shaft's razor-sharp spear point until it pointed straight at the heart of the South Carolina Captain.

The Captain waited until the two strange fugitive horsemen were safely past his rifles, then he called the order to fire. Fifty rifles cracked.

Horses screamed and fell into the mud. The guidon plunged point-first into a tussock and stuck there quivering while the Sergeant flailed back off the horse, blood spilling suddenly from his open mouth. A dozen horses were down in the mud and another dozen rode into the chaos of hooves and scrambling men. Horses screamed in pain. The surviving beasts would not charge through the tangle of blood and beating hooves, but swerved aside instead. A few riders fired their revolvers into the bank of rifle smoke, then spurred away before the infantry could reload. Colonel Thorne was among the fallen, trapped in the mud beneath his wounded horse. The Colonel's left leg was broken and his fine dream of galloping across a smoky field to his country's rescue was reduced to the stench of blood and the scream of wounded beasts and the receding thump of hooves as the other cavalry wheeled hard away. The South Carolina Captain wheeled his company back into line and marched on.

Colonel Jenkins galloped across to the newcomers. "Who the devil are you?"

"Captain Starbuck, Faulconer Legion, Virginia," Starbuck panted.

"Lassan, Colonel of the French army, come to see some fighting," Lassan introduced himself.

"You've sure come to the right place, Colonel. What's up ahead?"

"My official position as an observer forbids me to tell you," Lassan said, "but my companion, if he had his breath back, would tell you there are two separate regiments of Yankee infantry, one in a clearing beyond the next stand of trees and the other a quarter mile beyond them. After that you hit their main defense works at the crossroads."

"Then we'd best keep going," Micah Jenkins said, "and whip the bastards some more." He looked at Starbuck. "You were a prisoner?"

"In a way, yes."

"Then welcome home, Captain, welcome home." He turned his horse and raised his voice. "On, boys, on! Roll the bastards back where they came from. On, boys, on!"

Starbuck turned to look back at the left flank. A squad of rebel skirmishers had gone to put the wounded horses out of their misery and their shots sounded flat and low in the day's gloom. The remnant of the Yankee cavalry had gathered by the far trees and now stood there impotent and watched while the infantrymen looted the saddlebags and pockets of the fallen riders. The southerners pulled Thorne's horse off the Colonel, took his sword and pistol, then left him cursing their parentage. Still more horsemen emerged from the woodland, and Starbuck could see James among them. Poor James, he thought, and the guilt whipped though him like a bullet's strike.

"What is it?" Lassan asked, seeing the stricken look on Starbuck's face.

"My brother."

"You're playing a game," Lassan said brusquely. "He lost, you won, you're both alive. There are thousands of men who will do worse than that today."

"I don't want him to suffer."

"How has he suffered?" Lassan asked. "The worst that will happen to your brother is that he will go back to his law practice, where he will spend the rest of his life telling his colleagues about his wastrel brother, and do you think he won't be secretly proud of you? You're doing all he would never dare, but would secretly like to do. Men like him need brothers like you, otherwise nothing would ever happen in their lives. My mother used to tell my sister and me one thing over and over again. Geese, she would say, go in gaggles, but eagles fly alone." Lassan grinned mischievously. "None of that may be true, *mon ami,* but if the notion helps your conscience then I would cling to it as though it were a warm woman in a deep bed on a cold night. Now stop feeling guilty and look for a weapon. There's a battle to fight."

Starbuck looked for a weapon. He was back under his chosen flag with a battle to fight, a noose to escape, and a friend to betray. He picked up a fallen man's rifle, found some cartridges, and looked for a target.

Northern reinforcements finally began crossing the rain-swollen river. The weight of a field gun broke the damaged bridge, though miraculously neither man nor weapon was lost. Instead the team horses were whipped bloody until they dragged the heavy gun out of the water and up to the corduroyed road on the southern bank.

McClellan stayed in bed, dosing himself with quinine, honey, and brandy. He had taken so much medicine that he was dizzy and beset with headaches, but his doctor confirmed to the headquarters staff that the fevered General was aware that a battle was taking place, but claimed the patient was in no fit state to take command of the army. Tomorrow, perhaps, the Young Napoleon would be able to impose his granite will upon the battlefield, but till then he must rest and the army must manage without his guiding genius. The General's staff tiptoed away lest they disturb the great man's recovery.

General Johnston, waiting at his headquarters at the Old Tavern north of the railroad, had at last learned that the muffled noise of the guns was not an artillery duel, but rather a battle that had been raging without either his knowledge or his direction. General Longstreet had arrived at the Old Tavern to confirm that the first of his troops were now attacking south of the railroad. "I've lost Micah Jenkins," he told Johnston, "God only knows where his brigade is by now, and as for the rest, Johnston, they're exactly like virgins."

Johnston could have sworn Longstreet had said his men were like virgins. "They're like Virginians?"

"Like virgins, Johnston, virgins! Nervous of their flanks." Longstreet grinned. He was full of an excitable, quick energy. "We need an attack here"—he tapped a grimy fingernail on Johnston's map—"north of the rails."

Johnston rather believed he had given Longstreet specific orders to make just such an attack north of the rails, and that those orders had demanded the attack should have been made at dawn rather than now when the day was already dying. God only knew what had gone wrong with his careful three-pronged assault, but something had bent it dangerously askew and tomorrow, Johnston swore, he would find out exactly why it had gone awry and who was responsible. But that inquiry must wait for victory and so he curbed his normally sharp tongue and instead sent an order for one of the reserve divisions to attack on the northern side of the railway embankment.

The new attackers marched past the Old Tavern, and Johnston, fretting to know exactly what was happening on the battlefield, joined the advancing troops. As he rode forward he wondered just why everything in this army seemed so needlessly complicated. It had been the same at Manassas, he reflected. At that battle the rebel headquarters had waited ignorant on the right while a battle flared on the left, while here he had waited on the left as a battle flared ungoverned on the right. Yet still he might pluck victory from chaos if only the Yankees had not sent too many reinforcements across the Chickahominy.

President Davis arrived at the Old Tavern to discover that General Johnston had gone eastward. Johnston's second-in-command, Gustavus Smith, who had been New York's street commissioner before the war, professed himself uncertain about the day's events, but delivered the broad verdict that everything seemed dandy as far as he understood, though he admitted his understanding did not stretch very far. General Lee, accompanying the President, was embarrassed by such a reply from a fellow soldier and shifted uncomfortably in his saddle. The tavern keeper brought the President a glass of sweetened lemonade that Davis drank on horseback. In the distance Davis could see the two yellow balloons of the Federal army's Aeronautical Corps wobbling precariously in the gusting wind. "Is there nothing we can do about those balloons?" Davis asked testily.

There was silence for a moment or two, then Lee quietly suggested that cannons did not have the necessary elevation and that the best answer might be high-powered sharpshooter rifles to make the lives of the gondola's occupants uncomfortable. "Even so, Mr. President, I doubt such rifles will have the necessary range."

"Something should be done," Davis said irritably.

"Eagles?" General Smith observed brightly. Both Lee and Davis looked at him quizzically and Smith hooked his fingers to demonstrate the action of a bird's claws. "Trained eagles, Mr. President, might well be persuaded to puncture the balloons' envelopes?"

"Quite so," Davis said, astonished. "Quite so." He glanced at his military adviser, but Lee was staring into a puddle as though, somehow, the answer to the Confederacy's problems might be found in its murky depths.

While out in the fields the guns banged on.

"On! On! On! On! On!" Micah Jenkins seemed to know only how to hurl his men forward. He ignored his own casualties, leaving them in the field behind while he chivvied and encouraged and inspired his men to keep advancing. They were deep inside Yankee territory now, without any other southern troops to support them, but the young South Carolinian did not care. "On! On!" he shouted. "No stopping now! Give the bastards hell. Come on, drummers! Let me hear you! Keep marching!" A bullet whistled within an inch of Jenkins's cheek, the wind of its passing like a small, warm slap. He saw a puff of smoke drifting away from the bushy top of a pine tree and he spurred forward to one of his marching companies. "See the smoke? The pine tree, there! To the left of the hawthorn. There's a sharpshooter up in the branches; I want the bastard's wife widowed this instant!"

A dozen men knelt, aimed, and fired. The tree seemed to shiver, then a body slumped into view, held in place by the rope that had tied the northern marksman to the tree. "Well done!" Jenkins shouted, "well done! Keep marching!"

Starbuck had collected a Palmetto rifle, a haversack of cartridges, and a gray uniform jacket from the corpse of a dead South Carolinian. The jacket had a small bullet hole in its left breast and a big, bloody rent in the back, but it still made a better uniform than his dirty shirt. Now he fought like a mounted infantryman, loading and firing from horseback. He rode just behind Jenkins's front line, caught up in the mad daring of this lunge that had carved its bloody hook deep into the Yankee rear. The main battle still thundered to the brigade's right, but that battle seemed like a quite separate action from this inspired South Carolinian charge.

The rebels marched in line across a road, throwing down the snake fence at its far side before moving into a belt of trees. The dead Yankee sharpshooter dripped blood from his tether at the top of the pine tree. His rifle, an expensive target model with a heavy barrel and a telescopic sight, had fallen to lodge in one of the lower branches from where it was retrieved by a jubilant Georgian who caught up with his comrades just as they emerged from the belt of trees to face yet another battalion of northern infantry. The northerners had just been ordered to their feet when the rebels burst from the trees. Micah Jenkins roared at his men to hold their fire and just charge. "Scream!" he shouted. "Scream!" And the ululating rebel yell began again.

The Yankee line disappeared behind its own bank of gunsmoke. Bullets whistled past Starbuck. Confederates were down, gasping and kicking on the grass, but still the gray line surged forward with Jenkins whipping it mercilessly on. "Leave the wounded! Leave them!" he shouted. "On! On! On!" The Yankees began reloading, their ramrods showing spiky above their two ranks, but then the banshee yell of the attackers and the glimmer of bayonet steel in the smoke convinced the northerners that this day was lost. The battalion broke and fled. "Follow them! Follow!" Jenkins shouted and the tired rebels swarmed into the woodland where they opened fire on the fugitives. Some Yankees tried to surrender, but Jenkins had no time for prisoners. The northerners had their rifles taken and were then told to make themselves scarce.

One more Yankee battalion waited at the wood's far edge and they, like all the other northern regiments that Jenkins's brigade had faced that afternoon, were unsupported by any other northern infantry. The first they knew of a rebel assault was when fleeing Yankees appeared among the trees, but before the Colonel could organize his defense, the rebels were in sight, whooping, yelling, and screaming for blood. The Yankees fled, pouring back across an open wheat field toward the crossroads where the bulk of their army had checked the strong central thrust of the rebels' main attack. And now, in sight of that larger battle, Micah Jenkins stopped his men.

The brigade had come deep into the Yankee rear, but to go farther was to invite annihilation. In front of them now there stretched an open plain crammed with tents, wagons, limbers, and caissons, while to their right was the crossroads by the two shell-riddled farmhouses and the seven bullet-shredded pine trees. It was there, by the rifle pits and the big redoubt, that the day's main battle raged. The main Confederate attack had stalled in front of the redoubt where the Yankees were putting up a solid defense. Cannon fire scorched the wheat and mowed down rebels. It was there that Johnston had planned to catch the stubborn Yankee defense in the pincers of his flank attacks, but the flank attacks had never happened and the central thrust was being bloodied and decimated by the northern gunners.

Except, by chance, Micah Jenkins's twelve hundred men were now in the Yankee rear. The brigade had started with nineteen hundred men, but seven hundred lay dead or wounded in the path of chaos that the South Carolinian had carved across the battlefield. Now he had a chance to make more chaos.

"Form line!" Jenkins shouted and waited while his second line of men caught up with the first. "Load!"

Twelve hundred rebels in two ragged ranks rammed minie balls on powder charges. Twelve hundred percussion caps were fumbled onto firing cones and twelve hundred hammers pulled back.

"Take aim!" Not that there was anything particular to aim at. No enemy were immediately confronting Jenkins's brigade; instead the rebel soldiers faced a wide field of Yankee encampments under a wind-fretted sky of smoky clouds. The rebel flags were hoisted high behind the line, the Palmetto flags of South Carolina and the three-pillared seal of Georgia, and above them all the crossed stars of the Confederacy's battle flag. Six enemy flags lay on the grass by Jenkins's horse, all captured in the charge and held now as trophies to be sent to his parents' plantation on Edisto Island.

Jenkins raised his saber high, paused for a heartbeat, then swept the curved blade down. "Fire!"

Twelve hundred bullets whipped across the damp evening fields. The volley did little physical damage, but its massive splintering crack announced to the northerners that there were rebels deep in their rear, and that realization was enough to start the retreat from the Seven Pines crossroads. One by one the Yankee guns were dragged out of the redoubt, then the infantry battalions began to back away from their parapets. Rebel yells whooped in the gloom and Starbuck saw a gray line of men swarm through the long shadows toward the earthen fort. A last northern gun fired, hurling a knot of attackers back in a mist of blood, then a flood of bayonets was carried up and over the sandbagged parapets, and suddenly the wheat field in front of Micah Jenkins's brigade was dark with panicked men streaming eastward. The Yankees were abandoning their tents, their artillery, and their wounded. Horsemen galloped among the fugitives who ran toward the night, leaving the two houses and the shattered pines and the bloody redoubt to the rebels.

"My God." Jenkins spat a stream of tobacco juice that splattered onto one of the captured northern flags. "But Yankees sure make good runners."

There was enough light left to help the victorious rebels plunder the abandoned camps, but not enough to turn the day's victory into triumph. The northerners would not be driven into the swamps. Instead their officers halted the panicked flight a mile and a half east of the crossroads and there ordered the chastened battalions to dig new rifle pits and to fell trees to make new barricades. Guns came from the Yankee rear to stiffen the new defensive line, but in the day's dying light no rebels came to challenge the newly positioned batteries.

North of the railroad Johnston's flank attack waded through waist-deep swamps to attack emplaced guns protected by the infantry who had just marched across the river. The Yankee lines opened fire, their cannons cracking shell and canister and grape so that the gray lines reeled back, bloodied and shattered. The blue lines cheered in the twilight as they saw the shrieking enemy first silenced, then bloodied, then defeated. Wounded men drowned in the swamp, their blood oozing into the stinking mud.

General Johnston watched his men recoil from the sudden and unexpected Yankee defense. He was sitting on his horse atop a small knoll that offered a fine view across the battlefield that was suddenly touched red by an evening sunlight that slanted underneath the clouds and battle smoke. Bullets whiplashed overhead, ripping through the leaves of a small sugarberry tree. One of his aides kept twitching in his saddle whenever a bullet came near, and the man's timidity annoyed the General. "You can't duck a bullet," he snapped at the aide. "By the time you hear them, they're past you." The General had been wounded five times in the service of the old U.S. Army and knew what it was to be under fire. He also knew that the careful battle that should have fetched him glory and fame had gone disastrously wrong. By God, he thought vengefully, but someone would suffer for this. "Does anyone know where Huger is?" he asked, but no one did. The General seemed to have vanished as completely as Longstreet had disappeared earlier, but at least Longstreet had finally reached the battlefield. Huger was still nowhere to be found. "Who gave Huger his orders?" Johnston demanded again.

"I told you, sir," Colonel Morton said respectfully. "It was young Faulconer."

Johnston turned on Adam. "He understood them?"

"I think so, sir."

"What do you mean? You think so? Did he have questions?"

"Yes, sir." Adam could feel himself coloring.

"What questions?" Johnston snapped.

Adam tried not to show his nervousness. "About the troops you put under General Longstreet's command, sir."

Johnston frowned. "He didn't have questions about the attack?"

"No, sir."

"Well, tomorrow we'll get everyone into one room. General Huger, General Longstreet, then we'll find out just what the devil happened today and I promise you that whoever made a hash of this day's work will wish they hadn't been born. Isn't that so, Morton?"

"Absolutely, sir."

"And I want every aide who carried a message to be there," Johnston insisted.

"Of course, sir," Morton said.

Adam stared doggedly into the gunsmoke. Somehow, in the raw glare of Johnston's anger, his febrile idea of the previous night did not seem so very bright after all. He had planned to plead forgetfulness, or just plain carelessness, but those excuses seemed extraordinarily weak right now.

"I'll have the responsible man shot!" Johnston spoke angrily, still obsessed with the failure of his careful plans, then he made a flamboyant gesture with his left arm that seemed curiously out of place, and Adam, who was terrified of what the morrow's investigation would bring, thought for a second that the General was trying to hit him, and then he saw that Johnston had been hit in the right shoulder and that he had merely flailed his left arm in a desperate attempt to keep his balance.

The General blinked rapidly, swallowed, then tentatively touched his left fingertips to his right shoulder. "Damn it, I've been hit," he said to Morton. "A bullet. Damn it." His breath was coming in big gasps.

"Sir!" Morton spurred forward to help Johnston.

"It's all right, Morton. Nothing vital touched. Just a bullet, that's all." Johnston clumsily fetched out a handkerchief and began folding it into a pad, but then a Yankee shell exploded at the foot of the knoll and a piece of the shrapnel case struck the General full in the chest and threw him back off his horse. He gave a cry, more in astonishment than in pain, then his aides gathered around to strip away his sword belt, pistols, and jacket. Blood was soaking the front of Johnston's uniform.

"You're going to be all right, sir," one aide said, but the General was quite unconscious now, and blood had started to spill from his mouth.

"Take him back!" Colonel Morton had taken charge. "A stretcher here, quick!" Another Yankee shell exploded nearby, its shrapnel hissing overhead to tear more leaves from the sugarberry.

Adam watched as men from the nearest infantry battalion brought a stretcher for the army's commander. Johnston's eyes were shut, his skin was pale, and his breath shallow. So much for the inquiry tomorrow, Adam thought, and his hopes soared. He would get away with it! He had engineered failure and no one would ever know!

Across the plain the guns fired on. The sun sank behind cloud again and the dead lay in the wet fields and the wounded cried and the living crouched to bite their cartridges and to fire their guns. The dusk made the gun flames stab ever brighter in the gloom. Then twilight brought the fireflies out and the guns slowly stopped until the cries of the dying were the loudest noise left between the city and the White Oak Swamp.

Flames flickered in the dark. There were no stars and no moonlight, just lanterns and small campfires. Men prayed.

In the morning, they knew, the battle would stir again like embers breathed to fire by a whispering breeze, but now, in the damp dark where the wounded cried for help, the two armies rested.

The battle died on the Sunday morning. The rebels, led now by General Smith, pushed on in the center, but the Yankees had sent reinforcements from north of the Chickahominy and would not be budged from their new defense line. Then the Yankees pushed back and the rebels gave ground until, at midday, the two armies gave up the struggle in mutual weariness. The rebels, finding no profit in holding on to the sliver of ground they had gained, pulled back to their original lines, thus letting the Yankees reoccupy the crossroads under the seven fire-blasted pine trees.

Work parties cut timbers and made pyres on which the dead horses were burned. The heat contracted the horses' tendons so that the dead beasts seemed to twitch in dreamy gallops as the flames hissed around them. The wounded were taken to field hospitals or, on the rebel side, loaded onto wagons and flatcars to be carried into Richmond. The northerners buried the dead in shallow graves because no one had the energy to dig deep ones, while the Confederates stacked their corpses in carts that were taken back to the cemeteries of Richmond. In the city, as the carts and wagons creaked through the streets with their uncovered cargoes of the dead and dying, women and children watched aghast.

The Yankees celebrated. One of the spoils of their battle was a double-decker horse bus that the Richmond Exchange Hotel had once used to carry hotel guests to the city's rail depots. The bus had been brought to the battlefield as an ambulance, but the vehicle had bogged down in the mud and been abandoned, so now the Union soldiers dragged it about their camp, offering two-cent rides down Broadway. All aboard for the Battery, they shouted. The northerners declared the battle a victory. Had they not repulsed the vaunted, outnumbering Confederates? And when the sick, shivering, weak McClellan appeared on horseback amid the wreckage of scorched limbers and shattered cannon and bloodied grass and broken rifles, he was welcomed with cheers as though he were a conquering hero. A New York band serenaded him with "Hail to the Chief." The General gallantly tried to give a speech, but his voice was pallid and only a few men heard him declare that they had witnessed the last despairing lunge of the rebel army, and that soon, very soon, he would lead them into the heart of secession and there defeat it utterly.

On both sides of the lines regiments formed squares for Sunday worship. Catholic regiments took Mass, Protestants listened to the Scriptures, and all thanked God for their deliverance. Strong men's voices sang hymns, the sound mournful across a battlefield that stank of death and smoke.

Starbuck and Lassan had spent the night with Micah Jenkins's brigade, but in the afternoon, after the battle died, they worked their way back through the shell holes and past the rows of dead men cut down by canister until they found the army headquarters in a small shingled farmhouse north of the railroad. Starbuck sought directions there and afterward, standing in the road, he parted from Lassan, but not before he insisted that the Frenchman take his brother's horse.

"You should sell the horse!" Lassan remonstrated.

Starbuck shook his head. "I'm in your debt."

"For what, *mon ami?*"

"My life," Starbuck said.

"Oh, nonsense! Such debts come and go on a battlefield like a child's wishes."

"But I am in your debt," Starbuck insisted.

Lassan laughed. "You are a puritan at heart. You let fear of sin ride you like a jockey. All right, I shall take the horse as a punishment for your imagined sins. We shall meet soon, yes?"

"I hope so," Starbuck said, but only if the gamble he was contemplating paid off. Otherwise, he thought, he would be hanging from a high beam in a cold dawn and he felt the temptation to throw away Pinkerton's paper. "I hope so," he said again, resisting the temptation.

"And remember what I taught you," Lassan said. "Aim low for men and high for women." He shook Starbuck's hand. "Good luck, my friend." The Frenchman went to make himself known to the Confederate headquarters while Starbuck walked slowly north with his handful of spoils from the battlefield. There was a fine northern-made razor with an ivory handle, a small pair of opera glasses, and a stone jug of cold coffee. He drank the coffee as he walked, tossing away the empty jug as he reached the fields where the Faulconer Brigade was camped.

It was time to do what Sally had told him to do so long before; it was time to fight.

He walked into the encampment just as the soldiers were being dismissed from the afternoon's church parade. He deliberately avoided the Legion's lines, going instead to the headquarters ridge-pole tents that were grouped about two pine trees that had been stripped of their branches to serve as flagpoles. The taller tree flew a Confederate battle flag, the slightly shorter carried the flag adapted from the Faulconer coat of arms with its motto "Forever Ardent." Nelson, General Washington Faulconer's servant, was the first man to see Starbuck in the encampment. "You must go away, Mr. Starbuck. If the master sees you, he'll have you arrested!"

"It's all right, Nelson. I'm told Master Adam's here?"

"That's right, sir. And sharing Captain Moxey's tent, sir, till they find him a new one. The master's so pleased he's back."

"Moxey's a captain now?" Starbuck asked, amused.

"He's an aide to the General, sir. And you shouldn't be here, sir, you shouldn't. The General can't abide you, sir."

"Show me to Moxey's tent, Nelson."

It was a big tent, serving not only as sleeping quarters but as a brigade office. There were two camp beds, two long tables, and two chairs, all set on a floor of wooden slats. Moxey's bed was piled with dirty clothes and discarded equipment while Adam's luggage was stacked at the foot of his neatly folded blankets. The tables held the stacks of paperwork that soldiering engendered, the piles all anchored by rocks that kept the forms safe from the small wind that stirred through the laced-back tent flaps.

Starbuck sat in one of the canvas folding chairs. The midday sunlight, watery at best, was turned into a leprous yellow by the canvas. He saw a Savage Navy revolver among the tangled belongings on Moxey's bed and Starbuck retrieved the gun just as the first officers began arriving back in the headquarters. Horses stamped their feet, servants and slaves ran to collect reins while the officers' cooks carried the evening meal across to the mess tables. Starbuck saw that the Savage was unloaded, but, typical of Moxey's carelessness, had an unfired percussion cap left on one of the cones. He turned the cylinder until the cap was in the next firing position, then looked up just as Captain Moxey ducked under the eaves. Starbuck smiled, but said nothing.

Moxey gaped at him. "You shouldn't be here, Starbuck."

"People keep telling me that. I'm beginning to feel distinctly unwanted, Moxey. But I'm here anyway, so you go and play somewhere else."

"This is my tent, Starbuck, so—" Moxey stopped abruptly as Starbuck leveled the heavy revolver. He raised his hands. "Now, Starbuck. Please! Be sensible!"

"Bang," Starbuck said, then pulled the gun's lower trigger that cocked the hammer and turned the cylinder. "Go away," he said.

"Now, Starbuck, please!" Moxey stammered, then squealed as Starbuck pulled the upper trigger, making the percussion cap snap angrily. Moxey yelped and fled, while Starbuck levered the shattered and scorched scraps of copper off the cone. The tent was soured by a fine layer of astringent smoke.

Adam came in a few seconds later. He stopped when he saw Starbuck and his face suddenly seemed drained of color, though perhaps that was just the light-filtering effect of the canvas. "Nate," Adam said in a voice that was neither welcoming nor dismissive, but held a slightly guarded tone.

"Hello, Adam," Starbuck said happily.

"My father . . ."

". . . won't like it that I'm here," Starbuck continued the sentence for his friend. "Nor will Colonel Swynyard. Nor does Moxey approve of my presence, oddly enough, though why in the name of holy hell we should care what Moxey thinks, I don't know. I want to talk to you."

Adam looked at the gun in Starbuck's hand. "I've been wondering where you were."

"I've been with my brother James. Remember James? I've been with him, and with his chief who is a rugged little man called Pinkerton. Oh, and I've been with McClellan too. We mustn't forget Major General McClellan, the Young Napoleon." Starbuck peered into the Savage's barrel. "Moxey does keep a dirty gun. If he doesn't clean it he'll blow his hand off one day." Starbuck looked up at Adam again. "James sends his best wishes."

The tent gave a violent twitch as a man ducked through the entrance flaps. It was Washington Faulconer, his handsome face flushed with anger. Colonel Swynyard was behind the General, but Swynyard stayed out in the watery sunlight as Faulconer faced his enemy. "What the hell are you doing here, Starbuck?" General Faulconer demanded.

"Talking to Adam," Starbuck said mildly. He was suppressing his nervousness. He might dislike Washington Faulconer, but the man was still a powerful enemy and a full general.

"You stand when you talk to me," Faulconer said. "And put that gun down," he added when Starbuck had obediently stood. Faulconer mistook the obedience for subservience. The General had come into the tent with his right hand on the hilt of his own revolver, but now he relaxed. "I ordered you out of my Legion, Starbuck," he said, "and when I gave that order I intended it to mean that you stayed well away from my men. All my men, and especially my family. You are not welcome here, not even as a visitor. You will leave now."

The General had spoken with dignity, keeping his voice low so that the curious bystanders would not hear the confrontation inside the tent.

"What if I don't go?" Starbuck asked just as quietly.

A muscle twitched on Faulconer's face, revealing that the General was a good deal more nervous than his demeanor betrayed. The last time these two men had faced each other had been on the evening of the battle at Manassas, and on that night it had been Faulconer who was humiliated and Starbuck who had triumphed. Faulconer was set on revenge. "You'll go, Starbuck," the General said confidently. "There's nothing for you here. We don't need you and we don't want you, so you can crawl back to your family or go back to that whore in Richmond, and you can do it on your own or you can do it under arrest. But you'll go. I command here and I'm ordering you away." Faulconer edged to one side and gestured toward the tent door. "Just go," he said.

Starbuck opened the top pocket of the threadbare uniform jacket that he had stripped from the dead South Carolinian and took out the Bible that James had given him. He looked at Adam and saw that his friend recognized the book.

"Father," Adam intervened softly.

"No, Adam!" the General said firmly. "I know your nature, I know you will appeal for your friend, but there is no appeal." Faulconer looked scornfully at Starbuck. "Put your Bible away and go. Else I'll call the provosts."

"Adam?" Starbuck prompted his friend.

Adam knew what Starbuck meant. The Bible was a symbol of James, and James was Adam's partner in espionage, and Adam's guilty conscience was more than strong enough to make the connection between the Bible and his own betrayal of his father's cause. "Father," Adam said again.

"No, Adam!" Faulconer insisted.

"Yes!" Adam snapped the word surprisingly loud, astonishing his father. "I have to talk with Nate," Adam insisted, "and afterward I'll talk with you." There was an utter misery in his voice.

Washington Faulconer felt his certainty crumble like a battle line shredding under cannon fire. He licked his lips. "What do you have to talk about?" he asked his son.

"Please, Father!"

"What's going on?" Faulconer demanded. Swynyard was crouching at the tent flap, trying to listen. "What's happening?" Faulconer appealed. "Tell me, Adam!"

Adam, his face still pale and sickly, just shook his head. "Please, Father."

But Washington Faulconer was not ready to surrender yet. He put his hand back to his pistol and glared at Starbuck. "I've had enough," he said. "I'm not standing here while you make our lives a misery again, so just get the hell away from us. Now!"

"General?" Starbuck said in a tone so mild and respectful that it momentarily took Washington Faulconer aback.

"What is it?" Faulconer asked suspiciously.

Starbuck gave his enemy a glimmer of a smile. "All I'm asking of you, sir, is permission to rejoin the Legion. Nothing else, sir, that's all I want."

"I'm calling the provosts," General Faulconer said flatly and turned toward the tent's entrance.

"For whom?" Starbuck asked in a voice steely enough to check Washington Faulconer. "If I don't talk to Adam now," Starbuck went on remorselessly, "then I promise you that the name of Faulconer will go down in Virginia history alongside that of Benedict Arnold. I'll drag your family through mud so deep that even the hogs won't lie in your bedding. I'll break your name, General, and a whole nation will spit on its fragments."

"Nate!" Adam appealed.

"Faulconer and Arnold." Starbuck rubbed the threat home, and as he named the traitor, he felt the elation of a gambler, the same high feeling that had soared through him at the moment when he had turned the Yankee flank at Ball's Bluff. He had come here alone, armed only with a powerless shred of paper, and he was defeating a general surrounded by his own brigade. Starbuck could have laughed aloud for the arrogant success of this moment. He was a soldier, he was taking on a powerful enemy, and he was winning.

"Come and talk!" Adam said to Starbuck, and he twisted away toward the tent's entrance.

"Adam?" his father called after him.

"Soon, Father, soon. Nate and I have to talk first!" Adam said as he ducked out into the sunlight.

Starbuck smiled. "Nice to be back in the Legion, General."

For a second Starbuck thought Washington Faulconer was going to unstrap the holster and pull out the revolver, but then the General turned and stalked out of the tent.

Starbuck followed. The General and Swynyard were striding away, scattering the knot of spectators who had gathered to listen to the conversation inside the tent. Adam seized Starbuck's arm. "Come," he said.

"You don't want to talk here?"

"We'll walk," Adam insisted, and he led Starbuck through the ring of bemused and silent officers. They crossed the field and climbed to the summit of a wooded knoll where redbuds and hornbeams grew. The redbuds were in blossom, cloudy pink and glorious. Adam stopped beside a fallen tree and turned to stare across the camp toward the distant city. "So how much do you know?" he asked Starbuck.

"Most everything, I guess," Starbuck said. He lit one of his cigars, then sat on the fallen trunk and watched the distant smoke trail of a locomotive. He guessed the train was hauling casualties to Richmond, more bodies for the sheds on Chimborazo Hill or the blossom-shaded graves at Hollywood.

"I want the war to end, you see." Adam broke the silence. "I've been wrong, Nate, all along. I should never have worn the uniform, ever. That was my mistake." He was flustered, uncertain, maybe unnerved by Starbuck's stillness. "I don't believe in the war," Adam went on defiantly. "I think it's a sin."

"But not a sin shared equally by both sides?"

"No," Adam said. "The North is morally right. We're wrong. You can see that, can't you? Surely you can see that?"

For answer Starbuck took the oilskin packet from his pocket and picked its stitches apart. As he plucked at the tightly sewn waxed cotton he told Adam how one of his letters had been intercepted when Webster was arrested, and how the authorities had suspected Starbuck of being its author, and how, once that ordeal had been endured, he had been sent across the lines to entrap the real traitor. "A very frightening man in Richmond sent me, Adam. He wanted to know who'd written that letter, but I knew it was you. Or I guessed it was you." Starbuck took the tightly folded piece of paper out of its oilskin package. "I'm supposed to take this paper back to Richmond. It's the proof they want. It names you as the spy." The piece of paper did nothing of the sort; it was merely the list of questions that Pinkerton and McClellan had concocted before the General went down with the Chickahominy fever, but there was a circular impression of an inked rubber stamp on the bottom of the letter which read "Sealed by Order of the Chief of the Army of the Potomac's Secret Service Bureau," and Starbuck let Adam see that seal before he folded the letter into a neat square.

Adam was too frightened to challenge Starbuck's bald assertion that the paper was proof of his guilt. He had seen the seal, and he had seen the elaborate precautions taken to protect the paper from damp, and what he had seen was proof enough. He had no idea that it was all a bluff, that the paper failed to incriminate him and that Starbuck's frightening man in Richmond was lying white-faced in a coffin. Starbuck, in truth, held a lousy hand of cards, but Adam felt too guilty to perceive that his friend was bluffing. "So what will you do?" Adam asked.

"What I won't do," Starbuck said, "is go to the very frightening man in Richmond and give him this letter." He placed the folded letter into his breast pocket beside the Bible. "What you can do," Starbuck suggested to Adam, "is shoot me right now. Then you can take the letter and no one will ever know you were a traitor."

"I'm not a traitor!" Adam bridled. "My God, Nate, this was all one country just a year ago! You and I took our hats off to the same flag, we cheered each July the Fourth together, and we had tears in our eyes when they played the 'Star Spangled Banner.' So how can I be a traitor if all that I'm doing is fighting for what I was brought up to love?"

"Because if you had succeeded," Starbuck said, "men who are your friends would have died."

"But fewer of them!" Adam shouted in protest. There were tears in his eyes as he looked away from Starbuck to gaze across the green land toward the spires and dark roofs of Richmond. "Don't you understand, Nate? The longer the war goes on, the more deaths there'll be?"

"So you were going to end it, single-handed?"

Adam heard the scorn. "I was going to do the right thing, Nate. Do you remember when you sought the right thing? When you prayed with me? When you read your Bible? When doing God's will was more important than anything on this earth? What happened to you, for God's sake?"

Starbuck looked up at his angry friend. "I found a cause," he said.

"A cause!" Adam scoffed at the word. "The South? Dixie? You don't even know the South! You haven't traveled south of Rockett's Landing in all your life! Have you seen the South Carolina rice fields? Have you seen the delta plantations?" Adam's anger was eloquent and fierce. "You want a view of hell on earth, Nate Starbuck, then you take a journey to see what it is you're defending. You go down the river, Nate, and hear the whips and see the blood and watch the children being raped! Then you come and tell me about your cause."

"So what's your moral cause?" Starbuck tried to retrieve the upper hand in the argument. "You think by winning this war the North will make the slaves happy? You think they'll be served better than the poor in northern factories? You've been to Massachusetts, Adam, you saw the factories in Lowell, is that your new Jerusalem?"

Adam shook his head wearily. "America's had these arguments a thousand times, Nate, and then we had an election and we settled the argument at the ballot box, and it was the South that wouldn't accept that decision." He spread his hands as if to show that he did not want to hear any more of the old, pointless discussion. "My cause is to do what's right, nothing else."

"And deceive your father?" Starbuck asked. "Do you remember last summer? In Faulconer County? You asked me how I could be scared of my father and not be scared of battle. So why don't you tell your father what you believe?"

"Because it would break his heart," Adam said simply. He fell silent, gazing north to where a bend in the Chickahominy showed as a flash of light in the green landscape. "I thought, you see, that I could ride both horses, that I could serve my country and my state, and that if the war was over quickly then my father would never know I had betrayed the one for the other." He paused. "And that might still happen. McClellan only has to push hard."

"McClellan can't push. McClellan is a turkey cock, all strut and no puff. Besides, McClellan thinks we outnumber him. I saw to that."

Adam flinched at Starbuck's tone, but said nothing for a long while. Then he sighed. "Did James betray me?"

"No one betrayed you. I worked it out for myself."

"Clever Nate," Adam said sadly. "Wrongheaded, clever Nate."

"What will your father do if he finds out you were betraying the South?" Starbuck asked.

Adam looked down at him. "Are you going to tell him?" he asked. "You almost did already, so now you'll tell him the rest, is that it?"

Starbuck shook his head. "What I'm going to do, Adam, is walk down to those tents and I'm going to find Pecker Bird and I shall tell him that I've come back to be the Captain of K Company. That's all I'm going to do, unless someone comes to kick me out of the Legion again, in which case I'll go to Richmond and find a nasty, clever old man and let him deal with things instead of me."

Adam frowned at the implied threat. "Why?" he asked after a silence.

"Because that's what I'm good at. I've discovered I like being a soldier."

"In my father's brigade? He hates you! Why don't you go and join another regiment?"

Starbuck did not answer for a moment. The truth was that he had no leverage to join another regiment, not as a captain anyway, because his scrap of paper was only useful as a weapon against the Faulconer family. But there was also a deeper truth. Starbuck was beginning to understand that war could not be approached halfheart-edly. A man did not dabble with killing any more than a Christian could flirt with sin. War had to be embraced, celebrated, drunk deep, and only a handful of men survived that process, but that handful blazed across history as heroes. Washington Faulconer was no such man. Faulconer enjoyed the trappings of high military office, but he had no taste for war, and Starbuck suddenly saw very clearly that if he survived the bullets and shells, then he would one day lead this half-hearted brigade into battle. There would be a Starbuck Brigade, and God help the enemy when that day came. "Because you don't run away from your enemies," he finally answered his friend's question.

Adam shook his head pityingly. "Nate Starbuck," he said bitterly, "in love with war and soldiering. Is it because you failed at everything else?"

"This is where I belong." Starbuck ignored Adam's bitter question. "And you don't. So what you're going to do, Adam, is persuade your father to let me be the Captain of the Legion's K Company. How you do it is up to you. You don't have to tell him the truth."

"What else can I tell him?" Adam asked despairingly. "You've hinted enough."

"You and your father have a choice," Starbuck said, "to do this privately or to have it all dragged out into the open. I think I know which your father would prefer." He paused, then embellished his bluff with another lie. "And I'll write to the old man in Richmond and tell him the spy is dead. I'll say he was killed in battle yesterday. After all, you have finished your career as a spy, have you not?"

Adam heard the sarcasm and winced. Then he glanced sharply at Starbuck. "I do have another choice, remember."

"You do?"

Adam unbuttoned the flap that held the revolver in his holster and drew out the weapon. It was an expensive Whitney revolver with ivory sideplates on its handle and an engraved cylinder. He took out a small percussion cap and primed one of the loaded chambers.

"For God's sake don't kill yourself," Starbuck said in alarm.

Adam turned the cylinder so that the loaded chamber was ready to be turned under the hammer. "I've sometimes thought of suicide, Nate," he said in a mild voice. "In fact I've often thought how blessed it would be not to have to worry about doing the right thing, not to have to worry about Father, not to have to worry about whether Julia loves me, or whether I love her. Don't you find life complicated? Oh, God in His heaven, but I find it so tangled, except in all the prayer, Nate, and in all the thinking of these last few weeks, I did find one certainty." He gestured with the loaded revolver, sweeping the weapon around the whole wide horizon. "This is God's country, Nate, and He put us here for His purpose, and that purpose was not to kill each other. I believe in the United States of America, not the Confederate States, and I believe God made the United States to be an example and a blessing to the world. So no, I'm not going to kill myself, because killing myself won't bring the American millennium one day nearer, just as none of the battle deaths have brought it one day nearer." He straightened his arm and lowered the gun's barrel until it was pointing straight at Starbuck's forehead. "But as you said, Nate, I could kill you and no one would be any the wiser."

Starbuck stared into the gun. He could see the pointed cones of the bullets in the lower chambers and he knew that one such bullet faced him down the dark muzzle. The weapon shook slightly in Adam's hand as Starbuck looked up beyond the gun into his friend's pale and earnest face.

Adam cocked the revolver. The sound of the hammer engaging sounded very loud. "Do you remember when we used to talk at

Yale?" Adam asked. "How we took pride in the fact that God made being virtuous so difficult? It was easy to be a sinner, and so hard to be a Christian. But you gave up trying to be a Christian, didn't you, Nate?" The gun still shook, its muzzle catching and quivering the day's last sunlight. "I remember when I met you, Nate," Adam went on. "I used to worry so much about life's hardships, about the difficulties of knowing God's will, and then you came along and I thought nothing would ever be quite so hard again. I thought you and I would share the load. I thought we'd walk God's path together. I was wrong, wasn't I?"

Starbuck said nothing.

"What you're asking of me," Adam said, "is what you're not strong enough to do yourself. You're asking me to face my father and break his heart. I always thought you were the stronger of the two of us, but I was wrong, wasn't I?" Adam seemed very close to tears.

"If you had the courage," Starbuck said, "you wouldn't shoot me, but go fight for the Yankees."

"I don't need your advice anymore," Adam said. "I've had enough of your filthy advice to last me a lifetime, Nate." Then he pulled the trigger.

The gun crashed loud, but Adam had raised the barrel at the very last moment to fire into the tree above Starbuck's head. The bullet smashed through a bunch of redbud blossoms to scatter the petals across Starbuck's shoulders.

Starbuck stood. "I'm going to the Legion. You know where to find me."

"Do you know what they call that tree?" Adam asked as Starbuck walked away.

Starbuck turned and paused while he tried to find the trick in the question. He could find none. "A redbud, why?"

"They call it the Judas tree, Nate. The Judas tree."

Starbuck looked into his friend's face. "Good-bye, Adam," he said.

But there was no answer, and he walked down to the Legion alone.

"You've heard the news?" Thaddeus Bird said when Starbuck presented himself at his tent.

"I'm back."

"So you are," Bird said, as though Starbuck's sudden appearance were entirely ordinary. "Does my brother-in-law know you're under his command again?"

"He's finding out right now." Starbuck had watched Adam walk to his father's tent.

"And you think the General will approve?" Bird asked dubiously. He had been writing a letter and now rested his pen on the edge of the dry goods box that served as his table.

"I don't think he'll throw me out of the Legion."

"You are full of mystery, young Starbuck. Well, I'm sure Mr. Truslow will be pleased to see you. For some reason he seems to have regretted your absence." Bird picked up the pen and dipped its nib in ink. "I assume you've heard the news?"

"What news?"

"We have a new army commander."

"We do?" Starbuck asked.

"Robert E. Lee." Bird gave a shrug as if to suggest that the news were hardly worth mentioning.

"Ah."

"Exactly. Ah. It seems the President didn't trust Smith to replace Johnston, so Granny Lee, our King of Spades, has got the job. Still, even the King of Spades cannot be any worse than Johnston, can he? Or maybe he can. Perhaps the best we can hope for is that Lee is slightly better than his reputation."

"McClellan thinks Lee lacks moral strength," Starbuck said.

"You know that for a fact, do you, young Starbuck?"

"Yes, sir, I do. McClellan told me last week."

"Splendid, good, go away." Bird waved imperiously.

Starbuck paused. "It's nice to be back, sir."

"Get an early night, Starbuck, we're on picket duty from midnight. Major Hinton will have your orders."

"Yes, sir."

"And give Sergeant Truslow a dollar."

"A dollar, sir?"

"Give him a dollar! That's an order." Bird paused. "I'm glad you're back, Nate. Now go away."

"Yes, sir." Starbuck walked through the lines, listening to the distant sad sound of a violin. Yet the sadness did not touch him, not now, for now he was back where he belonged. The copperhead was home.

# ~ EPILOGUE ~

K COMPANY BEGAN ITS DYING THREE WEEKS LATER. Joseph May was the first. He was fetching water when a stray shell landed by the brook. His new spectacles were blown off his face, one lens was shattered, and the other so evenly coated in blood that it looked just like ruby-colored glass.

All that day the Legion waited while a battle hammered just to its north. The guns sounded from dawn to dusk, but the smoke plume never shifted, evidence that for all the rebel attacks the Yankees would not be moved back. Yet that night, after the fighting died, the northern army slipped away to new positions farther east and in the dawn they could be heard digging and the rebels knew there would be hard work ahead if the blue-bellies were to be pushed farther away from Richmond. James Bleasdale died that morning. He climbed a tree to get eggs from a nest and a Yankee sniper got him in the neck. He was dead before he hit the ground. Starbuck wrote to his mother, a widow, and tried to find words that might imply that her son had not died in vain. "He will be sorely missed," Starbuck wrote, but it was not really true. No one had particularly liked Bleas-dale, or disliked him either for that matter. A flurry of shots announced that Sergeant Truslow's expedition had located the Yan-kee sharpshooter, but Truslow came back disconsolate. "Son of a bitch skedaddled," the Sergeant said, then turned to stare at Major Bird. "He's gone mad."

Major Bird was indeed behaving more oddly than usual. He was progressing through the encampment with a curious, crablike motion, sometimes darting forward a few steps, then stopping with his feet together and one arm extended before suddenly turning com-pletely around and beginning the strange sequence all over again. Every now and then he interrupted the strange capering to inform a group of men that they should be ready to march in half an hour's time. "He's gone mad," Truslow said again, after a further examina-tion of the Major's strange gait.

"I am learning to dance," Bird announced to Starbuck and made a complete revolution with an imaginary partner in his ragged arms.

"Why?" Starbuck asked.

"Because dancing is a graceful accomplishment to high office. My brother-in-law has just made me a lieutenant colonel."

"Congratulations, Pecker." Starbuck was genuinely pleased.

"It seems he has small choice now that Adam has resigned from the fray." Pecker Bird, despite his avowed contempt for the formal military hierarchy, could not hide his pleasure.

"He had even less choice after everyone voted for you," Truslow growled.

"Voted! You think I owe my high military status to mere democ-racy? To mobocracy? I am a genius, Sergeant, rising like a comet through oceans of mediocrity. I mix metaphors too." Bird peered at the paper on Starbuck's lap. "Are you writing metaphors to Mother Bleasdale, Nate?"

"Just the usual lies, Pecker."

"Tell her some unusual ones, then. Say that her dull son is pro-moted to glory, that he has been loosed from his earthly bonds and now trills in the choir eternal. Say that he frolics in Abram's bosom.

Sarah Bleasdale will like that, she was ever a fool. Half an hour, Star-buck, then we march." Bird danced away, whirling an invisible part-ner over the cow pats in the field where the Legion had slept under the stars.

General Lee was beside the road as the Legion marched out of its encampment. He sat straight-backed on a gray horse, surrounded by his staff and touching his hat to each company in turn. "We must drive them away," he said to each company in a conversational tone, and in between made awkward small talk with Washington Faulconer. "Drive them away, boys, drive them away," Lee said again, this time to the company marching immediately ahead of Starbuck's, and when the General turned to Faulconer once again he found that the brigadier had inexplicably moved away. "Push them hard, Faulconer!" Lee called after him, puzzled by Faulconer's sudden departure.

Faulconer's abrupt leaving was no mystery to the Legion, who had noticed how their general assiduously avoided K Company. He had dined with the officers from each of his brigade's other regi-ments, but he ignored the Legion in case he was forced to acknowl-edge Starbuck's presence. Faulconer told Swynyard he wanted to avoid the appearance of showing favoritism to the regiment that bore his name, and for that same reason he claimed to have decided not to appoint his son to command the Faulconer Legion, but no one believed the tale. Adam, it was said, was sick in his father's country house, though some, like Bird and Truslow, suspected the sickness was connected with Starbuck's return. Starbuck himself refused to speak of the matter.

"Drive them away, boys, drive them away," Lee said to K Com-pany, touching a hand to his hat. Behind the general a stretch of woodland was splintered and charred from the previous day's fight-ing. A party of Negroes was collecting corpses, dragging them to a newly dug grave. Just around the corner another black man was hanging dead from a tree with a misspelled placard pinned to his chest. "This nigger was a gide to the yankees," the placard read. Lee, following K Company down the road, angrily ordered the corpse taken down.

Lee separated from the Legion at a crossroads where a tavern offered a night's lodging for five cents. A group of disconsolate northern prisoners was sitting on the tavern's steps under the guard of a pair of Georgia soldiers who looked scarcely a day over fourteen. A shell exploded in midair a half mile away, the smoke sudden and silent in the pearly sky. The sound followed an instant later, then a crackle of musketry ripped through the morning to scare a flock of birds up from the trees. A battery of Confederate cannon unlimbered in a field to the right of the road. Shirtsleeved men led the team horses back from the guns while other gunners filled sponge buckets with ditch water. They all had the efficient, unhurried look of workmen moving about their daily preparations.

"Colonel Bird! Colonel Bird!" Captain Moxey cantered down the Legion's line of march. "Where's Colonel Bird?"

"In the woods," Sergeant Hutton called back.

"What's he doing in the woods?"

"What do you think?"

Moxey turned his horse. "He's to report to General Faulconer. There's a mill down there." He pointed to a side road. "He's to go there. It's called Gaines' Mill."

"We'll tell him," Truslow said.

Moxey inadvertently caught Starbuck's eye and immediately slashed his spurs back to make his horse leap ahead. "We won't see him near the bullets today," Truslow commented drily.

The Legion waited beside the road while Bird learned their fate. The Yankees were clearly not far away, for rebel shells were exploding over some nearby woods. Rifle fire sounded in sudden bursts, as though the skirmishers of either side were probing forward to make contact. The Legion waited as the sun rose higher and higher. Somewhere ahead of them a great veil of dust hung in the air, evidence that wheeled traffic was busy on a road, but whether it was the Yankees retreating or the rebels advancing, no one could tell. The morning passed and the Legion made a cold dinner from hardtack, rough rice, and water.

Bird returned just after midday and called his officers together. A half mile ahead of the Legion, he said, was a belt of woodland. The trees concealed a steep valley through which a stream ran through marshland toward the Chickahominy. The Yankees were dug in on the far bank of the stream and the Legion's job was to drive the sons of bitches away. "We're the front line," Bird told his company officers. "The Arkansas boys will be on our left, the rest of the brigade will be behind us."

"And the brigadier behind them," Captain Murphy said in his soft Irish accent.

Bird pretended not to have heard the jibe. "The river's not far beyond the Yankees," he said, "and Jackson's marching to cut them off, so maybe today we can break them forever." Stonewall Jackson had brought his army to the peninsula after driving the Yankees out of the Shenandoah Valley. The northern troops in the Shenandoah had outnumbered Jackson, but he had first marched rings around them, then whipped them bloody, and now his troops were under Lee's orders and facing McClellan's lumbering and hesitant army. That army, after the fight around the seven pines at the crossroads, had neither advanced nor retreated, but had instead busied itself with making a new supply base on the James River. Jeb Stuart had scornfully led twelve hundred rebel cavalrymen in a ride clean around the whole northern army, mocking McClellan's impotence and giving every southern patriot a new hero. Colonel Lassan had ridden with Stuart and brought news of the ride to Starbuck. "It was magnificent!" Lassan had enthused. "Worthy of the French cavalry!" He had brought three bottles of looted Yankee brandy that he shared with the Legion's officers while he filled an evening with tales of battles far away.

Yet McClellan would not be defeated by horsemen, however brilliant, but by infantrymen like those Bird now led toward the woods above the stream. The day was sweltering. Spring had turned into summer, the blossoms were gone, and the peninsula's muddy roads had dried to a cracked crust that scuffed into thick dust wherever men or horses passed.

Bird deployed eight companies of the Legion into a line of two ranks. The small Arkansas battalion formed on the left of the Legion beside Starbuck's men. They raised their colors. One was an old-fashioned three-striped Confederate flag while the other was a black banner with a crudely depicted white snake coiled at its center. "Ain't really our flag," the Arkansas Major confided to Starbuck, "but we kind of liked it and so we just took it. Bunch of boys from New Jersey had it first." He spat a viscous stream of tobacco juice, then told Starbuck how he and his men had arrived as volunteers in Richmond at the very beginning of the war. "Some of the boys wanted to go home to Arkansas after Manassas, and I could understand that, but I kept telling them there were more live Yankees here than there were back home and so I guess we just stayed on to do a bit of killing." His name was Haxall and his battalion numbered just over two hundred men, all of them as lean and ill-kempt as Haxall himself. "Luck to you, Captain," he said to Starbuck, then slouched back to his small battalion just as Colonel Swynyard gave the order to advance. It was past midday so Swynyard was already hard put to stay in his saddle; by evening he would be incoherent and by midnight insensible. "Forward!" Swynyard shouted again, and the Legion trudged toward the shadowed woods.

"Does anyone know where we are?" Sergeant Hutton asked K Company.

No one did. It was just another piece of swampy woodland over which the shells began to burst. Starbuck could hear the missiles ripping through the trees, and every now and then a thrashing of leaves would show where a shell was passing through the upper branches. Some missiles exploded among the trees, others screamed over the Legion toward the Confederate battery in the field behind. The rebel guns answered, filling the sky with the thunderous wail of an artillery duel. "Skirmishers!" Major Hinton called. "Off you go, Nate!" he added more casually and Starbuck's company obediently broke ranks and trotted ahead to form a scattered line fifty paces ahead of the other companies. Starbuck's company formed teams of four men, though Starbuck, as an officer, was on his own and he suddenly felt very visible. He carried nothing that would denote to an enemy that he was an officer; no sword, no glint of braid, no metal bar on his collar, but his very solitariness suddenly seemed to make him a target. He watched the tree line, wondering whether northern skirmishers waited there or, worse, whether the green shadows hid a scatter of lethal sharpshooters with their telescopic sights and deadly rifles. He could feel his own heart beating and each step needed a deliberate effort. He instinctively kept his rifle's wooden stock over his crotch. A shell exploded just a few yards ahead and a scrap of shrapnel whipped past his shoulder. "Glad you came back?" Truslow called to him.

"This is how I always dreamed of spending my Friday afternoons, Sergeant," Starbuck said, astonished that his voice sounded so careless. He glanced around to make sure his men were not lagging behind and was astonished to see that the Legion was merely one small part of an immense line of gray-clad infantry that stretched away to his left for a half mile or more. He even forgot his fear for a few seconds as he gazed at the thousands of men in their wavering attack line who walked forward under their bright flags.

A shell exploded ahead of Starbuck, turning his attention back to the trees. He hurried past a scorched patch of turf where a fragment of shell smoked in the dirt. Another explosion sounded, this one from behind Starbuck and so huge that it seemed to punch a wave of hot air across the summer landscape. Starbuck turned to see that a Yankee shell had hit an artillery limber loaded with ammunition. Smoke boiled up from the shattered vehicle and a riderless horse limped away from the flames. A nearby gun fired, jetting a twenty-yard cloud of smoke behind its shell. The grass rippled outward in a shock wave from the gun's muzzle. The Faulconer Brigade's second line of men was deploying and somewhere a band was playing the popular Richmond song "God Will Defend the Right." Starbuck wished the musicians had chosen something more tuneful, then he forgot the music as he plunged into the trees where the day's harsh light was filtered green by the leaves. A squirrel ran ahead through the leaf mold. "When did we last eat squirrel?" he asked Truslow.

"We had plenty while you were away," the Sergeant said.

"I fancy some fried squirrel," Starbuck said. One year ago he would have gagged at the very idea of eating squirrels, whereas now he had a soldier's fastidious preference for young squirrels fried. The older animals were much tougher and were better stewed.

"Tonight we'll eat Yankee rations," Truslow said.

"That's true," Starbuck said. Where the hell were the enemy skirmishers? Where were their marksmen? A shell ripped through the treetops, provoking a clatter of pigeon wings. Where, for that matter, was the stream and the marshland? Then he saw the lip of a valley ahead, and beyond it the tall trees of the far slope, and under the trees there was a glimpse of freshly turned earth, and he understood that the Yankees were dug in on that far slope that would serve them like a giant earthwork. "Run!" he shouted. "Run!" He knew instinctively what was about to happen. "Charge!" he shouted,

And the world exploded.

The whole far side of the valley seemed to smother itself in a sudden, self-engendered fogbank. One moment the valley's far side was leaves and brush, then it was a layer of white smoke. The sound came a heartbeat later, and with the sound came a storm of bullets that ripped and shredded through the green woods. Men on the far slope were shouting and whooping; men on Starbuck's side of the valley were dying.

"Sergeant Carter's hit!" a man shouted.

"Keep running!" Starbuck bellowed. There was no point in lingering on the valley's lip to be the Yankees' victims. The gunsmoke was shredding and he could see a mass of blue-coated infantry among the far trees while, on the crest above, a line of cannon was emplaced behind newly dug ramparts. Rifle flames stabbed that blue line, then the cannon fired to roll a cloud of gray-white smoke among the trees. A man screamed as a canister ball disemboweled him, another crawled bleeding toward the bulk of the Legion that advanced into the wood behind the skirmishers. The trees above Starbuck sounded as if a sudden gale had snatched at their boughs. More cannon fired, and suddenly the whole wood was filled with the shriek and bellow of canister. Rifle bullets whistled and cracked. Fear was like vomit in Starbuck's craw, but survival lay in charging ahead and down into the green void of the valley. He leaped over the crest and half slid and half ran down the precipitous slope. The Arkansas men were giving the rebel yell. One of them was tumbling down the hill, blood smearing the dead leaves behind him. The Yankee gunfire was a constant splintering sound, a sustained, mind-numbing crackle as hundreds of rifles fired across the small valley. Amos Parks was hit in the belly, plucked backward with the force of a mule kick. More canister smashed overhead, bringing down a blizzard of leaf scraps and torn twigs. The Legion's only hope now was to keep running and so overwhelm the enemy with speed.

"Fix bayonets!" Haxall cried to Starbuck's left.

"Keep running!" Starbuck shouted to his men. He did not want his men slowing down to fix their clumsy bayonets. Better to keep moving into the morass at the valley's bottom where a stretch of black, stagnant water was broken by splintered trees, fallen logs, and marshy banks. The stream doubtless ran somewhere in the middle of the morass, but Starbuck could not see it. He reached the foot of the slope and leaped for a fallen log, then jumped again onto a bank of rich grass. A bullet churned water up ahead of him, another splintered a rotten length of wet timber from a log. He splashed through a stretch of water, then slipped as he tried to scramble up a short, slick bank of mud. He fell forward into grass, protected from the Yankees ahead and above by a huge, black, half-rotted tree trunk. He felt the temptation to stay behind the sheltering trunk, but knew his job was to keep his men moving. "Come on!" he shouted, and wondered why no one was using the rebel yell any longer, but just as he tried to stand up a hand banged him in the small of the back and drove him down.

It was Sergeant Truslow who had pushed him. "Forget it!" Truslow said. The whole company had gone to ground. Not just the company, but the whole Legion. Indeed the whole rebel attack had taken cover because the entire valley was whipsawed with Yankee bullets, filled with the shriek and scream of canister and thick with powder smoke. Starbuck raised his head and saw the far rim of the valley wreathed in smoke above which the red and white stripes of the Yankee banners floated. A bullet smacked the log just inches from his face, driving a splinter into his cheek. "Keep your head down," Truslow growled. Starbuck twisted round. The only men in clear sight were the dead. Everyone else was crouching behind trees or sheltering in undergrowth. The bulk of the Legion was still at the top of the slope, gone to ground in the main stretch of woodland. Only the skirmishers had reached the valley's floor, and not all the skirmishers had made it safely. "Carter Hutton's dead," Truslow said, "so God knows how his wife will manage."

"Did he have children?" Starbuck asked and chided himself for needing to ask. An officer should know these things.

"Boy and a girl. Boy's a slobbering idiot. Doc Billy should have strangled him at birth like he usually does." Truslow raised his rifle above the log's parapet, sighted briefly, then fired and ducked straight down. "The girl's deaf as a stone. Carter never should have married the damn woman." He bit the top off a cartridge. "The women in that family all have weak litters. It's no good marrying for looks. Marry for strength."

"What did you marry for?" Starbuck asked.

"Looks, of course."

"I asked Sally to marry me," Starbuck confessed awkwardly.

"And?"

Starbuck knelt up, aimed the rifle at the top of the slope, pulled the trigger, and dropped down just an instant before a whole hornets' buzz of bullets slapped into the tree. "She turned me down," he confessed.

"So the girl's got some sense left then?" Truslow grinned. He was reloading his rifle, doing it lying down. The Yankees were cheering because the Confederate assault had been stopped so easily, but then a rebel yell announced the arrival of the Faulconer Brigade's second line and the Yankee fire seemed to double itself as they tore at these new attackers among the trees. Some men of the first line managed to throw themselves over the valley's lip and scrambled down the slope to find shelter. Cannon fired at point-blank range, hurling men back from the gray line. Starbuck was tempted to try and advance a few yards farther, but the second attack went to ground even faster than the first and the Yankee rifle fire switched back to the valley bottom where water and mud were churned by the bullet strikes. "Bastards have got their dander up this afternoon," Truslow grumbled.

"Reckon we're here till nightfall," Starbuck said, then bit a bullet off a cartridge. He shook the powder into the barrel, then spat the bullet into the muzzle. "Only darkness will get us out of this."

"Unless the bastards run," Truslow said, though not with any optimism. "I'll tell you one thing. We won't see Faulconer down here. He'll be keeping his pants dry." Truslow had found a niche in the fallen tree that offered him an oblique view up the enemy slope. Most of the enemy had gone to ground in rifle pits or trenches, but Truslow found one target on the crest and took careful aim. "Got you," he said, then pulled the trigger. "She really turn you down?"

"Gave me a tongue-lashing," Starbuck said, ramming the new bullet down his rifle barrel.

"She's a tough one," Truslow said with grudging admiration. A barrelful of canister slashed through the topmost branches, provoking a shower of broken twigs and torn leaves.

"She takes after you," Starbuck said. He knelt up, fired, and ducked back. He wondered, as the retaliatory bullets thudded into the log, just what Sally's new job entailed. There had been no opportunity to visit Richmond, nor would there be till the Yankees were driven away from the city, but when that happened both he and Truslow planned to visit Sally. Starbuck had other errands in the city. He wanted to make a social call on Lieutenant Gillespie. The anticipation of that revenge was a pleasure he relished, just as he relished seeing Julia Gordon again. If, indeed, she would receive him, for he suspected that her loyalty to Adam would most likely make her keep her front door shut.

The northerners began to jeer the stalled rebels. "Lost your spunk? What happened to your yelling, Johnny? Your slaves won't help you now!" The jeers stopped abruptly when the rebel artillery at last got the range of the far crest and began dropping shells onto the enemy. Truslow risked a quick look up the slope. "They're dug in deep," he said.

Too deep to be easily shifted, Starbuck reckoned, which meant the company was in for a long, hot wait. He took off his gray coat and dropped it beside the fallen tree, then sat with his back against the decaying wood to try and determine where his men had gone to earth. Only the dead were in plain sight. "Who's that?" he asked, pointing to a body that lay facedown and spreadeagled in a patch of water thirty yards away. There was an enormous hole in the gray jacket through which a mess of blood, flies, and the glint of a white rib could be seen. "Felix Waggoner," Truslow said after a cursory glance.

"How do you know it's not Peter?" Starbuck asked. Peter and Felix Waggoner were twins.

"It was Felix's turn to wear the good boots today," Truslow said. Somewhere a wounded man was moaning, but no one could move to help him. The valley was a death trap. The Yankee cannon could not depress far enough to rake the valley's bottom with canister, but the northern riflemen had a fine sight of anyone who tried to move across the swamp and so the wounded man would have to suffer.

"Starbuck!" Colonel Bird called from somewhere beyond the valley's rim. "Can you move?"

"Come on, Starbuck! Move!" a Yankee shouted, and suddenly a score of the enemy were chanting his name, mocking him, inviting him to try his luck against their rifles.

"No, Pecker!" Starbuck shouted. The wood fell silent again, or as silent as a battle could be. An artillery duel still thrashed the sky overhead, and every half hour or so a crescendo of rifle fire and cheering would mark yet another rebel attempt to push a brigade or a battalion across the swamp, but the Yankees had the whip hand here and were not going to let it go. They were a rearguard placed north of the Chickahominy to protect the bridges while the rest of the army crossed over to the southern part of the peninsula that McClellan had declared would be his new base of operations. Till now the steamers had unloaded their supplies at either Fort Monroe or West Point on the York River, but from now on they would sail to Harrison's Landing on the James. McClellan described the southward redeployment as a change of base, and had declared that it was a move "unparalleled in the annals of war," but to most of his soldiers the change of base felt more like a retreat, which is why they were taking such pleasure in whipping the rebels into quiescence in the bottom of this swamp-fever valley that ran a mile north of the Chickahominy River. And every hour that they kept the rebels at bay was an hour in which more men of the northern army could cross the river's precarious bridges to the temporary safety of the southern bank.

Starbuck took his brother's Bible out of his jacket pocket, turned to the blank pages at the back, and used a stub of pencil to write down the names of the men who had died thus far in the afternoon. He already knew about Sergeant Carter Hutton, Felix Waggoner, and Amos Parks, but now he learned another six names by calling to men nearby. "We've taken a licking," Starbuck said as he laid the Bible on top of his discarded coat.

"Aye." Truslow fired through his loophole in the log, and the puff of his rifle smoke was sufficient to draw an angry response from a score of northerners. The bullets chewed into the rotten wood, thumping splinters into the air. An Arkansas man fired, then another from K Company, but the sniping was desultory now. There were no reserves to feed into this part of the valley, and General Faulconer was making no effort to stir his men out of their muddy refuges. Farther up the valley, well out of Starbuck's sight, a more sustained attack was generating a storm of rifle and cannon fire that slowly died away as the rebel assault failed.

A black snake slithered across the heel of the mudbank where Starbuck and Truslow had found cover. It had a diamond pattern on the back of its skull. "Cottonmouth?" Starbuck asked.

"You're learning," Truslow said approvingly. The cottonmouth paused at the edge of the water, tasting the air with its tongue, then swam upstream to disappear into a tangle of fallen branches. A fire had started on the far side of the valley, burning and flickering in the dead leaves under a fallen tree. Starbuck scratched his belly and found a dozen ticks had buried themselves in the skin. He tried to pull the ticks away, but their heads broke off and stayed buried in the flesh. The afternoon heat was thick and humid, the marsh stagnant. The water in his canteen tasted salty and warm. He slapped and killed a mosquito. Somewhere upstream, out of sight around the valley's curve, another attack must have just started, for there was a sudden splintering of fire and the sound of screams. The attack lasted two minutes, then failed. "Poor bastards," Truslow said.

"Come on, rebs! Don't be shy! We've got enough bullets for you too!" a Yankee shouted, then laughed at the rebel silence.

The day seemed to grow even hotter. Starbuck had no watch and tried to judge the afternoon's passing by the motion of shadows, but it almost seemed as if the sun were standing still. "Maybe we won't be eating Yankee rations tonight," he said.

"I was looking forward to some coffee," Truslow said wistfully.

"It's thirty bucks a pound for real coffee in Richmond now," Star-buck said.

"Can't be."

"Sure is," Starbuck said, then he twisted around, raised his head, and aimed the rifle at the scar of a rifle pit on the opposite slope. He fired and dropped, expecting the usual retaliatory fusillade of bullets to shiver the rotting trunk, but instead the Yankees began shouting at each other to hold their fire. A couple of bullets slapped at the log, but immediately an authoritative voice demanded that the northerners cease their fire. Someone plaintively asked what was happening, then a score of voices shouted that it was safe. Truslow was staring in amazement at the rebel-held side of the valley. "Son of a bitch," he said in astonishment.

Starbuck turned. "Dear God," he said. The northerners had ceased fire and now Starbuck shouted to make sure that his own men did the same. "Hold your fire!" he called. Colonel Bird was shouting the same order from the top of the slope.

Because Adam had come to the battlefield.

He was making no effort to hide, but just strolling as though he were enjoying a late afternoon's walk. He was dressed in civilian clothes and was unarmed, though it was not that which had persuaded the Yankees to hold their fire, but rather the flag that he carried. Adam was holding a Stars and Stripes that he waved to and fro as he walked slowly downhill. Once the firing had stopped he draped the flag around his shoulders like a cape.

"He's gone soft in the brains," Truslow said.

"I don't think so." Starbuck cupped his hands. "Adam!"

Adam changed direction, angling downhill toward Starbuck. "I was looking for you, Nate!" he called cheerfully.

"Get your head down!"

"Why? No one's firing." Adam looked up at the Yankee slope and some of the northerners cheered him. Others asked him what he wanted, but in reply he just waved at them.

"What the hell are you doing?" Starbuck kept his head below the makeshift bullet-scarred parapet of the rotting log.

"What you told me to do, of course." Adam grimaced because he needed to wade through a patch of filthy swamp and he was wearing his best shoes. "Good afternoon, Truslow. How are you?"

"Been better, I reckon," Truslow said in a suspicious voice.

"I met your daughter in Richmond. I'm afraid I was unkind to her. Would you apologize to her for me?" Adam limped through the mud and water to reach the patch of dryer land where Truslow and Starbuck were sheltered. He stood upright and careless, as though no battle were taking place. Nor, for the moment, was there a battle in this part of the valley. Instead men on both sides had broken cover to stare at Adam and wonder just what kind of fool would walk so brazenly into a nest of rifle fire. A Yankee officer shouted to ask what he wanted, but Adam just waved again as if to suggest that all would be made clear in a short while. "You were right, Nate," he said to Starbuck.

"Adam, for God's sake, get down!"

Adam smiled. "For God's sake, Nate, I'm going up." He gestured toward the enemy-held slope. "I'm doing what you did, I'm changing sides. I'm going to fight for the North. I'm deserting, you could say. Would you like to come with me?"

"Just get down, Adam."

Instead of taking cover Adam looked all around the green, humid valley as though it were a place where no dead lay festering in the stagnant air. "I fear no evil, Nate. Not any longer." He put his hand into a coat pocket and brought out a bundle of letters tied in a green ribbon. "Will you make sure these reach Julia?"

"Adam!" Starbuck pleaded from the mud.

"Those are her letters. She should have them back. She wouldn't come with me, you see. I asked her and she said no, and then things got kind of bitter, and the long and short of it is that we won't be married." He tossed the bundled letters onto Starbuck's folded jacket and noticed the Bible there. He stooped, picked up the Scriptures, and leafed through the pages. "Still reading your Bible, Nate? It doesn't seem like your kind of book anymore. I'd have thought you'd be happier with a manual on hog butchery." He looked up from the Bible and gazed into Starbuck's eyes. "Why don't you stand up now, Nate, and come with me? Save your soul, my friend."

"Get down!"

Adam laughed at Starbuck's fear. "I'm doing God's work, Nate, so God will look after me. But you? You're a horse of a different color, aren't you?" He took a pencil from his pocket and made a note in Starbuck's Bible, which he then tossed down beside the letters. "A few moments ago I told Father what I was doing. I told him I was doing God's will, but Father thinks it's all your doing rather than God's, but Father would think that, wouldn't he?" Adam gave the rebel slope one last glance, then turned toward the Yankees. "Goodbye, Nate," he said, then he waved the bright flag in the warm air and clambered over the black log to wade knee-deep toward the far side of the valley. He lost his good shoes in the muddy bottom of the stream in the swamp's center, but just pushed on in his stockinged feet. The slight limp caused by the Yankee bullet he had taken at Manassas was more pronounced as he began to climb the hill on the far side of the quagmire.

"He's gone mad!" Truslow said.

"He's a holy goddamn fool," Starbuck said. "Adam!" he shouted, but Adam just waved the bright flag and kept going. Starbuck knelt upright. "Adam! Come back!" he shouted across the fallen tree. "For Christ's sake, Adam! Come back!" But Adam did not even look back; instead he just climbed up into the trees on the valley's far side and disappeared where the turned earth marked the Yankee entrenchments at the slope's crest. Adam's disappearance broke the spell that had held the two sides in suspense. Someone shouted an order to fire and Starbuck ducked down behind the log just a second before the whole valley snapped and whistled with the sound of bullets. Smoke sifted among the leaves and across the black pools and broken tree stumps and dead soldiers.

Starbuck picked up the Bible. Adam had marked a page somewhere in the book's center and Starbuck now leafed through the pages to find his friend's message. Bullets whipcracked the valley as he flicked through the Psalms and the Proverbs and the Song of Solomon. Then he found it, a circle penciled around the twelfth verse of the sixty-fifth chapter of the book of Isaiah. Starbuck read the verse and, in the valley's mordant heat, suddenly felt cold. He closed the Bible fast.

"What does it say?" Truslow asked. He had seen Starbuck go pale.

"Nothing," Starbuck said curtly, then he put the Bible back into his jacket pocket and pulled on the frayed, threadbare garment. He pushed the letters into a pocket, then pulled the blanket roll over his head. "Nothing at all," he said and picked up his rifle and checked that a percussion cap was mounted on its cone. "Let's go and kill some goddamn Yankees," Starbuck said, then he flinched because the whole valley was suddenly crackling with the sound of killing. Artillery crashed and rifles splintered. The demonic rebel yell filled the trees as a new assault spilt gray over the valley's edge. Another infantry brigade had been sent to attack just to the left of Major Haxall's Arkansas men and the newcomers screamed their challenge as they leaped down the slope. The Yankees fired back, their rifle flames stabbing like fiery swords in the day's lengthening shadows. Shells burst on the far side of the valley, spreading patches of bitter smoke. Northern canister obliterated whole files of southern attackers, churning the leaf mold bloody where it struck, but still more men in gray and brown came surging from the upper woods and down the blood-slicked slope until the whole valley was filled with a scrabbling flood of yelling soldiers who charged through the mud and over the drowned dead.

Starbuck stood up. "K Company! Attack! Follow me! Come on!" He did not care now. He was accursed of God, a lost soul in the outer darkness. The slope ahead was dotted with smoke clouds, bright with flames. Starbuck began to scream, not the rebel yell, but a scream of a man who knows his soul is damned. He ran into the stream, forcing his steps through the clinging, sucking mud. He saw a Yankee take aim from a rifle pit ahead, then the man was snatched backward by a shot fired from the rebel side of the valley. Another northerner scrambled out of the hole and clambered upward and Starbuck looked past the fleeing man and thought this was how Ball's Bluff must have looked to the dying Yankees on the day when he and the other rebels had lined the crest and poured a dreadful fire down into their helpless ranks.

"Come on!" he yelled. "Kill the bastards, come on!" And he threw himself at the slope, pulling himself up on its roots and brambles. He passed two abandoned rifle pits, then there was a sudden movement to his right and he looked to see another pit half hidden by a screen of brushwood. A Yankee was taking aim at him, and Starbuck threw himself forward just as the man's rifle fired. Acrid smoke billowed around Starbuck's face. He was screaming defiance now, wanting the man's death. He rolled onto his back and pulled his rifle's trigger, firing from the hip. The gun crashed smoke and the bullet went wide. The Yankee scrambled out of his trench and began climbing to safety, but Starbuck was chasing him, screaming. The man turned, scared suddenly, trying to fend off Starbuck with an empty rifle, but Starbuck clumsily swatted the gun aside, then slammed his own rifle hard into the man's legs to tangle and trip him. The Yankee was keening in panic as he fell. He scrabbled for his sheathed bayonet, but Starbuck was above him with his rifle raised and its heavy brass-tipped butt pointing downward, and the man shouted something just as Starbuck struck. The blow jarred up through Starbuck's arms, blood spattered his boots, then he was aware that all around him the slope was moving with gray-clad bodies and the whole green valley was echoing with the murderous scream of a rebel attack. The star-crossed banners were moving forward and the Yankees' flags were going back. Starbuck left his victim bleeding and hurried upward, wanting to reach the valley's crest first, but all around him the rebels raced uphill, whipped on by the bugle calls that drove them up to a plateau skeined in smoke. A handful of Yankee gunners tried to save their cannon, but they were too late. A gray rush of men swarmed from the woods and the land between the swamp and the river suddenly became a chaos of panicked northerners.

A troop of northern horsemen tried to turn the rebels back. Two hundred and fifty horsemen had been waiting for the southern infantry to emerge from the trees and now, in three lines with their sabers drawn, the cavalry charged at the ragged rebel formations. The horses' hooves thumped the summer turf to make the whole hilltop shudder. The horses galloped, teeth bared and eyes white as a trumpeter sounded his challenge to the smoky sky and the guidon lance flags dipped into their killing slant. "Charge!" The cavalry commander drew the word out into one long, fine scream of defiance as he pointed his saber's blade at the rebel troops just forty yards ahead.

"Fire!" An Alabama officer called the command and the rebel infantry fired a volley that tore the guts and glory from the northern cavalry. Horses screamed and fell, their hooves flailing in an evening air misted by blood. Riders were crushed, impaled on their own swords, killed by bullets. The second line of cavalry tried to swerve around the bloodied carnage of the leading rank.

"Fire!" A second volley crashed smoke and lead, this volley fired from the left flank, and the surviving cavalry were swatted sideways. Horses ran into other horses, men fell from saddles and were dragged along by stirrups. Others fell clear, only to be trampled by panicked horses.

"Fire!" A last volley pursued the fleeing handful of defeated horsemen who left behind a slaughteryard of dying horses and screaming men. The rebels swarmed over the horror, shooting the horses and looting the men.

Elsewhere on the plateau the rebels captured northern cannons still hot from the day's battle. Prisoners, some wearing straw summer hats, were herded into groups. A captured northern flag was paraded up and down the victorious ranks, while in the swamp the wounded cursed and bled and called for help.

Starbuck climbed onto the hot barrel of a northern twelve-pounder. The gun's venthole and muzzle were black with burned powder, black as the shadows that now stretched long across the wide hilltop. The fleeing northerners made a dark mass in the dying light. Starbuck looked for Adam, but knew he would never see one man among so many. A silver streak betrayed where the river curled between the darkening marshes beyond which the setting sun illuminated a northern balloon that wobbled slowly down toward its winch. Starbuck stared for a long while, then shouldered his rifle with its bloody, sticky butt and jumped to the ground.

That night the Legion ate Yankee victuals around a Yankee campfire. They drank Yankee coffee and listened to Izard Cobb play a tune on a Yankee violin. The Legion had taken a whipping. Captain Carstairs and four other officers were dead, so was Sergeant Major Proctor. Eighty more men were dead or missing, and at least that number were wounded.

"We'll make eight companies instead of ten," Bird said. He had taken a bullet in his left arm, but had refused to take much note of the wound once it had been bandaged.

"Do we know what we're doing tomorrow?" Major Haxall of the Arkansas battalion had joined the Legion's officers around their fire.

"God knows," Bird said. He sipped at a captured flask of Yankee whiskey.

"Anyone seen Faulconer?" Haxall asked. "Swynyard, then?"

"Swynyard's drunk," Bird said, "and Faulconer is well on his way to being drunk, and even if he was sober he wouldn't want to talk to anyone."

"Because of Adam?" Captain Murphy asked.

"Yes," Bird said. "I guess."

"What the hell happened?" Murphy asked.

No one answered for a long time. A few of the men looked at Starbuck, expecting and wanting him to translate Adam's behavior, but Starbuck said nothing. He was just hoping that his erstwhile friend had the strength to be a stranger in a strange land.

"Adam thinks too much." Bird finally broke the silence. The firelight made the Colonel's thin face look more gaunt than ever. "Thinking isn't good for a man. It only confuses simple issues. We should make thinking illegal in our new and glorious country. We shall achieve the pursuit of happiness by abolishing education and outlawing all ideas that are deemed too difficult for the comprehension of snake-oil Baptists. In sublime stupidity will lie our nation's true contentment." He raised his flask in a mock toast. "Let us celebrate a notion of genius: legally imposed stupidity."

"Happens I'm a Baptist," Major Haxall said mildly.

"My dear Major, I am so sorry." Bird was immediately contrite. He might love the sound of his own voice, but he could not bear the thought of hurting people he liked. "You will forgive me, Major?"

"I might do more than forgive you, Colonel, I might just try to lead you to acknowledge the Lord Jesus Christ as your Savior."

Before Bird could even think of a suitable response a sudden blossom of red light suffused the whole southern sky. The great light grew and spread to illumine a vast tract of countryside, casting a lurid shadow almost to the edge of Richmond itself.

A moment later the sound of an explosion rolled across the land. It was a massive blast, and in its wake more explosions sounded and more fiery globes appeared, swelled, and died on the river's far bank. A thousand signal rockets whipped up into the night, trailing sparks. Flames leaped from gargantuan fires and burning rivers snaked across the dark earth. "They're destroying their supplies," Bird said in a tone of wonderment. He, like every other rebel on the plateau, had stood to watch the far inferno. More explosions echoed across the land and more great lights burst into the night. "The Yankees are burning their supplies!" Bird exulted.

The northerners were setting fire to a summer's worth of food and ammunition. Railroad wagons that had been fetched from northern depots and shipped to the peninsula were now put to the torch. All the massive shells, the two-hundred-pounders and the two-hundred-and-twenty-pound bombs that had been destined to tear apart the patchwork-quilt defenses of Richmond were detonated. The railroad bridge over the Chickahominy that had been destroyed and then rebuilt was now blown up again, and when the Yankees were sure that the bridge was gone into the dark waters they sent a train of burning ammunition cars at full speed toward the void. The locomotive plunged into the mud first, and after it a succession of exploding boxcars collapsed off the trestle and went on burning and exploding in the river's marshy edges. All night long the fires burned, all night long the ammunition cracked its flashes across the sky, and all night long the destruction went on until, by the dawn's gray light, there were no more Yankees left at Savage Station and no more supplies, just a great pyre of greasy smoke like the one the rebels had left at Manassas Junction three and a half months before. McClellan, still convinced he was outnumbered, was running south toward the James.

And Richmond was safe.

The Legion buried its dead, picked up its rifles, and followed the Yankees across the Chickahominy swamps. Somewhere ahead of the army a cannon cracked and a rattle of musketry sounded. "Pick up your feet!" Starbuck snapped at his new company that had been formed from the survivors of J and K companies. "Faster!" he shouted. "Faster!" Because far ahead of the tired men the gunsmoke had once again begun to rise, the sure sign of death on a summer's day and a pyre to beckon them onward.

Because they were soldiers.

# ~ HISTORICAL ~
# NOTE

THE BATTLE OF BALL'S BLUFF WAS A DISASTER FOR the North, not for its casualties, which were slight compared to the bloodlettings that were to come, or because of the battle's strategic effects, which were minimal, but rather because the Congress of the United States was prompted by the disaster to institute a Joint Committee on the Conduct of the War, and anyone at all conversant with the ways of the U.S. Congress will not be in the least surprised that the committee became one of the most obstructive, ill-informed, and inefficient institutions of the northern government.

Oliver Wendell Holmes, who survived to become one of the more celebrated justices of the United States Supreme Court, was indeed grievously wounded at Ball's Bluff. He recovered sufficiently to be back with his unit during McClellan's Peninsular Campaign. He was to be wounded twice more during the war.

Whether McClellan could have ended the war by a successful attack on Richmond in the early months of 1862 is, of course, a moot point. What cannot be disputed, however, is that the North lost its finest early chance to inflict a severe blow on the rebellion in those months, and it lost it through McClellan's pusillanimity. He constantly overestimated the numbers of the rebels opposing him, thereby justifying his own caution. His own men, perversely, worshipped him, considering him, in the words of one of them, "the greatest general in history." This was a judgment with which McClellan would undoubtedly have agreed, though he took great care not to test the reputation unless battle was forced on him, and when it was he usually contrived to be many miles away from the fighting. He marched his army to within six miles of Richmond, then marched away as soon as he was seriously challenged. Robert Lee then took the initiative so successfully that within two months the great northern invasion of the peninsula was but a memory. McClellan's opinion of Lee, quoted in *Copperhead*, is genuine; Lee, McClellan wrote, "is wanting in moral firmness when pressed by heavy responsibility, and is likely to be timid and irresolute in action."

The scene of the fighting at Ball's Bluff can be found just north of Leesburg in Virginia, off U.S. Route 15. The smallest National Cemetery in the United States is there, close to where the hapless Senator Baker was killed. A stone marks that supposed spot. The place is still relatively uncharged, and a happy local legend insists that a Confederate ghost can be seen in the shadows of twilight.

The scenes of the bigger battles near Richmond are mostly well-preserved (though not, alas, Seven Pines, which is known to northerners as the battle of Fair Oaks) and are best seen by following the battlefield routes that start from the Historical Center in Richmond's Chimborazo Park. The fort on Drewry's Bluff is well worth a visit. The battle described in *Copperhead*'s epilogue is Gaines' Mill, and the destruction of the northern supplies at Savage Station really did happen.

I could not have written *Copperhead* without Stephen W. Sears's marvelous account of the Peninsular Campaign, *To the Gates of Richmond*, and readers who want to know where the events in the novel coincide with the actuality of history could do no better than read Sears's work. Many of the characters in *Copperhead* are drawn from history, including all the general officers except, of course, Washington Faulconer. General Huger really did sleep late on the morning of Seven Pines and had no idea a battle was to be fought until Longstreet, advancing on the wrong road, informed him of Johnston's plans. Micah Jenkins's brigade really did tear a great hole in the northern army. John Daniels, editor of the Richmond *Examiner* and author of the South's most infamous pamphlet on slavery, was a real person, as was Timothy Webster, who died as the novel describes. The Englishman Price Lewis and the Irishman John Scully were lucky not to share Webster's fate. There is an unsubstantiated story that Scully's admission of espionage was indeed tricked out of him by a man pretending to take his confession. Pinkerton existed, of course, and fed his master McClellan with the fantasies of rebel strength that justified McClellan's innate timidity.

So, thanks to that timidity, the war is not over. The northern recruiting offices will soon reopen because, in Granny Lee, the South has discovered one of the great soldiers of all time. Rebellion is about to become legend, and near defeat will be turned into a series of dazzling victories and stunning reverses. The South, truly, has only just begun to fight, which means that Starbuck and Truslow will march again.

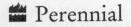
**Perennial**

## THE RICHARD SHARPE SERIES
### by Bernard Cornwell

**SHARPE'S TIGER:** *Richard Sharpe and the Siege of Seringapatam, 1799*
ISBN 0-06-093230-9 (paperback)
The first of Richard Sharpe's India trilogy, in which young Private Sharpe must battle both man and beast behind enemy lines as the British army fights its way through India.

**SHARPE'S TRIUMPH:** *Richard Sharpe and the Battle of Assaye, September 1803*
ISBN 0-06-095197-4 (paperback)
Richard Sharpe must defeat the plans of a British traitor and a native Indian mercenary army in this second volume of the India trilogy.

**SHARPE'S FORTRESS:** *Richard Sharpe and the Siege of Gawilghur, December 1803*
ISBN 0-06-109863-9 (paperback)
In this explosive conclusion to the India trilogy, Sharpe and Sir Arthur Wellesley's army try to conquer an impregnable fort in a battle with stakes both personal and professional.

**SHARPE'S TRAFALGAR:** *Richard Sharpe and the Battle of Trafalgar, 21 October 1805*
ISBN 0-06-109862-0 (paperback)
Having secured a reputation as a fighting soldier in India, Ensign Richard Sharpe returns to England and gets caught up in one of the most spectacular naval battles in history.

**SHARPE'S PREY:** *Richard Sharpe and the Expedition to Denmark, 1807*
ISBN 0-06-008453-7 (paperback)
Cornwell continues his popular series with Richard Sharpe's dangerous forays into Denmark, as he is fighting once again to keep the treacherous French troops at bay.

**SHARPE'S HAVOC:** *Richard Sharpe and the Campaign in Northern Portugal, Spring 1809*
ISBN 0-06-056670-1 (paperback)
It is 1809, and Sharpe finds himself once again in Portugal, fighting the savage armies of Napoléon Bonaparte, as they try to bring the Iberian Peninsula under their control.

**SHARPE'S ESCAPE:** *Richard Sharpe and the Bussaco Campaign, 1810*
ISBN 0-06-056095-9 (mass market paperback) • ISBN 0-06-059172-2 (unabridged audio)
Sharpe has made enemies among the Portuguese, and when the British army falls back through Coimbra, he and Sergeant Harper are lured into a trap designed to kill them.

**SHARPE'S BATTLE:** *Richard Sharpe and the Battle of Fuentes de Oñoro, May 1811*
ISBN 0-06-093228-7 (paperback)
As Napoleon threatens to crush Britain on the battlefield, Lt. Col. Richard Sharpe leads a ragtag army to exact personal revenge.

**SHARPE'S DEVIL:** *Richard Sharpe and the Emperor, 1820–21*
ISBN 0-06-093229-5 (paperback)
An honored veteran of the Napoleonic Wars, Lt. Col. Richard Sharpe is drawn into a deadly battle, both on land and on the high seas.

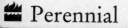 Perennial

## THE NATHANIEL STARBUCK CHRONICLES
### by Bernard Cornwell

**REBEL**
*The Nathaniel Starbuck Chronicles: Book One*
**Bull Run, 1861**
ISBN 0-06-093461-1 (paperback)
When a Richmond landowner snatches young Nate Starbuck from the grip of a
Yankee-hating mob, Nate turns his back forever on his life in Boston to fight against
his native North in this powerful and evocative story of the Civil War's first battle
and the men who fought it.

"The best thing to hit Civil War fiction since Michael Shaara's *The Killer Angels*."
                                                                    —*Washington Times*

**COPPERHEAD**
*The Nathaniel Starbuck Chronicles: Book Two*
**Ball's Bluff, 1862**
ISBN 0-06-093462-X (paperback)
Nate Starbuck is accused of being a Yankee spy. In order to prove his innocence and
prevent the fall of Richmond, he must test his courage and endurance and seek out
the real spy.

"A rollicking treat for Cornwell's many fans." —*Publishers Weekly*

**BATTLE FLAG**
*The Nathaniel Starbuck Chronicles: Book Three*
**Second Manassas, 1862**
ISBN 0-06-093718-1 (paperback)
The acclaimed Civil War series continues as Confederate Captain Nate Starbuck takes
part in the war's most extraordinary scenes.

"One of the finest authors of military historical fiction today." —*Washington Times*

**THE BLOODY GROUND**
*The Nathaniel Starbuck Chronicles: Book Four*
**The Battle of Antietam, 1862**
ISBN 0-06-093719-X (paperback)
The story of Nate Starbuck as he serves under General Robert E. Lee himself,
culminating in the famous bloody battle at Antietam Creek.

"A must-read for Civil War enthusiasts." —*Orlando Sentinel*

---

**Don't miss the next book by your favorite author.**
**Sign up for AuthorTracker by visiting *www.AuthorTracker.com*.**

---

**Available wherever books are sold, or call 1-800-331-3761 to order.**

# ◼ Perennial

## THE GRAIL QUEST SERIES
### by Bernard Cornwell

### THE ARCHER'S TALE
ISBN 0-06-050525-7 (mass market paperback) • ISBN 0-694-52609-6 (audio)
Determined to avenge his family's honor after a band of raiders brutally pillages his village, Thomas—a skilled and utterly fearless archer—joins the army of King Edward III at the start of the Hundred Years War, and embarks on a quest for the Holy Grail.

### VAGABOND
ISBN 0-06-621080-1 (hardcover) • ISBN 0-06-051080-3 (audio)
ISBN 0-06-053268-8 (mass market paperback) • ISBN 0-06-051743-3 (large print edition)
In this sequel to *The Archer's Tale*, Thomas of Hookton continues his quest for the mysterious relic, rumored to be the Holy Grail itself, as he weaves through the bloody battlefields of the Hundred Years War.

### HERETIC
ISBN 0-06-053049-9 (hardcover) • ISBN 0-06-056613-2 (audio)
ISBN 0060569980 (large print edition) • ISBN 0-06-053284-X (mass market paperback)
For three years, Thomas has fought alongside the English troops as they made their way through France. But to seek revenge and reclaim what's rightfully his, Thomas finds himself in a murderous race with the dangerous black rider who keeps eluding his grasp.

## Also by Bernard Cornwell

### GALLOWS THIEF
ISBN 0-06-051628-3 (mass market paperback) • ISBN 0-06-009301-3 (audio)
A historical novel featuring a private investigator in 1820s London whose explorations into a mysterious murder case may help rescue an innocent man from the gallows.

**"A thing of literary glory."** —*Sunday Telegraph* [London]

### STONEHENGE: *A Novel*
ISBN 0-06-095685-2 (paperback) • ISBN 0-06-109194-4 (mass market paperback)
An epic tale about one of the most mysterious and compelling monuments ever built, and the three men, brothers and rivals, who will be marked by its long shadow.

**"[A] wild tale, rich with sorcery, pagan ritual, greed, and intrigue."** —*Publishers Weekly*

### REDCOAT
ISBN 0-06-051277-6 (paperback) • ISBN 0-06-101264-5 (mass market paperback)
A young Redcoat, Sam Gilpin, has seen his brother die. Now he must choose between duty to a distant king and the call of his own conscience as he fights in some of the most dramatic battles of the American Revolution.

**"A rousing adventure. . . . Excellent."** —*Washington Post Book World*